ALSO BY E.E. H

THE WORLD OF THE GATEWAY

The Gateway Trilogy (Series 1)
Spirit Legacy
Spirit Prophecy
Spirit Ascendancy
The Gateway Trackers (Series 2)
Whispers of the Walker
Plague of the Shattered
Awakening of the Seer
Portraits of the Forsaken
Heart of the Rebellion
Soul of the Sentinel
Gift of the Darkness
Rise of the Coven
Tales from the Gateway

THE RIFTMAGIC SAGA

What the Lady's Maid Knew
The Rebel Beneath the Stairs
The Girl at the Heart of the Storm

THE GIRL AT THE HEART OF THE STORM

THE GIRL AT THE HEART OF THE STORM

The Riftmagic Saga Book 3

E.E. HOLMES

Lily Faire Publishing

Townsend, MA

Lily Faire Publishing
Townsend, MA

www.lilyfairepublishing.com
www.eeholmes.com

ISBN 978-1-956656-07-7 (Print edition)
ISBN 978-1-956656-00-8 (Digital edition)

Publisher's note: This is a work of fiction. Names, characters, places and incidents are either the product of the author's imagination or are used fictitiously.

Cover design by James T. Egan of Bookfly Design LLC
Author photography by Cydney Scott Photography

For Norman who, somehow, could always find just the right words.

Prologue

H E STUMBLED DOWN the rubbish-strewn alleyway, feeling
along the walls, searching for meaning with the tips of his
fingers. His eyes were still blurred and blinded with the smoke,
his mind adrift in a fog of confusion, but something like recognition
was tingling in his fingertips and he forced his wobbling legs forward,
step by agonizing step.

The fire was everywhere, it seemed. He had left the flames behind
him, but pain burned in his veins, charring him from the inside out.
He wondered what he would see if he looked in a mirror—if the face
he'd once had would stare back at him, or if all would be twisted and
blackened—a log in the grate, crumbling to embers. He pushed the
thought down. He needed to keep moving.

The Barrens were strangely quiet. He supposed many had been
drawn to the commotion of the fire, but still he was not safe. His heart
pounded, sure that every turn in the road would reveal a patrol running
toward him, and when it didn't, his fear only ratcheted higher still. His
luck was sure to run out, and soon.

He had snatched a cloak off the feebly stirring body of an orderly
and wrapped himself in it to disguise his patient uniform. He pulled it
more tightly around himself, noting as he did so that there was no way
to hide his filthy, bare feet. Then again, there were stranger things to
be seen in the Barrens than the occasional bloke whose shoes had been
stolen—at least, there had been, the last time he'd set foot on these
cobbles. How long ago had that been? Years, surely. It had been so
long since time had meant anything to him that he had lost all track of
it.

He turned the corner into the High Street to see a knot of children

1

arguing playfully over a marble game. As he hobbled closer, one of the children looked up and caught his eye. He looked away, but not before he saw the confusion and then, unmistakably, fear, twist the child's expression. Exhausted though he was, the man quickened his step, forcing his shuffling feet forward as fast as his wasted muscles would allow.

At last, he arrived at the dark and narrow entrance to Butler Lane. Here, in this familiar place that meant he was nearly home, he hesitated for the first time. Would she know him, he wondered? Would she know him when he hardly knew himself? Perhaps it was kinder to seek shelter elsewhere. Perhaps she had moved on, found herself someone else. He had often wished it, prayed to an empty sky that happiness would find her as surely as it had abandoned him. She deserved to be happy. There was nothing at all in the world like her smile. He couldn't have survived that place if he thought she wasn't somewhere, smiling.

He took a deep breath that ended in a gasping, rattling cough. His lungs still felt full of smoke. His eyes still stung with it. He had nowhere else to go, he reminded himself. If she was still there, even if she had built a whole new life for herself, surely she would not begrudge him a meal and a place to sleep for the night. And then tomorrow he would move on, figure out something else.

And if she wasn't there... well, hopelessness was a feeling with which he'd grown quite comfortable.

A neighbor scrubbing out clothes in a washtub looked askance at him as he hobbled down the lane, but otherwise he met no one. The door to their tiny brick flat swam out of the gloom. She had painted it blue. She'd always wanted to paint it blue. A cheerful color, she'd insisted. And in a place like the Barrens, cheerful was hard to come by. There was a small pot of yellow flowers in the window, their faces turned to drink in the tiny sliver of sunlight that filtered down into the lane.

He smiled. The expression felt like a stranger on his face.

Keeping his eyes fixed on the little pot of flowers, he lifted a shaking fist to the door and knocked. The silence that followed seemed to stretch on endlessly. He kept staring at the little flowers, hoping.

When the door opened, it opened just a crack, enough so that a piercing green eye set in a pale, freckled face could examine him suspiciously.

"What is it you need, love? I've got nothing in for tea, or I could spare you some bread. If it's begging you're doing, you'll find no joy here, I'm sorry to say."

He raised his head so that the cloak fell back from his face. Then he held his breath, waiting for the same fear to appear upon her face, for the door, perhaps, to slam closed between them once again.

But the door did not close. The green eye widened, as did the gap of the door as she pushed against it, the better to take him in.

"Peter?"

"Yes, Tillie. It's me."

Tillie stood motionless for what felt like an eternity, her complexion milky beneath its collection of freckles. Then, as if in a dream, she reached out a small, work-roughened hand and pressed her fingertips to his face, prodding at him, making sure he was solidly before her, and not a dream she'd conjured from her years of longing.

"It can't be you, can it?" she whispered.

"It is. It's me," Peter answered, hoping she would hear a shadow of the man she once knew in the hoarse ghost of his voice.

The smile that broke upon her face was like the sun breaking over the horizon. She threw herself into his arms, tears and laughter and kisses and cries all jumbled together so that he hardly knew what to do but fight to stay on his feet.

"I knew it! I knew you were still alive! They all told me I was mad to wait for you, the whole lot of them, but…" her voice trailed off as, too soon, she pulled away from him, looking him over from head to foot, concern blossoming out of her joy. "But Peter, love, whatever's happened to you? Where have you been? And who in the world has done this to you?"

"The Illustratum. The Illustratum did this to me." The words felt like venom being sucked from a wound. He already felt freer having simply spoken them aloud. The truth, at last.

Tillie sucked in a gasp, pressing her hands to her mouth. Then, with a swift glance around the deserted lane, she reached out and tugged at Peter's hand. "Come on inside, quickly, before a patrol sees you. We must get you fed up, you poor darling, and you must tell me everything."

And the door closed behind them, sealing all the joy and sorrow of their reunion behind it.

1

F IGURES FLOATED THROUGH the smoke-haunted grounds
like ghosts.

Ghosts. Everywhere.

Some keened and moaned like lost souls. Some staggered. Others
flew about like apparitions, white smocks and filthy hair streaming out
behind them. Some simply stood, eyes staring, faces like blank pages
as they watched their prison burn.

And sunken into the grass, shaking and folded upon legs that
would no longer hold her, another figure. Her teeth chattered. Her
throat burned. Shock and grief snatched at her breath in equal
measure, and her chest rose and fell shallowly as she gasped for air.
All she could do was stare—stare at the place where the figure had
slipped away over the wall and out of sight. Her very own ghost,
returned to haunt her.

"Eliza?"

The voice that whispered in her ear startled her so badly that
she cried out and raised her hands in front of her—she did not even
know why. To defend herself? From what? Ghosts couldn't hurt
people—not like that, anyway.

"Eliza, are you all right? Are you hurt?"

The sound was not the rattling whisper of a ghost, but the crisp and
anxious snap of her mistress's voice, and Eliza lowered her hands and
focused her eyes through the smoke to see Jessamine crouching down
beside her in the grass.

"I... I don't... no, I'm not hurt." She couldn't answer the first question. She hardly knew who she was, let alone how she was. The last few moments had changed everything.

"We've got to get you away from all this smoke," Jessamine muttered. Her forehead crinkled with concern as she laid a hand on Eliza's clammy forehead and took in her papery complexion.

"It's not the smoke," Eliza muttered, meeting her mistress's eye and watching the realization appear there, like a candle catching flame.

"Yes, of course. Your mother. The shock. You poor darling. I can't imagine."

Jessamine's words seemed to bring Eliza back to herself. Suddenly she was looking around her with clear eyes as the realization sunk in: they were still on the grounds of Bethlem Hospital, and the ghosts were very real patients run amok as the building burned. As though to confirm her realization, a large section of roof chose that very moment to cave in, tumbling down into the depths of the inferno with a deafening crash and sending great plumes of smoke and showers of fiery ash spewing up into the sky.

"Come on, now. Up you get. We must alert the staff that we're all right. Mr. Brown looks like he might drop dead with worry, not that I'm much bothered about that after what we saw of that place, but we must keep up appearances," Jessamine said, hooking an arm under Eliza's and pulling her upright. Eliza scrambled to get her feet under her, and hastily patted at herself to make sure that her appearance was in order—her cap in place upon her hair, her gloves upon her hands. Her hem was torn and there were smudges of soot on her apron, but that seemed to be the worst of it. Jessamine's elaborate hat was slightly askew, and there was grass and mud stuck to the toe of her boot, but other than that she looked remarkably unscathed.

"Yes, miss. Let's go. I'm... I'm all right now."

Jessamine was still looking at her with concern, but they set off together across the lawn, leaping to the side as a patient came tearing across the grass toward them, spitting profanity, only to be tackled to the ground by an orderly a moment later. There was an awful crunching sound, and the man did not get up again. Eliza could feel that Jessamine's hand on her arm was now shaking. They passed another shape on the ground. Eliza averted her eyes quickly but not before the moaning of the figure had caught her attention and she got a glimpse of black and flaking skin and the pungent smell of burnt flesh.

She felt the vomit rise in her throat and had to swallow it back down again.

They were making their way toward a group of men standing under a gnarled tree. One of the men looked up as they drew nearer, relief spilling over his features like the sunlight over the horizon.

"Miss Hallewell! My dear!" Mr. Brown broke away from the men, mostly Praesidio guards, and hurried over to meet them. "I cannot begin to express my relief at seeing you. I thought... but you're here. My word, are you hurt? You must be seen to at once."

Jessamine opened her mouth to protest, but Mr. Brown was waving his arms frantically at a doctor who had just finished bandaging the arm of a wailing patient on the ground. Jessamine snapped her mouth shut again, looking resigned. It would be much easier to let them fuss over her than to argue.

"Right, then, well if that's all, Mr. Brown, we'll move along to questioning some of the other staff," said the most senior of the guards, the many medals and patches emblazoned upon his sash designating him as the officer in charge. "We'll alert the Elders at once."

"The Elders? Is that really... well, yes, I suppose it is," Mr. Brown mumbled to himself, his face now the color of porridge. He dragged a handkerchief over his forehead.

"Have you located the Riftborn who started the blaze?" asked the guard.

Mr. Brown shook his head. "I'm sorry, I don't know. It's been absolute chaos. The patients who have been caught and subdued by the staff are being moved to the medical outbuilding on the back of the grounds. You can check in with the doctors there. I'll be along shortly; I must see to Miss Hallewell."

"Mr. Brown, please do not concern yourself with me," Jessamine said. "I am quite well, and you must have so many other things to tend to..."

But no. No, Mr. Brown would not hear of it! Mr. Brown could not dream of being anywhere else but by her side! Mr. Brown saw it as his Creator-given duty to ensure that she had everything she required and was safely on her way home before he could possibly spare a thought for anyone else on the grounds! It was not hard to interpret the bowing and scraping and overattentiveness; whatever else he may have claimed to feel, Mr. Brown was downright terrified of what would happen when Elder Hallewell discovered that his only daughter had been endangered on his watch.

"Insufferable man," Jessamine huffed, once the doctor had finally declared her fit and Mr. Brown had bowed and groveled them right into their carriage and shut the door. "Pretending to care about me when it's his own hide he's worried about. And all those patients!" She shook her head, her eyes full of tears. "I can't believe the conditions they're kept in. It's abominable! When my father hears about this..." Jessamine's voice faded away as Eliza met her eye and she let out a soft gasp. "You think he already knows."

Eliza merely nodded.

"And you... you still think he knew that Bridie was there?"

"Yes."

The struggle played out clearly on Jessamine's face, like a scene being played on the stage. She struggled to believe that her father could be so cruel. Eliza did not bother to try to disabuse her of this notion. She would know soon enough, one way or another, just what Josiah Hallewell was capable of, and Eliza did not relish the idea of being the one to break her mistress' heart like that. Let Elder Hallewell break it himself. Eliza was done doing the cruelest of his bidding where his daughter was concerned.

Her head was still swimming, and she felt like she was clinging to her composure by the very thinnest and frayed of threads. She knotted her hands together in her lap in an effort to still their violent trembling. She didn't trust herself to discuss the matter with her mistress—she was afraid that if she started, the dam would break and everything she knew—about the Illustratum, about Riftmead, about the Resistance—would all come spilling out of her in a flood that could quite possibly drown them all.

"Speaking of my father, we really ought to go over our story, for when he arrives home," Jessamine said. "He's going to be angry that I was there, I'm sure of it."

"I am sure of it, too," Eliza agreed, although she did not divulge that any anger he showed today would be a mere shadow of the anger to come. She cowered inside to think what Josiah Hallewell would say when he discovered that both Bridie and Emmeline had escaped in the chaotic aftermath of the fire. His entire façade of benevolence would slip away in that moment, and he would never be able to rebuild it. From that moment on, his daughter—and the world—would always know what he truly was. And although there was a part of Eliza that longed for it, her sensible side was praying—though she hardly knew to whom anymore—that their knowledge of Emmeline's plight and their role in her escape would remain deeply buried.

"Eliza?"

"Hmm?"

"Did you hear me?"

"No, I'm sorry, miss, what did you say?"

"I asked whether you thought there was any chance my father won't know we were there?"

"Oh, I don't think so, miss. You heard the guard. They are going to alert the Elders at once, and I can't imagine they would leave out the detail that the daughter of an Elder had just barely escaped a burning building. No, I think we must accept that your father will know everything before we even arrive back at Larkspur Manor."

Jessamine bit her lip. "Yes, you're right, of course. It was a silly question."

"It wasn't silly. Merely hopeful," Eliza said with a weak attempt at a smile.

"Well, never mind that now," Jessamine said, with an impatient wave of her hand. "I can't believe I'm even talking about it. What must you think of me?"

Eliza frowned at her mistress. "What do you mean?"

"Imagine me, prattling on about my father after what's just happened," Jessamine said, reaching down and taking Eliza's hand. "Your mother, Eliza! I'm talking about your mother!"

Eliza looked down at her mistress's hand enclosed over her own, but her voice felt lost inside of her and she didn't answer.

"You poor creature," Jessamine went on. "What a shock that must have been. Did you... had you any idea she was there?"

Eliza shook her head and held her breath, but the question came anyway, as she knew it must.

"But my goodness, why was she there in the first place?" Jessamine murmured. "I knew she disappeared, but..." She broke off her speculation at the look on Eliza's face. "But of course, you cannot know any more than me, can you? Please forgive me, Eliza. I won't bring it up again, not until you're ready."

"Thank you, miss," Eliza replied in barely more than a whisper, grateful for the chance to avoid the topic.

"I'll just say one last thing," Jessamine said, turning to face Eliza and taking both of her hands. "I'm sure you'll want to see her, when it's safe. I just want to tell you that I will never begrudge you that. I will cover for you, I swear it. Whenever you want to see her, you go, and never mind about me. I can bloody well lace up my own boots, understand?"

Eliza's eyes widened.

"What?" Jessamine asked, sounding anxious.

"Nothing, it's only..." Eliza shook her head. "I can't believe I just heard the word 'bloody' come out of your mouth."

Jessamine laughed. "Yes, well. Quite. Although, I rather think breaking patients out of an asylum for the insane is rather the more shocking of the things I've done today."

A laugh burbled up in Eliza's throat, which broke the stranglehold on her emotions. The laugh was quickly followed by tears, and before she knew what was happening, she was sobbing unrestrainedly in Jessamine's arms. Jessamine did not try to calm or placate her. She simply stroked Eliza's hair and let her cry herself out. By the time Larkspur Manor loomed up at them through the gloom of a foggy afternoon, Eliza felt as dry and fragile as kindling.

One spark, and up she would go, just like Bedlam. She almost longed for it.

To the Most Honorable Elder Hallewell,

Sir, I write to you this morning with great urgency, and yet I do not wish to cause you alarm. Be assured that the conclusion of my tale shall bode no illness nor injury to any person you hold dear. I cannot continue with my letter until I have satisfied myself that you shall not be ill at ease as you read.

I had the pleasure this morning of offering my services to your charming daughter, who, as I am sure you are aware, wrote to me last week requesting a tour of our fine facility at Bethlem Hospital. I was most pleased to hear of her interest in our work here and offered most heartily to be her tour guide. We fixed upon an appointment this morning, and I met her promptly at 8 o'clock as agreed.

She very kindly brought with her an assortment of items for donation, for which I thanked her profusely. We then embarked on a tour of the site, for she was very interested in the manner of care our patients receive, as well as the therapies and activities we provide. I answered her questions and introduced her to our staff. She was quite pleased and, I daresay, impressed with all she saw. We take great pride in being able to allow the Dignus to interact safely with the public-facing areas of the hospital, and having a guest of your daughter's social stature was a great privilege for us.

When we arrived in the women's common area, however, a regrettable incident occurred, and one which I could not possibly have foreseen, or I assure you, your daughter would never have been exposed to it. A confrontation with a doctor resulted in an outburst from a usually docile patient, which quickly riled the others into a frenzy. A fire broke out—it appeared to have been started by a patient who is a Catalyst—and we were forced to evacuate the building. We did so swiftly, and your daughter was escorted to the grounds. I saw to her well-being personally and made sure she was looked over by

11

the medical staff on site before seeing her safely off home by her own conveyance. Her maid, who attended her throughout the visit, was also unharmed.

By now, I am sure you have heard of the fire from the Praesidio, but I could not settle myself until you were reassured of your daughter's safety. I cannot put into words my regret that such a disastrous event should take place on the very same day as her visit. But the Creator shone his protection upon her, as he surely must always do, and so I am most grateful to be able to conclude my letter thus.

I remain,
Your humble servant,

Thomas Brown

2

J OSIAH HALLEWELL STARED DOWN at the letter, the words blurring in and out of focus as his hands shook with shock and anger and something else less definable, but which left a bitter tang on his tongue that tasted suspiciously like fear.

Jessamine had been at Bedlam, of all places. *Bedlam*.

"Josiah, are you quite all right? You look as though you've seen a ghost!"

Josiah whirled to see Francis charging toward him. Without offering a word of explanation, he thrust the letter at him and watched Francis' eyebrows disappear into his hair as he read it.

"Bloody hell," Francis whispered.

"My thoughts exactly," Josiah replied. He swallowed hard and then added, "Of course, I knew she'd been on the grounds because you'd informed me so, but this... she was in the very room where the fire broke out, Francis! Do you think this was meant to be an attack on me?"

Francis frowned. "The fire? I don't see how."

"I may have been tempted to say the same an hour ago, but the more I think about it, the less likely it seems. A fire breaks out at Bedlam on the very morning my daughter traipses off there on some foolish philanthropic whim? That doesn't seem suspicious to you?"

Francis snorted. "We'll have to wait for the official report, but the Praesidio are saying it was a Riftborn patient who set the fire after a confrontation with a staff member, and this letter confirms it. I understand your concern, Josiah, but I think we must chalk this up to an unfortunate coincidence."

Josiah wanted to argue, but a bell rang out through the halls, assaulting his ears and what remained of his composure. The Council meeting was about to begin, and another horrifying thought had just occurred to him.

"Francis, the patients..."

"Are being accounted for as we speak," Francis said. He reached out and gripped Josiah's shoulder. "I think the bigger concern is the other Elders getting wind of your daughter's presence there. Do not mention it unless it becomes absolutely necessary, understand? It's not clear yet who among them may be privy to that information, and frankly, the fewer the better."

Josiah nodded absently. His mind had already sped away from Jessamine, had already barreled into a future catastrophe that was unfurling faster than he could gain control of it. He could hear that Francis was still talking to him in soothing tones, but not a word could penetrate the buzz of panicked speculation that now filled his head. Without knowing what he was doing, he obeyed Francis' tug on his arm and began the long walk toward the Council chamber.

The room, upon their entering it, was as silent as a funeral and equally as somber. Josiah scanned the sea of faces on the benches. Each one had contracted into expressions of misery or disbelief. He could still feel the shock sitting upon his own features like a mask he could not take off. How could so much have gone so disastrously wrong in such a short span of time? It was enough to make the mind reel.

"Let us all take our places. The Praesidio has another update coming for us in just a few moments," the Moderator called from his place at the top of the hall.

There followed a great rumbling as the Elders took their seats, mumbling to each other in tones of dismay. It was clear they all expected the update to confirm whatever dire consequences they'd concocted in their imaginations the moment they first heard the news of the fire.

Madmen running through the streets. Bedlam ablaze. Public uproar as the volunteer brigades fought to keep the flames from spreading beyond the asylum's boundaries.

And then, of course, there were the very real consequences that were now running riot in Josiah's mind. It took every ounce of self-control to remain in his seat, to remain stationary and calm while the carefully constructed future he'd been on the verge of seizing crumbled in front of him. He felt a hand come to rest on his forearm and looked over to see Francis beside him. The warning in his eyes was clear. *Keep yourself together. Be patient.* He was right, naturally, but it did not stop Josiah from shaking his hand off.

At that moment the High Elder entered the door at the top of the hall and took his place above the Moderator. He moved slowly, laboriously, and it was with considerable difficulty that he lowered himself into his chair. Josiah frowned. Morgan was failing more quickly than he'd realized. They were running out of time.

"Let us begin," the High Elder called out, an audible quaver in his voice.

"This extraordinary meeting of the Council is hereby called to order," the Moderator bellowed, slamming his gavel upon the desktop and clearing his throat importantly. "I invite the representative from the Praesidio leadership to present his report on the incident at Bethlem Hospital as it stands thus far."

A very tall man in a Praesidio colonel's uniform unfolded his lanky frame from the bench by the rear door and walked to the podium. He shuffled a stack of papers in front of him and began to drone in a monotone voice.

"At ten o'clock this morning a fire broke out in the main building of Bethlem Hospital. According to the statements from staff taken on the premises, the fire was started by one of the patients, a Catalyst who first attacked a staff member and then set fire to the draperies in the common area of the women's ward."

A chorus of muttering broke out, but the colonel carried on with his report as though he did not hear them.

"The staff attempted to evacuate as many patients as possible, but the flames spread quickly. It is unclear at this time how many of the patients may have perished within the walls of the hospital, but it is believed to be in the dozens."

Josiah heard a throat clearing loudly to his left and turned in time to see Elder Carpenter give him a smug look before turning and raising a hand into the air. The Moderator acknowledged him with a wave of his hand.

"What news of the Dignus present?" Elder Carpenter called out.

"The doctors, nurses, and other staff are all being accounted for as we speak," the colonel rattled off, flipping to the next page of his report. "We know for sure that at least one doctor, the physician in charge, a Dr. Blakewell, is deceased. His body has been pulled from the building and has been identified by the hospital manager, a Mr. Brown. There are others dead and wounded among the staff, but we will not know the details until the full report comes in from the soldiers on site. And of course, there may still be others who were trapped inside. We cannot know the full extent of the casualties until the building has been fully searched, and that could take days. We are still not confident that the place is structurally sound enough to enter, now that the flames have been quenched."

"What about visitors on the premises?" continued Elder Carpenter, his dramatic voice carrying easily over the low rumblings of response. "There was a rumor there were Dignus visitors on the premises when the fire broke out."

Josiah swore under his breath. Francis was right. There could be no hiding Jessamine's presence there that day. And of course, Elder Carpenter would be the one to seize on it and use it to bludgeon him publicly. That jumped-up little bastard had been angling for attention for months, trying to set himself up as an alternative to Josiah, a sort of dark horse candidate. At first, Josiah had thought of it as little worth his notice—nothing more than a way for Carpenter to build his reputation now for a real run at the highest seat in a decade or so. But he had been growing bolder in his attacks on Josiah, and it was a boldness that refused to be ignored. Josiah could not hand him this victory of being called out in such a manner. It was best to own the news rather than be forced to react to it under the intense scrutiny of the entire Council. While the colonel searched his notes for the pertinent information, Josiah stood up and signaled his intention to speak.

"I can answer that, Elder Carpenter," he said, his voice clear and carrying. Nothing to hide, nothing to fear. "My own dear daughter, Jessamine, happened to be at Bethlem Hospital today, taking a tour as part of her charitable endeavors. I hardly dare to think what might have happened to her, but I am glad to report that I have already been brought the news that she is safe and well, and on her way back to Larkspur Manor, Creator be praised."

There was an answering chorus of "Creator be praised" as the rest of the Council had no choice but to echo his sentiments. The colonel gave a curt nod as though to acknowledge that Josiah's words

16

confirmed his report. Josiah turned and looked Elder Carpenter coolly in the eyes. Elder Carpenter, who looked as though he'd just been made to swallow castor oil, had no choice but to repeat the sentiments of relief that courtesy demanded. Josiah stared Elder Carpenter down into his seat before sitting himself, pulse thudding in his temple as he fought to remain calm. He felt as though the fires of Bedlam were raging in the Council Room itself while the others sat so calmly amidst the flames.

"We have had reports of patients loose in the streets of London," the colonel continued. Josiah stiffened at once. "Two have been apprehended by patrols and one by a pair of concerned Riftborn citizens. We must assume that others remain unaccounted for and have therefore increased the presence of patrols in the areas surrounding the hospital. Search parties will be formed and dispersed once we know precisely which and how many patients we are looking for."

"We ought to alert the public, ask them to be on the lookout for the escaped patients," Elder Smythe bleated from his seat in the front.

"Official notices have already been drawn up, sir," the colonel replied flatly. "Soldiers have been assigned to post them throughout the Barrens and neighborhoods in close proximity to Bethlem. In the absence of names and descriptions, citizens have been asked to keep an eye out for anyone acting in a suspicious manner and have been provided with a description of the patient uniforms."

"I hardly think uniformed lunatics will be hard to spot," Elder Garrison announced with a derisive snort. "Surely it won't be difficult to round them up."

"I wouldn't get too complacent on that score," Francis replied, rising to his feet. "Let us remember that madness presents itself in many ways and can be insidious. We cannot assume the patients will be babbling nonsense and swinging from the trees. There is cunning and guile among the mad just as there is among the sane. We must be wary and assume these patients will not be easy to apprehend."

There was a rumbling of general approval at these words, and Elder Garrison sat down, looking surly. Josiah stood again. It was time to broach the subject he had wished to avoid.

"My brothers, there is another issue at hand which we must discuss. I know it is easy for us to dismiss the ravings of lunatics, but the fact remains that the Riftborn of the Barrens are easily influenced. Need I remind you of the important research that was taking place within the walls of Bethlem and other institutions across our great city? Research involving the miraculous properties of Riftmead upon the sin of Riftmagic?"

The Elders went quiet. Some were solemnly nodding their heads, having already scented the danger but others, Elder Smythe among them, wore expressions fitting to being clubbed over the head. Evidently, not all of them had foreseen the problem. A glance at the High Elder revealed him slightly hunched, his face pale and drawn. Josiah frowned and continued.

"As we all well know, the recent initiative to increase the dispersal of Riftmead among the greater Riftborn population has been a definitive success. We've seen a dramatic reduction in violence and unrest within the Barrens, and that is a direct result of the research and implementation of regular Riftmead dosing within places like Bethlem Hospital. But now the patients upon whom the Riftmead has been tested have escaped. This could create another very messy and volatile situation for us."

Elder Carpenter rose, his expression snide. "I fail to see how. You are suggesting that the word of escaped lunatics will be believed over the word of the Elder Council? I, for one, can hardly imagine a less likely scenario. We chose the lunatic population precisely for this reason. Indeed, it was argued for strongly on the sole fact that a lunatic cannot be trusted or believed, therefore using them for experimentation was ideal."

"Yes, and while I believe that using lunatics was the safest choice, there is still a risk that some of the patients who have escaped could convince others that—"

"I'm sorry, Josiah, but I think you are being paranoid here," Elder Carpenter announced, breaking through the end of Josiah's statement with all the subtlety of a sledgehammer. "It's the word of a half-naked lunatic shouting in the streets over the entire Elder Council. I fail to see who would be convinced by the former in the face of the latter."

"Do I need to remind you that not every patient within the walls of Bedlam is actually insane?" Josiah asked, his voice rising. "You know as well as the rest of us that we have used the place to dispose of some of our more difficult Riftborn criminals."

"But those criminals are now discredited, tainted by the same lunacy as the true lunatics. Once someone has been locked up in Bethlem Hospital, their true mental state becomes irrelevant. They cannot be trusted, even by the other Riftborn." Elder Carpenter spoke the words with a ringing finality that meant he knew the argument had been won, an assessment confirmed by the sea of heads nodding along behind him.

Josiah felt his hold on the room slipping away. With a slight edge of panic in his voice, he appealed directly to the High Elder.

"High Elder, I humbly beg your opinion on the matter," Josiah said, turning his face to the uppermost seat. He realized a moment too late that this was a terrible mistake. Morgan's face was twisted with pain, and it was only with a visible effort that he was able to turn his attention back to the discussion happening in front of him. When he did so, it was with an impatient wave of his hand.

"We cannot waste resources trying to round up a handful of Riftborn patients. Elder Carpenter is correct. No one will listen to them anyway. Put up the notices if you must, but let us concentrate our efforts on continuing our work with the patients that remain. Let me hear some proposals on where we might find the space and resources to house the patients that remain in our custody."

It took every ounce of his self-control (as well as Francis' warning hand on his arm) to prevent Josiah from arguing right then and there with the High Elder, a prospect that would never have so much as crossed his mind a mere month ago. He felt like he was watching a tapestry being unwoven, the men around him standing there, pulling at the stray threads. "It's just a single thread," they seemed to say. "What does it matter?" But it did matter. Every thread mattered. Every thread was part of the pattern, every thread lent its strength to the integrity of the whole. With each thread carelessly pulled, they were in very real danger of everything unraveling, and no one could see it but him.

§

"Francis, we must do something. This situation is spinning out of control. Surely you see that," Josiah said, nearly an hour later, when they were at last adjourned and could retreat to the privacy of Francis' office.

"Would you stop pacing, man? For Creator's sake, you're in danger of wearing a hole right through my rug. And blast it, I love that rug. Sit down and have a drink, steady your nerves," Francis said, inclining his head toward the pair of chairs by the fire and pulling the stopper from a cut crystal decanter of scotch.

Josiah glared at Francis but did as he was bid and threw himself into the chair. Francis handed him a glass with a generous measure of amber liquid sloshing around inside it, but he did not drink. He did not think he could bear to dull his senses, not when so much was at stake. Francis settled himself into the chair opposite him, took a long sip of scotch, rolled it around his mouth in an exaggerated manner, and then swallowed. Only then did he speak.

"Josiah, your picture is not the big picture," Francis said.

"I beg your pardon?" Josiah snapped, affronted.

"I'm not saying you aren't right to worry, but you need to understand why the others do not share your fears," Francis said patiently.

Josiah bit back the retort that had been waiting restlessly on his tongue. Damn it all, he hated when Francis was right.

"You've got a horse in this race, Josiah, and you cannot let them know it. If we are to repair the damage and prevent any future threats to your political career, we may need to handle this ourselves."

"What do you mean, handle it ourselves? I can't very well patrol the streets in search of escaped patients, although Alexander Carpenter would be nothing short of delighted to see me resort to it," Josiah snapped.

"You're not letting that jumped-up little blighter get to you, are you?" Francis cried, a laugh rumbling in his chest. "Good Lord, Josiah, if I didn't know any better, I'd say you were losing your nerve."

"Losing my nerve? Losing my patience is more like it. Who does that cheeky little weasel think he is, calling me out like that in front of the rest of the Council?!"

"He thinks he's his father's son, that's bloody well who. Ever since he stepped into his father's seat, he's had his eye on you. You remember how bitter George Carpenter was when you were named Morgan's counselor. He never got over it. And that boy of his has been raised on a steady diet of vitriol aimed at you since he was in short pants."

"Someone ought to teach him his place," Josiah growled.

"Yes, they ought to, but it cannot be you. You've got bigger fish to fry, and you're letting that upstart distract you."

"I'm not distracted!"

"I'm glad to hear it. Now, to the matter at hand, which is the escaped lunatics."

Josiah opened his mouth to argue, but a sharp look from Francis induced him to shut it once again. He would make no more headway on the topic of Alexander Carpenter, that much was clear.

"That's more like it," Francis said with satisfaction. "Now, first, we don't need to go charging off in search of a solution if there's no problem. Remember, we are not yet sure if the maid and the Braxton woman are accounted for. You may be working yourself up into a frenzy for nothing."

Josiah took a deep breath. "Yes, of course."

"Get Brother Goodwin down to Bedlam. Task him with ensuring that both women are identified and back in custody. If they are, you're in the clear. If not, then we decide what to do next."

"But Francis, you must understand my urgency. At this very moment either one of them could be in search of allies, telling their story to anyone who will listen!" Josiah countered.

"I do not deny it. But the chances are slim. There's a better chance they've both been reduced to cinders," Francis said, in a tone that suggested this was all just friendly banter. "But let me ask you this: where would either of these women go, if they were looking for allies?"

Josiah thought for a moment. "Home," he said at last.

"Precisely," Francis said.

"But they would have to be mad to try to return to Larkspur Manor!" Josiah said. "Escaping a madhouse only to return to the home of the man who put you there? They aren't actual lunatics, I'm sure I need not remind you."

"Yes, but with nowhere else to turn, they might just be desperate enough to try it," Francis said. "Hire a few Praesidio guards to keep watch over your grounds. If they are mad enough to try to return, they'll be apprehended before they can find a single servant to hear them out. Speaking of your servants, have you any you mistrust?"

Josiah bristled. "Of course not! What do you take me for?"

"What about Braxton? Would you worry he might try to aid his wife if she returned?" Francis asked, narrowing his eyes shrewdly.

But Josiah was shaking his head before the question was even finished. "Absolutely not. Braxton is faithful to his core; I'd stake my life on it."

"Staking your life on a Riftborn? That's saying something," Francis chuckled, but seemed to accept Josiah's assessment at face value. "Very well, then. If you cut them off from the place, they'll have no choice but to hide or flee. Either way, they disappear, and with them, any threat to your future."

Josiah could see the logic laid out before him, but the sense of relief he expected refused to sink in. His fear had created a barrier, and not even Francis' well-reasoned arguments could penetrate it. Still, he knew he would have to play along, at least for now. After all, he needed Francis by his side just as much as he needed the Braxton woman and the scullery maid to vanish.

"Very well. I will see to the added security. But I will do it privately, not through the Praesidio office. I don't need other Elders nosing around in the official requests and asking questions."

Francis nodded his approval of this strategy. "Very good. Now that we've settled that particular distraction, let's remember that there's a more pressing issue at hand, and that is getting the Council to reschedule the election preparations. You saw Morgan today."

Josiah nodded, his expression grim. "Yes, I did. He is failing quickly. Too quickly."

"Precisely. And all of this chasing around and disposing of Riftborn threats will mean nothing if your name isn't on the ballot with the official recommendation of the High Elder himself stamped beside it. Secure that in writing, and you've as good as won, Josiah."

"Yes. Yes, you're right."

"You're damn right, I am. Now, we'll return after this recess and push through the popular measures quickly. I know you want to act more aggressively and divert more resources to the missing patients, but the subsequent arguing and bargaining will eat up valuable time we do not have. Push for a quick resolution to this Bedlam catastrophe so that we can return to the very important business of getting you installed." Francis raised his glass. "To reaping the benefits of our hard work, Josiah."

Josiah raised his own glass and forced his mouth into the grim approximation of a smile. "Yes, indeed, friend. I'll drink to that."

3

I T WAS WELL PAST DARK, but Jessamine was not yet in bed.
She sat by her window in her dressing gown, eyes fixed on the
long gravel drive that would bring her father home to Larkspur
Manor.

Word had come earlier in the evening, as Jessamine dressed for
dinner, that her father would not be able to join her. This was
unsurprising. With the burning of Bedlam, the Illustratum must surely
be in a state of chaos. Jessamine knew the asylum was much too
far away for her to see from her window, and yet she fancied a
deeper darkness to the sky in the direction of the river, a darkness
born of smoke and destruction. She wondered if the flames had yet
been quenched, or if the fire had spread beyond the boundaries of the
grounds.

A soft snore sounded behind her, and Jessamine looked over her
shoulder to gaze upon Eliza, curled like a cat upon the chaise, a
hairbrush still clutched in her hand. She had insisted on waiting up
with Jessamine so that the latter wouldn't have to face her father's fury
alone, but shock had sapped the last of her energy hours ago. Her sleep
at first had been fitful, almost feverish, but in the last little while she
had settled into a deeper, calmer slumber, for which Jessamine was
grateful; each whimper and cry that had escaped Eliza had felt like a
dagger to Jessamine's heart.

Jessamine's own mother was a source of great heartache, and yet
she felt that Eliza's heartache must be worse. At least Jessamine had
known where her mother was, even if she was just as unreachable.
But for Eliza to discover her mother had been nearby for so many

23

years, and to know what they had been doing to her all that time... Jessamine shuddered. That place... the state of those poor patients... she could hardly imagine a danker cauldron of misery, and suddenly found herself fiercely glad that the place was likely little more than a pile of blackened stones now.

The familiar grinding sound of hooves and wheels upon gravel dragged Jessamine's attention back to the window. Her father had arrived home at last. Jessamine jumped to her feet, fear licking up her insides like the flames that had engulfed Bedlam. She knew she had only minutes before she was summoned, and she had to force herself not to hide under her covers like a child and feign slumber. Putting off the confrontation would do nothing but feed her choking sense of anticipation. Best to get it over with.

It could not have been five minutes later—though arguably five of the longest minutes of her life—that a tentative knock sounded upon her door. She hastened to answer it and found one of the footmen waiting on the other side of it, blushing furiously and staring pointedly at his own feet.

"Miss Jessamine, your father would like to see you in his study."

"Yes, of course. I shall be right down," she replied, and closed the door again.

Jessamine glanced back at Eliza once more but had not the heart to wake her. Eliza did not need a share in her father's fury on top of all she had suffered that day. Jessamine tucked a blanket carefully around her and slipped out without disturbing her. By the time she reached her father's study door, there was hardly a cell in Jessamine's body that was not alight. Though she despised herself for it, she could not help but peek around the doorway like a naughty child to catch a glimpse of what she might be facing.

He stood over the fire, staring down into the flames with a brooding expression that sapped the last of Jessamine's remaining courage. She had seen that expression before, and it had never been a harbinger of anything but anger of the most unreasonable sort. Jessamine hoisted a look of meek obedience onto her face and entered the room, clearing her throat to announce her presence.

"You asked to see me, father?"

"Jessamine!" He looked up at her, and a strange spasm of emotion crossed his features. He started forward; a hand outstretched toward her before he seemed to take possession of himself once more. He let his hand swing back down to his side and he stepped back again, placing a hand upon the fireplace mantel as though to anchor himself. "You... you are all right, then? You are not injured?"

"No, father. I assure you, I am quite well," Jessamine replied. For a moment, she had thought her father was going to reach out and embrace her, and the sudden, unexpected ache for it left her breathless and confused.

He looked her up and down for a moment longer, as though he did not trust her own assessment, as though he might spy a bandage or a mark somewhere upon her person. When he found none, he turned his eyes back to the fire.

"What in Creator's name were you doing at Bethlem, Jessamine? You have no business in such a place," he said.

The sharpness in his tone stabbed at her. "I am sorry, father. I had no idea you would disapprove, truly. My charity group has visited many such places, and we have never felt ourselves in jeopardy."

"It is not down to you, a mere child, to decide what is or is not dangerous. You ought to have told me your intention. I would never have allowed it."

The ring on Jessamine's finger seemed suddenly to weigh a hundred pounds. "I am not a child," she muttered.

"You are barely eighteen."

"I am a woman, engaged to be married."

"Then you ought to have behaved like one!" Elder Hallewell snapped. "What sensible woman would place herself in such a position?"

Anger came to Jessamine's defense now, and her voice, shaking a moment before, had a note of steel in it now. She would not be infantilized like this. "A woman who desires to better understand the society in which she lives so that she can find her place in it!" she replied. "We have always been told to take to heart our duty to the less fortunate, and I was only trying to—"

"Your silly meetings and little projects are all well and good, Jessamine, but you cannot place yourself in harm's way like that. It's irresponsible."

Silly meetings? Little projects? Jessamine could barely hold back her anger. For the second time in her life, she came dangerously close to shouting at her father. It was with a herculean effort that she kept her voice calm and even as she replied, "Many of the Dignus

25

have visited Bethlem Hospital, some of my friends included. I can't imagine Mr. Brown thought it irresponsible for me to be there or he would not have agreed to the tour."

"Don't speak to me of that man!" Elder Hallewell growled, banging his fist upon the mantelpiece, and causing the whisky in his glass to slop onto the polished surface. "He'll be lucky to keep his freedom, let alone his job. His incompetence is now the subject of an official Illustratum inquiry."

"The fire wasn't his fault, father," Jessamine said softly. She did not care for Mr. Brown, but she hardly thought he deserved to be locked up.

"We'll let the investigation decide that, thank you very much," Elder Hallewell said. "That fire is only the last in a very long list of complaints that man must answer for. I shall be interrogating him personally, I assure you."

"I have no doubt of that," Jessamine said dryly, though her father seemed too preoccupied to miss the sarcastic edge to her voice. "But you must see, father, that I am equally blameless. The fire was a fluke—a danger I could not possibly have predicted."

"There are other dangers in a place like that—dangers you can't even begin to conceive of."

He seemed to be struggling with what he wanted to say next. He kept clearing his throat and opening his mouth. Jessamine waited patiently.

"I need to… to know what you saw there," he said at last.

"What I saw?"

"Yes. I need to… you need to tell me."

Jessamine frowned. "I'm afraid I don't…"

"For Creator's sake, Jessamine, what did the man show you?!" Elder Hallewell shouted. Jessamine took a step back. Her father looked half-mad in the firelight, his hair in disarray from running his fingers through it, his collar askew.

"I… I saw what anyone might see on a tour, father. I was taken through the grounds, the common areas, the women's ward…"

"He took you through the women's ward?" Elder Hallewell asked, his voice rising unnaturally.

"Well, yes, of course! He couldn't take me through the men's ward. That would have been highly irregular, not to mention dangerous, I should imagine," Jessamine said, somewhat indignantly.

26

"But in the women's ward, what did he show you?" Elder Hallewell pressed. His knuckles were white on his whiskey glass and his eyes were wide and glazed with something very like fear.

"He... he showed me the places they bring the patients to socialize, the places where they employ different therapies, and so forth..."

"And what of the patients?"

"What of the patients? Yes, we saw many, of course, but I assure you he did not let any of them get too close. The dangerous ones are locked up, aren't they?" Jessamine felt so wrong-footed that the floor might have been the swaying deck of a ship at sea. Something was terribly off. What was the man so riled up about? She had anticipated his anger about the danger of the fire, but this was something altogether different. What was he so scared she might have...?

And suddenly the truth slammed into her with such force that she only just managed to stop herself from gasping out loud. He knew. All along, he knew Bridie was there, and perhaps even Eliza's mother, too. Two of his former servants, locked up together in Bedlam, neither of them mad, which he knew all along. She did not need him to say it out loud; the naked animal panic in his eyes was all the confirmation she could ever hope for. The reason his questions seemed strange was because he could not directly ask her what he really wanted to know: whether she had recognized either of their former servants while touring within those walls. Eliza had warned her, but she had not wanted to believe it, had fought against the abhorrent notion with all her might. Now, all the fight went out of her. She could see the truth as plainly as if it was written in ink upon his brow.

All of this flashed through her mind in the span of a second, a second during which she miraculously managed to keep control of her facial expression. Her father, on the other hand, seemed to deflate, an unabashed sigh of relief fluttering through his lips as his chin dropped to his chest.

"I see. That's... that's good." He picked up his head, drained his glass, and cleared his throat, trying to re-assume some semblance of calm and authority. "I'm glad to hear he restricted you to appropriate areas of the hospital at least. Given the man's lack of propriety, I shouldn't have been surprised if he'd allowed you to mingle with the violent and criminally insane they keep in the basements."

"Of course not," Jessamine said, somewhat coldly. "Nor would I have wanted to see such things. I hope you know I have more sense than that."

Elder Hallewell met his daughter's eye, and she watched the last of the fear ebb away. "Yes, of course. But I must ask you, from now on, to consult with me before you take it upon yourself to tour any of the Illustratum-run institutions. I have much more knowledge about what goes on in such places than you could hope to have."

Yes, you certainly do, Jessamine thought. Out loud, she replied, "Yes, father. I would have done so on this occasion as well, but I've hardly seen you since the visit to the palace. I did not like to bother you. I know that your work must come first."

Elder Hallewell's face broke into something like a sad smile. "I shall never be too busy to ensure your safety, Jessamine. But you must assist me. Our family cannot afford to be caught up in a scandal, especially now, with your nuptials just around the corner."

"Of course, father," Jessamine bleated obediently, feeling sick with herself. "A scandal is certainly the last thing we want."

"That's right, my dear. We are so very close to achieving everything this family has ever wanted. We must tread carefully and keep our eyes firmly fixed ahead. We cannot afford distractions and mistakes. Do you understand?"

"Yes, father," Jessamine said, and for the first time, she felt it was true. She did understand. She understood that when her father said "this family" he meant himself. After all, what was left of their family, truly? Her brother, gone. Her mother, lost to an endless reverie of grief. And she, Jessamine, promised to a man she despised, and sacrificed like a pawn upon the political battlefield. Her father was the only one left standing, the only one poised to attain... whatever it was he wished to attain. Power? Wealth? Titles? Whatever it was, she knew now that her own happiness played no part in it.

And it felt, in that moment, that the last fragile thread of connection between them had snapped. She turned her back on him and, as she ascended the stairs to her chambers, wondered just what the most direct route to a scandal might be.

4

B RIDIE WOKE WITH A GASP, staring around into the
pressing darkness with a terror that clawed at her innards. Her
fingers scrabbled around her, feeling for the rough stone floors
and filthy scraps of blanket, but found clean, dry cotton instead. She
blinked, letting her eyes adjust and the fog of sleep lift from her brain.
The shapes and smells of an unfamiliar room resolved themselves, the
darkness peeling back just enough to reveal a bed, a chair, and a small
table with a burnt-out candle still smoking gently.

Then she remembered.

Eliza. The fire. An escape in a stranger's coach.

"You're awake."

Bridie meant to shriek, but her dried out husk of a voice would not
comply. A figure rose from the nearby chair, arms raised in a kind of
surrender.

"It's all right. You're safe. It's Eli Turner, remember? I'm Eliza's
friend."

Bridie felt her insides unclench slightly, but she remained on edge
as the figure approached the bed. A moment later, the sulfurous scrape
and flare of a match brightened the space between them, and she
recognized Eli's face as he lit the candle that had gone out. She
examined his features in the wavering orange light. His under-eyes
were heavily shadowed, and his jaw was dark with stubble, but the
smile that spread across his face was genuine.

"How are you feeling? All right?" Eli asked.

A hysterical bubble of laughter fought its way out of Bridie's
throat. "Is that a joke?"

Eli ran a hand through his hair and chuckled. "Sounded a bit like one, didn't it? Look, I told Sully I'd keep an eye on you, and send Cora in when you woke up, so…"

Bridie shook her head, and then instantly regretted it. It felt like rocks tumbling around inside her skull. "Sorry, but who's Sully?"

"Of course, you wouldn't… she was the one who picked us up in the coach. This is her house. She's my… well, she raised me. She's going to keep you hidden while you're on the mend, and then we'll find a safe house for you."

Bridie was silent for a moment, absorbing this. More memories came back to her, sticky and faded, like old photographs. "The loud woman in the trousers?"

Eli let out a bark of laughter, before clapping his hand over his mouth and composing himself.

"That's the one. You'll be safe here until we sort out what to do next."

"And… Cora, was it?"

"She's an herbalist, very knowledgeable about remedies. We can't get a proper doctor in without giving you away, but she'd like to examine you, if that's all right."

Bridie's fingers relaxed on the edge of the blanket. "Oh, I see. I suppose so."

"Are you sure?"

Bridie shrugged. "I was surrounded by doctors in that place, and never once did they listen to me. She can't be worse."

"She's not, I promise you. She'll have you right as rain before long."

"All right, then. You can… um, send her in."

Eli nodded and slipped through the door, closing it quietly behind him.

Bridie located the ticking sound in the room and squinted at the clock. It was eleven o'clock at night. She'd been asleep for almost twelve hours in a stranger's house. There had been little time for explanations in the coach. They were all just trying to hold themselves together, stay out of sight and be inconspicuous until they could get undercover. Every patrol they drove past, every shout in the street had been another breathtaking punch of panic. Even when they finally arrived at the house in which she now sat, they had had to keep crouched in the coach with the curtains drawn, the door pulled up to

30

the mouth of a neighboring alleyway, waiting for the all-clear to jump down out of the coach, and run down the alleyway, and in through the partially concealed kitchen door. They had huddled in the kitchen, Emmeline barely conscious and leaning heavily on the two men, until Sully had gone through the house and pulled all the curtains, locked the doors, and given them permission to move through the house.

Bridie had been escorted up to a bedroom on the second floor and told to rest while the others found help for Emmeline. There had been no time to ask the thousand questions she had pounding through her head like a stampede of beasts. There had only been whispered warnings to keep the curtains drawn, and a promise to return soon. Bridie had paced for a while, pulse still thudding in her ears, jumping at every footstep and muffled voice that bled through the walls of what she could only think of as her new cell, but eventually, the wild excitement of the escape wore off, and she had surrendered to marrow-deep exhaustion. She had been confident her slumber would be poor, riddled with nightmares, but she had slept like the dead.

Now she was just counting her lucky stars that she wasn't *among* the dead.

A gentle knock sounded on the door, and she tensed as she answered. "Come in."

Eli had returned, a kind faced woman peering around his shoulder. "This is Cora. She's here to help. It's okay, she's one of us."

Bridie stiffened. "One of us? What does that mean?"

Eli pressed his lips together as though he'd said too much. "I just mean she's safe. That's all you need to know."

"Thank you, Eli. I'll take it from here," Cora said, pushing past Eli and settling herself on the bed beside Bridie. "I'm going to give you a quick going over, all right, love?"

Bridie chewed her lip. "Eli said you're a... what was it?"

"An herbalist. Natural remedies, love. I'm the closest you'll get to a doctor in the Riftborn sections of the city. May I?" She reached out a hand toward Bridie's. Bridie shrugged and then nodded. Cora took her wrist and pressed her fingers to it, against the rushing of blood.

"How are you feeling, then?" she asked.

"Tired. In my bones tired. I've slept for ages, and I can still barely keep my eyes open," Bridie replied. "I can't think what's wrong with me. I've never been the lazy sort."

Cora snorted. "Lazy? Don't be daft, child. After what they put you through in that place? Lazy's got not a jot to do with it. You've been through an ordeal, and it's going to take time to heal up properly. You've got to be gentle with yourself, understand?"

Bridie quirked a half-smile. "I've never been much good at being gentle with myself."

"I don't doubt it. I've never known a servant who was. But it's what you need now, so do as I say."

Bridie nodded, shifting on her pillows. Even the ginger movement made her wince.

"What about pain? Any pain?"

"Yes."

"Whereabouts, love?"

Bridie swallowed hard. "Everywhere," she whispered.

Cora nodded, her expression grim. "That's to be expected."

"Is it?"

"Oh, yes. It's the Riftmead what does it. Pain, like a burning in your muscles, your very skin. It will pass, love, I promise you."

"Riftmead? Whatever do you mean? I've had Riftmead all my life, and it's never made me feel this way," Bridie said, her face wrinkled in confusion.

Cora gave her a pitying smile that made Bridie feel defensive. "That's because you've never had it in the amounts they dole it out at a place like Bedlam."

"I still don't understand," Bridie mumbled.

Cora put Bridie's hand back on her lap and began pressing her fingers along the sides of Bridie's neck, though what she was feeling for, Bridie could not fathom. "How often did they give you Riftmead while you were in there?"

Bridie stiffened. "Three times a day."

"And how much did they give you?"

"I'm not sure exactly."

"But more than the sip or two you have at services, I expect?"

Bridie nodded warily. "Yes. Some days it was the only thing I had to drink all day. But how did you know that?"

"Bedlam is one of many places they've been using patients for Riftmead experiments. You're fortunate you were only there for a short time—the symptoms are likely to disappear in a few days, and I don't think they gave you enough to cause any permanent damage."

"But what do you mean? How can the Riftmead have been hurting me?"

It was Eli who answered. "I'm sorry to have to be the one to tell you this, but Riftmead isn't at all what the Illustratum claims it to be. It's not blessed, and it's not sent from above to save the Riftborn. It's manufactured and distributed to dull our magic and keep us subdued."

Bridie shook her head. "I don't believe that."

"Believe what you like. Doesn't change what's true," Eli said softly.

Bridie looked up at him, searching his eyes for something to explain away his words: madness, dishonesty, even a twinkling of poorly executed humor. All she found was earnestness. The lump in her throat seemed to expand, and she swallowed convulsively again. Eli's expression softened.

"I know it isn't easy to hear," he said. "But look at what they did to you. Do you truly think them incapable of what I've said?"

Bridie shuddered. The weight of the truth felt like a living thing pressing down upon her, smothering her.

"I'm sure it's not easy to talk about, but can you tell me what they did to you in there? It will help me treat you," Cora said, and her voice was gentle now.

Bridie's mouth twisted into a little knot, and her eyes were suddenly bright. "I suppose I'll have to."

"I'll not make you, child. I can come back when you've—"

"No, that's all right. I'll tell you about it." She glanced over at Eli.

"I can leave," he said at once, placing a hand on the doorknob. "It's none of my business, and I don't want to make it harder on you."

"It is your business. I'd still be in that place if it wasn't for you," Bridie said.

"Still, I'll not make this harder for you, Miss Sloane."

"Call me Bridie. You saved my life, after all."

"Very well, then, Bridie. If you prefer."

"I do. And I prefer that you stay, Mr.—"

"Eli."

"Eli," she corrected herself with another ghost of a smile that vanished before anyone could be sure it had really been there at all. "Where should I start?"

"Start at the beginning. It's all important," Eli said.

She considered this, then took a deep breath. "They knew I wasn't mad. I went to the workhouse, y'see, in Clerkenwell. I was there to find out about my parents, but before I could get any records or anything, there was a commotion, and we all ran to see what had happened. It was Mrs. Braxton. They'd had her there, locked away for ages, and she'd fought her way downstairs. I recognized her right away, from the photograph Eliza's got by our bed. It's been a long time, and she's much changed, but it was her. I was certain of it."

"And what happened, when they realized you had recognized her?" Eli asked.

"They kept denying who she was. Told me I was mistaken. Then Mrs. Langford—that's the matron—she rang for tea, and the tea had something in it. It made me dizzy and confused, and I tried to run, but I got trapped in the courtyard. I woke up locked in a room upstairs, and they left me there for two days, just screaming for them to let me out. I tried not to eat or drink anything they gave me, but I got too hungry and thirsty in the end. They drugged me again, and when I woke up, both Mrs. Braxton and I were in Bedlam. I have no memory of getting there."

"And once you were there?" Cora prompted.

"It was horrible," Bridie croaked, tears filling her eyes and spilling over down her cheeks. "I wasn't chained up, but some of the others were. The other women, I mean. I think they would have chained me up if I'd fought back too much. The cells were filthy. I think they... they must have examined me when I arrived because when I woke up, I was wearing that." She pointed a violently trembling finger at the stained white linen heap of fabric that had been her patient uniform. "And I... I had bruises on my arms and legs. Some of them... some of them looked like *handprints*." Her voice broke. She thought she heard Eli swear under his breath, but when she looked at him, he was merely nodding encouragingly, his expression rapt with attention.

"They never let us out. I could see patients being walked around the grounds outside and out in the corridors, but no matter how much I begged, they wouldn't let me leave the cell. I was the only one in there who seemed... well..."

"Sane?" Eli offered.

Bridie nodded. "Well, Mrs. Braxton isn't mad, really. At least, I don't think she is. Just sick. But the others..." She shuddered. "I tried to reason with the doctors and the nurses. Every time someone came to take away the waste buckets or bring us food, I pled with them.

They wouldn't talk to me. They wouldn't even look at me! It was as though I wasn't even there. The only time I had anyone's attention was when they came around with the Riftmead. Then they would stand and watch us, to make sure we drank it. Once, one of the women stumbled and spilled her Riftmead on the floor. They beat her until she stopped moving."

"Creator save us," Cora whispered.

Bridie shuddered. "And then there were the tests…"

Eli stood up straight. "Tests? What tests?"

"The doctors would come 'round and test our magic. It was the strangest thing, although I suppose, now that you've explained to me about the Riftmead, it makes more sense. They would hand me things and see if I could ignite them—I'm a Catalyst, see. And they kept a kind of log where they wrote down the time and what I was able to do. But after a week in that place, I could barely produce a spark."

"And how did you feel? Apart from the magic, I mean?"

"Terrible. Like I was rotting away on the inside. My brain felt like mush, I could hardly string a sentence together, the words kept getting lost on their way to my mouth. And the pain…" She shook her head.

"That's okay. You don't need to go on," Eli said, and his expression was nauseated. "That's enough for now. Just one last question, Bridie, and then we'll let you rest again. The reason you went to Clerkenwell in the first place—you said you wanted to find out about your parents?"

Bridie stiffened. "Yes, that's right."

"When you spoke to Mrs. Langford, did you tell her about the book?"

Bridie's eyes widened like saucers. "How did you know about—"

"Eliza found it, inside the mattress. The Praesidio came and searched your things, but they missed it."

"And you… you know what was in the book?"

"I do."

"But how—"

"Don't trouble yourself with that now. It's enough that we know. Now listen, Bridie, this is really important. Think back. Did you mention the book to anyone? Mrs. Langford, or anyone else?" Eli asked.

His voice was calm and even, but there was a slight edge to it that made Bridie feel very grateful that she could return the answer, "No. I never mentioned that book to anyone."

"You're sure?"

"Quite sure. I was... I was too scared to admit I'd read it," she mumbled, dropping her eyes to her hands now twisting in her lap.

Eli reached out a hand and tucked a finger under her chin, forcing her face up to look at him. She met his eyes reluctantly.

"You listen to me, Bridie Sloane. You've done nothing wrong, do you hear me? All you've done is discover the sins of others. They'd like you to believe it's a crime, but it's not. Nor is being a Riftborn. Do you understand me?"

Bridie's voice stuck deep in her throat. "Yes," she barely managed to whisper.

Eli nodded his satisfaction. "Now, get some rest. Cora, what should we do for her?"

Cora was already measuring and pinching and grinding up something fragrant with her mortar and pestle. "Put the kettle on. I'm knocking up a tea that will ease the muscle pain and lessen the fatigue. Then I've got to go check in on Emmeline."

"How is she?" Bridie cried. She was ashamed of herself for not asking after the woman immediately.

Cora did not look up from her work, but her face folded into a frown. "She's still very unwell. They've kept her subdued for years. It's a bloody miracle they didn't kill her. She must have discovered what they were doing, found ways to protect herself. I can't see how else she could have survived it."

"Will she... do you think she'll be all right?" Bridie asked.

Cora tipped her newly ground mixture into a tea strainer and balanced it atop a chipped old teacup. "I can't say for sure. I may be able to make some improvements, but only time will tell how much of the damage can be undone."

"Why did they do this to her? What could she possibly have done to deserve that?" Bridie whispered, more to herself than to the others, but it was Eli who answered.

"I intend to find out the answer to that question," he replied. He nodded again, first to Cora, and then to Bridie. "Now, if you'll excuse me, I'll see to that kettle."

5

A FTER SENDING LOUISE UPSTAIRS with a steaming teapot full of water and some bread and cheese, Eli could put it off no longer. He mustered up the courage to go down to Sully's workshop. He was not sure why he was avoiding her, despite the questions burning inside him, questions to which he had longed his whole life to find the answers. But now that those answers were a mere flight of stairs away, he suddenly found it difficult to coax his feet down those steps.

Whatever it was he was about to learn, he could not unlearn it. And he would have to find some way to live with that. The thought was nearly as unbearable as the emptiness of not knowing.

Nearly, but not quite.

He found Sully at her worktable, glasses hanging on precariously to the tip of her nose, the documents Jasper had rescued from Bedlam spread out before her. For a moment, he felt like a small child, working up the courage to ask for something when he knew the answer must be no.

But Sully did not wave him away when he appeared like a shadow in the doorway. She settled her eyes on him for a long moment, her expression utterly indecipherable. Then she waved him in and resumed her examination of the documents. Eli crossed the room and walked around the table until he was looking over her shoulder at the papers. He opened his mouth and, like a coward, asked the question he cared least about first.

"Is it enough?" He gestured to the papers on the table in front of them.

"Oh, yes. I haven't been through all of it yet, but it's exactly what we've been looking for—conclusive proof that Riftmead is poison, developed expressly for the purpose of draining us of our magic: Disarmament by poison, staggering in its scope and nearly unfathomable in its cruelty." Sully leaned back in the chair, arching her back with a groan and plucking the glasses from her nose so that she could rub at the deep purple shadows nestled under her eyes.

"Does that mean we're forgiven for the way we came in possession of it?"

Sully gave a dry snort of a laugh. "On any other day, I'd still rake you over the coals. But not today, Eli. Not now."

Eli pressed his lips together, unsure what to say next. Sully spared him the trouble, however.

"There's only one person who should be talking of forgiveness right now, Eli, and it certainly isn't you," she said. She looked up and met his eye, and for the first time in his life, he thought Sully looked old. "Sit down, please."

Eli dropped into the chair beside Sully as suddenly as if her words had cut his legs right out from under him. His heart felt swollen in his chest, his heartbeat messy and uneven.

"I've put this off for too damn long, and that's the truth. I'm sorry for it, but know that it came from a place of good intentions. I was trying to protect you. I couldn't see what good could come from it, how it could possibly serve you to know what I know. But you bringing Emmeline Braxton to my doorstep feels like the world's way of telling me that this secret isn't mine to keep anymore. Maybe it never was."

Eli could feel the truth sprouting up like a bud forcing its way up out of the soil that had tried so hard to bury it. As Sully spoke the words, they fell upon him like memories rather than revelations; his mind seemed to open them up to him even as Sully did.

"The night you came to me, it was Emmeline Braxton who brought you. The Lamplighters Confederacy had fallen, and the Resistance was in tatters. But the wheels had already been in motion to get you out, and Emmeline would not hear that I could not take you. She would not hear that you had to go back. She had promised to make you safe, and that's what she did. She saved your life."

Eli swallowed hard against something. "Emmeline Braxton worked at Larkspur Manor."

"Yes."

"For the Hallewells."

"Yes."

"So that means... are you telling me that..."

"That you are a Hallewell, yes. William Elias Hallewell, the eldest and only son of Elder Josiah Hallewell, and the rightful heir to enormous wealth and power," Sully finished in a toneless voice.

Eli felt the truth of this wash over him. There was no disbelief, no shock, no denial. Only rightness, the rightness of the words settling upon him like the mantle he had always been meant to take up.

Sully was watching him carefully, leaning away as though bracing herself for an explosion. When it didn't come, she dared speak.

"I'm sorry, Eli."

"No, enough. Enough of that," Eli whispered. "I'll not have you apologizing for saving my life."

"But keeping it from you—"

"Was necessary," Eli said. "I couldn't know who I was. It wasn't safe."

Sully nodded, grateful tears in her eyes. "It was. But as you got older, I didn't know how or when to... it's been years now that you should have known. I told myself it wasn't safe, but really I think I just didn't want to see the hurt in your eyes when you realized where you came from. That was selfish, lad, and I'll never feel right about it."

"You say Emmeline saved my life. From what?"

"Our exchange was brief the night she left you with me, but she said you weren't safe. I can only assume your family was making plans to..." she stopped, pressing her lips together again, watching him anxiously for that pain to unfurl in his eyes.

"You think they would have had me killed," Eli finished for her.

"I do." She gestured toward the printing press, where a copy of the book they'd distributed to the Barrens still lay upon the plates. "I think we all know what they were willing to do to keep Riftmagic out of their family lines. And an Elder as powerful as Hallewell? The stakes would have been that much higher."

Eli tried to imagine a situation in which an Elder would admit to having a Riftborn child. His mind could not even construct the hypothetical, so outlandish was the premise. The reality of how close he'd come to death bloomed in his stomach, and he swallowed back bile.

"Are you all right?" Sully asked quietly.

"I am. Well, I will be," Eli said, looking up into the face of the only mother figure he'd ever known and trying, for her, to scrape together a smile. But the moment he'd managed to hoist it onto his face, a realization hit him with such force that he gasped.

Sully winced. "I know, it's a lot to take in, but I promise Eli…"

"No, it's not that!" Eli said. "I mean, yes, it is a lot to take in but… it's… that means Jessamine Hallewell is… my God, I saw my *sister* yesterday. I spoke to her. I shook her hand!"

Sully had already realized this, of course, so she sat quietly while Eli tried to absorb it. "You can imagine the terror when I realized you'd encountered each other in that mad scheme of yours. I would have panicked at the thought of you working together with any member of the Dignus, but her…" Sully shook her head. "Thank the Creator you were both too young when you were separated to remember each other now."

Eli was barely listening. He kept thinking back to the moment of looking into Jessamine's face; how her expression had twisted in the oddest way, how she had asked whether or not they had ever met.

"What did you tell her, Eli? I need to know what the Hallewell girl—what your sister knows."

Eli ran his fingers through his hair, forcing his scattered thoughts into formation. "Nothing, honestly. She knows our first names. That's all."

"What of the book? Of the Resistance?"

"Nothing. She knows us as Eliza's friends who agreed to help find Bridie Sloane. That's the whole of it. And Eliza is too smart to reveal more than that."

Sully nodded, and a small burst of air escaped her, a bubble of relief.

"I asked Jasper, but he didn't know. How on earth did you discover Emmeline Braxton was in there?" Sully asked.

"We didn't have to. Bridie had already found her. She recognized her back at Clerkenwell Workhouse. They transferred them over to Bedlam together," Eli replied.

Sully raised her eyebrows. "At Clerkenwell? All this time?"

"She'd been locked away in one of the wards there—Bedlam

wasn't the only place they were experimenting on Riftborn, you know that."

"Yes, I certainly do. It's just... to think she was right here in London all these years. I thought for sure she'd been killed, or else thrown into the Praeteritum. I wonder why they let her live," Sully murmured to herself.

"Seems like it would have been a mercy to kill her," Eli mumbled as his mind vividly conjured Emmeline's frail, skeletal appearance.

"Well, Creator knows the Illustratum leadership isn't famed for its mercy," Sully said. "I expect your f—Elder Hallewell wanted to sweep her under the rug. The scandal it would have caused—one of his own servants turning on him—might have been enough to topple him."

Eli's insides twisted, like a wet cloth being rung out. "I think you were right."

"I usually am, but about which bit in particular?" Sully asked dryly.

"I think it was better not knowing. I always knew my parents were Dignus, and that they'd abandoned me, but..." He shook his head. "How am I supposed to make peace with the fact that my father is a monster?"

Sully reached out and squeezed Eli's arm. It was as close as she came to anything resembling an embrace, and Eli felt his throat tighten at the gesture. "We've all had to make our peace with something, lad. That man might have sired you, but he's not even a tiny part of who you really are, you hear me?"

Eli nodded because he knew he had to, not because he really believed it. He cleared his throat, desperate to change the subject.

"I didn't want to pester Cora with too many questions, because she was working, but how is Emmeline doing? I promised Eliza I'd send her word when I could."

Sully grimaced. "She's been poisoned by Riftmead within an inch of her life. Hasn't woken yet, so Cora can't really know the extent of the damage. Tell Eliza to give things a day or two to settle. I don't think we were followed or spotted, but we've got to be sure. We should lay low, avoid any unnecessary risks. Then we can arrange for her to come visit."

The very thought of Eliza having to see what had become of her mother almost undid him. He dropped his face into his hands.

"They tortured her for years… she went through all of that… because of me."

"No." Sully's voice was sharp, a knife slicing through the space between them, and Eli's face snapped up. "Don't you give them that, Eli Turner! Don't you dare sound like the subservient Riftborn they want you to be! She went through all of that because of *them*. Don't you dare shoulder a burden that ought to be theirs. This is their fault, not yours. Never yours, you hear me?"

Eli met her eye, and let the anger there burn some of his guilt away. Not all, but a tiny portion of it. Because of course not all of that guilt had to do with what happened to Emmeline. It was her daughter he was thinking about now.

Eliza had grown up without her mother—and not only that, but with the mistaken perception that her mother had left her by choice. She'd spent nearly her entire life thinking she'd been abandoned, and all along, it hadn't been true. Eli couldn't fathom what that must have done to her. And even now, the knowledge that her mother had left her to save another child—and that that child was him—would that make her despise him even more than she must already after that night at Madam Lavender's? How in the Creator's name could he ever admit to her who he really was, and that his very existence had wrought more chaos and heartache in her life than she ever could have imagined?

"I can't bear to tell her. I can't, Sully. She'll hate me, I know it."

"If you believe that, then you don't know that girl half as well as you think you do."

"Sully…" There was a note of pleading in his voice that he despised, but he couldn't suppress it.

She sighed. "You don't have to ask. It was my decision to keep this from all of you. I'll be the one to tell her who you are."

Eli seemed to deflate. "I know I'm a bloody coward, but I just can't face it. I'll make myself scarce when she visits. It can be her choice if she ever wants to see me again. I'll not force myself on her."

"If you like. But in the meantime, write to her and tell her what I said, about waiting a few days."

"I'll let her know. That much I can do," Eli agreed. "And Sully?"

"Hmm?"

"Thank you."

Sully scoffed. "For what, lad."

Eli's voice softened. "Does it really need saying? For everything."

And he closed the door, leaving Sully alone with his gratitude, either to absorb it or to deflect it with that hardened shell of hers, exactly as she chose.

6

I T HAD BEEN A MOST UNUSUAL DAY in the Barrens. Penny was unceremoniously shaken from a deep sleep close to noontime to be told that Bedlam was on fire and the city was overrun with lunatics. Her wry observation that the Barrens was overrun with lunatics on any given day was thoroughly ignored.

None of the girls seemed to want to leave the relative safety of Lavender's, though they lingered by the doors and windows incessantly, hoping for a glimpse of a real-life Bedlam patient skipping down the road in broad daylight. By nightfall, however, all they'd seen was an increase in Praesidio patrols and a great deal of baseless rumor-trading between housewives and merchants. It was all rather anticlimactic if Penny was being honest. She would have preferred to be left sleeping, even if the lunatics had thrown a bloody parade down the middle of the High Street. She was descending the stairs after concluding her business with her first customer of the night, still longing for a nap, when the guard first walked in.

Penny had her eye on him from the moment he crossed the threshold. It wasn't that it was so very unusual to see a Praesidio guard paying his custom at Madam Lavender's; indeed, she'd bedded more of the jumped-up little blighters than she cared to remember, and there were bound to be a few more around the place than usual tonight, given the number of the patrols throughout the day. But this one was different somehow. Penny tried to put her finger on it as she watched him from the shadowy corner by the bar where she was nursing the one whiskey she was permitted to have.

He had none of the swagger of the guards that usually frequented the place. More often than not they came in on wage day, puffed up like popinjays, loudly announcing their intentions to spend said wages recklessly on too much booze and too many women. They were conceited and intoxicated on their own borrowed authority, and their disdain for the Riftborn didn't stop them from slavering all over them. Penny ran a finger along her cheekbone, where the powder was layered extra thick to obscure the shadow of a bruise. They were also sometimes violent. She supposed any man who pursued such a profession might have a taste for causing pain. Then again, her choice of profession might suggest she was a glutton for punishment.

In other words, appearances could be deceiving.

Penny studied the man over the rim of her glass— though 'man' was very nearly a misnomer. He had such a lanky frame and boyish features that he seemed hardly out of short pants. But it was his face that held Penny's interest. His eyes were raking each of the girls in turn, but there was nothing lascivious or covetous in his gaze. He seemed to be searching for something—or someone—and there was a kind of sad desperation in his eyes. Penny decided she was too curious to let it go. She drained the dregs of her whiskey, plunked the glass down on the bar, and slunk toward him, patting at her hair as she went.

"Looking for some company, soldier?" she purred, tapping him on the shoulder. The guard whirled around, looking almost alarmed. His eyes were wide and very blue, and his nose was dotted with a smattering of freckles. He pulled off his cap, revealing a haystack of yellow hair. He cleared his throat.

"No, I... that is to say, that's very kind of you, but I'm not looking for company, delightful though I'm sure yours is," he said, inclining his head. Penny blinked, unaccustomed to such politeness. And mistaking her advance for something resembling "kindness?" This poor boy was so very, very lost. She smiled her most seductive smile.

"Well, you certainly seem to be looking for something," she said, reaching out and plucking a stray thread from the man's shoulder and twirling it between her fingers, letting it flutter to the ground.

The guard pressed his lips together into a tight smile. Penny found herself wanting to reach out and ease those lips apart, spilling the words sealed inside. She wasn't sure what compelled him, but he went on.

"I'm, uh... looking for someone," he said.

"I'm someone," Penny cooed.

He smiled that tight smile again. "Indeed, you are. But I'm looking for a specific someone."

"Well, I know everyone around here," Penny said, gesturing to the room at large. "Maybe I can be of some help?"

The guard hesitated. She could see a battle raging in his eyes, his desperation to find whomever it was he sought warring against his mistrust of a woman he did not know.

"I'm Penny, by the way," she said sweetly.

"Is that your real name?" the guard asked.

Penny's smile almost slipped—almost. Real names and real faces and real intentions were something of a hazard in her line of work. And yet, something about the earnestness in the guard's face disarmed her just enough to answer truthfully. "A nickname, if you please. Short for Penelope."

The guard nodded, and scanned the room again, searching.

"Am I not to have the courtesy of your name, soldier? After all, I've given you mine."

The guard looked startled by the request, but obliged. "Daniel. Daniel Byrne."

"That's more like it," Penny said, her voice like honey. "Well, Daniel, can you tell me anything about this person you're hoping to find? If they've set foot here, it's odds on I've noticed them. I'm the eyes and ears of this place, apart from Madam Lavender herself, of course."

Daniel's face twisted. Again, he seemed to struggle with the decision to trust her. Finally, with a grim nod, he pulled a small gold frame from the breast pocket of his jacket.

"I'm looking for my sister. I've not seen her for many years. This is the only photograph I have," Daniel said, flipping the catch on the frame so that it unfolded in his hand, like butterfly wings.

Penny took a hesitant step forward and reached for the photograph. "May I?"

"Please do."

She scooped the frame out of his palm and gazed down at the daguerreotype. It showed a small girl, no more than three or four, perched upon a child's rocking chair and clutching a porcelain doll. She wore a frilly dress, buttoned boots, and a lavish bow in her crown of curls. Penny could make out a sprinkling of freckles across the fair nose and cheeks, nearly identical to the man now standing before her. The child was trying to hold a solemn expression, but she had a pixie mischief curve to the corners of her lips that hinted at an impish charm.

Penny looked up. "But this is just a child. How old would she be now?"

Daniel frowned. "She would be nearly nineteen years old now."

Penny let out a low whistle. "That's a tall order, trying to find a grown woman with naught but a child's photograph. Why are you looking here? Run off, has she?"

Daniel shrugged. "Something like that."

Penny took in the frills, the bows, the fine doll clutched in the girl's arms. "I can't imagine a girl from such a respectable Dignus family ending up in a place like this," she murmured, before handing the picture back to him. "The girls what work here are all Riftborn, love."

"Yes, I... I know that."

"Then why...?" Penny began, swallowing the rest of the sentence. A strange thought had occurred to her—a thought she barely dared to voice aloud, lest she insult the man. And yet...

"Are you... is this girl Riftborn?" she asked in barely more than a whisper.

Daniel froze for a moment, and Penny braced for an angry tirade, but then his shoulders sagged, his expression hangdog and drooping. "Yes."

Although she knew it was impossible, Penny's eyes darted to Daniel's wrist, searching for a Riftmark there, but of course, there was nothing. Riftborn were not allowed to work as Praesidio guards—it was one of the Exceptions. That meant Daniel was from a Dignus family that had produced a Riftborn child. Penny knew from the Resistance's latest stunts with the books that such things were possible, but she had never encountered it in the flesh, as far as she knew. One of the older girls, Mira, would tell anyone who would listen that she dreamed almost nightly of her former life, before she'd been abandoned in the gutter as a wain. She swore she had once lived in a fine house, had worn fine frocks, and had memories of being pushed about in a pram by a nursemaid who sang to her as she fell asleep. Her assertions were met with skepticism all around, the other girls insisting she needed to lay off the mead. She'd left Madam

Lavender's a year or two back, having run off to marry a butcher. But she'd been dark-haired and nearly ten years too old to be mistaken for Daniel's sister. Still, the faraway look she used to get in her eyes, when she spoke of the dreams—it was easy to let yourself believe something like that. People want to believe beautiful things, after all.

Just like Daniel wanted to believe that the little girl in the picture would be somewhere in London, waiting to be found, like a lost toy or a stray dog. If that child really had been Riftborn, it was odds on she'd been killed rather than risk the world discovering what she was. Penny pitied him, a dangerous emotion in a place like Lavender's. She cleared her throat and looked back down at the picture, squinting again. "That was quite the head of hair. What color was it?"

"Red," Daniel replied, gazing back down at the photograph with a wistful expression. "Red as could be."

Penny closed the frame carefully and handed it back to him. "I'm sorry, love, but I haven't seen her. I'll be happy to keep an eye out for you, though."

Daniel's face snapped up, and he dug into his pocket, pulling out a handful of *venia*. "Would you? I'd appreciate it. Here, let me…" He began counting out coins.

But Penny shook her head, pushing his hand away. "You don't need to pay me. I've got eyes that work. T'ain't no trouble."

Daniel's face went slack with shock, which made Penny grin.

"Never met a brothel girl who turned down a coin, have you?" she asked teasingly.

Daniel grinned sheepishly, running a hand through his hair, and returning the coins to his pocket. "You are certainly the first," he said.

Penny waved her hand in an airy gesture, a queen surveying her domain. "I'm not hurting for customers. Now, if you wanted to pay for *that*…"

Daniel blushed from the collar of his jacket to the roots of his hair. Penny smirked. It was endearing. She had always loved the power she had to fluster a man. It was one of the few powers left to a girl in her position, and she wielded it with delight.

"But of course, you've no time for that, have you. You're a man on a mission today," she said softly, letting him off far more gently than she would normally have done. Creator above, was she going soft?

Daniel looked grateful for the escape and took it gladly. "Perhaps some other time, Miss…"

"Penny," she reminded him.

"Penny."

"You've come a long way for nothing. Can I at least get you a drink?" Penny asked.

Daniel hesitated, then nodded. "Yes, I think I could do with a drink, actually. It's been a long night."

"Too right, it has," Penny said dryly as she made for the bar. She'd only just managed to escape the merchant who'd been pawing at her all night. Mercifully, their time upstairs had been very brief—thank the good Creator for men who couldn't hold their liquor. In his drunken stupor, he'd gifted her a pearl necklace. She'd pawn it the very first chance she got before someone discovered she had it and stole it from her room. Trinkets of value might be pretty, but they were too dangerous to hang onto for very long in the Barrens.

Penny returned to Daniel with a generous measure of whiskey and a smile. He accepted it gratefully. "I can pay you for this, at least?" he asked, extracting the coins from his pocket, and placing them in her upturned palm.

"Oh, that you can, and must. Madam Lavender don't let no one drink for free," Penny said. *Or at bloody all,* she added silently. Still, at least she felt no pressing need to dull her senses around Daniel. What a novelty, interacting with a man without the customary buzz of underlying dread. She felt she could rather get used to it.

"So, where have you looked for this sister of yours, anyway?"

Daniel sighed into his glass, looking suddenly exhausted. "Everywhere, it seems. All through the Commons, and well enough every corner of the Barrens. And now, here."

"So, this was your last resort, then," she observed, somewhat amused.

Daniel nodded. "I suppose I dreaded coming here. Dreaded finding her here, of all places." He looked up, eyes suddenly wide as he realized what he'd said. "Please accept my apologies. I didn't mean to imply…"

But Penny was waving his apology away, laughing. "No need to apologize. I reckon I know better than anyone why you'd not want to find your sweet baby sister here."

Daniel flushed again. "Still. That was dreadfully rude of me."

Penny smirked. "I can think of a dozen ways you could make it up to me, if you took the notion."

Daniel mumbled something into his glass that sounded like a further attempt at an apology. Penny let it pass.

"What about the workhouses?" she suggested, plucking an errant curl from her shoulder and twirling it around her finger. "I'd think that a far likelier place to find your sister than here."

Daniel shook his head. "I can't risk asking after her in a place like that. The Dignus... they'd rather not acknowledge that children like my sister exist, you see."

Penny did see. She'd had enough people avert their eyes from her in her garish make-up and revealing frocks to know what it felt like to be erased. Over time she'd learned to protect herself from the sting, but she still remembered the way it used to make her insides shrivel.

"This might be a silly question, given what you've just told me, but... have you asked your parents about her?" Penny asked. Then she held her breath, sure she'd pressed too hard, sure he'd stand up and berate her for her insolence before storming out.

He did neither. His face crumpled, and he let out a sigh that seemed to come from a very deep place inside him. For just a moment, he resembled a much older man.

"I tried when I was younger. My father refused to speak of her, and forbade her name to be mentioned in the house. Worst thrashing I ever got. My mother... well, when my father made a rule, my mother dared not break it." He looked up and found Penny looking at him. "They're gone. My mother a few years ago, and my father just last month. With both of them buried, I felt like I was finally free to start looking."

Daniel picked up his whiskey and took another sip, rolling it around in his mouth as though working up the courage to speak again. When he did, his voice was low. He leaned in conspiratorially toward Penny, who found herself drawn toward him.

"I understand that Madam Lavender is... well connected," Daniel murmured.

Penny raised an eyebrow. "You might say that."

"Do you think... do you suppose she might be willing to help me?"

"Madam Lavender is not one for charity. She helps those who can help her in return," Penny said carefully.

"Yes, I... well, that is to say, I know some of the other lads... they've worked for her before. Just little tasks, a bit of information here or there."

51

Penny shrugged. "I wouldn't know too much about that."

Daniel eyed her shrewdly. "And you wouldn't admit it, even if you did."

"A girl's got to look out for herself around here."

"Well, let's say, just for the sake of argument, a Praesidio guard needed help finding someone," Daniel said, a smile tugging at the corner of his mouth.

Penny leaned on her hand and batted her lashes dramatically, playing into the bit. "I see. An imaginary guard, is it?"

"Yes, completely imaginary," Daniel replied, clearly glad she was playing along. "Let's say this guard was willing to compensate Madam Lavender for her help."

"In what way?" Penny asked.

"In whatever way Madam Lavender prefers. Money. Information. Some hitherto undiscovered form of currency."

Penny's smile broadened. "I suppose she might be persuaded."

"And who ought to do the persuading? The guard himself? Or might it be better—more prudent—to go through one of her trusted inner circle?" Daniel pressed.

Penny hesitated. A tiny little seed of an idea was taking root in her mind, a seed which, if tended to just right, might very well blossom into something useful. Of course, she thought dryly, there was a much better chance of it tangling wildly out of control and throttling her in the process.

But she liked a risk, Penny did.

"Well," she said slowly, "this imaginary guard you've dreamed up, if he's serious about finding his sister, he may have to dig in places that dredge up some ugly things. Is he willing to do that?"

"Perhaps you underestimate some of the digging he's already done," Daniel said, a lightness in his tone that did not entirely mask the intensity of his eyes. "I can safely say there isn't anything he wouldn't be prepared to do if it meant finding her."

Unbidden, a lump rose in Penny's throat. She choked it down, annoyed with herself. What was wrong with her? Flirting with a man who had no intention of making it worth her while? Feelings accosting her, breaking through her carefully constructed defenses meant to contain them? She really needed to get a grip on herself.

"Lucky girl," she managed to mumble, before clearing her throat forcefully and getting suddenly to her feet. "Well, I'll talk to her for you, but I can't promise anything. It's likely as not she'll tell you to sod off."

Daniel kept his face smooth. "I understand. I can't thank you enough for helping me, Penny."

Penny shrugged, trying for all the world to look unbothered. "Don't thank me yet. Ain't hardly done nothing at all."

Daniel reached out and snatched her hand as she bent to take his empty glass. "You've shown me kindness. You listened to my story. I haven't found that anywhere else in the streets of this town. Most Riftborn are glad to see the back of me."

Penny looked down at her hand in his. She at once wanted to slap it away, and keep it there forever. But after all, she had a reputation to maintain. She pulled her hand back from him and waved him off with a dramatic sigh. "Oh, I'm surely glad to see the back of you—distracting me from paying customers when I've got a living to make." But she'd not gone a step before she turned back to him. "Where do I find you, when I've got an answer from Madam Lavender?"

"I work the north wall of the Praeteritum, morning shift. You can find me there," Daniel replied.

"Right. Well, don't hold your breath," Penny huffed.

Daniel smiled. "I wouldn't dare."

Penny watched him for a few minutes from the bar, staring down at the picture in the golden frame, running his thumb over the glass, his eyes heavy with sadness. Then a pair of boisterous merchants came banging through the front door. By the time she'd had them seated and entertained, a primped and powdered girl lolling in each of their laps, the chair that had contained Daniel Byrne and all his sadness was empty once more.

7

F AR FROM THE SHADOWY TRYSTS of Madam Lavender's
establishment, Eliza slept a deep but troubled slumber and
hardly moved until the morning, awaking with a crick in her
neck and a throat raw and dry from sleeping too close to the fireplace.
Her brain felt fuzzy, and it took several long seconds for her to piece
together the events of the previous day. Once her sluggish memory
caught up with her, she sat up straight, staring first in confusion at the
hairbrush still clutched in her hand, and then in alarm in search of her
mistress.

"It's all right, Eliza," Jessamine called from her perch on the
windowsill. "I'm here. Everything's fine." She made a face as she said
the last word, as though she knew perfectly well how very far from
true it was.

"Your father!" Eliza cried out, her voice hoarse. "Did he—"

"He summoned me when he arrived home. You were right. He
knew we had been at Bedlam."

Eliza's stomach was suddenly full of bubbling fear. "You should
have wakened me. I would have faced him with you."

"Nonsense. You needed to sleep after the day you had, and I was
perfectly capable of confronting my father on my own."

"And? What did he say?"

Jessamine's smile was sad. "Don't worry. He doesn't suspect us
of anything but poor timing, and perhaps a markedly female brand of
stupidity. But you were right. He knew Bridie and your mother were
there. He was terrified we had seen them."

"How do you know that?" Eliza gasped.

"Of course, I'm only guessing. He couldn't come out and ask me directly without giving himself away, but I could tell the way he danced around the question, the fear in his eyes. You were right. He knew. I think he was more scared that we'd discovered his secrets than that we might have been injured in the fire." Jessamine was trying to keep her voice light, but there was an undertone of sadness in it. Eliza pitied her; it could not have been easy, coming to terms with who her father really was.

"I'm sorry," Eliza whispered.

Jessamine merely shrugged. "It's better to know. Terrible, but better, somehow."

Eliza's pity was immediately overtaken by a new fear. "What if they didn't get away, Jessamine? What if that carriage ran into a patrol, or Bridie or my mother were spotted in their uniforms? We have to—"

"Eliza, stop," Jessamine said, her voice firm but not without kindness. "What we need to do is wait. I know it must be agony, but your friends seemed a reliable sort. I'm sure they'll find a way to contact you."

Eliza knew the advice was sound and tried to convince her brain to accept it as such, but the constant buzz of terror and the agony of not knowing would not be quieted easily. They rang for tea, and Jessamine insisted that Eliza take a long, hot bath in her own tub. Eliza objected strongly, but Jessamine would hear none of it, and soon Eliza was sunk up to her neck in hot steaming water, breathing in flowery fumes from the lavender oil and vanilla soap her mistress always used. It was hard to feel desperate when every muscle in her body had turned to jelly, and by the time the tub had been drained and she had been wrapped head to toe in fluffy white towels, Eliza wasn't exactly calm; but, she had at least convinced herself not to go charging off to the Bell and Flagon to demand answers.

"There, now. That's better, isn't it?" Jessamine said, sitting Eliza down at her own vanity and beginning to comb the tangles from her mane of silvery blonde hair. "I always have a fresh perspective after a good long soak."

Eliza had never in her life, until that very moment, had a good long soak, so she could not venture a response.

"Now that we've scrubbed the events of yesterday off you,"

Jessamine said with a sigh, "what's next? We've been granted a reprieve from my father, at least for now."

"I wonder if we'll be so lucky when he realizes Bridie and my mother are gone," Eliza mused out loud.

Jessamine bit her lip. "Do you think that's likely?"

"It doesn't seem in character for your father to leave it to chance. He's going to make sure they're accounted for if he has to dig through the ruins himself."

Jessamine's shoulders slumped. "Yes, I'm afraid you're right about that. Well, even if he does discover they're missing, I'm fairly confident he won't suspect our having had a hand in it."

"Let us hope not," Eliza said, taking a deep breath. A fluttering of anxiety had already overcome the soothing effects of the bath.

"What about your father? What will you tell him?" Jessamine asked.

"I have no idea," Eliza replied. "Nothing, until I can see my mother again and see for myself that she's safe and also what kind of state she's in. She..." Eliza swallowed back a lump in her throat, "she was so frail, so sickly looking."

"Yes, and no wonder after so long in a place like that," Jessamine agreed. "But I'm sure she'll be fine, Eliza. If she survived that long, she's shown herself to be quite tough, hasn't she?"

Eliza nodded but kept her lips pressed tightly together. Part of her wanted to scream, another to burst into tears, and still another to talk herself hoarse asking a million questions to which neither of them had the answers. How had her mother wound up in such a place? Where was she now? Had they made it to Sully's house, or taken her somewhere else to hide her? And poor Bridie—how was she faring? It was utter agony, the not knowing. And yet she did not see that she had any choice in the matter. It wasn't safe to contact Eli or the others, not now. She would have to bear the pain and wait to hear from them.

"Unfortunately for the both of us, I think we'll have quite a lot to keep us distracted," Jessamine said, and her voice was full of apathy. "I have my first dress fitting today."

"You... what?" Eliza asked, pulling herself with difficulty out of the dark whirlpool of her own thoughts.

"My wedding dress. I've got the first fitting this afternoon," Jessamine said.

"My goodness, I'd all but forgotten!" Eliza cried, jumping up from the stool and gazing around for her uniform. "I've got to get ready, and I'd better check in downstairs, or the others will surely start asking for me."

Eliza hastily dressed herself in yesterday's uniform. It smelled strongly of smoke and grass and the salt and musk of sweat. Then she helped Jessamine dress for the day and escorted her downstairs. They gave each other's hands a last meaningful squeeze, and then parted ways, Eliza for the servants' quarters and Jessamine for the breakfast room.

Downstairs, everything was hustle and bustle and efficiency. In the kitchen, Mrs. Keats was scolding the new kitchen maid about a batch of overdone eggs. In the storage room, Millie was singing a Riftborn hymn to herself as she cheerfully polished some cutlery. The back door to the garden had been thrown wide; Eliza could hear a few of the valets laughing boisterously about some nonsense like a pack of schoolboys skipping their lessons. She slipped past them all, breath held, until she arrived back in her room. She stripped off her dirtied clothes and shoved them into the back corner of her wardrobe until she could wash them properly. Then, she changed into a crisp, clean uniform. She took one last look in the mirror to make sure she was presentable, smoothing her hair and staring into her own face.

"Just hold yourself together, Eliza. Just until you hear from Eli. You can do that much. If your mother and Bridie can survive in that hellhole, you can grin and curtsy through your work for a day or two," she whispered to her reflection, which, despite her firm tone, still looked unconvinced. Then she lifted her chin and marched out to take her place as a cog in the Larkspur Manor machine.

She checked in with Mrs. Keats about the preparations for the wedding food, a conversation that ended with Mrs. Keats slightly hysterical and needing a strong cup of tea. Then she popped in to check on Millie and give her a hand with the polishing. She interacted with a dozen servants over the course of the morning, and not a single one of them asked about Bedlam—it seemed that news of her adventure with Miss Jessamine had not yet trickled downstairs.

She kept her eye on her father's office door, knowing that she would have to face him sooner or later, but the door remained closed all morning. Twice she saw someone knock tentatively upon it only to be turned away with a gruff, "Not now." She grew uneasy. Was she reading too much into her father's conspicuous absence, or had news of Bedlam trickled down to him at last? She knew she ought to see him, to tell him she had been there, if only to stave off accusations of having kept it from him deliberately. And though she walked by it several times, and even paused in front of it, she could not bring herself to knock on the door. She was afraid to face him, afraid that every word of the truth would come spilling out and she would have no way to gather it all up again. She decided she would rather face her father's wrath for keeping him in the dark than the unknowable consequences of enlightening him, at least until she understood more about what had happened to her mother. And whatever the reason for her father's continued isolation, it helped her to stick to that decision.

There was one conversation she needed to have, but the opportunity didn't present itself until close to noontime. Liesel had been sent out on some errands, and Eliza began to fear that she would not catch her before she had to accompany Jessamine to her fitting. Luckily, however, Liesel shuffled through the door with her arms full of parcels just as Eliza was tying on her bonnet.

"Liesel, let me help you with those," she said at once, hurrying forward before Liesel could object and starting to shift packages out of her arms. As she did so, she leaned forward and whispered, "Follow me. I have news."

Liesel's face remained completely impassive as she and Eliza walked down to the pantry. Once inside, Eliza shut the door and pressed her back against it.

"Well go on then, out with it," Liesel said, and Eliza could hear the sharp bite of anxiety in her voice.

"Bridie is safe. I found her."

For a moment, all Liesel could do was blink. Then she swayed on the spot, a hand shooting out to catch the countertop and steady herself. She closed her eyes and took a long, deep breath.

"You're sure?"

"Yes. She's with friends."

Liesel made a strange sound, half-laugh, half-sob. "How?" she managed to ask.

"You were right. They detained her at Clerkenwell. Then they transferred her to Bedlam."

"Bedlam?!" Liesel gasped.

"It's all right, Liesel. She isn't there anymore. I got her out."

"But how did you—"

Eliza silenced the question with a raised hand. "Liesel, I don't mean to sound cryptic, but the less you know about it, the safer it is for you."

Liesel just nodded, eyes wide.

Eliza went on, "I expect to get word from a friend soon, and then with any luck, I'll get the chance to see her."

Liesel dropped her eyes for a moment, and it was clear she was trying to get control of her face. When she looked at Eliza again, she was making a valiant attempt at her usual sour expression. "Well, you tell that girl when you see her that she's to mind her manners, wherever she's staying. And she's to make herself useful and stay out of what trouble she can avoid. If I hear otherwise, I'll find out where she is and tan her hide myself."

Eliza smothered a smile. "I will be sure to pass that along."

There was a knock on the door. Eliza stiffened, and then hastened to answer it. It was Peter.

"I thought I heard your voice. The carriage just went around front. You don't want to keep Miss Jessamine waiting," he said.

"Thank you, Peter. I'll head up now," Eliza said, hastening to tie the bow on her bonnet. Liesel took the opportunity to sneak out past Peter without another word, though she tossed a shadow of a smile over her shoulder at Eliza as she left.

Eliza hastened out of the kitchen entrance and walked around the side of the manor. The sun beat down on her. She lifted her face to its warmth and inhaled the balmy air, laden with the heady scent of flowers from the gardens, but not even the long-anticipated arrival of early summer could penetrate the chill of anxiety that nested in her bones. The rays of the sun seemed to mock her, reminding her that people she loved would have to hide from it in darkened rooms and dank basements for fear of someone discovering them. She could find no joy in the warmth until she could share it with them. She thought she might go mad for lack of news, and yet she knew she had no choice but to wait it out. Eli would contact her when it was safe, and no amount of impatience would hasten that moment. Even so, as the carriage set off along the gravel drive and to the dressmaker's, Eliza could not help peering into every shadow for a glimpse of movement, lest a clever little messenger might be cloaking himself in darkness to bring her news.

But the shadows, for the moment at least, were empty.

8

J OSIAH'S FOREHEAD DROPPED HEAVILY into his hands. He
had been staring down at a draft of a proposal to the Riftborn
Social Policy Committee for so long that his eyes had started to
blur, and still he had not made a single note upon it. The sigh that
escaped him seemed to be dredged up from his very toes, and he
tossed his pen aside, watching as it rolled across his desktop and
clattered to the floor. It was a sign of his distraction that he did not
even bother to pick it up, but let it land where it may; a spot of ink on
his expensive oriental rug the very least of the problems he sat mired
in. He had been able to assure himself the previous evening that
Jessamine, at least, had not come away from Bedlam any the wiser
about his business there, but there was still no word about the
whereabouts of the patients, and he had had a sleepless night as a
result. He was so distracted that he did not even look up when his door
opened.

"Creator above, Josiah. You look like hell in a cravat, man!"

Josiah closed his eyes and sighed again. "I feel it. And I'm sorry,
Francis, but I haven't made much progress on this draft you sent over
to me, so if you're here for my thoughts, I fear you're going to be
disappointed."

Francis shuffled into the room, waving his hand impatiently. "I
sent that to you so that you'd have something to do other than pace a
hole through your floor, not because I actually expected you to finish
it." He paused, and the sudden silence caused Josiah, at last, to glance
up.

"Well, if you're not here for my commentary, then what can I do for you?"

Francis' mouth twisted into a frown. "Morgan missed his morning communion with the Rift."

Josiah sat straight up, all else forgotten. "Missed it? What do you mean? He was late?"

"He didn't show up," Francis clarified. "The Prayer Gatherers stood outside with their baskets and candles for over an hour."

"Well, where is he? Has anyone sent a missive to the palace?"

Francis nodded. "He was too ill. The doctor had already been sent for."

Josiah swore under his breath, running a trembling hand through his hair, which seemed to have greyed considerably over the last several months. "Who knows?"

"Just me and Morgan's staff. And the Prayer Gatherers, of course, but I was able to feed them another story."

"There's not a chance we can keep this secret."

"I paid handsomely to ensure they keep their mouths shut, but you're right. We're running out of time here, Josiah."

"I am well aware of it," Josiah hissed between tightly clenched teeth. "Damn it all, what do we do? I can't appear to be pushing this matter, or my opponents will find a way to interfere. They're all just aching for the chance to—"

"Josiah, calm down. I do not deny the opposition is a problem, but regardless of Morgan's health, they will try to interfere. You know it, I know it, and what's more, they all know that we know it. We push forward, man. Only thing we can do."

Josiah squeezed his hands into fists as tightly as he could, and then released them slowly, along with a long, deep breath. "Very well. What do you propose? I don't think I can proceed with the speech I was intending to give, unless…"

"No, I agree, the time for speeches has passed. There's no time for the traditional nomination process. We need to get Morgan's recommendation in writing now before he fails and we miss our chance."

"In writing? Do you think he'd do it?" Morgan had always followed tradition to the letter, and the traditional nomination process was always carried out in person.

"The only thing that might stand in his way is his pride, and

I'm not sure how much pride a dying man has left," Francis said, his expression thoughtful. "On the other hand, we might be able to play the pride angle. He doesn't want to be seen in such a weakened state. Making the recommendation in writing will help him avoid that scrutiny."

"People will still speculate," Josiah said dismissively.

"Yes, but that's all they'll be able to do: speculate," Francis said. "And if we get out ahead of it, circulate a plausible reason for him to be away from the council chambers, that may just throw enough doubt into the discussion to buy us a little more time."

"A very little," Josiah grumbled. "But I suppose we ought to be grateful for what we can scrape together at this point."

"You agree then?"

"Yes. Grudgingly, but yes."

Francis gave a satisfied nod. "Good man. I'll draw something up personally. We can't afford even our staff to know what we're up to. With the stakes this high, there's not a man in this building who couldn't be bribed or blackmailed to let this slip."

At that very moment, as though to put a fine point on Francis' words, there was a tentative knock on the door.

"Yes, come in." Josiah cringed at the exhaustion in his own voice.

Brother Goodwin entered, though judging by the look on his face, he would rather have been anywhere than stepping over the threshold into Josiah's office. His normally pasty complexion had a grey tinge, and he licked his lips nervously. A sealed letter trembled in his hand.

"Elder Hallewell, please pardon the intrusion, sir, but you ordered me to notify you at once if there were any updates from Bedl—um, Bethlem Hospital, sir," Brother Goodwin stammered.

Josiah crossed the room in two long strides and snatched the letter from Brother Goodwin's fingers. Then he glared at him until Brother Goodwin took the hint and backed out of the room again, bowing and muttering until the door had closed between them.

Josiah broke the seal and unfolded the stiff parchment. He stared at it for so long that Francis gave a huff of impatience.

"Well, are you going to stare at it all day, or are you going to bloody well tell me what's happened?"

Josiah had to swallow back a nervous spasm in his throat before he was able to answer. "It's a list of the missing patients from Bethlem."

"And?"

The room suddenly seemed to sway. Josiah's hand shot out and groped around until it found a chair back against which he could attempt to steady himself. Unable to speak, he held out the paper wordlessly to Francis, who grabbed it at once. Josiah stared numbly into the fire, waves of fear crashing over him, waiting for Francis to understand his silence. He knew the moment it happened.

"Damn it all to hell!"

Josiah looked up to see Francis staring at him.

"The Braxton woman is missing then. And the housemaid? Her name has escaped me."

"Bridie Sloane. She's on there as well."

Francis cursed again. "What of the bodies they've pulled out? How many are left to be identified?"

"Only three they haven't been able to identify."

Francis opened his mouth, but Josiah forestalled him.

"I don't want to hear it, Francis. Don't you dare insult me by telling me there's so much as a prayer those women are both laying there in the ashes."

Francis sighed and put the paper down on the corner of Josiah's desk. "No. I wouldn't be foolish enough to suggest it. But... Josiah, I must ask you... do you truly believe either of these women to be a threat to you now?"

Josiah whirled around, his temper instantly ablaze. "Of course they're a threat! Don't you understand—"

"Josiah, I know what they know," Francis said, raising a hand. The calmness in his demeanor was so utterly infuriating that Josiah had to look away or risk flying at the man with his fists. Whether Francis knew how close he was to being assaulted, Josiah did not know, but Francis continued talking, unflappable as ever. "I know that, in the right place, before the right audience, they could do great damage to you. But you must ask yourself: what earthly chance do they have of reaching the right place or indeed the right audience?"

Josiah risked a glance at his friend. "Any chance at all is too great," he hissed.

"Oh, come, now. You don't mean that, Josiah."

"I assure you, I do," Josiah replied with a bark of bitter laughter.

"No, you bloody well don't, and I'll tell you why," Francis replied. "You are logical. You understand the odds. You understand the difference between a long shot and a good bet. You seem to have forgotten it all in this moment of panic, but if you manage to calm yourself down for a damn minute, I'm fairly certain it'll all come back to you."

Josiah blinked. Part of him still wanted to slap the calm expression from Francis' features, but he managed to keep his hands firmly clutching the chair back instead.

"There we are," Francis said with an approving nod. "I don't need you calm, but I do need you in possession of your senses, Josiah, or I can't help you. Now, let me remind you of the reasons you chose to lock those women up in the first place, rather than simply having them done away with, which would have been much neater and easier to bet on."

"Francis, I really don't—"

"Oh, I think you really do," Francis cut him off sharply, "because you are at serious risk of coming apart at the seams. Now, I am your friend, but I am not a fool. Your rise to power benefits me nearly as much as it benefits you, and I have calculated my involvement accordingly. I have placed my bet on you, Josiah, and I do not intend to lose."

"Then you should be the first person sending out the search parties for those two women!" Josiah cried.

"And draw attention to them, when they've likely done all they can to go to ground? Not bloody likely," Francis said with a snort. "Josiah, those women have no credibility. They are escaped patients from a lunatic asylum. They cannot risk contacting anyone who knows them, and the general public will be terrified of them. Nothing they say can be trusted, if they were ever foolish enough to risk opening their mouths in the first place. They have no money, no resources, nothing. If they don't turn up dead in an alleyway or floating in the Thames, it's because they're in hiding somewhere, and if they are lucky enough to manage to disappear, they will not be foolish enough to reappear. They know how powerful you are. They know what fate awaits them if they are caught. They may not be among the bones in the ruins of Bedlam, Josiah, but they may as well be."

Josiah's eyes were closed now. He was taking deep breaths, trying to force Francis' logic to penetrate the solid barrier his fear had built within his chest. Francis took his silence as an invitation to continue.

"Now, let's look at that smallest of chances that either one of them will find a friendly ear to listen to their story and actually believe it.

What then? You think a half-mad, Riftmead-poisoned servant without resources or credibility is going to lead a revolution against you? You think they can rile up the masses and lead them in the streets, torches ablaze? Bollocks."

"But Francis, what if... just... just what if—" He couldn't even complete the sentence. His fear was choking off the words.

"I don't bet on what-ifs," Francis said baldly. "But even if that 'what-if' were to come to pass, it would have to come awfully quickly. Because once you're installed as High Elder, it won't matter what madwoman rises from the ashes to point her finger at you. And so that is why I need you, for the sake of everything we've worked for, to forget about what may or may not have happened at Bedlam and focus every fiber of your being on ascending to the highest seat in this country, or I promise you, Josiah, I will lay my bet elsewhere and I will not look back."

Josiah stared at his friend, who stared calmly back, cigar dangling unconcernedly from the corner of his mouth, and knew that he meant every word of it. At last, he felt the fear loosen the iron grip around his heart. He was being a hysterical fool, and if he wasn't careful, he would send his own carefully constructed future crashing to the ground out of sheer panic.

"You're right, Francis, as usual," he managed at last, and was relieved to hear his voice sounded almost normal again.

"It's the reason you keep me around, after all," Francis said with a smirk. "Now, throw that blasted letter in the fire where it belongs and let's get to work, for you have more obstacles to face than you realize. Have you seen the afternoon agenda yet?"

"No, I'm afraid I... why?"

"There's a meeting scheduled in the north committee chamber."

"I fail to see why this is newsworthy."

"There are no committees scheduled to meet today. The chamber was reserved by Elder Carpenter for purposes described only as 'confidential,'" Francis replied.

Josiah groaned, dragging a hand over his face in frustration. "Bugger it all. I knew it. I told you. Didn't I tell you? Alexander's forming some sort of faction to try to fight this nomination, isn't it obvious?"

"Yes, I daresay it is quite obvious, hence my coming here to inform you of it," Francis drawled.

"Well, then? What do you advise? I confess myself stretched too thin by the events of the past few days to have prepared for this as I ought, and would appreciate whatever suggestions you have."

"I'd gathered as much, and so I've already spoken to Brother Goodwin about procuring the list of those Elders in attendance. Once he has it, we will know exactly which and how many Elders we will need to pull away from Carpenter's ranks."

"I hardly see how we can be expected to lure anyone away from Elder Carpenter's clutches. He and his comrades are thicker than thieves."

"Yes, but if you ask me, this meeting smacks of desperation. Elder Carpenter knows he hasn't got the level of support that you have, even among the backbenchers. We must be ready to offer enticements he cannot offer."

"Such as?"

"Such as cabinet seats and committee assignments. Make the kind of promises only the assumed heir apparent can make."

"And surround myself with men who would betray me at the first opportunity? I hardly think that's wise."

"I suppose you could always stand by and allow them to betray you before you've even had a chance at the nomination, but I fail to see how that would be a savvier choice," Francis said.

Josiah cursed under his breath. He appreciated Francis' cool head in a crisis, but it was maddening the way he never seemed to get flustered. Just once he'd like to see the man fumble for the path forward rather than coolly strolling down it while beckoning him on.

"You really think Elder Carpenter is a threat?" Josiah asked.

"On his own merits? No. I think he's an upstart hooligan whose father neglected to teach him his own insignificance. A handsome face and a fiery rhetoric does not a leader make."

"Leaders have been made of less," Josiah pointed out.

"Yes, but they've never lasted long."

"He only needs to last a few weeks to unravel everything we've worked for," Josiah said.

"He's a flash in the pan, Josiah, but you're right, we must smother him nevertheless. It would be foolish to let his opposition to you go unchecked— it could be seen as a sign of cockiness at best, and weakness at the worst. He is only dangerous if he is able to surround himself with enough support. You must siphon them away from him, one by one, starting with the most prominent and powerful. I'll have a list to you by the end of the day."

Josiah's thoughts were swirling. The thought of having to woo so many colleagues he despised was infuriating. Surely there had to be a simpler solution to the problem...

"Josiah? Did you hear me?"

Josiah yanked himself back into the present moment and focused on Francis. "No, I'm sorry, Francis. What was it you said?"

"I said, have Goodwin ready your carriage."

"My carriage? Why?"

"You have urgent business at the palace. Now, have a drink, pull yourself together and decide what you're going to say to convince Morgan."

"Very well. And... thank you, Francis, as always," Josiah grumbled.

Francis frowned. "Don't fall apart on me, Josiah," he said, almost under his breath, and strode from the room.

Josiah was left alone to stew in his roiling tempest of fears. He stood for a very long time, statue-still on the outside, mind working relentlessly on the inside. When at last he managed to move again, he was decided.

He knew what he must do.

And he also knew that, for perhaps the first time ever, he could not breathe a word of his plan to Francis.

9

J OSIAH SAT IN THE CORRIDOR outside Morgan's private
chambers, his heart pounding against his ribs like an animal trying
to escape a cage. Never, in all his time as an Elder, had he felt
such crippling anxiety about what would happen when he was at last
admitted into the High Elder's presence. Even on the day he was to
find out if he had been named to the position of counselor, he had been
calm, filled from head to toe with a kind of surety, a sense of rightness
that he was precisely where fate, and the Creator, had determined he
should be.

He ached now for that surety, ached with a fear that he would
never know it again.

As it was, it was only by virtue of his position that he had a prayer
of seeing the High Elder today. Though he had sent Francis' letter
along ahead of him, his presence at the doors was met with a good deal
of agitation. The valet seemed hardly to know where to put him, and
he was left standing in the entry hall for much longer than a man of his
position should ever be kept waiting by anyone. At last, the servants
seemed to conclude that the outer sitting room to the High Elder's
chambers would do until they could determine how to proceed, and
Josiah was left to his own devices, along with a hastily assembled tea
tray, until the High Elder was ready for him.

The tea went cold. Grim-faced servants slipped in and out of the
doors. No one so much as looked at him. He had never in his life been
made to feel superfluous by mere servants, and the sensation gnawed
at the already raw edges of his temper. He had finally resolved to

confront the next servant he saw and demand to be brought through when Mrs. Morgan appeared alongside a pair of uniformed nurses.

"...and I don't care what the doctor says, he is still in pain, I can see it in his expression. If you cannot give him any more laudanum, then I wish you would consider supplementing with—"

She stopped cold in her tracks, a look of utter bewilderment on her face. For the second time in a few moments, Josiah felt completely wrong-footed. He cleared his throat and made a bow.

"Mrs. Morgan. I trust you are well."

"Elder Hallewell! I am sorry, I was not expecting—"

"My decision to come today was made only slightly before I set out," Josiah explained. "It is a matter of some urgency, you see."

"Yes, I'm afraid most everything is a matter of some urgency today," Mrs. Morgan replied with a wan smile. "If you will allow me to ask, what is the nature of your business? Perhaps it is something I can help with?"

But Josiah would not be deterred so easily. "I wish that were the case, Mrs. Morgan, but I can only discuss the matter with the High Elder."

Mrs. Morgan bit her lip. "I see. Well I cannot promise you will be able to see him, he is very—"

The door to the chambers opened and a weary-looking valet emerged. "Elder Hallewell, sir. The High Elder apologizes for keeping you waiting and would like to see you now."

Mrs. Morgan opened her mouth as though to argue, but Josiah did not give her a chance. With a swift bow he turned his back on her and followed the valet through the door and into the chamber beyond.

The place was swelteringly hot. The heavy brocade curtains were drawn and the fire was roaring in the grate. The air was thick and smelled of something sweetish and rotting that made him taste panic on his tongue. He squinted through the dimness and saw Morgan propped up in a wingback chair beside the fireplace, blankets tucked around him as though holding him in place. The skin on his face and hands looked waxy and yellow. Despite how poorly he looked, Josiah felt a stab of relief that he was, at least, sitting up. He moved forward, trying to keep his eyes fixed on Morgan rather than on the alarming number of bottles, pills, salves, blankets, jars, and other medical supplies assembled around the room.

It seemed to take a moment for Morgan to recognize him, but

when he did, his face broke into a wry half-smile. "Blast it all. I knew I wouldn't escape a visit from someone today," he said with a sigh. His voice was wavering, cracked and dry as an autumn leaf.

"How are you, John?" Josiah asked with an attempt at lightness.

"Oh, I think you can answer that question for yourself," Morgan replied with a feeble flick of the wrist, gesturing around himself. "Who knows?"

"That you missed your Communion with the Rift? I think we've managed to keep it from nearly all of the other Elders, with the exception of Francis and myself."

Morgan chuckled, a wheezy sound that ended in a wracking cough. "That must have been expensive."

Josiah forced a laugh in return. "A small price to pay, sir."

"I'm actually glad you're here. I think we've reached an impasse now that I'd hoped to avoid. I thought I could fight this longer, make a better showing of it. But even I must admit at this point that my time here is growing very short indeed."

Josiah opened his mouth, ready with a half dozen flattering placations to the contrary, but they died on his lips. He couldn't insult the man with lies, not now. They had to speak the truth—they were running out of time. Morgan watched this all play across Josiah's face, nodding with satisfaction as Josiah closed his mouth again and simply nodded his agreement.

"There are many arrangements that must be made," Morgan said. "The grimmer among them, I shall foist upon my wife. But there are matters that must be settled between us. Matters that cannot wait."

Josiah expelled a breath, relief washing over him. "Yes, that's why I'm here. I want to discuss—"

"The wedding must be moved up," Morgan said.

Josiah blinked. "Pardon?"

"The wedding. It must be moved up. We cannot delay."

Josiah cleared his throat. The words had been so unexpected that he felt quite discomfited. "I must admit I was not thinking of the wedding, sir."

"Well, you ought to be," Morgan said. "Given the complexity of the arrangements, the security, the banquet, the invitations— we have not a moment to lose."

"I... I agree, sir, it would be a great undertaking to shift it all."

"Then you best get to work. A month. That is all the time I can hope for."

"A month, sir?" Josiah repeated, feeling as foolish as a caged bird parroting its master's words.

"The doctor has told me I cannot expect much more than that," Morgan said. "The disease has—"

"Sir, please pardon the interruption, but when you spoke of 'matters to be settled' I thought we were discussing the nomination," Josiah blurted out.

It took several seconds for the confusion etched into lines on Morgan's brow to smooth itself into understanding. "Ah, yes. The nomination. Yes, of course."

"I am sorry to force the topic upon you, sir, but you must see that our political readiness must surpass even our social readiness. The children will find their way down the aisle regardless, but we cannot allow your health to throw the very system of our power into disarray," Josiah said, the words tumbling out over each other in his rush to make himself understood.

"Naturally, you are correct," Morgan said. "And I have agreed that I will nominate you, Josiah. I have promised as much. I am not sure what else I can do."

"Perhaps you would consider putting my nomination in writing, sir," Josiah said, with a lightness of tone that one might adopt when discussing a menu for dinner. "It would settle your choice to everyone's satisfaction, and then you could focus energy on keeping well rather than lengthy political proceedings."

Morgan was nodding slowly, staring into the fire. Josiah paused to see if he would respond, but he did not. Josiah went on.

"Not knowing the state of your health, sir, Francis and I took the liberty of drawing up a draft of what such a nomination might look like." He pulled a scroll of paper out of his bag and held it out for Morgan.

"That was quite a liberty," Morgan said, reaching out for the paper.

Josiah had the good grace to appear penitent, though impatience was beginning to bubble just under the surface. "I realize that sir, but we had a spoken agreement, and so I hope my presumptuousness can be forgiven. There is direction for written nominations laid out in the procedurals, as you know, and so I thought it would be prudent to have something drafted just in case we—"

"No."

Josiah blinked. "I'm sorry?"

"I said no."

Josiah stood there stupidly, the rest of his speech shriveling to nothing on his lips. "I'm afraid I don't underst—"

"Josiah, you have been a loyal and reliable counselor over these last fifteen years. I do not doubt your fitness to take over for me when I have passed along into the arms of our Creator. But you must understand that there is an order to things."

"Of course I know there's an order to—"

"I need my son to be settled," Morgan said.

"Sir, he *is* settled. The engagement has been announced, the wedding preparations progress apace, and—"

"Josiah, I am not blind. I know who my son is. I know what he is. I did not take it lightly when I asked you to form this alliance between our children. I knew what I was asking of you. I knew what I was asking of your daughter," Morgan went on. "I imagine that both of you have reservations."

Josiah took his time choosing his words. "The Hallewell family does not shirk its responsibilities."

"You have many responsibilities, Josiah, and not all of them are to me. When I am gone, I imagine those priorities will shift. I cannot risk that they will shift so much that Reginald is left behind."

"Sir, I would never go back on my word to you!" Josiah said, appalled.

"I am sure that is true, now. But things change, Josiah. I cannot plan for a world in which I no longer play a part. I cannot hope that what holds true now will always hold true. I must exercise what influence I have left while I am still here to wield it, and I am telling you that I will not proceed with a nomination, written or otherwise, until the wedding has taken place."

Josiah's hand clenched and unclenched at his side, his nostrils flaring as he breathed through his fury.

"I thought you trusted me."

"I trust you now, Josiah. But you would be a fool to remain beholden to a dead man, and I know that you are certainly no fool."

"That is what you think of me? After all this time?" Josiah spat.

"I think you will always do what is right for you, Josiah. It is the reason you have come so far, and the reason you will climb higher still. And when the wedding has concluded, when the flowers have been admired, the cake eaten to the last crumbs, and the happy couple whisked off on their wedding tour, I will sign my name on whatever you thrust at me. But not until then."

Josiah wanted to rage at the shriveled little man before him. He wanted to slap him, to take him by the shirt and shake some sense into him. He very may well have if it wasn't for the fear that one good shake would kill the man, and then where would he be?

Sensing his victory, Morgan held out the paper. "Hand this back to me at the wedding reception, and I will sign it readily."

What choice did Josiah have? He took the paper and placed it back into his satchel. "As you say, High Elder."

Morgan managed a smirk. "How eager you must be to be addressed with such sentiments rather than having to speak them."

Josiah did not answer; he could not decide if the remark was a jab at him or merely an observation. But Morgan, it seemed, did not expect an answer. He sighed, lifting a glass of water to his parched lips with a shaking hand. The simple gesture seemed to take enormous effort and the sight of it drained some of Josiah's anger away.

"I will arrange everything as you have requested. The wedding will take place within the month."

"Thank you, Josiah. It is but a short journey left, you to your earthly reward, and me to my heavenly one. The last leg of the journey is bound to be the most difficult. Courage, man."

"Courage, indeed," Josiah muttered.

"The Creator is testing your mettle, Josiah. Do not disappoint Him."

"I assure you, I have no intention of doing so."

"Good man. Now, pray with me."

Josiah dropped automatically to his knee and bowed his head. There was no greater honor, no place closer to the Creator than to pray beside the High Elder. That is, until the title of High Elder is just out of one's reach; and then, it seemed, no place in the world felt farther.

Eliza,

I will not waste your time with pleasantries, as I am sure you are desperate for news. Your mother has been under Cora's care since we arrived back at Sully's house, and she has fared well in her capable hands. She was feverish at first, but Cora managed to break that fever quickly with her ministrations. I would like nothing better than to tell you that she is not in pain, but the damage from the Riftmead has been extensive, and Cora has determined that it is likely pain that is preventing your mother from trying to communicate. Cora is keeping her well-supplied with teas and salves that will help to ease that pain, and is also keeping her sedated to minimize her suffering. She has slept most of the time, but Cora says that is the best thing for her, to have some uninterrupted rest.

During the brief periods she is awake, she has not been lucid. She is mumbling and making sounds, but not speaking or answering questions. The only word we have been able to make out, definitively, is your name. I hope this does not distress you, but I thought you should know.

We have been carefully monitoring the area around the house over the last two days and feel confident that it is safe for you to visit at your earliest convenience. We would not keep you from your mother a moment longer than is necessary. Now that we know it is safe, you are welcome any time, day or night. We will take good care of her until you can get away to see her.

Sincerely,

Eli

10

W AITING UNTIL NIGHTFALL WAS AGONY. Throughout
the entire afternoon, Eliza kept Eli's letter in the pocket of
her apron, a talisman she could run her fingers over in the
moments when she wanted to scream from the weight of the
anticipation.

Soon, the letter seemed to whisper to her. *Soon.*

Not bloody soon enough, she wanted to shout back.

Jessamine was no help, either, encouraging Eliza to abandon her
duties for the day and set out for the Commons at once.

"Honestly, Eliza, I'm fine. There's not a thing I can think of that
I can't handle well enough on my own today. What's the point of
torturing yourself further?"

The point, as Eliza patiently explained, was to wait until the safety
and cover of darkness. She could not hope to arrive at Sully's house
unnoticed in broad daylight, and the other servants would surely ask
questions if she simply disappeared for the day. She was particularly
keen not to arouse her father's suspicions, although he had been nearly
as elusive as Colin over the last day, barely emerging from his office
and having little to say when he did so. And then there was the matter
of the patrols.

They arrived mid-morning and presented themselves at the front
doors while Eliza was carrying a tea tray upstairs. Her father made
a rare appearance from his office to greet them and then followed
them back outside. Eliza hurried up the stairs so that she could try to
glimpse them from the windows of Miss Jessamine's chambers. She

answered Jessamine's questioning look by beckoning her over to join her.

"Why are there so many of them?" Jessamine whispered, though they were in no danger of being overheard.

"I don't know," Eliza murmured.

"It looks like he's positioning them around the borders of the grounds," Jessamine said after several tense seconds of watching Braxton gesture broadly and the guards setting off around the sides of the manor and out of sight.

"Your father must have ordered them," Eliza replied. "Additional protection."

"Protection from whom?"

"Bridie. My mother," Eliza suggested.

"What possible threat could they be to anyone here?" Jessamine asked, her expression incredulous.

"He wants them caught. If there's even the slightest chance they might come back here, he's going to prepare for it," Eliza said.

"But what about you? They're going to make it terribly difficult for you to sneak out, aren't they?" Jessamine asked.

Eliza pressed her lips into a tight smile. "Yes, I daresay they will."

In the end, though, when darkness fell and Eliza was at last able to sneak away, getting past the guards was much easier than she had anticipated. After all, she had been practicing her Influencer magic with Eli for weeks and hadn't allowed a drop of Riftmead to cross her lips since she had learned the truth about it. Her gift, always powerful, was easier than ever to wield, and the guards at the borders were her first opportunity to test just how much progress she had made.

She chose her exit point carefully, a gap in the hedgerow that opened into the field beyond. Eli had promised Colin would meet her in the lane, so she didn't need to bother with saddling a horse or risk being caught in the stables. She decided to remain in her uniform rather than change into street clothes. She could always make some excuse for being out on the grounds where she worked, but it would be harder to explain why she was dressed like a Riftborn from the Barrens who didn't belong there to begin with.

She watched quietly for several minutes from behind the rose bush that grew near the gap. The guard positioned here couldn't be more than twenty years old. He sagged against the trunk of a tree, picking at his fingernails with the blade of a pocketknife, whistling softly to himself. Eliza removed her gloves, stowed them hastily in the pocket of her cloak, and edged forward. The hydrangea would hide her until she was within a few feet of the tree, and then she would have to chance a dash across the open garden to where the guard now stood. Praying there would be no crunching of twigs to give her away, she held her breath and crept across, setting her feet down as slowly and carefully as she dared. She reached the far side of the massive old yew and then froze, listening to the guard on the other side. There was no pause in his whistling, no hitch in his tune. She stepped carefully, edging her way around until his shoulder came into view. Then she bit back her terror, reached out, and rested a single finger upon the man's shoulder.

What was that loud sound near the stables? Quickly, go investigate! She felt the strength of the command shoot down her arm. The soldier did not so much as turn, but gasped in sudden alarm and ran off in the direction of the stable, drawing his weapon as he did so.

Eliza exhaled, elated with her victory, but wasting no time in celebrating it. By the time the soldier found himself in the stables, blinking around confusedly and searching for the source of a sound he no longer remembered hearing, Eliza was already gone.

§

Eliza entered Sully's dimly lit kitchen an hour later to see Bridie sitting alone at the table clutching a cup of tea, an overlarge nightshirt hanging off one shoulder so that she looked like a small child who had slipped into her father's clothing for sport.

"Bridie!" The name bubbled up from her chest along with a slew of emotions she had not been prepared to confront the moment she walked in the door.

"I waited up for you," Bridie said, jumping to her feet with a sheepish grin and gesturing unnecessarily to her cup.

Stumbling forward and tossing her cloak to the floor in a heap, Eliza flung her arms around her friend, easing up at once as the force of the embrace nearly knocked her back into her seat. Through the thin muslin fabric, she could feel Bridie's shoulder blades poking out, sharp and pronounced. She'd lost so much weight in such a short period of time!

But Bridie did not seem to care in the least that a hug was enough to topple her. A laugh burst from her lips, punctuated by a sob. She clasped her hands together around Eliza's neck, pulling her closer.

"I've been so worried about you!" she gasped.

"Me?! You're the escaped prisoner hiding out from the Praesidio and you were worried about me?" Eliza replied, echoing the laugh. "How are you feeling?"

"Better every day," Bridie replied, pulling away at last, but keeping a hold of Eliza's hand. "Everyone's been so kind. Cora's been here every day, checking in on me and bringing me tea and salves. I don't know what's in them, but they're helping. Louise is nearly as good a cook as Mrs. Keats, so though I haven't got much of an appetite, I'm eating well. And I have a bookshelf in my room with the most *interesting* books." Bridie's eyes widened. "I don't know what to make of them! They aren't anything like our primers …" She shrugged, blushing. "I never took myself for much of a reader before, but I can't put them down!"

Eliza smiled. "Wait until you're well enough to explore the library! You'll not believe what she has hidden away down there."

Bridie returned the smile. "I'm starting to think I *would* believe it."

Eliza led Bridie to the table and settled her in the chair she'd just vacated, pushing the cup of tea toward her. "Here. You should still be resting, not venturing out of bed to see me."

"I didn't want to miss you," Bridie said. "Eli told me you were coming tonight. I could hardly sleep, I was so excited."

"Well, you mustn't tell Cora that, or she'll scold me for hindering your recovery," Eliza said. "But I'm glad you waited up. I've missed you so much."

"How is everything at Larkspur Manor?" Bridie asked, her face dropping at once. "I was so scared, knowing you were going back there."

"Elder Hallewell knows we were visiting Bedlam. He was angry, of course, but only because he was afraid that we'd discovered you or my mother there. Miss Jessamine was able to convince him we'd seen nothing out of the ordinary—well, ordinary for Bedlam, that is—and that it was simply a coincidence that the fire broke out while we were on the premises. He seemed satisfied… for now, anyway."

"Does he know I escaped?" Bridie asked, chewing anxiously on the nub of a fingernail.

Eliza shrugged helplessly. "If he does, I certainly won't hear about it. It's his greatest fear, I think, that someone will discover what he'd done to you and so many others." *And to my mother,* she added silently to herself.

"And what about everyone else? Do they still think I'm in a Riftward somewhere?" Bridie asked, a catch in her voice.

"Everyone except Liesel," Eliza said, reaching out to pull Bridie's finger out from between her teeth before she drew blood. "I didn't tell her everything, of course, but I did tell her enough to let her know that you are safe. I hope that's all right."

Bridie's smile was tight with emotion. "Of course it's all right. I know she must have been worried about me."

"Yes, she certainly was," Eliza said. "Worried enough that she would have marched right down to Clerkenwell workhouse if I hadn't promised to find you. She sends her love."

Bridie nodded, wiping away the tears that had snuck into her eyes. "Really?"

Eliza laughed. "Well, she told me to tell you to mind your manners and keep out of trouble. But from Liesel that's as good as a love letter, wouldn't you say?"

Bridie laughed. "Oh, it is that." A silence fell, during which Bridie turned the teacup in her hands, trying to warm her fingers. "So are you..." She bit the question off.

"It's all right, Bridie. You can ask me," Eliza said softly.

Bridie met her eye. "Are you nervous to see your mother?"

Eliza sighed. "I'm not sure if I've ever been so nervous about anything in my life."

"I understand. What do you say, after so much time?" Bridie whispered.

"I can't decide if I'm more scared that she might be able to talk to me, or that she might not ever be able to."

"She... she really couldn't say much, when we were together in Bedlam, but Cora thinks that could change," Bridie said softly. "I couldn't believe my eyes when I saw her at the workhouse. I thought I must be imagining it."

Eliza caught Bridie's hand and squeezed it gently. "But you weren't, and you refused to leave her behind, and that's the only reason they did what they did to you. Bridie, thank you. Thank you for finding her. I'm so sorry it brought such wrath raining down upon your head."

Bridie flushed and tucked a loose red curl behind her ear. "You don't need to thank me, Eliza. I didn't do anything extraordinary. It's what any decent person would have done."

Eliza smiled. "No, Bridie. It was far, far more. And I'll never be able to properly repay you for what you've done, but I promise you I'll spend the rest of my life trying."

Bridie started to mumble something in which the words "ridiculous" and "nothing special" were barely audible, but Eliza didn't stop to listen, instead leaning over and pulling her friend into another hug that she fervently hoped said all of the things she couldn't say. Bridie's eyes were bright with unshed tears.

"So, what happens now?" she asked. "I can't ever come home, can I?"

Eliza shook her head. "No, you certainly can't."

Bridie had already known it, Eliza was sure, but it did not lessen the blow. "Where am I to go, then? I can't risk seeking out another position, not in a Dignus house. How shall I find work without references?"

"Let's not worry about work just yet. Even if there was a place that would hire you, we can't risk you traipsing about out in the open. There are notices up all over the Barrens offering rewards for turning in any of the patients who escaped Bedlam, and Creator knows there's no shortage of desperate folks who'd do anything for that kind of money. You'll have to stay here for now and lay low."

Bridie groaned. "But I'm tired of laying low, Eliza! I want to do something! I want to help!" She lowered her voice, although they were alone in the kitchen. "Eliza, these people who took me in—Sully, Eli, and the others—how do you know them?"

Eliza bit her lip. She'd been hoping to put off this conversation, but she ought to have known better. Bridie was far shrewder than anyone who'd heard her prattle on about gowns and balls would ever guess. The Resistance had taken a chance on Eliza, though her position in the Hallewell house made her much more of a threat than an asset. Perhaps it was time to take a chance on Bridie as well. After all, she was going to figure out she was in a Resistance safe house one way or the other. It was far better she hear the whole truth from Eliza than try to cobble together some garbled version of it from what she picked up by listening at keyholes. Still, she wanted to make sure...

"Bridie, when you say you want to help, what do you mean? Help with what?" Eliza asked.

Bridie bit her lip, and Eliza watched as she struggled to find the right words for the way she was feeling. The struggle felt very familiar, like she was watching herself from weeks ago when she herself was deciding she could no longer sit by. "I understand that the Illustratum runs the workhouses and the asylums. But they can't be allowed to continue that way. They're... they're torturing people! Those places are using Riftmead in ways it should never be used, Eliza! They're poisoning people with it! The Illustratum has to know! Someone has to make them realize how wrong it is!"

"And you want to be that person?"

Bridie made a movement that was half-shudder, half-shrug. "I don't know why anyone would listen to just me. I'm nobody. But if we could get more people, if we all spoke up together, maybe the Elders would listen and look into it!"

Eliza's heart nearly broke hearing the note of hope in Bridie's voice. She knew she was about to kill it, and she took no pleasure in that knowledge.

"Bridie," she said slowly, picking her words carefully, knowing they would wound, and yet needing them to, "what if I told you that they already know? Elder Hallewell and the rest of them? What if I told you that those places—Bedlam and the workhouses—were using Riftmead exactly as the Elders intended? What if I told you that it was the only purpose that Riftmead has ever had?"

Bridie swallowed hard. It looked painful. "I would say I hope you're wrong. I would really, really want you to be wrong."

"And what it if I wasn't wrong? What then?"

Bridie's lips trembled, and then she pressed them together, hard. She closed her eyes for a moment, and when she opened them again, something had hardened within them—something that looked very much like resolve. "Then I would say they should be stopped. I know who they are. I know who they answer to. But they still need to be stopped." A spasm of pain shot through with fear rippled over her face. "It's not right, what happened to me in there—what's happening to all of them. People wouldn't stand for it if they knew."

Eliza smiled gently. "You're right. And what if I told you we could help? Would you want to?"

Bridie's eyes widened. "Of course."

"Even if it was dangerous? Even if it meant we could be arrested? Thrown in the Praeteritum, or worse?"

A pause. And then...

"Yes. Even then. This has to stop, Eliza. Someone has to stop them."

"People are already trying. The people in this house—Sully, Eli, Jasper, Cora, and many others. They've formed a Resistance, Bridie. And not long ago, I joined them as well. Do you remember the book? The one that you read, and then hid? The one that led you to Clerkenwell in search of your family?"

Bridie nodded, stunned into silence.

"I was the one who put that book—and hundreds of others—into the charity baskets we delivered all over the Barrens. It was the book I took from Elder Hallewell's office, the night of the Presentation Ball. You remember the one, I'm sure. You carried it downstairs for me, concealed in your apron, remember?"

"That... that was the same book?" Bridie whispered.

Eliza nodded. "Well, copies of it. I brought the original to Sully, and she reproduced it with her printing press. Then I placed the real book back in Elder Hallewell's desk and he was none the wiser that it had ever been missing."

"Oh, Eliza! That was so dangerous! Did you really do all of that?"

"Yes, I did. And I would do it all over again if it meant that the Riftborn of London would finally know the truth about the Illustratum. And as to dangerous, I've done far more dangerous things since, I can assure you." She did not elaborate. Impersonating brothel wenches was not a memory she cared to share the details of.

"Will it all be dangerous?" Bridie whispered.

"Honestly? Yes," Eliza said. "I won't soften the edges of this for you, Bridie. If you want to be a part of the Resistance, you have to know the truth. It's only going to get more dangerous now. If you agree to join, you will be putting your life in danger."

Bridie nodded solemnly. She dropped into quiet contemplation, and Eliza pressed her lips together, waiting. "It isn't right, you know," Bridie said at last. "It isn't right that we should have to risk our lives just so people can know the truth."

"You're right. None of this is fair," Eliza agreed. "But when those in charge maintain their power through lies, the truth can't emerge without a fight. If we want to make this world a better place for Riftborn people, we will have to risk our place in it."

"I want to help," Bridie said, and her voice, though small, was strong. "Can you tell Sully and the others? They can count on me."

Eliza smiled and wrapped her arms around her friend once again. "Yes, I'll tell them. And I'm proud of you, Bridie."

"I'm proud of you, too," Bridie whispered back. She pulled away, tucking a strand of Eliza's flaxen hair back into place. "What will you do now? Stay here?" There was a hopeful note in her voice, and Eliza hated to dampen it with her answer.

"No. I've got to go back to Larkspur Manor. I'm more useful there, for now."

"I'd feel braver if you were here with me," Bridie pressed.

"But I'll feel much braver knowing you're here, looking out for my mother. Can you do that for me?" Eliza asked, squeezing Bridie's hand.

"Yes, of course I can," Bridie said, and she sat up a little straighter. "I can't speak to anything else the Resistance might ask me to do, but that I can promise, Eliza. I won't let you down."

"You could never let me down," Eliza said. "And when this is all over, Bridie, I'll make you a promise of my own. We won't rest until we find out exactly where you came from. That is, if you still want to know."

Bridie nodded her head vigorously, resolve hardening the sharp planes of her face. "Oh, yes, I do. Now more than ever."

"Very well, then," Eliza said. "I'd best stop stalling and go see my mother. It's already very late and wedding preparations will be in full swing tomorrow."

Bridie leaned forward, that familiar eager gleam in her eye. "Will you come back and tell me everything? About the gown and the flowers and—"

Eliza laughed. It was good to know she could still manage to laugh. "Of course I will. Not a detail spared. But only if you promise to stop waiting up for me and go to bed!"

Bridie smiled—a fleeting but very real grin. "All right, then. Don't wait too long to come back."

Eliza gave Bridie one last squeeze but was careful to make no promise about when she would return. After all, there was a better chance now than ever that she might have to break it. The last thing she saw as she slipped out of the kitchen to climb the stairs was Bridie, alone at the table with her cold cup of tea, tracing a finger over the raw wounds still visible on her wrists from the restraints at Bedlam. The sight of her friend's injuries sent pain, like a lightning bolt, shooting through her heart.

She stared up the staircase into the darkened hallway above, where she knew far greater pain awaited her.

11

"**M**ANOR GIRL? IS THAT YOU?"

Sully's voice drifted down the stairs, and her shadowed form appeared on the landing.

"Yes, it's me," Eliza said. The nickname didn't carry the animosity that had once accompanied it. It sounded more like an inside joke now—a chummy sort of nickname. "You're going to have to start calling me by my name soon. You've got more than one manor girl under your roof now."

Sully tutted. "Don't I know it. This place really is going to the dogs."

Eliza arrived on the landing. Sully's pipe was clenched between her teeth, but she wasn't smoking it—just gnawing nervously on the end. Her dark curls sprang out at random from the scarf she had tied around her head.

"I'm sorry it's so late," Eliza said. "It's hard to get away during daylight hours, and Elder Hallewell has hired additional patrols around the manor."

Sully nodded. "He must know by now that Bridie and your mother are unaccounted for. I'd wager he's afraid they'll return to the manor."

"That's what I thought as well. If it weren't for you, they mightn't have had a choice!" Eliza whispered.

Sully shrugged away the implied gratitude. "Well, I expect you didn't come all this way just to yammer away with me. I'll take you up." She started to climb the rest of the stairs with a quiet groan. Eliza followed behind her, her pulse beginning to race. Sully led her up to

87

the third floor and along a gaslit hallway almost to the very end and then turned abruptly on her heel.

"That's your mother's room there," she said, jerking her head over her shoulder toward the very last door. "I'll leave you to your visit."

Eliza approached the door and stood in front of it as though turned to stone. After two days of desperately wishing she could be exactly where she was, she suddenly found she could not move her feet forward another step, could not will her arm to reach out and turn the knob.

"You don't have to do this right now, you know," Sully said. Her voice was gruff, but not unkind.

It took a moment for Eliza to force her mouth to form the words. "Of course, I do. I didn't come all this way in the dead of night with Praesidio guards swarming the streets not to see her," Eliza said, the businesslike snap in her voice not quite enough to hide the tremor. And still she stood there, unmoving, trying to remember how to take air into her lungs, to shift her feet forward. After several long, silent seconds, Sully took pity on her and reached out to turn the knob herself. The door swung forward into the room beyond where it was swallowed into the darkness, broken only by the dim circle of light cast by a lone candle on the bedside table. Eliza found it easier to move forward if she focused on the candle. She kept her eyes fixed firmly on it, and let its wavering light draw her gently into the room, a moth to the flame. It was only when she stood right in front of it, her hands resting lightly on the tabletop, the warmth from the flame tickling her chin, that she allowed her eyes to wander to the woman in the bed.

Behind her, Sully eased the door shut once more, leaving them alone.

Emmeline's eyes were closed, her breathing shallow and fluttering, like something caught in a breeze. Though she slept, no peace nestled in her features. Deep lines creased the space between her eyebrows, as though her very dreams weighed upon her. Her long eyelashes shuddered against her cheeks, worry gathered in the corners of her mouth, pooling like stagnant water. Upon her chest, one hand rested, fingers twitching incessantly. Despite her assurances that she would hold herself together, Eliza felt the sting of tears trying to force themselves into her eyes. She wished she could reach right into her mother's head and pluck out the darkness that lent such restlessness to her slumber.

Trying not to make a sound, Eliza sunk into the rocking chair that had been placed at her mother's bedside. The table beside it was littered with the remains of Cora's ministrations: smudges of powdered herbs, a tea towel half submerged in a bowl of lukewarm water, a teacup, empty but for a sticky brown residue in the bottom. Eliza's eyes drifted from these remnants to her mother's restless face again. Everything that had happened at Bedlam had transpired so quickly that she had had little time to take in the details of her mother's appearance, but she thought she looked better now. Certainly, she looked cleaner, the curtains of her white-blonde hair fluffy and clean against her pillow, her hollowed out cheeks smudged with just a hint of warmth. When she had first laid eyes on her, curled up on the floor of that filthy cell, she had looked like little more than a corpse. Now, under Cora's careful care, she looked by no means healthy, but she looked like a woman with a spark of life inside her, a spark she might just be able to cling onto.

"Hello, mum," Eliza whispered softly. She reached out a tentative hand and laid it on her mother's. The fingers, though thin as twigs, were warm to the touch. Eliza did not expect it and felt a tiny, hopeful bubble in her chest that sent a sob up her throat. She swallowed it down again. Damn it all, she would not cry. She took a deep breath and found, to her relief, that she could keep talking. "It's me. It's Eliza. I'm here with you. I've found you. It's all right now. We're taking care of you. You're safe."

She could almost believe it was true, in the warm, quiet darkness of Sully's house. She could almost forget the dangers lurking around every corner outside, the forces converging upon them, desperate to snuff them out. The light of that tiny candle was holding it all at bay, forcing it back into the shadows, if only for this moment. She hoped her mother could believe it, too.

"I know you didn't mean to leave me," Eliza went on, finding it much easier to talk to her mother's fingers than to risk a glance at her face, a glance that could shatter her tenuous hold on her self control. "I know why you left. Mrs. Hallewell told me everything, and I'm not angry with you. I would have done the same thing. You... you had to try."

If Eliza had had the courage to watch her mother's face as she spoke to her, she would have seen her words landing there like raindrops, would have seen the way Emmeline's eyelids fluttered at the sound of her daughter's voice, and the way her mouth began to twitch at the corners. She would have seen something like a flush creeping into her cheeks, bringing just the faintest signs of life and recognition to her papery skin. Cora's brews were working their powers, but Eliza's words contained a magic of their own. But Eliza, whose eyes were still fixed firmly on her hands, saw none of this.

"I can't undo what's happened. I can't get back all those years that they took from you—from us. And when I say I would have done the same thing, those aren't just words. I am fighting. I know what they are now, the Illustratum, and I'm fighting back, just like you did. And I'm... I'm very scared. I'm scared of what may happen." She swallowed hard, forcing back a lump of fear in her throat that seemed hellbent on choking her. "I'm afraid that people will die... that we will lose. I'm afraid it will all be for nothing." The words trailed off in a strangled whisper as she thought of the many nights she had longed to whisper her fears into her mother's ear, and longed for the comfort she would have received in return for her confidences. Just as the emptiness of the silence threatened to swallow her up in return, she felt something that made her heart skitter up into her mouth like a frightened rabbit.

The fingers beneath hers moved—a small twitch. In response, without even thinking, Eliza slid her own trembling fingers between her mother's, applying a squeeze of gentle pressure. A moment later, Emmeline's hand contracted, returning the pressure. Eliza cried out, a sound filled with joy and grief in equal measure, and the sound was so heart wrenching that the door behind her swung open.

"What is it? I heard a cry! Is everything okay? Is she... did she...?" Sully couldn't seem to finish the thought aloud, but Eliza was already shaking her head.

"No, she's okay, she... she squeezed my hand!"

Something like a smile passed over Sully's face. "That's... I'm glad to hear it. I'll leave you to it, then." And she closed the door again at once.

Eliza, who had not taken her eyes from her mother, began to watch her face for further signs that she was being understood. "You can't imagine how I wondered what had happened to you. I am so sorry you were trapped in that terrible place for so long. We had no idea you were there, I promise you, or we would have tried to get you out! That letter you left us — well, of course, I understand now. You were just trying to protect us. You didn't want us to come looking for you. When you're more rested and feeling better I'll find a way to tell father that I've found you, and then we can all—"

An odd, strangled cry escaped Emmeline's lips. Her hand clenched convulsively around Eliza's fingers, squeezing them with more power than Eliza thought possible. Emmeline's eyebrows contracted and she began to whimper. Eliza gasped.

"Oh, I'm sorry, what did I... did I hurt you? Are you in pain? Do you want me to fetch Cora?" She half-rose from her seat, but Emmeline's hand was suddenly a vice grip upon hers, and she sat smartly back down again. She leaned close to her mother, watching her lips move, trying to divine meaning from the stream of agitated mumbling.

"I'm sorry, I... please don't worry yourself. Just stay calm. I won't... it's all right, you're safe, mother," Eliza said, as soothingly as she could manage while her voice shook.

But Emmeline would not be calmed. Her muttering became wilder and more insistent, and Eliza leaned all the way down, so that their faces almost touched, to try to understand what was being said. Individual words broke through, barely intelligible, but charged with a quiet terror.

"...*mustn't... know... your father... never... never tell...*"

Eliza's eyes widened, but she kept her voice even. "I... I understand, mother. I won't tell him. I won't tell anyone. We'll keep it a secret, all right?" She continued to repeat this until, at last, it seemed to penetrate her mother's fear. Her breathing eased, the muttering slowed and quieted, and her hand relaxed enough so that Eliza could pull free her numb fingers from its grip. Then she scooped up the soft cloth from the bowl of water and patted it gently against her mother's forehead, repeating her promise over and over again even as her mind spun.

Why such a powerful reaction to the idea of telling her father that she had found Emmeline? Surely no one would be more relieved than Eliza's father when he discovered what had really happened to her? Perhaps Emmeline was simply scared that they would all be caught, that she would drag her husband and child into the consequences of the decision she made on a dark night so many years ago. After what she had been through, that fear was certainly not unfounded. Eliza herself had barely slept two hours together since they had fled the burning halls of Bedlam and she'd barely had a taste of the place. No, there was no reason to upset her mother now. There would be plenty of time to decide whom to tell, and how, once she had more time to rest and recover. Eliza was giddy with relief that she had listened to her gut, and hadn't gone running to her father the moment she'd arrived home from Bedlam. It was safer for everyone that she keep the secret, for now.

As she pulled her hand away to dampen the cloth again, Emmeline reached up and caught Eliza's hand. Slowly, she pulled it to her face, pressing it to her cheek. Her eyes fluttered, fighting to open for just a moment, to catch a glimpse at the startled face swimming above her out of the gloom.

"My... Eliza..."

The words were half-murmur, half-sigh, and they tore right through Eliza's heart as easily as tissue paper, shredding what remained of her self control, and reducing her to tears that sprung from that deepest place inside her—the one that never healed, the very heart of the hollow ache.

And for once, the carefully ordered lady's maid, the one who had mended herself so tightly and so precisely, allowed herself to come apart at the seams.

12

W HEN AT LAST SHE CLOSED THE DOOR BEHIND HER, Eliza found Sully still sitting on the stool in the darkened hallway, a book abandoned on the delicate little table by her elbow.

"I'm sorry to keep you so late. You didn't need to stay," Eliza whispered.

But Sully waved the apology away. "I wanted you to have your time, and I wanted to make sure no one disturbed you. I owed you that, at least."

"You don't owe me anything, Sully," Eliza said, frowning.

"If you like," Sully said with a shrug.

"Will you please pass along my thanks to Cora, for all her care and attention? I can see my mother is in very good hands. She already looks better than when we found her."

"I'll be sure to do that, yes," Sully agreed. "Cora seemed pleased with her progress."

"She understood me," Eliza said, doing her best to sound robustly clinical even as her heart threatened to swell through her ribs. "She said my name. She knew it was me, she recognized me. And she responded to me as well."

Sully sat up straighter, her eyes going wide enough to jostle her spectacles out of place. "She spoke to you?"

"She tried. Couldn't seem to keep her eyes open, but she definitely replied to me," Eliza confirmed.

Sully pressed her lips together into a thin smile. "That'll be Cora's work. The poultices and teas she's been using have a sedative effect.

She is hoping to help your mother avoid the pain of her withdrawal from the Riftmead. Downside is, she's real groggy."

Eliza smiled back. "I'd rather she be groggy than in pain. Again, please thank Cora for me."

Sully nodded, chewing on her lip. She looked like she was trying to come to a decision. Then she said, "I know you've got to get back, but would you come down to the sitting room with me? There's something I've got to tell you, and there's no good to come from putting it off any longer."

She turned and marched down the stairs before Eliza could open her mouth to answer, so she closed it again and followed Sully downstairs.

"Sit down, Eliza." Sully pointed to the settee but chose to stay standing herself, pacing back and forth while Eliza settled herself.

"Please don't kick me out of the Resistance!" Eliza cried out, so suddenly that she even startled herself. She hardly knew this was what she had feared until the words were halfway across the room.

Sully squinted at her. "What are you on about?"

"I... I thought... aren't you kicking me out? For bringing too much trouble your way?"

Sully snorted. "Of course I'm not! We've made more progress in these last few months than we'd made in years. You're invaluable, Eliza, surely you can see that by now?"

It took a moment for Eliza to collect herself. "No, I suppose I hadn't."

"Look, I was cautious in the beginning, but the time for caution is past. We're going to need all the help we can get in the coming days, and I'll not be turning anyone away with a true devotion to the cause, regardless of how useless I think them; and you, child, are far from useless."

Eliza felt herself flush, but she did not suppose Sully would notice in the dim light of the dying fire. "Well, then, what was it you wanted to tell me?"

"It's about Eli."

Eliza felt her heart plummet into her shoes. "Eli? What's wrong? Has something happened to him? Is he all right?" She began looking around the room as though he might be hiding in a darkened corner.

"Calm yourself, lass, he's fine."

"Oh. But you made it sound—"

"I know, I know. It's simply... ah, bloody hell..." Sully ran a hand over her face. Eliza had never seen her looking so lost for words—after all, the woman's tongue was famously sharper than a butcher's knife. She waited patiently, this time with her lips pressed together, so that Sully could gather her thoughts. After what felt like an eternity, Sully seemed to pull herself together. She sat down on the settee beside Eliza and kept her eyes fixed on her feet as she talked.

"Eli never knew anything about his family except that they were Dignus. Like so many other Riftborn children, his family was horrified at his powers and wanted to keep them a secret from the world. His father planned to stage his kidnapping and murder, but his mother discovered his plan and begged a servant to escape with him instead. The plan was to deliver him to the Resistance by means of the Lamplighters Confederacy, but Davies was caught and the Confederacy disbanded just days before he was meant to be smuggled out of the country by means of our network."

Eliza listened with rapt attention, and with the increasing feeling that something loomed just beyond her peripheral vision, something huge and important, something she knew and yet did not know. She had heard this story before...

"Eli was delivered to me, but I had nowhere to send him. It wasn't safe to send him back, and so I kept him here, hidden away until enough time had passed that I could be sure he wouldn't be recognized. I reared him up as best I could, Jasper alongside him, never telling him who he really was because that information was too dangerous for a child to have. But two nights ago, the secret ran out of road. I had no choice. The time had come to tell him who he was."

"Who is he?" Eliza whispered.

Sully raised her head, looking at Eliza with eyes that seemed suddenly, impossibly old.

"William Elias Hallewell. And it was your mother lying upstairs who risked her life to save him."

Eliza closed her eyes and waited for the shock to hit her, but what settled upon her, into her bones, was something very different than shock. It was... rightness. Understanding. As though she had been staring for years at the scattered puzzle pieces of her life, and at last the picture had emerged. Each piece fitted so perfectly. And now she could feel nothing but relief.

95

"Are you going to pass out, child? Or vomit? Should I fetch a bucket?"

Eliza opened her eyes to see Sully staring at her in alarm. Rather than answering, she flung her arms around Sully's neck and hugged her tight. Sully went as rigid as a lamppost as Eliza laughed and cried into her shoulder.

"Blast it all, she's lost her blooming mind," Sully muttered, patting Eliza awkwardly on the back.

Eliza laughed again. "I have not lost my mind! I'm... it's just... to finally understand it all... you can't know how it feels. I-I hardly know myself!"

"I can see that."

Eliza took pity on Sully and released her, jumping to her feet. "Where's Eli? I have to see him!"

Sully was still looking warily at Eliza. "He's not here."

"Is he... when do you expect him back?" Eliza asked. Her heart was pounding.

"Honestly?" Sully hoisted an eyebrow. "I'd say I expect him back when he's sure you're already gone for the night."

"What do you mean?" Eliza asked.

"Oh, Eliza, isn't it obvious, love? He's avoiding you," Sully said, in as gentle a tone as someone as sharp as Sully could coax from herself.

"Avoiding me? But why?"

"Come on, now. Surely you must realize he's ashamed to face you."

"What could he possibly have to feel ashamed about?"

"Can you not imagine how he must feel?" Sully prompted. "He can't bear to face you, Eliza. He blames himself."

"He was little more than a baby!"

"Such logic, while sound, has never had much success in the burning away of shame and guilt."

"Where has he gone?" Eliza asked.

"He didn't tell me where he was going."

"But you know all the same, don't you?" Eliza asked, reaching out and placing a hand on Sully's arm. "Please, Sully, I have to find him. I have to tell him... please, where is he?"

Sully hesitated a moment, then sighed. "He'll be down by the river's edge. Follow the water to the foot of the bridge."

"Thank you," Eliza breathed, and then raced down to the kitchen entrance and out into the night.

§

The water lapped gently against the muddy shore in the darkness as Eli sat upon the bottommost step leading down to the water, turning a single smooth rock over and over in his palm. In just a few hours, the Thames would be swarming with boats—pleasure boats, fishing boats, steamers, houseboats, skiffs, all clogging the waterway, turning it as bustling, noisy, and smelly as any roadway. In the predawn hours, a few small craft drifted quietly along, most likely eager to escape notice as they smuggled goods or avoided tariffs, slipping a few quiet coins into well-greased palms at the wharves to look the other way as they unloaded whatever contraband they'd hidden below deck. Sully used to receive smuggled books that way before the Illustratum cracked down on the borders. Now it was nearly impossible to bring anything into the country by boat.

A pair of men were shouting raucously at each other on the opposite shore. A slip of cloud bisected the full moon, casting its long, thin shadow over the water. And down the river, the Illustratum rose up out of the gloom, stretching the long, covetous fingers of its shadow over the shoreline. Eli half expected it to reach for him, to gather him in its ghostly fist and squeeze him to dust.

Without warning something small and round hit the back of his head. Rubbing at the place, Eli turned around, already knowing who he would see standing there.

Jasper smiled down at him, tossing a second small rock up and down in his hand.

"Sorry about that. I was trying to skip it."

"You're a terrible liar," Eli grumbled, rubbing the back of his head.

"I thought I'd find you here."

"So you came to murder me?"

"Nah. If I'd wanted to murder you, I would have used a bigger rock."

Jasper tossed his second pebble aside and descended the stairs to the shore, coming to a stop beside his brother, staring out over the river.

"So Sully told you, too, I suppose," Eli said after a moment.

"She did."

"Were you surprised?" Eli asked. He'd begun to wonder if everyone had already guessed the truth but him, if he mightn't have guessed it himself, had there not been a part of him determined to hide from it.

"Surprised? No. I knew there had to be a reason you were so insufferable."

Jasper grinned at his own joke, but Eli could manage little more than a grimace. Jasper's smile quickly fell away.

"It could be worse, you know," he said.

Eli turned to him, incredulous. "Jasper I know you're trying to cheer me up, but I honestly don't see how this could possibly be worse."

"At least you know," Jasper said. "At least you have the answer to the question."

"And never mind that it's the worst possible answer?" Eli asked.

"When you have an answer you can stare it in the face, Eli. You can deal with it. You can make your peace with it or you can rage against it. But without it..." He gave a sad shrug, and Eli understood. For someone like Jasper, the not knowing would always be worse.

"Did you ask Sully? About your family?"

"I didn't have to. Blurted it out the second she saw me standing in the doorway—I guess after your little chat, she wanted it all out in the open. She really doesn't know who they were. I was a foundling already when the Confederacy brought me to her, and the member who found me is long since dead."

Eli clapped his brother on the back. "Bad luck, mate."

"Yeah, well, we can't all have fortunes and titles waiting for us, can we?"

"You know I don't want any of that," Eli muttered.

"Is that so? Well, I'll gladly take it off your hands. The fortune, I mean. You can keep the title."

Eli snorted. The thought of bearing the name of Hallewell, and all that went with it, made him feel ill.

"Look, when it comes down to it, this could be a really good thing," Jasper said, and when Eli gave him a black look, he held up his hands in surrender. "I just mean for the movement. After all, if we really do manage to force a change—and for the first time, I think we may just be able to—it's going to mean something that we've got you on our side. You're walking proof that we're all connected: the highest of the high and the lowest of the low, tied inextricably together. How can they argue how different we are then?"

"They'll still try," Eli said.

"Of course they will. But it's going to ring pretty hollow, don't you think?" He slapped Eli on the back, and then left his hand there, giving Eli's shoulder a squeeze.

"Why are you being so nice to me?" Eli asked, his eyes narrowing.

Jasper shrugged. "I thought about taking the mickey out of you, but then I remembered how rich you're going to be. I figured I'd better start being nice to you if I want a slice of that pie."

Eli threw back his head and laughed then. It felt good—a release. Jasper chuckled along with him.

"I keep thinking about what's next," Eli said, looking back out over the water. "I mean, I suppose that's nothing new. I've always tried to imagine what the future might be like if we actually win—what would I do? Where would I go? I never had a solid answer, but I loved the possibilities. But now..."

"Now you've got a family. A home, maybe. But just remember, you can walk away from it."

"Can I?" Eli asked under his breath. Jasper heard him anyway.

"Yes, you bloody well can. You aren't beholden to anyone, Eli. When this is all over, if we survive it, you do what makes you happy. And if that means staying Eli Turner of the Commons forever, then that's what you do. They've taken enough from you, mate. Take back what you want, and leave the rest."

Eli took a silent moment to absorb these words. Then he looked at Jasper. "You're actually making sense."

Jasper patted his back again. "Enjoy it while it lasts. I'll be spouting nonsense again for the foreseeable future."

A skittering of pebbles made both of them turn suddenly and jump to their feet.

Eliza was descending the stairs to the shore. She had a shawl drawn around her head and shoulders, and Eli wouldn't have known it was her but for the way the moonlight shone off the tendrils of silvery blonde hair that had slipped out of her cap, blown about by the fetid breeze off the water.

"I'll see you later," Jasper whispered.

"You don't have to go!" Eli whispered back, an edge of panic in his tone now.

"I might be a fool when it comes to most things, but I know when to make myself scarce," Jasper said with a wink. Eli opened his mouth to argue, but Jasper had already turned his back on him and was walking briskly along the shoreline.

Eli watched helplessly as Eliza walked toward him. He realized he was still clutching one of the river stones, and released it, dropping it to the ground with a muted thud. He wished he could do the same, drop unnoticed to the ground, indistinguishable from the other stones rubbed smooth and featureless by the relentless waters.

She came to a stop a few feet from him, her arms stiff at her sides, her hands clenched into fists. Eli forced his eyes up to her face, but her expression was unreadable, tucked away in the shadows of her shawl. All he could see clearly of her face was her mouth, pressed tightly into a line. The sight of it made his heart sink right into his boots.

"Hello," he said, the word escaping him before he could get a hold of it. He felt his cheeks burn.

"Why are you here?" Eliza asked. Her voice was thin and strained.

"I… thought you might not want to see me, after… after you talked to Sully," Eli replied, stuffing his hands into his pockets. Yes, it was really much easier to embrace his cowardice and stare at his own feet. "So I made myself scarce, as it were."

"Why wouldn't I want to see you?" The question was so brittle it seemed to shatter the moment it left her lips. Eli could have cheerfully flung himself into the river for causing such fragility in her voice. He half wished she'd reach out and give him a proper shove. And yet, what she was asking for was not his imminent swim in the Thames, but an answer to her question, and he knew he owed her one.

"I would have thought that would be obvious," he said, with a weak attempt at a grin. "I'm the reason your mother was locked up. I'm the reason you had to grow up without her. Please believe me when I tell you that you could not possibly hate me more than I hate myself, though you are, of course, welcome to try. Creator knows I deserve it."

Eliza stepped forward, and as she did so, a gust of wind off the river caught at the shawl, tugging it back from her face to reveal her eyes burning with intensity in the pale planes of her face. Once their eyes had locked, Eli could not bring himself to look away. He simply stood there, statue-like, as she closed the distance between them step by step, until she stood barely a foot in front of him. She stared at him for a moment, and then, without warning, reached a hand up toward his face. He flinched slightly, expecting a slap, and then froze again in shock as she ran her fingers softly over his cheekbone.

"I don't hate you. I *remember* you," she whispered, her fingers tracing his features like she was drawing them from memory. "I remember playing together. I remember your eyes. I ought to have known you from the first, that day when you hid in my carriage."

Eli could not speak. He was so shocked that she was not shouting at him that he felt quite wrong-footed. His face tingled at every point where she let her fingers trail over his skin. He could almost feel the promise of her magic in her fingertips, though she was not using it.

"I'm so sorry, Eli," she whispered.

The words were so antithetical to what, by rights, should be coming out of her mouth, that a bark of incredulous laughter left Eli's throat before he could stop it. "What the devil do you mean by apologizing to me?" he breathed. "It's me who should be apologizing! I'm the one who—"

"The one who what?" Eliza asked. "You were a child—what could you possibly have to apologize for?"

"I... I was the reason she left. I..." The enormity of his guilt rose up, a tidal wave threatening to drag him under.

"You were a victim," Eliza said, her voice as calm and reassuring as a lullaby. "So was my mother. So was I. Don't let them do this to you, Eli. They've taken so much from you, from all of us—don't let them twist their crimes into a burden strapped to your back. It's not yours to carry. It never was."

Tears welled up, transforming Eliza into little more than a blur, and with the tears came the words. "I'm sorry, Eliza. I'm so very sorry. God, I am just so, so... how can I ever..."

"Shhhh," Eliza shushed him, wiping the tears from his cheeks, even as she blinked away her own. "You already have, don't you see? You saved her. You saved me. I never knew, never understood what was right in front of me, until you... Don't you see? You owe me nothing, Eli. Nothing."

And then, before he quite knew what was happening, she had thrown her arms around him and buried her face in his neck. He cried out in surprise and then relief flooded him. He wrapped his arms

101

around her, drawing her close, letting his tears fall into her hair. Her fingers were gripping him so tightly it hurt and yet all he could think to do was pull her closer. Her hair smelled like lavender and wood smoke. Her breath was hot and sweet against his neck. Her fingers reached up and clutched at the back of his neck, sending tremors down his spine like an electrical current. Startled, he pulled back from her, opening his mouth to make some excuse, some apology for the way he had forgotten himself, the way he had lost control.

Their eyes met, blazing with something other than fear now.

"Eliza, I..." He licked his lips, dry with fear and something else. "Eliza... would it... can I...?"

"Yes."

The word shivered in the air between them and Eli, gobsmacked, seemed unable to reach past it. Eliza, however, popped it like a bubble as she lifted herself onto the balls of her feet, closing that last unbearable space between them.

"Yes," she whispered again.

When their lips met, Eli forgot everything—where he was, who he was, and what he had to be so gutted about only moments before, because now he was kissing Eliza, and she was kissing him back, and there was nothing else left in the world. There surely could not be, for the world had been reduced to the taste of her lips and the softness of her cheek, and the sound of the breathless sigh that escaped from her mouth into his like some euphoric elixir. At last, he pulled away, staring into the sky-deep grey of her eyes.

"Eliza, I—"

"Don't say it," Eliza whispered, pressing a finger to his lips.

Eli frowned in confusion. "But I want to tell you. I want you to know it, the way I've known it since nearly the first time I laid eyes on you."

But Eliza shook her head. "No. Please."

"But why?" He took a step back, feeling all at sea. Had he misunderstood all he thought he'd read in that kiss? "Unless of course you don't—"

Eliza shook her head violently, and then stretched up to kiss him again, feather soft. "No, it's not that. Please don't tell me yet. Wait. Wait until this is all over."

"But why?" Eli asked with an incredulous chuckle. "Why not say it while I have the chance? Who knows what may happen tomorrow?"

"Exactly! If you haven't told me yet, then you have something left you must do, don't you see? None of us knows what will happen. The danger is only going to get worse, day by day. But I know you won't let us be parted from each other without telling me."

"You want me to wait? But what if—"

"You have no choice, don't you see? You haven't told me, and you can't let anything happen to yourself until you do," Eliza said, her tone light, but her voice trembling. "We are going to succeed and we are going to come out of this, when it's all over, and you are going to say those words to me, and I am going to say them back."

Eli smiled at her. "Are you sure?"

"Completely. Now, go on. Promise me."

He bent down and kissed her softly once more. "I promise you."

Eliza's lips pulled up into a smile that could surely have undone him faster than any Riftmagic. He carried it with him long after she left him, still reeling, upon the fog-threaded shoreline.

13

"**P**IPE DOWN, ALL OF YOU!" Madam Lavender barked. Her voice rang out through the room, bringing the girls assembled there to an uneasy hush. It was unusual for Lavender to gather all of her girls together like this, and it usually boded ill. The last time they'd had a meeting like this, Penny thought darkly, it had been to inform them they could no longer drink with impunity. If Lavender was here to take away her last remaining whiskey, Penny thought she might just have to hang up her corset and find some honest work elsewhere. She continued lacing up her boot as Lavender cleared her throat.

"I know we have customers clamoring at the doors, so I'll make this quick," she said. "You all know where the sympathies of this establishment lie. You agreed to adhere to them when I hired each of you. You know that my husband's money started this place. You know what the Illustratum did to him."

All the lingering whispers faded out. Every face was turned in solemn attention now. If Madam Lavender was speaking of her husband, the situation was serious. Penny abandoned her laces and turned her full attention to the staircase where Lavender had positioned herself so that she could look out over the entire room. She did not continue until every eye in the room was fixed steadily upon her.

"You also know that things have gotten heated in the Barrens, what with the escaped prisoners. That's likely to get worse before it gets better. I'm urging you all to stay on your guard when you're out in the streets, and take care where and with whom you spend your off hours. I know you can all look out for yourselves, but you'd be smart to keep your guards up. There's something brewing out there, and it's bound to boil over soon. You can set your watch to it."

The girls exchanged wary glances. A few put their heads together to whisper. These words came as no surprise to Penny, privy as she was to Resistance communications. There were rumors that the fire at Bedlam was no accident, and that Colin lad had been seen coming and going, correspondence in hand. But even apart from that, you could feel it in the air out there—a tension that hung like a fog.

Lavender shushed them again. "There's a chance we may be taking in some folks in the upper attic rooms for a spell. Because of the recent unrest and the fire at Bedlam, there may well be some Riftborn seeking refuge, and we must do our part."

The attics were nearly always empty, except for quarantining the occasional illness and, once or twice, when one of the girls found herself in the family way. Penny knew the Resistance had used the space in the past, but that had been years ago, before she'd come to work there.

"Stuffing the attics full of lunatics? Bloody hell, Lavender!" Tabitha grumbled too loudly. Penny snorted. Tabitha never knew when to keep her mouth shut, and today was no exception.

"Sorry, Tabby, could you speak up? I didn't quite catch that," Lavender barked, cupping a hand around her ear and leaning forward for dramatic effect.

Tabitha looked uncomfortable, but stood up nevertheless. "I was just sayin', it sounds a bit... risky, bringing mad people into a place like this. Aren't you afraid they'll cause trouble and get us all into hot water?"

Lavender dropped her hands to her waist. "Tabitha, what kind of fool do you take me for?"

All eyes turned rabidly on Tabitha, scenting blood. The girls were always game for sport, especially when Lavender was the one dishing it out.

"I don't think you're a fool—" Tabitha mumbled, red-faced, but Lavender wasn't finished.

"Is that so? Because only a fool would take in Riftborn who would threaten the safety of her operation. Only a fool would take that kind of risk."

Lavender let Tabitha sink down into her chair again, the silence spiraling horribly before continuing.

"Now, everyone in this room understands what it means to be looked down upon. You've shouldered the snide remarks about your virtue and the aspersions cast on your morality, and you know it's all a load of bollocks. Well, a stay in Bedlam will brand a person as easily as a stint working for me. The Illustratum is counting on it. But we've got our own code here, haven't we ladies? We know there's more to the people that live and work in the Barrens than the Illustratum wants the rest of London to believe."

A murmur ran through the crowd like a breeze through petticoats. Penny smirked. If the Illustratum was half as adept at silencing dissension in the ranks as Lavender was, the Praesidio patrols would be looking for new work.

"Now, that said, I'm asking you all to keep your eyes and ears open, especially with your Praesidio customers. Any morsel of information, you bring it straight to me. The more we know, the better we avoid getting caught up in the trouble, you mark me?"

"Yes, Lavender," came the chorus of replies.

"That's my girls," Lavender said with a satisfied nod of her head. "Now take up your posts, Jack's set to open the doors. Let's see some of that famous High Street hospitality, savvy?"

There was a great scraping of chairs as the girls hurried to their posts. Penny, however, shoved her way toward the stairs, hoping to catch Lavender before she disappeared into her chambers.

"Lavender! A word, yeah?" Penny called.

Lavender turned, her hand on the railing. "Penny, for the love of England, if this is about the damn drink limit again..."

"No, no, it's nothing like that," Penny scoffed, making her way onto the staircase with a final push. "I've got something... well, that is to say, I *think* I've got something that might interest Sully."

Lavender raised a quizzical eyebrow. "Is that so? She's been pressing me to meet. Let's have it, then."

Penny dropped her voice as she arrived on the same stair where Lavender had paused. "There's this Praesidio guard. He was in here a few days ago, poking around."

"Poking around? You think he's digging up dirt on the place, and you waited until now to tell me?" Lavender asked, her voice turning sharp.

But Penny was already shaking her head. "It's not like that. He's looking for his sister. His *Riftborn* sister."

Lavender's eyes went wide. "Follow me upstairs," she murmured, and began to climb the stairs.

Penny followed in silence, not daring to speak again until she had shut the door behind them. "This guard, he goes by Daniel Byrne. Says his sister vanished when she was just a small child, and he's trying to find out what's happened to her."

"And he turned up here, did he? He must be desperate," Lavender said dryly.

Penny nodded. "I think he is, rather. Which got me thinking."

Lavender had the good manners to look intrigued, so Penny pressed on.

"Do you remember when the John Davies business went south?"

"Not likely to forget it, Penny," Lavender drawled.

"Yes, but do you remember why it went south?"

Lavender only just managed not to roll her eyes. "I do. They lost their inside man on the guard, didn't they?"

Penny nodded. "That's right. He got transferred from the patrol, and they didn't have the information they needed to go through with the extraction."

Lavender stared at her for a long moment before throwing her hands up. "And? I fail to see how these two matters are in any way related to each other, Penny, so if you've got a point to make, please make it."

"All right, all right!" Penny cried. "My point is, this Daniel Byrne, he might be what the Resistance is looking for! A new man on the inside, a spy to help the cause."

Lavender cackled. "Penny, just because the lad is looking for his Riftborn sister doesn't mean he's prepared to overthrow the whole of the Illustratum."

"You didn't talk to him, Lavender. If you could have heard the way he spoke about her... I think he'd do anything to find her, including breaking the law. He's already risking his neck flashing her picture around."

"But the Resistance isn't fixing to track down abandoned Riftborns, Penny. Just because he agrees to help doesn't mean he'll find his sister. That child is probably dead, and you well know it."

"I know, I know, but... I've just got a feeling about this, Lavender.

You've told me before I've got good instincts, that I should trust my gut."

"A girl in your position should always trust her gut, as long as she's got sense," Lavender agreed.

"Well, then. I've been with you five years now. You ought to know by now I'm not without sense. My gut is telling me we can trust this soldier. He told me himself he'd be willing to trade information. I think we should recruit him."

"And what if you're wrong? What then?"

Penny bit her lip. The stakes were high. She didn't need Lavender to remind her of that.

"Look, Pen, I know you want to help. We all do. If my instinct about this Bedlam business is right, then the Resistance is cooking up something big. But that means we've got to be more cautious than ever. I'm sure that soldier turned on the charm. I'm sure he was the picture of politeness and good manners. But you've got to remember, just like all men who walk in here, he wanted something from you. Not what the others want, to be sure, but he wanted something all the same. And unless you're the one who can deliver it to him, I'm not convinced he'll even so much as speak to you again."

Penny shook her head. "You're wrong, Lavender."

Lavender shrugged, looking unbothered. "It wouldn't be the first time, and it certainly won't be the last. I've been wrong about many things, Penny. But men? Well, they ain't often one of them."

Lavender settled herself behind her desk and looked pointedly at the door. Penny sighed. She recognized the dismissal and decided not to push her luck. A girl could talk to Lavender easily enough, but she did not like to be argued with. But as Penny eased the door shut behind her and made her way down to start her shift, her surety about Daniel sank heavily like a stone into her stomach. She had never been much tempted to disobey Lavender—well, aside from the occasional nip of whiskey. But now, as she plastered on her false smile and settled into her nightly role of pretending to give a damn, her mind set to scheming. It was dangerous to let her mind wander while she was working, but she could not help it.

Many things had been said of Penelope Lynch, but perhaps the truest of all of them was that she knew precisely which rules to follow and which to grind cheerfully beneath the heel of her boot.

14

ELIZA FELL INTO BED FULLY CLOTHED at half past two in the morning, and yet she could not sleep. She had barely evaded the patrol on the edge of the manor grounds, and nearly woken the whole of the downstairs when she slammed her foot into a milk jug that had been tucked into a corner of the larder where she hid her travel cloak; but it was not this harrowing return that kept her awake. Her mind was abuzz with everything that she had learned that night.

And of course, the kiss. Oh, the kiss. The memory of it filled her with such a strange and wonderful mixture of feelings that she didn't know whether to laugh or cry or dance or lay perfectly still so she could recall every detail. Her dreams when she finally settled were a confusing tumult of images, intimate one moment, and full of terror and anxiety the next.

When Liesel's sharp knock came upon the door at six o'clock, Eliza had to bite back tears of exhaustion. She wasn't sure how long she could keep sneaking out until all hours and still manage to rouse herself to do her work in the morning. Well, she told herself dryly as she slapped cold water onto her face and examined the deep purple circles under her eyes in the looking glass, at least she wouldn't have to deal with awkward questions from Jessamine, who knew perfectly well why she was likely to fall asleep over her mending.

Eliza shuffled out into the kitchen and stopped short in the doorway. A girl was standing by the sink, a small, battered suitcase clutched in her hand. Her dark hair was tucked up inside a straw hat, and she wore a traveling cloak. Her boots were caked in mud, and Liesel was tutting over them.

"I daresay it's not your fault, you had to come here on foot, and you certainly didn't make the mud. Still, I don't know what we'll do—you'll have to borrow a pair from one of the uniform cupboards until we can get those sorted."

"Yes ma'am," the girl replied, her voice a trembling little squeak. She pulled anxiously at her dress, examining the hem for mud. Her sleeve shifted, and Eliza spotted a Catalyst Riftmark inked upon her wrist.

"What's going on?" Eliza asked, looking from the girl to Liesel.

"Ah, Eliza, good, you're up. I'll need you to help Sarah here learn the ropes," Liesel said briskly. She did not meet Eliza's eye. Nor did Mrs. Keats, who continued to bustle around as though the conversation was not taking place.

"Learn the... is she here to replace Bridie?" Eliza asked, her voice rising despite her best efforts to control it.

"That's right. Sarah's just arrived this morning from the workhouse in Clerkenwell," Liesel said, giving Eliza a warning look. "She's the new scullery maid."

Eliza pressed her lips into what she hoped would pass as a smile, and nodded her head at Sarah in a cursory greeting. Sarah bobbed a curtsy in reply, then returned to examining her hem. Eliza turned back to Liesel. "You didn't tell me you were going to Clerkenwell for a new scullery maid," she said pointedly.

Liesel's face spasmed with emotion, forcing her to turn toward the sink and busy herself. "That's because I did no such thing. It was your father who decided we need not wait until Bridie is recovered. He wrote to Clerkenwell just two days ago, and they sent Sarah over to fill the position."

"Recovered?" Sarah asked, her face snapping up.

"Our former scullery maid took ill. She's in one of the Riftwards," Liesel said, still keeping her back turned on them.

Sarah's eyes went wide, which was saying something, as she already looked like a frightened baby bird. "Riftsickness? You... you needn't worry about that with me, ma'am. I'm a good girl, I am. Memorized my Riftborn primer cover to cover, I have," she squeaked.

"Yes, yes, I'm sure you have. Get on with you, now," Liesel said impatiently. "Eliza will show you to your room. Once you've laid off your things, come back here to me and we'll get you fed up before you start. You look half-starved, child."

Anger pounded through Eliza's body as she turned and walked wordlessly back down the hallway, Sarah scurrying along behind her, still murmuring apologies for the mud. Eliza pushed open their door and gestured inside.

"You'll share a room with me. That's your side of the room there, and that's your bedside table. You can put your things inside that wardrobe," Eliza said blankly.

"Is… is this where that other maid slept?" Sarah asked, wrinkling her nose distastefully, as though afraid she could contract Riftsickness from the sheets.

"Yes, and if it was good enough for her, it's good enough for you, I daresay," Eliza snapped. Sarah blushed and bobbed another hasty curtsy before scuttling across the room to remove her boots and hang up her cloak. Eliza did not bid her farewell, but turned on her heel and marched out of the room. She knew she'd been rude to the girl, that the circumstances of her arrival weren't at all her fault, but she couldn't find it inside herself to care at the moment. She'd apologize to Sarah later. Right now she had something else she had to do.

She ignored several calls of her name from the kitchen as she passed and continued toward her father's office. She discovered him just outside the door, giving orders to Peter.

"And we'll need to get all of the rooms ready in the East Wing. There will be guests who require lodging after the wedding, and we must be ready to accommodate as many as possible. Ask Martin to have all the linens brought down to be aired and the spare bedrooms opened up and prepared." She paused and drew a long, deep breath. She had to play this carefully. If she allowed her anger to get the better of her, her father would take offense and she wouldn't get a single word out of him.

"Father!" she called, and he looked up from his list, from which he was wearily striking another to-do. She watched his face carefully. It was the first time they'd seen each other since she had been to Bedlam. She couldn't be sure, but she thought she saw a spasm of emotion pass over his face before he regained control of it—was it fear? By the time Peter had taken his leave and she stood before him, he was once again the picture of composure.

"Eliza! I'm glad you're here, I have something I need you to—"

"I just met the new scullery maid," Eliza said, as blandly as she could manage.

She could have imagined it, but she thought she saw her father's shoulders tense. He certainly dropped his eyes back to his paper as though he suddenly found it much more interesting than anything she might have to say to him.

"Ah, good, she's arrived then, has she? I'm glad to see the workhouse is punctual with its placements, if nothing else. I assume Liesel is seeing to her?"

"Yes, of course," Eliza said. She squeezed her hands into fists to stop them from shaking.

"Does she seem competent?" Braxton continued, still poring over his list.

"It's hard to say. I only just met her. But I'm sure she knows how to work hard and take orders. She's a workhouse orphan, after all," Eliza said.

"Well, keep an eye on her, and let me know how she fares. We can't afford a chink in the armor with the wedding coming up. Everyone must be on their toes," he replied.

"Father, does this mean you've... had news about Bridie?" Eliza asked.

Braxton hesitated only a moment before raising his head and saying, "Ah, yes. I've been in contact with the staff at the Riftward. I'm afraid we shouldn't expect Bridie back any time soon."

There it was. Not an evasion. Not a half-truth. A bald-faced lie. It stole Eliza's breath right out of her lungs.

"When you say you've been in contact..."

She might not have noticed the pause if she hadn't been looking for it. "That's right. A letter."

"Why didn't you tell me?" she asked, heart hammering.

He frowned. "Surely, I don't need to remind you how busy we are with wedding preparations. I'm afraid it slipped my mind."

"But how is she? Where is she? Can I go see her?"

Braxton looked alarmed. "Certainly not! A Riftward is no place for a young woman of your position."

"But surely if she recovers—"

"Enough of this!" Braxton looked taken aback at the way the words had exploded from him, and he endeavored to compose himself before he continued. "Eliza, listen to me carefully. You must forget about Bridie."

Forget. The word punched a hole in her chest. She couldn't breathe.

"Regardless of her recovery, Bridie will not be returning to this house. Riftsickness may not be catching, but the weakness of mind that causes it certainly can be. We don't want such weakness infiltrating our well-ordered system downstairs. Elder Hallewell will not allow her back in the house, and I must say I agree. Once a servant betrays such a weakness of character, a master cannot be expected to rely on them again in his service."

"But... this is her *home*," Eliza whispered. She was less successful at stilling the tremor in her voice than in her hands.

"This isn't her home, Eliza, it is her place of employment, and I'm sure she can find another one more suitable if she finds the strength of character she will need to recover." Eliza let slip a sound that might have been a dry sob, and Braxton's expression softened. "I realize you miss your friend, Eliza. But you must be sensible about this. What kind of friend is she for you, a lady's maid to one of the most powerful families in the country? Why, you'll be off to the palace before long! It was foolish of me to allow you to get so attached to her in the first place, but I didn't see the harm in it at the time. I was too soft for my own good, and now I fear you are suffering for it. You've never been one to give in to pride, Eliza, but you would do well to remember who you are."

Eliza bit down on her tongue so fiercely she tasted blood. She had wondered how or if she should tell her father that her mother was still alive. Now she knew, her mother's warnings were not merely fevered ravings of a poisoned mind. Eliza looked at her father, and for the first time in her life, she knew that she could not trust him—could perhaps never trust him ever again.

"Yes, of course you're right, father," she murmured.

"Such a good girl," Braxton said with a satisfied smile. "Now, I must go speak to Mrs. Keats. The master will be home for dinner, and we must see to it that he has everything he requests. And you will be sure to tell Miss Jessamine to prepare to dine with her father tonight."

"I will, sir," Eliza said, and turned her back on him. The act felt terribly final.

§

Jessamine hardly knew what to expect as she opened the door to the dining room that evening. She hadn't spoken to her father once since the morning of the fire. In fact, she had barely even glimpsed him but for a moment or two from her window as he hurried to the waiting carriage. Jessamine was used to the distance between them, but she was accustomed to at least exchanging a few pleasantries over breakfast and dinner. And so when Eliza arrived at her door and announced that her father would like her to dine with him that evening, she couldn't decide if she ought to feel relief or apprehension. She still couldn't decide, even as she took her seat. Her father's expression was inscrutable.

"Good evening, Jessamine."

"Good evening, Father."

"I trust you are well?"

"Very well, thank you. And you?"

"Tolerable, I thank you."

A lengthy silence followed, during which Jessamine reached gratefully for her wine glass as soon as the valet filled it and took a sip. Her mind had gone blank. A moment ago she was so full of questions she couldn't even sort through them to find her own feelings, and now, try as she may, she found herself utterly incapable of formulating a solitary sentence to begin the conversation. She stared down at her consommé as though she might find a suggestion floating around in the bowl. She had just decided to start with a mild remark about the weather when her father cleared his throat and she was saved from the embarrassment.

"I visited the palace yesterday."

Jessamine blinked. She wasn't sure what she had expected her father to say, but it certainly had not been that. She scrambled to reply. "I didn't realize you had planned to visit the palace."

"I hadn't, but the need arose, and I cleared my afternoon meetings to make the trip."

Jessamine's hands squeezed together tightly in her lap. She wasn't sure what she was permitted to ask about the visit. Her father did not appreciate her curiosity about Illustratum affairs.

"I hope it was a pleasant and productive visit," she said finally.

"I thank you, yes, it was quite productive. In all honesty, the subject of the visit was the planning of your union with Reginald."

Jessamine kept her face composed. "I see. I... would have been happy to attend with you, father. I know that the details of wedding planning can be tedious, and you know I am eager to lend my hand in that regard."

"Certainly, Jessamine, and you shall have your little projects to attend to, I promise you. I daresay I have no objection at all to your putting your stamp upon such details as fabrics and flowers," her father said, with what he obviously considered to be an indulgent smile, even as Jessamine's temper quietly flared. "But my aim was not to dabble in such trivial details. I have important news for you."

Jessamine's stomach clenched, but she tried to look politely interested.

"The High Elder and I have decided it is in the best interest of all parties to move up your wedding date. His health is poor, as you know, and he is eager to see his son settled."

Jessamine clutched at the arm of her chair to steady herself. "I see. And what date have you settled on?"

"July the 5th," her father replied.

Jessamine nearly dropped her wine glass. "But that's only a month away, Father!"

"I am aware of that, versed as I am in reading a calendar," Elder Hallewell said dryly. "Surely you do not object?"

"It's... it's not that I object, it's just... there's so much to do! It doesn't leave nearly enough time to plan all of the—"

"Nonsense," Elder Hallewell scoffed with an airy wave of his hand. "There is plenty of time. Our staff is the best and most capable to be found in the country."

"But my dress..."

"My dear, if a dressmaker cannot complete a single dress in a month, I would seriously question the skill and competence of said dressmaker." He raised an eyebrow, in a familiar expression that always made Jessamine feel like she was about five years old. "I hope you are not going to allow your vanity to overshadow what ought to be a joyous turn of events. You have the opportunity to unite two of the most powerful families in London. You will not only secure your future happiness and standing in our society, but bring hope and spectacle to the masses, all while fulfilling the Creator's grand plan. Surely the shorter the wait, the better?"

Jessamine bit her lip. There was no way to argue without sounding, at best, like a selfish, petty child, at worst, a faithless blasphemer. And so she did the only thing she could do; she swallowed every objection raging inside her and pasted what she hoped was a bland and pleasant smile on her face.

"Of course, Father. I apologize. Your news caught me off-guard. Naturally, I am delighted that the union shall take place so much sooner."

Elder Hallewell smiled a satisfied, indulgent smile and launched into a lengthy description of all the preparations already being made, passing a folder full of papers down the table so that she might peruse them. Jessamine flipped through the papers without actually seeing them and moved her food around her plate with her fork in an effort to appear as though she was actually eating. The moment she thought she could excuse herself without appearing rude, she did so, and escaped up the stairs to her bedroom, a sob building against the dam she had shored up inside her, threatening to burst the barrier at any moment. If she could just get inside, if she could just shut the door...

She barely made it. She pressed her back against the door panels and slid to the floor, her papers scattering everywhere. It felt like everything inside her was collapsing and washing away in her grief and her pain. The sound that escaped her was almost unrecognizable. So consumed was she in this sudden storm that she did not even notice she was not alone.

§

"Miss Jessamine! What in the world?" Eliza was across the room at once. She dropped to her knees beside her mistress, who seemed barely aware of her presence even as she stroked her hair away from her tear-stained face and started gathering up the papers from the floor.

Jessamine's reply was disjointed and nearly unintelligible, punctuated by sobs and shuddering breaths that clawed at Eliza's heartstrings.

"The... wedding is... my father, he... I can't, I just can't..."

"What is all of this?" she asked, looking down at the papers now gathered in her arms.

"I... I... it's all been moved up... the wedding... oh, I can't bear it!"

It took several minutes to calm Jessamine enough that Eliza could finally understand what had happened. When at last she did, she felt some of Jessamine's panic flooding her own body.

"It's... it's all right, miss," she murmured, stroking her mistress' hair and knowing that it was a lie.

"Eliza, I can't marry him. I thought if I... I had time to get used to it, to make my peace with it, that I might be all right, but... I just... I can't marry that man, I just can't do it!"

"I know. I know, and I'm so sorry," Eliza whispered.

"You have to help me!" Jessamine gasped suddenly, clutching at Eliza's apron and pulling her closer. "You have to help me escape. I can't bear it, Eliza. If I have to marry that man, I will die!"

"Miss Jessamine, calm yourself. You... you don't know what you're saying, you're upset..." Eliza stammered.

"Don't you dare patronize me!" Jessamine cried hysterically. "I know exactly what I'm saying! I can't marry Reginald Morgan. He is a rake and a scoundrel and I can't bear the thought of him touching me, do you understand?! I have to escape!"

"Miss Jessamine, you must consider what you would be giving up! You would have no money, no connections, nothing!" Eliza said, doing her damnedest to sound rational even as she hated herself for saying the words.

"I don't care! Do you hear me, I don't care!" Jessamine shrieked. "If I must go through with this, I shall go mad, Eliza! I shall become my mother all over again, driven mad with grief and despair. I shan't survive it!" And she dissolved once again into stormy tears.

As Eliza sat stroking Jessamine's hair, the helpless feeling inside her began to shift and condense, solidifying into something hard and bitter and angry. She thought of Mrs. Hallewell. She thought of Bridie and her mother. She thought of Eli and Jasper, and the countless others who had had their lives upended and destroyed by Elder Hallewell's cruelty and ambition. And now he would sacrifice his only daughter to the most reprehensible of men, all to shore up his own position in the Illustratum leadership. Eliza had ignorantly lived her life as a cog in that machine of cruelty. But no more.

No more.

"It's all right, miss. It will be all right." Eliza said, surprised at how calm her voice sounded even as her rage at Elder Hallewell boiled just beneath her skin. "You aren't going to marry Reginald Morgan. We'll find you a way out of this. I promise."

Jessamine raised her tear-stained face from Eliza's shoulder and stared at her, wide-eyed. "Do you truly mean that? Will you help me?"

"Yes. I will help you. And I know others who may be able to help as well."

"You... you mean your friends from Bedlam? The ones who helped us find Bridie and your mother?"

Eliza nodded. "I do. And there are others. Many others."

Jessamine's eyes widened, still glistening with unshed tears. "What do you mean? What have you gotten yourself mixed up in, Eliza?"

Eliza hesitated only a moment. She had made her decision. Jessamine's father had taken more from her than she even realized. She, of all people, deserved the truth. She deserved the chance to fight back. An idea was forming as she looked first at Miss Jessamine and then at the pile of papers in her hands, an idea that might just pull all of the pieces together at last for the Resistance, for Miss Jessamine, and for herself.

"I will tell you soon, Miss Jessamine, I promise. But first, I have a letter to write."

"A... a letter?"

"Yes. And these papers... can I borrow them?"

Jessamine looked utterly bewildered. "Of course, but... but what could you possibly want with them?"

Eliza smiled. "All in good time, miss."

Sully,

I know it has been scarcely a day since I saw you, but something has happened, something serious, and I need you to gather the rest of the Resistance for a meeting right away. Rest assured, no one has been caught, and I am not in danger. But I've learned of something that everyone needs to know, and it cannot wait. Can you ask Colin to get the word around and see who can meet me at the Bell and Flagon tomorrow night at midnight? I will not wait for your reply—I will plan to be there. Just gather as many of the others as you possibly can.

Sincerely,

Eliza

15

NIGHT ENVELOPED THE BARRENS, but the back room of the Bell and Flagon flared like a little candle in the blackness. Within its walls, the occupants buzzed with a mix of excitement and wariness. Eliza felt every eye in the place turn upon her when she entered, following her as she took off her cloak and helped herself to a flagon of mead from the table. She ignored them all as she knocked back a few gulps of the sweet golden liquid and felt the warmth flood through her. Liquid courage, she'd once heard Mrs. Keats call it. She needed all the courage she could get.

"I didn't know you were calling us here just to get pissed," an amused voice whispered into her ear.

Eliza whirled around and let out a sigh of relief. It was Eli. The sight of him instantly calmed her, and yet made her pulse race strangely. Part of her wanted to reach out and kiss him again, but she knew she couldn't, not with so many people watching. He seemed to be thinking the same thing— he reached a hand down to give hers a quick, clandestine squeeze before returning it to his pocket.

"Thank goodness you're here," she said. "I was afraid you might be out on Resistance business or something."

Eli smiled at her. "You made quite sure all Resistance business was here tonight," he said.

"I wasn't expecting to see Bridie," Eliza said, returning Bridie's timid wave from where she sat hesitantly in the corner, looking like she was unsure whether she should even be there.

"She's one of us now, so I invited her along. You don't object, do you?"

"Certainly not. I'm just glad no one else did."

Eli shrugged. "What can I say? You've changed our minds about manor girls in general. Would you like me to call them to order for you?"

"For me?" Eliza repeated blankly.

"You are the one who called the meeting, aren't you?"

"Yes, I suppose so." Eliza took one last sip of mead and cleared her throat, her heart hammering. "Very well, then."

Eli turned over his shoulder, jammed two fingers into his mouth and gave an ear-piercing whistle. All of the conversation died away at once, and Eli made a sweeping gesture for Eliza to take the floor. Reluctantly, she crossed the room and stood in front of the fireplace.

"Thank you all for coming," Eliza said, silently cursing the audible tremble in her voice.

"Your letter said it was urgent. Of course we came," Sully said dryly. "Now get to it, lady's maid. What's so important that it couldn't wait?"

"There's been a development involving the nuptials of my mistress to Reginald Morgan," Eliza said.

Sully sat up a little straighter. Jasper dropped his feet from the tabletop to the floor, all trace of sleepiness gone.

"As you all know, the wedding was planned for the fall. They were discussing plans for a big public spectacle, an event that all of the city could celebrate."

"So, what's happened, then? Has it been called off?" Zeke asked.

"No. It's been moved up. The wedding will now take place in only a month, on the 5th of July."

"A month?!" Sully cried. "Why would they do that? Why would they rush such an important event? All that pomp and circumstance doesn't happen overnight. Are they scaling it back?"

Eliza shook her head. "From what I can tell, the plan is the same. It will just happen much, much sooner."

Jasper looked flabbergasted. "The rumors must be true— about the High Elder. They say he's been appearing at fewer and fewer services, and that he looks frail."

"They are true," Eliza confirmed with a nod. "Miss Jessamine has confided in me that the High Elder is indeed very ill. The truth of the matter is... he's dying."

The words settled over the room like a muffling blanket of snow. Every voice went quiet, every body still.

"Bloody hell," Zeke whispered.

"So then, it must also be true that Elder Hallewell is expecting to take the highest seat," Eli spoke at last into the quiet. "It's the only explanation that makes sense. He's moved the wedding up to ensure the match and secure his own political position in the process."

"Miss Jessamine herself confirmed it," Eliza said. "Evidently, Reginald Morgan told her as much when he proposed to her. But now the High Elder has taken a turn for the worse, and they feel they cannot wait."

"It makes sense," Sully said, gnawing on the end of her pipe. "They know the death of the High Elder will be met with despair in many corners."

"Not this bloody corner, I'll tell you that for free," Jasper growled.

"Perhaps not, but in corners enough, especially now that they've got so many of the Barrens inhabitants half-addicted to Riftmead. They'll need something to give people hope again, and nothing captures the masses like the pageantry of an Elder family wedding," Sully said. "The joining of the Hallewells to the Morgans will be seen as both a spiritual and a political union."

"So, when Hallewell ascends to the highest seat, it will be seen as a perfect, crowning moment, rather than a political maneuver," Eli said. "Say what you will of my father, but he's certainly no fool."

The statement was punctuated by an awkward silence. No one had ever heard Eli call Hallewell his father, and though they all knew it to be true now, it did not lessen the shock of hearing it stated so baldly. Eli weathered the silence with a truculent expression on his face, as though demanding they all absorb this truth as he had done, uncomfortable though it may be. Jasper, in a rare show of brotherly support, was the first to break it. He stood up, clapped a hand on Eli's shoulder and cleared his throat.

"I can't be the only one in this room who is listening to all of this and hearing an opportunity," he said, looking around, meeting each gaze. His eyes landed last upon Sully. "Sully? Come on, now."

Sully pushed her answer out around the pipe, her tone grudging. "I won't deny it. The transfer of power is always a tumultuous time. The Illustratum itself will be deeply divided in its selection of new leadership. Factions will form, grudges will deepen, and desperate men will make the only plays they've got. It's an opportunity to be sure, if we can figure out how best to exploit it."

"That's why I've come to you," Eliza said. "I think the wedding is the chance we've been looking for."

She felt the blood rush into her cheeks as every pair of eyes turned on her, but she did not look down or sit or hide in her own apron. She lifted her chin and went on.

"My mistress does not want to go through with this wedding. She is desperate to find a way out of it. I think we can help her and use the chaos of an upended wedding to further our own ends," Eliza said. She chanced a direct glance at Eli, whose mouth was hanging open.

"She... doesn't want to marry him?" he asked, gobsmacked. "But... the power! The prestige! She'll be living in the palace for Creator's sake!"

"She doesn't care for any of that, not now that she knows the price she will pay for it. Reginald Morgan is an utter monster, and her father is no better. I don't think there's anything she wouldn't do to avoid a union contrived by the two of them."

Eliza could tell that very few in the room believed this assessment, and she couldn't blame them. A pampered daughter of an Elder was a highly unlikely ally and they all knew it. Then again, so was she, when they first took the risk to trust her and welcome her into the fold.

"You say she'd do anything to avoid shackling herself to that man," Sully drawled. "And does that include betraying all of the Dignus, her own family included?"

"What family?" Eliza asked pointedly. "Sully, she has no family left! Her father has taken her brother and her mother from her. He is all that remains, and rather than looking out for her and her future happiness, he has sacrificed her as a pawn in his own political machinations. She knows what he is... or at least, she's beginning to. Certainly her eyes have never been so open as they have been in the wake of the events at Bedlam."

"Are you suggesting, then, that we use her as an ally in... whatever plan we may come up with?" Jasper asked. Eliza had flinched as soon as he started to speak, but there was none of the anticipated ire or even sarcasm in his voice. He sounded as though he actually cared about her opinion.

"I trust her with my life," Eliza said solemnly. "I don't think she needs to know everything, but I do know that she could be useful. Certainly there's not a soul alive who would suspect a Hallewell."

"Not a legitimate one, anyway," Eli said with a bitter little smirk.

Jasper was looking thoughtful. "I was impressed with Jessamine Hallewell," he said at last, and Eliza's mouth very nearly fell open. "She was brave. She didn't bat an eyelid when we leaped into the carriage at Bedlam. She seemed smart and ready for an adventure. We could do worse." He looked at Eli and winked. "Had a bit of her brother in her, I think."

Eli blinked, then smiled.

Bridie stood up suddenly, her chair legs scraping against the floor and making everyone jump. She reddened at once, her mouth working like a fish out of water.

"Bridie? Is there something you'd like to add?" Cora asked, her voice gentle.

Bridie's hands twisted anxiously in her apron as she spoke. "It's only... well, I know Miss Jessamine as well. Not the way Eliza does, of course, but well enough to say that I... I trust her, too. She were always kind to me, even though I was only a scullery maid. She traded places with me, disguised herself as a maid, just so that she could better understand what life was like in the Barrens. And then, when she learned what had happened to me, she took a terrible risk in helping to rescue me. She didn't need to do any of that. She could have ignored my very existence, and it would be no more than a scullery maid might rightly expect from a woman of her position. I think we can trust her. I certainly do."

Bridie sat down again smartly, expelling a nervous breath. Cora reached over and patted her hand with an encouraging smile.

"I'm sure we're all grateful for your opinion, love," she said. "Don't be afraid to speak up. Creator knows the rest of us spout our mouths off when we've got no cause to."

She threw a cheeky look at Jasper, who merely grinned.

"Well, that's all well and good, now, but let's not put the cart before the horse here," Zeke said, waving his arms and letting his chair fall back down onto all four legs. "Hadn't we better come up with a plan before we try to decide if we're going to get all chummy with the Dignus to pull it off?"

"I agree with Zeke," Sully said, rousing herself from some deep pool of thought. "I won't rule out our making use of the Hallewell girl, knowingly or not, but I want a plan first."

"Well then, here," Eliza said, reaching into her cloak and pulling out the envelope, which she tossed down onto the table between them.

"And what, pray tell, is that?" Sully asked, gesturing to the envelope with the butt of her pipe.

"That is the plan for the wedding procession," Eliza said. "I copied it over from the original, so no one will know the information has left Larkspur Manor.

Sully reached out for the envelope and pulled the papers gingerly from it, as though jostling them might cause them to explode. "How in the bloody blazes did you manage to get your hands on this?"

Eliza shrugged, trying not to look too pleased with herself. "I'm the lady's maid. Believe it or not, wedding details are among the most important of my duties at present."

Jasper raised an eyebrow, smirking. "Really? Guest lists and all?"

Eliza returned the smirk. "Let's just say I stumbled upon them in my travels," she replied.

Everyone rose from their chairs to get a better view of the papers Sully was now spreading out over the tabletop, muttering excitedly together. Under cover of this sudden interest, Bridie sidled over to Eliza and slipped a hand into hers.

"I can't stay. I've got to be getting back. We left Louise in charge of your mum."

"How is—"

"Stronger every day, just like me," Bridie said before she could even finish her question. "I'll tell her you've been asking after her."

Eliza nodded her thanks. "And tell her I'll be over to see her again just as soon as I can."

"Of course," Bridie said, and with a last squeeze, released Eliza's hand and slipped out the back door. Colin went with her, tipping his cap and trailing shadows from his grubby fingertips.

Eliza watched her friend go with a sense of trepidation. She didn't like the idea of her being out in the street, but she knew Colin would keep her hidden. Eli got up from his seat, edging his way around the table until he was standing beside her.

"Well done," he said, gesturing toward the documents now being passed around.

"Thank you," Eliza replied. "I saw the opportunity, so I took it."

"A natural double-crosser if ever I saw one," Eli teased.

Eliza frowned. "You make me sound like a criminal."

"Aren't you?" Eli asked, amused.

"Not really. Not in the sense of right and wrong."

"Ah, but see, you've hit the nail on the head. When the wrong people make the laws, you sometimes have to break them to do the right thing," he said.

"So... calling me a criminal is actually a compliment?"

"That is correct."

"Oh. Well, in that case... thank you?"

They both laughed, but Eli's face fell quickly back into lines of contemplation. Eliza did not miss it.

"Are you all right, Eli?"

Eli shrugged. "Are any of us all right, really?"

"No, I suppose not. But even so, if you have something on your mind..." she trailed off, hoping he would take her up on the implied invitation to confide in her. And a moment later, he did.

"Does she know? About me?"

Eliza didn't need to ask whom he meant. She shook her head. "No, she doesn't. I haven't told her about you, or about what her father did to you and to your mother. It... didn't feel like my place."

Eli closed his eyes for a moment and nodded once, slowly. "Thank you," he whispered.

"I'm not sure you should be thanking me," Eliza said softly, "because I'm not entirely sure that keeping her in the dark about all of this is the right thing to do. I find myself biting my tongue ten times a day. After all, if I'm not the one to tell her, who will be?"

Eli pressed his lips together. "Hmm. I suppose you're right. Our mother is in no fit state, and as far as Jessamine knows, I'm just some Riftborn upstart. I can't imagine why she'd believe anything I told her, even if I got the chance."

"Oh, I wouldn't be too sure about that. She has better cause to believe you than she does anything her own father might say to her. Think of the web of lies he's woven just to reach this point."

"But that's just it! How could she ever forgive me for shattering what's left of her perceptions? If I tell her what our father's done... who he is... she'll have nothing left."

"That's not true. She'll have you."

Eli laughed bitterly. "Ah, yes. What a consolation prize."

Eliza looked suddenly so stern that she rather resembled Sully, and Eli took an involuntary step back from her. "I don't want to hear another word like that come out of your mouth, Eli Turner. Your sister would much rather have you, a brother who will be honest with her and look out for her, than a father who has done nothing but lie to her and break her heart."

"I… well, quite," Eli said, allowing himself a flash of a grin.

Eliza returned it, though tightly, before her face fell into serious lines again. "What do you want me to do?"

"I'm… I'm not sure."

"Why don't we wait, just for the moment," Eliza advised. "Once we have an idea of what the plan is, perhaps that will make it clear when Jessamine should know the truth, as well as from whom she should hear it."

Eli sighed, his shoulders sagging with relief. "Yes. One thing at a time. Mustn't get ahead of ourselves."

"I know it can be overwhelming," Eliza said, glancing around to be sure no one was watching, and then slipping her hand into Eli's to give it a squeeze. "I'm still trying to come to terms with the fact that my mother is alive, and that everything I thought I knew about her, about why she left, was a fabrication. Part of me wants to shout from the rooftops that she hasn't left me after all. The other part wants to take the truth with me to my grave. I'm not sure what the right answer is. I just know that my world has been turned upside down, and I haven't gotten my bearings yet. I imagine you feel very much the same."

"A fairly accurate depiction, yes," Eli said. Eliza could hear the pain behind the bravado.

"Well, no better time than when the world is upside down to make a new one," she said.

Eli gave a genuine smile this time. "No better time, indeed."

Eliza squeezed his hand once more, and then let it drop, moving forward to rejoin the others. Sully was deep in conversation with Zeke and Seamus, discussing the various entrances to the Illustratum and the Praesidio's possible plans to guard them. Jasper looked up as Eliza approached the table.

"This is tremendous, manor girl. Well done," he said with a grin, and for the first time, the words 'manor girl' held not a hint of sarcasm nor contempt. Eliza could not help but grin in return.

130

"Thank you, Jasper," she replied.

"Now, I don't suppose you've come across any security plans in your travels, have you? Because that would be really helpful," Jasper asked.

Eliza's face fell. "No, I'm afraid not. Miss Jessamine wouldn't be likely to be included in that sort of discussion, I'm afraid, so I haven't seen anything like that."

Jasper looked disappointed but rallied almost at once.

"Jasper's right," Zeke said, tapping his finger agitatedly upon the map in front of him. "This is too good a chance to pass up, but we can't do it with the people in this room. We've got to go bigger, lads. Much, much bigger."

All eyes turned to Sully, who was nodding slowly. "If we had the numbers to overpower the Praesidio and get inside the Elder Council chamber, we might just be able to demand a parley vote."

The room grew quiet. Eliza looked from face to face, but no one's expression mirrored her own confusion.

"What is a parley vote?" she asked at last.

"It's down in the Illustratum Code of Governance," Sully said. "It was put in to give the appearance that the Elders would be held to the will of the people—a promise they've never kept, which is why you've never so much as heard of it."

"But what is it? How does it work?" Eliza pressed.

"It's a rule which states that any person who brings a petition to the Elder Council floor must be heard, and that every person there present may vote upon it. It is written in such a way that it excludes no one, not even a Riftborn, from bringing their grievance before the Elder Council. It was adopted to appease the members of Parliament who opposed Illustratum rule, a feeble attempt to avoid a monopoly on power."

"And why is it feeble? It sounds fair," Eliza said.

"Fair on paper, yes, but in practice? Have you ever heard of a Riftborn entering the Elder Council chambers? Have you heard of anyone but an Elder being allowed a voice in that space?"

"No," Eliza said.

"Of course you haven't. It was a promise the Illustratum never intended to keep," Sully spat.

"They promised any man who stood upon the chamber floor

would have a voice," Zeke added with a bitter, twisted smile, "but they never promised to allow him *access* to the floor in the first place."

"Which is why, in all the years of the Illustratum running this country, there has never *been* a Riftborn on the Elder Council chamber floor," Sully finished.

"But you don't have to take our word for it," Jasper said lightly. "You were there the last time a Riftborn attempted to gain access to the chamber floor."

"What do you mean I was there when… oh!" And she recalled, with gut-wrenching clarity, sitting in the servants' pew at Sunday services and hearing the desperate cries of a man out in the atrium. The man had come demanding justice for John Davies, and within seconds, a shot rang out. Eliza had seen the blood upon the atrium floor where the man had fallen.

It had been right in front of the Elder Council chamber door.

"He was a bloody fool, but at least he was a bloody fool with a purpose. He knew that the chamber would be empty with all the Elders in the service, which meant it would be less heavily guarded. If he'd been able to get through that door and onto the chamber floor, they would have had no choice but to hear his petition."

"I still don't understand why he risked it," Cora said, shaking her head.

"Davies was his uncle," Fergus said, his voice solemn. "Helped raise him from when he were no higher than me knee. He had to do something, even if it was bound to fail. Because that's what you do, innit, for family."

No one spoke for a few moments. Such heavy words fell hard, and could not be so easily sifted through and pushed aside. For many in the room, after all, the concept of family was not so cut and dried. At last, Sully's sharp voice sliced through the silence.

"We're going to need numbers. Big numbers. The Praesidio will be concentrated on areas other than the chamber floor, but the Illustratum will still be heavily guarded. We can't expect to sneak past them. We'll have to target the weak points and overwhelm them with sheer manpower."

"We ain't got them kind of numbers," Zeke said, shaking his head. "And I'm not sure we can get 'em."

"We haven't got them now, but the wedding is a month away!"

Jasper cried, jumping to his feet so fast that he knocked his chair to the floor. "We haven't a moment to lose! We've got to get recruiting!"

"Hang on now, lad," Fergus wheezed. "I admire your fire, but we can't just start shouting in the streets or we'll all be swingin' from a noose by week's end."

"Saints alive, Fergus, I'm not talking about making a speech in the bloody High Street! I'm talking about the papers from Bedlam, the ones we smuggled out the day of the fire. Sully's got a printing press. We need to deliver a copy of that information into as many hands as possible!"

Zeke was shaking his head. "That's what we did with the truth about the Lamplighters Confederacy. We were hoping to light a fire under the Barrens, but it all came to nothing."

"Yes, but this is different! The last time, the Elders were already anticipating upheaval. They got out ahead of us with the Riftmead. They had the whole of the Barrens subdued within days. This time they think they've got everything back under control."

Zeke opened his mouth to argue again, but it was Eli who cut him off this time.

"I think Jasper's right. Their sense of control comes from the Riftmead, and the information we've got is going to undermine that control directly. Not only will people stop drinking it, but they'll be beside themselves knowing they've been unwittingly poisoning themselves, their children, and their elderly relatives. And just as that anger is coming to a head, we give them a call to action."

Sully nodded slowly. "We don't just tell them they're being poisoned and leave them to reckon with it alone. We tell them exactly what they can do to hold the Elders accountable."

Eli nodded, sharing a grim smile with Jasper. "That's right. We tell the Riftborn of London that if they've had enough of their children being poisoned and their livelihoods being ground into the dust, that they need to come to the gates of the Illustratum on the day of the wedding and stand with us!"

"But... the Praesidio will still be plentiful, and armed to the teeth. Without a doubt, people will be killed," Eliza said.

Sully looked up, a grim understanding sparkling in the darkness of her eyes. "That's right, child. We'll be asking people to risk their lives for a chance at a future that doesn't freeze them out of all possibilities of health, wealth, and prosperity. We know the risk, and we do not take it lightly."

Eliza's stomach roiled. For the first time, they were discussing plans that meant assured casualties. She looked around the room, half hoping to see the same fear and hesitation in someone's features. But every single face that stared back at her was full of nothing but resolve. They'd all been in this fight so much longer, seen so much of the darkest corners of Riftborn life. They'd made peace with those kinds of fears long ago. All they feared now was failure.

"This is going to take a lot of planning," Cora was saying now. "We're going to need more people in this inner circle, to help us recruit and organize in the lead up to the day, more people to take point on different parts of the plan. And we should consider very carefully who we're going to ask and how."

"I'll go to the lads at the docks," Zeke said at once. "They've been involved in smuggling long enough to know what we're up against, and the recent crackdowns have hit them hard. I reckon we can find some good recruits there if we promise them action."

"Oh I reckon there'll be action enough for them that want it," Jasper said with a grin that folded almost instantly into a grimace as Sully stood and cuffed him on the back of the head.

"I'll go to Lavender," she said. "We've got no better resource in the city. If we can convince Lavender to throw her weight and considerable resources behind this scheme, I'll like our odds a lot better, and no mistake."

"We'll want to group people by gift," Michael piped up, leaning forward and trying to shake off the stupor his mead had cast over him. "Catalysts of a kind, and so forth, to use their powers to greater effect."

"I think we should reach back into the Praeteritum," Jasper added. "Security will be decreased, with the number of soldiers they're going to need near the Illustratum itself, and the ones who get left behind won't be the cream of the crop. We might be able to stage the kind of mass break out that will give us the numbers we need to overwhelm the Praesidio."

"All right, all right, everyone, rein it in," Sully said suddenly, slamming her hand down on the table. "We're getting ahead of ourselves. First, we recruit other organizers. Once we know who we've got, and what their gifts and connections are, we can plan the rest. Until then, all this chatter is nothing but a congress of dreamers spouting nonsense into the bottom of their empty pint glasses."

The Resistance members broke off into mumbling, and Sully cocked her head in Eliza's direction. "Talk to the Hallewell girl, but do it carefully. Tell her as little as possible, and assess how far she's willing to go to help us."

Eliza threw a quick look at Eli, now bent over the table examining a timetable with Jasper. "I think I know one way to ensure she's on our side," she said softly, "But I'll have to ask Eli."

Sully met her eye, and it was clear from her flat expression that she understood exactly what Eliza meant. "Yes, I think that would do it."

16

S ULLY PACED THE FLOOR, the plumes of pipe smoke marking her trail like the steam engine of a locomotive. Every few passes of the sitting room floor, she'd divert to the window, pull aside the curtain, and scan the street. Then, with a restless sigh, she would drop the curtain and resume her pacing once again.

There were very few people of her acquaintance who could elicit this level of anxiety from Lila Sullivan, but Madam Lavender was one of them. Sully cursed herself and demanded that she get a grip, but it was useless. Too much was riding on this meeting.

It did not help that the last time she and Lavender had stood in this room together was the day they received word that Lavender's husband had died in exile in France. Sully's palms broke into a cold sweat just remembering how her stomach had roiled, how she had forced her mouth to form the words, how Lavender had crumpled into a heap upon the rug, her strings cut, her heart shattered.

Sully shook her head to clear it. She could not afford to sink back into the mires of those memories—she needed to stay sharp and focused in order to secure what might very well be the most crucial element of their scheme, the solid foundation upon which it could all stand. After the previous night's revelations, it had become clear that the wedding was the moment to which they must pin all their nebulous hopes. No better opportunity was going to present itself. If they had Lavender, they had a chance. Without her, well… Sully shuddered and resumed her pacing.

Bridie entered the room, dropping into a respectful little curtsy before setting a tea tray down on the table. "Louise was fixing to take this upstairs, so I thought I'd make myself useful. Do you need anything else before your guest arrives, Miss S—um, Sully?"

Sully's mouth quirked into the suggestion of a smile. Bridie had been having trouble settling into a household that didn't adhere to such stringent rules of hierarchy. It seemed she wasn't sure what to do with herself if she wasn't curtsying or otherwise showing deference to someone. Still, she was a helpful little thing, eager to please, and it was nice to give Louise a bit of a break with the housework.

"That's just fine, Bridie, thank you. I've got everything I need for now," Sully replied. "You know, you don't have to work. You've still got a fair bit of recovering to do."

Bridie made a face. "I don't think I can lie in that bed another second. If I don't stay busy, I think too much."

Sully nodded sagely. She knew all about combatting emotion by throwing herself into work. "Well, thank you for the tray then, child."

Bridie curtsied again, flinched as she corrected herself, and then turned to go, but she had not yet crossed the threshold when she hesitated. She stayed frozen there in apparent indecision for so long that Sully took pity on her.

"Was there something you needed, Bridie?" she asked, trying to soften the bite in her own voice so that the girl might find the courage to just have out with it.

"Yes," Bridie said, whirling on the spot and dropping her eyes to her hands, which had twisted the hem of her apron into a wrinkled ball. "Or, rather… well, I suppose it isn't really something I need so much as it's something I… hoped."

Sully raised an eyebrow, intrigued in spite of her nerves. "What's this, then?"

"It's only… well, Eliza told me about… about your library."

"Is that so? And what did she tell you about it?" Sully prompted.

"Well, she told me you've got more books than she's ever seen in one place, more even than the Illustratum collections. And she said that some of the books—well, all of them, really—are illegal?"

Bridie hooked the last word up into a question mark, looking anxious now that she might have offended Sully by suggesting she was a criminal. But Sully merely chuckled at the look on her face and gave a confirming nod.

"That's right. Now, what about that has got you hopeful?"

"Well, it's just that... I was wondering if I might... might read some of them?"

Sully, who had not been expecting intellectual curiosity from a scullery maid, did not answer right away, and Bridie, no doubt misinterpreting her hesitation for a denial, flushed a mortified scarlet and began backing toward the door again.

"I'm so sorry, I shouldn't have asked. Of course you have to be careful who you trust with such—"

"Bridie, for Creator's sake, calm yourself, child. I'm more than happy to let you read whatever you'd like—I didn't rescue those books to hoard them like a jealous dragon in a cave. What kind of book are you looking to read?"

Bridie turned, if possible, redder still. "Well, now, I suppose you might not have any of these kinds of books, but Liesel over at Larkspur Manor, she told me once there used to be books called... called *novels,* and that they could be tragic or romantic, or... and I thought maybe...something with a happy ending?"

Sully threw back her head and laughed. "Lass, if anyone ever needed to escape into a good novel, I do believe it might be you. You like balls, dancing, romance, that sort of thing?"

Bridie had now reached a level of embarrassment so acute that it prevented her from offering any other answer but a violent nod and a squeak that was more rodent than girl. Sully, however, was delighted. "I know just the books for you, Bridie Sloane. You leave it with me. I'll pop a few on your bedside table before I set to work for the afternoon."

"Oh, I don't even know what to... only if it's not inconvenient, of course. Thank you, Sully." And with a final truncated curtsy, she backed out of the room, closing the door behind her.

Sully had barely time to watch her go when there was a knock on the door that nearly startled her clean out of her skin. She snorted ruefully at herself as she crossed into the entryway to open the door; she was starting to lose her edge. She'd been cooped up with her books for too long—she would have to relearn how to become a woman of action, and she wouldn't find that lesson on her shelves.

Sully pulled her door open to reveal Lavender waiting on the landing, a carved ivory walking stick in her hand and a feathered peach confection of a hat perched upon her head so that she looked rather like a bird of paradise desperately lost among the sooty pigeons of London.

"Sully," she said with a gracious incline of her head.

"Good to see you, Lavender. Come on in," Sully replied, stepping aside.

"I told my driver to pull the carriage into the alley to wait for me. I see no reason to draw any unwanted attention to the fact that I've made this little early morning sojourn."

Sully smirked as Lavender swept past her into the sitting room. It was only "early" to someone who kept hours like Lavender's. For the rest of the city of London, half their day's work was already behind them. Sully shuffled in after Lavender to find her looking around the room with a somewhat disappointed expression.

"Something wrong, Lavender?"

"Well, I just assumed that if you'd invited me all the way here, I'd be sure at least to see a house full of escaped Bedlam patients or maybe a stockpile of weaponry. I'm almost disappointed."

"In the front room? What do you take me for, an amateur? We keep the prisoners and weaponry in the basement," Sully said. She waved Lavender over to the settee. "Tea?"

"Oh go on then, unless you've got something stronger," Lavender said, settling onto the settee with a creaking of whalebone and crinkling of satin. She propped her walking stick against the fireplace bricks and heaved a sigh. "And then let's get right down to it, Sully. I was never one for suspense."

Sully poured out the tea and passed over the plate of biscuits. Then she did as she was told, and bloody well got right down to it.

"I didn't want to risk having this conversation at your place, Lavender. I know you trust your girls, but there's too much riding on this."

Lavender simply nodded in acknowledgment. She knew the dangers of running her business on the farthest edges of legality, and how a bit of trust in the wrong person could bring the whole operation toppling down like a deck of cards.

Sully went on, "You and I have known each other a long time. We both know things that could land the other on the gallows before sundown, and I don't take that lightly."

"Nor do I."

"You know we've been looking for an opportunity to tear the

140

Illustratum down. You know the schemes we've hatched and the risks we've taken. You also know it has amounted to very little, at least since the days of the Lamplighters Confederacy. I was starting to fear, once Davies and the others were captured, that the Illustratum's hold was too deep. That we'd missed our chance."

Lavender quirked an eyebrow, clearly intrigued. "And now?"

"And now some information has come into my hands that could change all of that." Sully took a sip of tea, steeling herself. "No doubt you've heard through your sources that the Hallewell girl and the High Elder's son are to be married?"

"Naturally," Lavender drawled.

"Have your sources yet informed you that the wedding's been moved up to a mere four weeks from now?" Sully asked.

Lavender's teacup stopped in midair, halfway to her mouth. Sully repressed a smirk. It was unusual to catch Lavender by surprise with information of any kind, and they both knew it.

"Go on," Lavender said, recovering herself enough to take a sip of her tea.

"The High Elder's health is failing more quickly than the general population knows. They've pushed up the wedding in hopes that he will live to see it, but even that possibility is slipping away."

Lavender let out a low whistle. "And therein lies the opportunity."

Sully nodded solemnly. "The wedding itself, along with the political upheaval of installing a new High Elder might just be the chaos we can cloak ourselves in. It's hard to imagine another opportunity presenting itself like this."

Lavender stared off into the middle distance, her eyes unfocused but her voice sharp. "Yes. Yes, we'd be fools not to take advantage of such a moment."

It was Sully's turn to be brought up short. Could it truly be so easy? "We?"

Lavender did not refocus on Sully right away, swept up as she was in the tide of possibility that had just washed over her, but when she finally did, her face betrayed nothing. "I see now why you wanted me to come here. I think you'll be unsurprised to know that I can't definitively include myself in that general 'we' until I have a few more details about exactly *how* you're planning to take advantage of this moment."

Sully snorted. No, of course it wasn't going to be so easy, and she was a fool for thinking, even for a moment, that it might be. She stirred some sugar into her own tea, took a sip, and set it down.

"We've come into possession of some documents we mean to distribute among the Riftborn, but it's got to be on a massive scale, far greater than what we did with the charity baskets."

Lavender sighed wearily. "Sully, I know you cling to this notion that the pen is mightier than the sword, but I really think you need to start thinking beyond the radical distribution of reading material before you—"

"The documents prove the Illustratum is using Riftmead to poison and therefore subdue the Riftborn population," Sully said flatly.

It was with no small satisfaction that Sully watched as Lavender's mouth fell open with a distinct popping noise.

"How in the bloody hell did you— ah, of course. Bedlam. That was your people, was it? I had a feeling. And is that why you lit the place on fire, to cover your tracks?"

"We didn't light the place on fire— a disgruntled inmate took that upon herself, I understand. But yes, one of the objectives in entering the place was to retrieve what proof we could, now that the Illustratum is practically pouring the stuff down Riftborn throats."

"One of the objectives?" Lavender asked.

Sully cursed internally. "That's right. There was a prisoner there as well who needed to be... extricated."

"It all sounds a bit risky for your taste, Sully. You expect me to believe you signed off on that?"

Sully's face twisted like she'd bitten into a lemon. "It all worked out."

Lavender threw her head back and laughed, slopping tea into her saucer. "Of course. How that Jasper of yours isn't swinging from a noose already, I'll never know. That boy's got more lives than an alley cat."

"Actually, that particular adventure was Eli's idea," Sully admitted.

"Is that right, then?" Lavender remarked, smirking as she set down the saucer and mopped the tea from it with her napkin. "I must give that boy more credit. He's got a bit of Jasper's gumption after all, tempered with some common sense."

"Well, regardless of whose hide I had to tan as a result, we've got the documents now, and we want to get them into as many hands as possible, with a call to action. If you're fed up with the Elders poisoning you and consigning you to the gutters of this city, come to the gates of the Illustratum on the day of the wedding and join our cry for change."

"And you think people will come?"

"When they understand that the Elders are poisoning them? Their children? Yes, I do."

Lavender nodded. "All right. I'll allow you may get a crowd, perhaps even a large and angry one. What then? What happens when they all turn up?"

"We use them as a means of diversion at the gates to get ourselves onto the chamber floor with a petition to call a parley vote."

Lavender actually threw back her head and laughed. "A parley vote? You might as well call for divine intervention, a lightning bolt to the tower."

Sully grimaced "I realize that. But if we can actually get a quorum..."

"Sully, how long have we known each other? I know how much you value the written word, and what can be learned from it. I know you think your books are going to change the course of history —"

"Books have already changed more of the course of history than perhaps any other human invention," Sully replied, annoyed at the sulky edge to her voice.

"Except perhaps war," Lavender said dryly.

"And if you think those wars weren't spurred by the ideas circulating in books, you might need to read a few more of them," Sully snapped.

Lavender raised her hands in surrender. "Touché, my dear friend. Regardless, though, the idea that you are going to stage this coup with nothing but a pretty speech and a ream of paper is awfully naive."

"Naive? We are plotting a mass breakout from the Praeteritum to swell our ranks. We will be attacking not only with a mob at the front gates, but at ten strategic points around the Illustratum. We have procession plans. Guest lists. Seating charts."

In spite of her best efforts to appear unimpressed, Lavender's eyes widened at this scrap of information— a scrap that Sully had purposely held back in order to entice.

"Is that so? But how... of course. The lady's maid."

Sully nodded. "Eliza has turned out to be a most invaluable

resource. In fact, she has given us a window into the lives of manor servants that has been most enlightening. I think, even among the servants of the Elders themselves, there are many who would stand with us if given the chance."

Lavender gave a dry chuckle. "Well, I'm not sure about 'many,' but I admit the child has surprised me. So, she's been feeding you wedding preparation details, has she?"

"She has, indeed. I admit, we'd be in better shape if we had security plans from the Praesidio end of things, but even so, we have more information than we could have ever dreamed of collecting on our own. And we know we will have to face it with determination and with weapons. I have no illusions, Lavender. You think I don't know that there will be violence? That I will likely have to participate in it? You think I don't realize that the costs will be steep and that it may very well be more than we can pay? I might be a lowly academic and a woman of ideas, Lavender, but the chief benefit of being so is that I am *not* a fool."

Lavender gave her friend a long, hard stare, which Sully met, unflinching. At last, Lavender nodded her head once, slowly. "Very well. You are right, friend. You are not a fool and I would do well to remember that. And so... where do I fit into this grand plan, do you suppose?"

Sully felt her body tense. She knew exactly how much of their chances of success rested on Lavender's participation. "We are going to need to spread the word about the Riftmead. Without the Riftborn riled and present in huge numbers, we are lost."

"And how do you propose I could help with this?" Lavender asked, delicately stirring a lump of sugar into her tea.

"You have more connections in more places than any Riftborn in London, and more than half the Dignus, at that. If I needed mass distribution on the very eve of that wedding, where do you think I could find it?"

"You need help producing the leaflets?"

"I wouldn't turn it down. My printing press could handle it if we had the ability to man it continually between now and the wedding day, but I'd rather not waste the manpower we have with so tedious a task. What I really need is the bodies to manage the distribution around the Barrens and even out here into the wealthier Riftborn sectors. It must be coordinated. We can't risk that the Illustratum has gotten wind of the leaflets, or the entire plan collapses."

Lavender nodded, clearly deep in thought. Then, quite without warning, she set her cup and saucer upon the table with a clink and rose to her feet. "I know just the man. I'll... renew our correspondence and see if I can't persuade him."

Sully blinked. "So you'll... you'll help us?"

Lavender looked down at Sully, looking almost affronted. "That is why you asked me here, isn't it? For my help? Did you expect me to refuse it?"

"I... I guess I just expected you to... look out for yourself," Sully said.

The stern lines of Lavender's face seemed to soften for a moment. Her eyes, before she cast them to the floor, were glinting with unshed tears.

"I do not forget what you did for my husband, Sully."

"I know that. But I do not expect you to thank me by placing yourself in danger."

"I will call in this favor. I am fairly confident it will be carried out to my satisfaction. Beyond that, I am not sure. But this much I can do."

"Thank you," Sully said.

"Don't thank me yet," Lavender said. "We've set things in motion we won't be able to stop. We may all be very sorry indeed that I agreed to help in the end."

"Well," Sully said, rising to see her guest to the door, "We'll just have to wait and see, won't we?"

Lavender grinned. "Isn't the suspense just delicious?"

Dear Mr. Harlowe,

   I trust this correspondence finds you well. It has been a few years since we have seen each other, but I was delighted to see in the Weekly Word Bulletin that circulation of your publications are well up. I trust that you and your charming family are enjoying the fruits of your success.

   While I fancy I could write to you about the weather with thorough enjoyment, this missive is more than simply a fond greeting. I have a favor which I must ask of you, and I know you are not the sort of man who would begrudge his aid to a worthy subject, not when said subject had done him a great service in the past. (And on that topic, may I just take a moment to say that I appreciate the timeliness and exactness of your payments to me. I was only too delighted to arrange for the loan for you, Mr. Harlowe, especially given the fact that the debts had been run up as a result of your being a regular and loyal customer at my place of business. Your trustworthiness in meeting your obligations on that score is commendable, and no less than I would expect from a man of your status and importance.)

   If you are amenable to meeting with me to discuss this favor, please do respond with a time and place that would be most convenient for you. If not, please do not make yourself uneasy. I understand that you may find yourself hesitant to acquiesce to my request for assistance. If this is the case, simply respond your intention to decline it, and I promise I will harbor no ill feelings whatsoever.

   On an unrelated subject, I just stumbled across a box of letters that I held on to from the time of our most intimate acquaintance, as well as some documents that outline the nature of our financial arrangement. I had not realized I'd held on to them, and they brought back such fond memories. I wondered whether you had ever told your lovely wife any amusing stories of those days, and wanted to assure you that, even if we do not meet, I will find a way to deliver them to her. I simply cannot bear the thought of her missing out on such a fascinating correspondence, the contents of which must surely be of great interest both to Mrs. Harlowe and her father, without whose money, I understand, you could never have launched your great publishing enterprise.

I look forward with great pleasure to receiving your reply promptly, for I fear the matter to be of a time-sensitive nature. I remain,

Yours affectionately,

Lavender

Dear Lavender,

What a pleasure to open my mail this morning and see that a letter from your illustrious self was included amongst my incoming correspondence. As you know, I receive many letters from readers and spend a great deal of my time answering them. Yours is the first I have read today, and also the first I am taking the time to answer.

I would be delighted to meet with you at your earliest possible convenience. I promise you that, whatever the favor, I will be only too happy to grant it in whatever way I am able. I likewise think back on the earliest days of our acquaintance with much fondness and promise you I have told my wife all that she could ever wish to know on that subject. I assure you that your offer to share your treasure trove of correspondence with her, while very kind, is entirely unnecessary.

If the date and time are convenient for you, please meet me two days hence at 11 o'clock in the morning, in the private room on the second floor of Mrs. King's Tea Room. There I am sure we can come to an arrangement that will be to everyone's satisfaction.

Cordially Yours,

Thomas Harlowe

17

I T WAS TOO BLOODY EARLY. Penny tugged her shawl around her shoulders and blew into her numb hands. The sun had not yet been up for long enough to take the nighttime chill out of the air, and she could still see her breath hovering in the air around her as she walked. Everything about this time of day felt strange and unfamiliar. She couldn't remember the last time she'd dragged herself out of bed in time to watch the sun break, rosy and new, over London's smog-threaded rooftops, but it had been years. She supposed she ought to be thanking Lavender for her new rule about drinking, or she'd no doubt have a blinding headache to accompany her morning grogginess.

Penny didn't dare venture out any later. Her plan, cobbled together between customers the previous evening, was fairly simple: sneak out before any of the other girls were up, find Daniel at his post along the North wall, convince him to join the Resistance, and get back to Lavender's before anyone realized she had left her room. And even with all her careful planning she was nearly spotted by Lavender herself, who left just as early in a carriage, dressed to the nines and also headed in the direction of the Commons. The close call had nearly sent her scurrying back to bed, but she was up now, and she wasn't going to waste all that effort. She'd just have to be extra careful sneaking back in and pray that, whatever Lavender's business was, it took longer than her own.

Although she had to admit as she was hurrying along, she wished she'd spent just a bit longer deciding how she was going to convince Daniel. For all her scheming, she'd had no real strategy in place for that particular part of the plan. Well, she told herself as she arrived at the outer edge of the Barrens that bordered the market district of the Commons, she had always been good on her feet. She'd just have to improvise.

Improvising. In the Commons. Surrounded by Praesidio guards. What a lark.

A bit of flirting and more than a bit of mead had loosened the tongue of another Praesidio guard the previous evening, which meant that Penny now knew precisely what time the morning shift change occurred. All she needed to do was get there before Daniel had to start his patrol and pull him aside for a private word, hopefully without attracting the attention of any of the other guards. She wasn't made up as she normally was, and without her gaudy frocks and painted face, she hoped no one would recognize her. She barely recognized herself, she thought dryly, catching her rippling reflection in a cobbler's window. She dropped her eyes at once, laughing at herself. Here she was, stripped bare of her usual costume, hoping to blend in, and instead, she felt vulnerable and naked. A costume meant she was performing, after all—playing a part. Now she had no choice but to play herself, and she had far less confidence in that performance.

The market district was just waking up. A handful of shop owners were unlocking doors and dragging out carts and stalls, eyes swollen and sleepy. A stray dog trotted out from the alleyway, nosing hopefully at Penny's pockets. She shooed him away toward the greengrocer to try his luck. In another hour or two, the street would be crowded with shoe shiners and paper sellers, truant children and harried shoppers consulting their lists of purchases. Penny could see them clearly in her mind's eye, like ghosts.

At last, she arrived at the narrow alleyway that cut down to the north wall of the Praeteritum. As she approached its mouth, a vagrant emerged, mumbling incoherently and rattling a can in which a single coin echoed with a dismal clunk. Penny sidestepped the woman and continued on her way, reaching her hand into her pocket to ensure the pearl necklace was still there. She planned to pawn it on her way home. If any of the girls spotted her sneaking back in, she would have a few coins jingling in her purse to back up her cover story as to where she had been.

The wall loomed up at the end of the alley, a solid, hopeless stretch of stone topped with barbed metal stakes. The borders of the Praeteritum were marked with walls on the North and South boundaries, and with metal fences along the East and West boundaries. Penny was relieved to be facing the wall, and not one of the border fences, through which the tableau of human misery was clearly visible. Once, she had wondered why they didn't just put walls up all around the Praeteritum. Surely walls would make security easier. But in the years since, she'd seen enough from beyond the bars to understand: the fences served as a warning. By displaying the misery within, the Illustratum hoped to deter others from committing the kinds of infractions that could land them on the other side of the bars. The stench alone would have been sufficient, Penny thought with a shudder.

Penny hovered in the mouth of the alley, watching for the patrol to come by. She checked the battered old brass pocket watch she kept clipped to her waist; Daniel should be arriving any moment. His shift began in less than five minutes. She began to count the seconds in her head to distract her from her own nerves. Then before a minute had passed, she spotted him, head bent against the morning chill. She stepped out of the alleyway as he approached to catch his attention, but he seemed lost in his own thoughts, and she had to clear her throat loudly to get him to look up.

Daniel stared blankly at her for a moment, and then recognition dawned in his eyes and his face broke into a genuine smile.

"Penny! What are you doing here? I almost didn't recognize you with…" his voice trailed off in embarrassment and he pulled his gaze from her simple, modestly cut dress.

Penny smirked. "Yes, I tend to put the girls away in the daylight," she said dryly. "They're nocturnal, see."

Daniel smothered a laugh under his hand, then gave an anxious glance up and down the road. Taking his cue, Penny stepped back into the alleyway shadows and he followed her. She supposed he wouldn't want to be seen with her in public.

"What are you doing here?" he asked again when they were well concealed. "I don't suppose…" His eyebrows shot up, his expression suddenly hopeful. Penny hated to dash out that hope, but she couldn't tell him what he wanted to hear, so there was no avoiding it.

"No, I haven't found your sister," Penny said, pushing through the words to get it over with more quickly. "But I have another sort of… proposition for you, and I think it might help you with your search."

Daniel's disappointment lifted at once into eager interest. "Go on, then," he said.

"Well, the truth is, the Illustratum doesn't want girls like your sister found. They want to keep the truth about them buried, and they've gone to great lengths to do it," Penny said. Her heart had begun to pound like mad. Once she said the words, she couldn't take them back. What if she was wrong? What if Daniel wasn't the kind of man she thought he was?

"Yes, I know. Why do you think I've taken to wandering brothels at night with a fifteen-year-old photograph?" Daniel said with a humorless chuckle. "There would be much faster ways of finding her if I weren't so worried about rocking the boat."

"What if I told you there were others already rocking that boat? What if I told you they need help? What would you say then?" Penny asked, her voice tentative.

"I'd say keep talking," Daniel said, looking intrigued.

Penny took a deep breath. "Look, the fact is, I spoke to Lavender and she's not convinced she can trust you, but there are others who might. You aren't the only person who wants to know what happened to Riftborn children born to Dignus families. There are others, others who put their lives on the line to rescue those children before anything terrible could happen to them. They found safe houses for them, and even smuggled some of them out of the country, all to protect them from their own families."

"You're speaking of the Lamplighters Confederacy," Daniel whispered, sounding breathless. "I've heard of it, of course, but the official documents are very sparse. I've found little in the Illustratum archives other than the arrest records of the alleged perpetrators, and no information at all on what became of the children. I thought perhaps it was a cover for the Dignus, blaming the disappearances on Riftborn upstarts they wanted out of the way. Are you telling me it was real?"

"Yes, it was real. And many of the Riftborn involved are still doing what they can to bring the truth to light."

"How do you know this?"

Penny shrugged, hoping she looked more collected than she felt. "I work at Lavender's. I know a lot of things."

"What has all this got to do with me?" Daniel asked.

"If these people—this resistance, let's call them—are successful, everyone will know the truth about what the Illustratum has done to the Riftborn. And it goes deeper than missing children, Daniel. Much, much deeper." There was no playful edge to her voice, no sardonic note. They had reached the heart of the matter, and there was no room for joking here.

"Yes, I thought it might," Daniel murmured.

"You were right," Penny said. "With the right help, there's no telling what or who they might be able to find."

Daniel hesitated, letting the significance of the words wash over him. "And when you say, 'the right help,' you mean me?"

Penny nodded. "They need people on the inside, people with access to places and information they cannot get for themselves."

"And you think, if I help them, that I could find my sister?" Daniel asked. His hand fluttered almost unconsciously to his breast pocket, where Penny knew he must keep his sister's photograph. She felt a stab of guilt.

"Look, I'm not trying to sell you on a fairy tale here, Daniel," she said, being careful to catch and hold his gaze. She had to be clear with him. "Happily ever afters are few and far between where I come from. I don't know if your sister is alive or where she is, and there's a good chance we'll never find out. But if the Resistance never succeeds, if you just keep coming to this wall day after day, doing the Illustratum's bidding, you've got no chance at all of finding out what's become of that child, and that's the truth."

Daniel swallowed hard, his Adam's apple bobbing at his high collar.

"I ain't gonna try to persuade you any further than that," Penny said. "This has to be your choice, and yours alone. I ain't doing the others any favors by dragging you somewhere you don't want to walk to on your own two feet. Just... think on it, all right? Have a good long think and, when you're sure, come find me. You know where I'll be, sure enough."

Daniel stared at Penny for a long time, so long that Penny felt a flush beginning to creep up her neck. The sensation caused mild surprise—she'd thought herself quite impervious to blushing these days. When he finally spoke, it was in a whisper.

"You took a great risk, coming here today, telling me this," he said. "I'm a Praesidio guard. What are the odds I'd simply turn around and report you to my superior?"

Penny managed a small smile. "In my neighborhood, you have to learn to trust your instincts. I meet a dozen men every night I wouldn't trust with my last name, let alone tell them what I've told you."

"So why did you tell me?"

Because I've never seen a man look at a photograph the way you look at that one, and it was the purest damn thing I've ever witnessed, Penny thought. Out loud she said, "Just call it a hunch, soldier."

"Oi, you there! Byrne! Get a shift on, you're late!"

The voice rang out, loud and belligerent, from a knot of soldiers positioned a hundred feet or so down the North wall.

"Aw, look, he's gone and found himself a ditch rat lover," another voice added, and the men broke into a chorus of obnoxious guffaws.

Daniel gave Penny a shadow of a wink before raising his voice and saying, "Look, I'm sorry, but I can't help you. If you want to arrange for visitation, you have to submit a request at the Praesidio office like everyone else. Now bugger off, before I have you arrested for loitering."

Penny took her cue, dipping into a curtsy and turning to go. She'd only just taken a step when she felt a hand on her shoulder.

"So, what is your last name, then?" he whispered.

She crossed her arms, trying to look offended. "I can't just go tellin' you top secret information like that. What kind of girl do you take me for?"

And she slipped away up the alleyway, whistling to herself and thinking that, after she pawned the necklace, she might just treat herself to a scone from the bakery cart in the High Street.

18

"**I**'M NOT GOING."

"You have to go."

Jessamine and Eliza stood in front of Jessamine's full-length mirror, Eliza clipping the last of the pearls into Jessamine's hair, where they shone like stars winking into existence in a deep night sky.

"No one will notice my absence, surely," Jessamine said.

"At your own engagement party, thrown by your dearest friend? Oh, yes, I'm sure your presence will hardly be noted," Eliza said with a laugh.

"Kitty will understand."

"Miss Price will be devastated and you well know it," Eliza said with one last pat to an errant curl. She took Jessamine by the shoulders and turned her around so that she had no choice but to look her in the eye. It was bold of her, but the old days of servant and mistress were long behind them. They were compatriots now, fighting on the same side.

"Come now Miss Jessamine," Eliza intoned. "Remember what we agreed to."

Jessamine heaved the heaviest of sighs. "I will play along with all of the preparations with a smile on my face."

"And why?"

"Because not doing so will raise suspicions," Jessamine answered dully.

"Precisely. We all need to play our parts."

"Will you never tell me what you're planning? I promise you can trust me, Eliza," Jessamine whispered, snatching up Eliza's hand as she made to put down the hairpins.

"I do trust you. But I also mean to keep you safe, which means telling you as little as possible, and not until everything is in place," Eliza replied, prying her hand away. Jessamine had made a new habit of trying to wheedle details out of Eliza about the Resistance's plans for the disruption of the wedding, but so far Eliza had not budged an inch.

It was not an easy promise to keep, because so much progress had been made over the last week, and Eliza was now bursting with things she couldn't divulge to anyone. Eli, Jasper, and Zeke were quietly recruiting people from their circles to help lead the effort. Madam Lavender had worked her special influence over a local newspaper publisher, and he was organizing the distribution of the pamphlets about Riftmead. Meanwhile, Cora had gleaned much from the papers Eli and Jasper had stolen from Bedlam, and was working on an antidote to Riftmead. The plan, if she succeeded in creating one, was to use it at the source, infiltrating the Riftmead bottling factories and rendering their supply harmless. Even Bridie was playing a part, attending meetings and carrying messages between Resistance members, as well as helping Cora. Everyone was working as quickly as they could, but the days left until the wedding felt like they were slipping past much too quickly.

Eliza continued to feed Sully whatever information she could find about the wedding arrangements, but said arrangements had left her much busier than usual and she was finding it harder and harder to slip away. She had only been able to see her mother once since that first visit. Emmeline was still quite heavily sedated, but she had mumbled a few replies and squeezed Eliza's hand when it was time for her to leave. Eliza hoped that, when Cora at last hit on the right formula for an antidote, she might see some real improvement in her mother's condition. This hope sustained her through the worry and the exhaustion, and she clung to it as tightly as she could.

There was only one aspect of their plan upon which they had made little headway, and that was their hope to infiltrate the Praeteritum. Jasper had exhausted his contacts of former inmates and turned up empty-handed; not one of them wanted to risk another stint on the inside of those walls by helping him. Sully's next tactic was to see if Lavender had any Praesidio customers that could be coerced with a bit of blackmail or bribery, but thus far Lavender's girls had come up empty-handed. Sully was getting more and more anxious by the day, wondering if they would have the numbers they needed to overwhelm the guard and get through the Illustratum doors, and time was running out.

"Are you sure you don't want me to come with you, miss?" Eliza asked.

"No, no. I am perfectly capable of handling this on my own," Jessamine said, though with less conviction in her voice than Eliza would have liked to hear.

"I really don't mind, you know," Eliza pressed. And it was true. Better busy at a social gathering than stuck at home, pacing and wishing she could be with the other Resistance members. She couldn't even find refuge in her own bedroom anymore, not since Sarah had come to replace Bridie.

"No, I can't ask you to do that," Jessamine said, closing the door on that opportunity for distraction. "It will be tedious, but nothing worse than that. I assure you, I will be just fine."

"Very well, then, miss, if you say so. The carriage is waiting, so let's get you downstairs," Eliza said.

They were crossing the entrance hall when raised voices caused them both to stop in their tracks. They traded a wide-eyed glance, and then wordlessly agreed to stop and listen, edging closer to the door from which the shouting had emanated. It was Elder Hallewell's study.

"...and I suppose he promised them all manner of favors he's in no bloody position to grant," came Elder Hallewell's voice, fairly trembling with rage and indignation.

"I cannot say, sir, but I can't imagine Elders like Smythe throwing their weight behind him for anything less," answered a second voice, trembling as well, but with fear.

"Brother Goodwin," Jessamine mouthed, answering Eliza's unspoken question.

"And what does Francis advise?" Hallewell went on. "I suppose I'm just meant to sit back and let them all conspire right under my nose, is that right?"

"Well, sir, he... he did say we ought to reach out, diplomatically speaking, and see what counter-offers we can—"

"These men don't want counter-offers, they want blood!" Elder

Hallewell shouted. "They can smell it in the water, like predators, and they can't wait to pounce on it. Oh, wouldn't they just love to watch me shunted to the side after all these years of steady climbing?"

"Nevertheless, sir, Elder Potter provided me with this list of who he thinks you should meet with first. I can contact them and set up—"

"No."

"I'm… I'm sorry, sir?" Brother Goodwin stammered.

"I said no. I am done handling this Francis' way."

"Then wh-what should I tell him, sir?"

"Tell him I will take care of it."

"T-take care of it? But how—"

"That is none of your concern. Thank him for the list and tell him I shall manage it. That is all, Goodwin."

"Very well, sir. Good night."

"One last thing, Goodwin. Ring for Braxton and have him send for a carriage."

"Send for? Don't you mean—"

"No, I certainly do not. I do not want one of my own carriages. My daughter is already going out for the evening and will require the best of the horses. Send for a carriage for hire."

"I arrived in a carriage for hire. I shall be more than glad to see you to your destination, sir."

"No!" The word was sharp. "But you can send it back for me once you have returned to the Illustratum."

"Very good, sir."

The sound of footsteps on the other side of the door sent Eliza and Jessamine scurrying back to the foot of the stairs so that when the study door opened, they appeared to just be descending to the entrance hall. Goodwin started when he saw them, but did not appear suspicious as he folded himself into a bow.

"Miss Jessamine. Looking as lovely as ever you have," he simpered.

"Thank you, Brother Goodwin," Jessamine said with an ingratiating smile. "Have you been to see my father?"

"Yes, indeed, miss, but I am just taking my leave. Please permit me to escort you out to your carriage."

Jessamine smiled again, a smile that shifted into a significant look as she turned to Eliza. "I shan't be terribly late, Eliza. Please wait up for me. I shall require your assistance upon my return."

160

"Of course, miss," Eliza said, bobbing a curtsy.

"Jessamine."

Eliza, Jessamine, and Goodwin all jumped. Not one of them had heard the door open. Elder Hallewell stood on the threshold, his hand upon the doorknob. He looked at his daughter, his expression impassive, but with a strange burning in his eyes.

"Father?" Jessamine took an uncertain step toward him, but he was already stepping back into his study.

"Have a lovely time," he said, and the door closed between them once more.

§

Essex Park was a neat and unpretentious little estate, as estates go. Elder Price's family had always erred on the side of humbleness when it came to demonstrations of their wealth. There was always a vicious buzz of gossip circulating that Elder Price's grandfather had had a penchant for gambling, and so the sparseness of the estate was merely a matter of necessity as the family fortunes ran dry. But the truth was that there were some Elders who considered their homes a reflection of their faith, and for the Price family, that meant decorum and an almost puritanical abhorrence of extravagance. Jessamine often felt for her best friend Kitty, the eldest of the Price children and the least shiny bell at nearly every ball. She was fortunate she had an abundance of natural beauty and a sparkling personality to make up for the shortcomings in her dress allowance; her two younger sisters, bless them, favored their dour-faced mother and therefore had little hope of shining their way through the gloom in such a manner. In fact, Jessamine had often mused that all the ribbons, lace, and jewels in the world would hardly have made a difference.

It was one of these dreary young siblings who was the first to greet Jessamine as she arrived. The child looked unutterably bored, which Jessamine considered a sin when there was a dance to be had. If the girl was this indifferent already to the lush, music-filled nights of society life, she would be insufferable by the time she was being Presented. Jessamine smiled at the girl, whose mouth struggled to mimic the expression as she dipped into an off-balance curtsy and slumped away to tell Kitty that Jessamine had arrived. A few moments later, Kitty appeared, all peaches and cream in a gown of mauve satin that, despite its simple design, brought out the natural glow of her complexion.

"Good heavens, you'd think I'd assigned her a place on the rack rather than at the front door," Kitty said, rolling her eyes before breaking into a dimpled grin. "Jessamine, you look divine! Your Eliza is so clever with your hair, I've half a mind to steal her away from you!"

Jessamine laughed, patting unnecessarily at the curls cascading down the back of her neck. "She has got quite the knack for it," she admitted. "But you keep your greedy little paws off her, Kitty. She's coming to the palace with me."

Kitty heaved a great fake sigh. "Some girls have all the luck."

The girls caught each other's eye but neither of them laughed. Kitty might look like a porcelain doll, but she was shrewd.

"But where is Reginald?" Kitty asked, looking out into the entryway.

"He's meeting me here. He insisted on coming from the palace, but I wanted Eliza to dress me, and I didn't feel right dragging her across the city on a whim," Jessamine replied.

"I'm sure she wouldn't have minded, Jessamine. After all, she'll be dressing you there every day before long."

Jessamine tried to smile and found, to her great relief, that she could manage one. If Kitty noticed anything off about it, she didn't mention it.

"Come along. Mother wasn't going to let me plan the menu, but when we had to move up the date, she was already committed to her ministry group banquet, and so I got to manage everything!"

Jessamine flushed. "Yes, Kitty, I'm so sorry about that. I didn't mean to inconvenience you."

"Oh, fiddlesticks," Kitty scoffed. "I don't know when I've ever been so pleased. You know mother never lets me organize anything on my own. Even when she insists I can, she always swoops in at the last minute and gets her hands into every last detail until I simply give up and hand it all over to her."

"Which I daresay was her aim in the first place," Jessamine laughed.

"Too right it was! But anyway, this time she had no choice, so whatever the reason for moving up the wedding, I was delighted." She dropped her voice. "What *was* the reason for moving up the wedding? I'm ever so curious."

Jessamine sighed. "Yes, I daresay everyone will be. It wasn't my decision."

"I should think not!" Kitty murmured. "You must be terribly rushed now with all your preparations! You know I'd be happy to lend a hand if you're in need of help." She gave Jessamine a terribly pitying look that Jessamine had no trouble understanding. For all Kitty's complaints about her mother's interference, she knew Jessamine would give anything to be squabbling with her own mother over fabric swatches and appetizers.

"I assure you, we have everything well in hand," Jessamine answered and, eager to steer the conversation in another direction, added, "I can't wait to see what you've planned for tonight!"

It worked. Kitty took her arm and began gushing. "I can't wait for you to see the petit fours! They are so very darling, and I've never seen the likes of our cook for making sugar flowers!" She pulled Jessamine through the entrance hall and along into the front parlor where the guests were beginning to gather.

As soon as Jessamine entered the door, announced loudly by the footman, the other girls were upon her like honeybees on a particularly toothsome summer rose. They hovered, they twittered, they whispered and giggled. They each simply *had* to see the ring again, simply *must* know all the details of the wedding planning, about her dressmaker, about her flowers, about the reception; no detail was too insignificant to be beneath their flutter of enthusiastic interest. Jessamine was quite light-headed after just a few minutes of interrogation and realized this evening, which she had assumed would be simply tiresome, was destined to become positively insufferable. At least Sadie Carpenter had not arrived yet. Jessamine would take whatever respite from the girl that she could get, for she was sure to be fending off her barbed compliments for the rest of the night.

Before the second round of questioning could begin, however, Reginald arrived, and the men there gathered became so boisterous in their congratulations to their friend that Jessamine was able to slip away from the other ladies in the commotion, only to be grasped unceremoniously by the arm and steered to her fiancé's side.

Out of the frying pan, into the fire, she lamented silently to herself.

"There you are, my darling," Reginald said, tucking her in against him in a proprietary manner that made it challenging to keep the smile on her face. "I was afraid you'd have all the fun and drink all the champagne before I could slip away."

"Oh, nonsense," Jessamine said, her voice low enough that the others would not catch it. "We know better than to leave you without a drink in your hand." The comment was mild enough that Reginald could choose to ignore it, and he did. Jessamine knew she ought not to provoke him, but she found she could hardly muster the will to care. She could already smell the whiskey on his breath; it seemed the wrapping up of his business dealings could not delay his getting started on the celebration. She ached with dread wondering how she would manage it if he should grow too intoxicated, and then with a stronger pang, realized that much of her time as his wife would be occupied with such worries.

If I become his wife, she thought to herself, remembering Eliza and her nebulous plans that might just mean her escape from such a future.

"Has everyone arrived?" Reginald asked, glancing around at the assembled company. He seemed to be looking for someone.

"Very nearly so, I imagine," Jessamine replied.

"Oh I think there may still be a guest or two on the way," Reginald said, a dangerous smirk playing at the corners of his lips.

At that moment Kitty invited them all through to the ballroom, where there was more room for mingling about and dancing. Jessamine snatched a glass of champagne from a passing tray and drank it much more quickly than propriety allowed. Then she took advantage of Reginald's distraction to detach herself from him and disappear back into the nearest cluster of frocks. She was relieved to see Adelaide Shaw among the group and pounced on the opportunity at once to draw focus onto someone else's upcoming nuptials.

"Adelaide, you must tell me how your own wedding preparations are coming along," Jessamine said, smiling broadly.

But while Adelaide returned the smile, it faded quickly. "No, indeed. I will not be accused of stealing your spotlight, Jessamine Hallewell."

"Nonsense! I insist. It is I who should be apologizing for stealing your spotlight. After all, you were engaged before I was," Jessamine said, reaching out and squeezing the girl's hand.

"Yes, but your wedding is coming before mine. We'll have plenty of time to talk about my wedding after you've been settled at the palace," Adelaide said, and it was a testament to the sweetness of her temper that there was only the mildest edge of bitterness in her voice.

"Why has the wedding been moved up, Jessamine?" Bette Smythe asked, narrowing her eyes shrewdly. "It must be very inconvenient, given all of the planning that you must still have to do."

Jessamine looked around at the eagerly staring eyes surrounding her and was glad she had prepared an answer to this question. "It was my father's request," she said, dropping her eyes to the floor. "In a rare show of sentimentality, he asked if we might not get married on the same day as he and my mother were wed. I could hardly say no."

The effect on the circle was instantaneous and predictable. Cheeks flushed crimson, eyelashes fluttered, and voices dropped to solicitous murmurs. Jessamine breathed a sigh of relief. She had been afraid rumors may have begun to spread to the ladies' circles about the High Elder's failing health, and the thought of everyone knowing that her wedding was nothing more than a masterstroke on the chessboard of her father's political strategy was almost more than she could bear. Happily though, it seemed the Elders had closed ranks around their leader, at least for the time being. Jessamine highly doubted that she would be able to conceal the truth for much longer, but at least on this night, she would escape with her dignity intact.

That was, until the footman arrived at the door of the ballroom to announce that more guests had arrived.

"Mr. Theodore Potter and Miss Sadie Carpenter."

Jessamine's blood turned to ice water in her veins. It could not be—she had provided Kitty a list of guests, and Teddy Potter's name had not been on it. She looked up and caught her friend's eye. Whatever expression had settled on her features caused Kitty's complexion to blanch, but she had no choice but to float off across the room and play the hostess. Jessamine turned her back firmly on the new arrivals and tried to rejoin the conversation, but her friends, chittering cheerfully like a flock of birds mere moments before, were now as silent and still as statues, each one of them staring at her as though she might burst into flames at any moment. Jessamine dropped her gaze and focused on suppressing the overwhelming urge to run out of the room until she felt a hand on her elbow and Kitty was steering her away from the others and into a private corner by the windows.

"Jessamine, whatever is the matter? The look on your face!"

"What is he doing here, Kitty?"

Kitty's face crumpled with confusion. "Whatever do you mean? He was on the list. To be sure, I was surprised when you added him, but—"

"When I added him? I never added him! He was the last person I would have wanted here tonight!"

"Well, yes, that's what I'd thought, but then when his name was on the updated list from the palace, I assumed you'd simply decided to keep up appearances. Stiff upper lip and all that," Kitty said.

"From the palace?" Jessamine repeated, her voice a mere whisper.

"Yes, but your name was included on the..." Kitty gasped, a white-gloved hand flying upward to clamp over her mouth. "Do you mean to say you didn't know?"

"Of course I didn't kn—" but Jessamine's eye had caught sight of another face just over Kitty's shoulder, a face that was smirking at her with such unadulterated glee that she suddenly understood everything. She snapped her mouth shut again.

"Jessamine?" Kitty ventured, and Jessamine turned back to her friend to find her looking tearful. Conscious of many pairs of eyes now on her, Jessamine tried her best to pull herself together.

"Never mind, Kitty. Please don't concern yourself. It was just a miscommunication. I am perfectly at ease. Now, where are these petit fours you keep going on about?"

Kitty looked like she wanted to argue, but decided against it. She took Jessamine's arm and steered her across the room to the beautiful display she had arranged for the guests before dinner. Jessamine did her best to look delighted at everything, and thanked her friend profusely, but even as she smiled and simpered, her attention was divided. She listened to her friend gush, but also she was listening to snatches of Teddy's voice as it wove through the fabric of the conversation. She knew she would have no choice but to greet him and graciously receive his congratulations. It was impossible that she might be able to avoid speaking to him. Sure enough, a few minutes later, she heard Reginald's voice boom out, too loud.

"Thank you, thank you. And no hard feelings I hope, old boy. All's fair in love and war, after all, and war is not at all to my taste."

Jessamine chanced a glance and saw that Teddy and Reginald were shaking hands. Teddy's face was smiling, although tightly. Sadie

Carpenter was still on his arm, and her expression could not have been more smug.

"We look forward to celebrating with you what will surely be the wedding of the season," Teddy said diplomatically, and Jessamine had to look away again. The sight of them shaking hands put a terrible tight knot in her stomach, twisting her insides. She silently berated herself. What had she wanted him to do, make a scene? Start a fight? He was behaving exactly as he ought to, and yet it made her want to scream.

Kitty had cottoned on to Jessamine's state and was watching Teddy and Sadie move about the room while describing the party arrangements in an increasingly hysterical tone until, with a significant look to Jessamine, it was quite clear that the latter had run out of time.

"Ah, Teddy! Sadie! So pleased you could make it!" Kitty said with a manic giggle, and Jessamine had no choice but to turn around. Teddy and Sadie did indeed stand before them. At least Teddy had the good grace to look embarrassed.

"Why, Kitty Price, we wouldn't have missed it for the world!" Sadie answered. All of the girls dipped into identical curtsies while Teddy bowed deeply. Sadie looked pointedly at Teddy, who cleared his throat.

"Yes, indeed. Delighted to be invited, and to share in the happiness of the couple," he said, looking Jessamine in the face for the first time. Though his expression was carefully blank, his eyes were burning with unsaid things.

"I thank you both for coming, on behalf of Reginald and myself," Jessamine heard herself reply. She'd meant to smile as well, but it didn't feel like her face was bothering to cooperate.

"Well, the big day certainly is approaching quickly!" Sadie said. "I hope you aren't too overwhelmed with your preparations, Jessamine! I'm sure I would hardly know which way was up, with so many details to finalize in so short a time. However are you managing?"

"As best I can, Sadie," Jessamine said.

"I must say, we were all surprised when the date of the wedding was announced! I suppose you just couldn't wait, could you?"

"I... suppose not," Jessamine replied.

"I should say not! And why should you? What good is a long engagement when one knows precisely what one wants? When you love someone, it's natural to rush things along, isn't it? The sooner you marry, the sooner the happily-ever-after can begin, right?" Sadie said, turning and gazing up through her eyelashes at Teddy. Jessamine's stomach heaved.

"Please, excuse me," she managed to whisper, before crossing the room to the nearest door and escaping into the hallway, where she wanted to claw the corset from her body so she could breathe.

She had overestimated herself. She could not do this. She could not pretend, for the sake of appearances or propriety or whatever hellish social rule demanded her submission. She wanted to scream. She wanted to—

"Jessamine?"

She gasped and spun away from the wall at the sound of his familiar voice so near to her. Teddy was watching her warily, like she was an animal he wasn't sure was tame. This only angered her further.

"Teddy! I'm sorry, you... you startled me." She cursed herself for apologizing, but the words had slipped from her mouth automatically, a reflex she could not suppress.

"I didn't mean to..." he looked angry with himself, running a hand over his face. "I didn't want to miss this opportunity to speak with you."

Jessamine glanced back at the room they'd just left. "You really mustn't keep Sadie waiting."

"Hang Sadie!" Teddy growled. "It's you I want to speak to."

Jessamine sighed. "Teddy, there's nothing to say."

"There's everything to say!" Teddy cried out before dropping his voice again with a nervous look over his shoulder. "I wrote to you. Over and over and over again. You never replied to me. Not a word."

"And I've just told you, there is nothing to say," Jessamine said wearily.

"How can you say that after everything we've... did you even read my letters?"

"I did not."

"Then how can you—"

"Because none of it matters anymore!" Jessamine cried. "Whatever it is you think you need to say, don't you see that the moment for it is passed? I don't want to hear that you love me, if you even still do. I don't want to hear excuses or explanations or apologies. It's all too late! If you wanted to say any of those things, you could have said them to me before the Presentation, instead of leaving me to be publicly humiliated!"

Teddy flushed. "You know why I couldn't do that."

"Oh yes, I certainly do. Because you're a coward. A coward who wouldn't fight for me."

"That's not fair!"

"Oh, isn't it? Do set me right then, Mr. Potter, for I admit my memory of the night is somewhat of a blur."

"I couldn't make a scene in front of all those people, Jessamine," Teddy said, looking flabbergasted at the very idea. "It would have ruined your Presentation!"

"So you decided to ruin my life instead?"

"I haven't ruined your... you're going to live at the palace! You'll have everything in the world you could ever want, your father promised me that!" Teddy insisted.

"Oh, yes, my father loves making promises on my behalf," Jessamine said. "And I suppose you thought you could assuage your guilt like that, imagining me swanning about the palace, jewels and finery dripping off me. Never mind that my heart was shattered into a thousand pieces. Never mind that I loved you... that I trusted you. Never mind that we made plans together, plans to live our lives with one another."

"We never should have made those plans," Teddy said stiffly. "They weren't ours to make."

"They ought to have been," Jessamine said quietly. "They could have been if you had had a scrap of fight in you."

Teddy lifted his chin defiantly. "And what about you? You're doing just as daddy says, wearing that ring on your finger, smiling and making wedding preparations. How are you any different from me?"

Jessamine laughed. "How dare you suggest I have the same power to refuse them that you do. What woman does? And yet, I daresay I put up more of a fight than you did, enough so that my father panicked and forced my maid to subdue me."

Teddy looked taken aback. "*Subdue* you?"

"Yes, that's right. I'm told I danced with Reginald when I returned to the party, but I cannot recall it. I was reduced to a puppet, with Riftmagic tugging at strings to keep me upright. And what were you doing, pray tell? I suppose it was as good a time as any to decide which girl you would replace me with."

"That's not fair!"

"I suppose it's not. But I don't care, Teddy. I count fairness among the many things I do not believe in anymore."

Teddy's expression softened. "Jessamine, please…"

"Please what? Please assuage your guilt? Please lie to you, tell you that I'm fine, that I'll get over it? That I'll be happy?"

"You… you will be," Teddy replied, in so uncertain of a voice that Jessamine laughed out loud.

"You know Reginald Morgan. I daresay you know even more about him than I do. I've seen the way men laugh together in drawing rooms. You know what he is. How could you, Teddy Potter? How could you give me up to such a scoundrel?"

Teddy opened his mouth, and Jessamine watched him with satisfaction as he choked on the words. Because what could he say? What excuses could he possibly make?

"I was in love with you, Teddy Potter. Creator help me, there's probably a small foolish part of me that still is. But please, never speak to me again."

The reality of the situation finally seemed to sink in; there was no fixing this, and he was a fool to keep trying. Teddy snapped his mouth closed again, slumped his shoulders, and walked back into the ballroom, snatching a glass of champagne off a tray as he passed.

For one exhilarating moment, Jessamine felt like she was soaring. She had held nothing back, said everything she always wondered whether she'd have the chance or the courage to say. She was proud of herself. That pride was a fleeting thing, however, and it drained away from her within seconds, leaving her cold and exhausted.

She couldn't stay here another moment. Hang propriety, she had to get out of here, and she didn't give a damn how they talked about her after she was gone.

She glanced down the hallway, but it ended in a closed door. She jogged along it, trying doorknobs as she passed, but as she expected, the private rooms had all been locked for the duration of the party, and the only rooms that were not locked—a small library and a sitting room—had no other doors she could escape through. She had no choice but to walk back through the ballroom.

Thanking her lucky stars she hadn't walked back into the ballroom with Teddy—a sight that surely would have been much remarked upon—she squared her shoulders and walked back down the hallway and into the ballroom. A waltz was in full swing. Before she could even make sense of the couples whirling past her in a blur, Reginald had grabbed her by the hand and whisked her into the throng.

"Reginald, I am hardly in the mood to dance," Jessamine groaned.

"As the party is in our honor, we can hardly avoid it," Reginald said. "I thought it best to get it over with early, before they start serving the wine. Wouldn't you agree?"

Jessamine did not reply. She was too busy trying to gain her balance and find the beat of the music. By the time she felt confident she wasn't about to fall, Teddy and Sadie had joined the dancing as well. Jessamine turned her face away as they passed, a gesture that did not go unmissed by her partner.

"I say, everything all right between you and young Theodore?" Reginald said, an entirely unconvincing note of innocence in his voice.

"You did this, didn't you?" Jessamine hissed back. The venom in her voice would have cowered a man with any sense of shame, but Reginald had none.

"Did what?" he asked, drawing his hand away from her waist and using a single finger to trace an invisible halo in the air above his head.

"Don't you dare mock me!"

"I'm not mocking you. I just have no interest in playing guessing games. If you'd like to accuse me of something, just come out with it. I assure you I am a big boy who owns my decisions, however poorly made."

"You invited Teddy Potter here tonight out of spite."

Reginald raised his eyebrows in mock surprise. "Hmmm, an intriguing theory, but only partially correct. I invited him here, yes, but out of common courtesy. We can't be leaving families of Elders off the guest list, my darling, it sends the wrong message."

"You knew how painful it would be for me, to see him here," Jessamine whispered.

Reginald spun her enthusiastically and she had to grasp at his sleeve to stay upright. "Well, then, I did it for your own good. The Potters run in our circle, my dear, however heartily you may wish to avoid them. Best to get it over with and move on."

"Spoken like someone who's never loved anyone more than he loves himself."

"Well, I am a delight, it has to be said, but you underestimate my affection for you, Jessamine!"

Jessamine smothered a bitter bark of laughter behind her glove. "Affection? You call this affection?"

"I made the hard decision for you that you could not make for yourself," Reginald replied. "I've done you a favor."

"A favor? All you've done is provide yourself with perverse entertainment for the evening. Tell me, whose pain do you find more diverting, mine or Teddy's?"

"Oh dear, did I look like I was enjoying myself?" Reginald chuckled. "Very well, I admit that Potter's discomfort was mildly amusing, but that wasn't my aim. I wish you could see how this has really been an act of love."

The music came to an end. Jessamine joined in politely with the applause, using the sound as a cover to continue the argument. "Love? What could you possibly know of love? Falling in love with someone requires a heart."

Reginald pretended to stumble backward, clutching his chest dramatically. "Dear heart, you wound me to the core!"

"I only wish that were true," Jessamine hissed, and walked right back out of the ballroom into the entrance hall. She thought she might have heard Kitty call her name, but pretended she had not. She managed to make it all the way to the front door, but just as her hand closed around the gilded handle, Reginald's fingers closed around her arm.

"I am leaving," Jessamine hissed.

His fingers tightened around her arm. "Nonsense. You can't leave now, we haven't even had dinner. The party's in your honor, for Creator's sake!"

"Let go of me. I said I'm leaving."

"Is that so? And are you going to walk all the way back to Larkspur Manor?" Reginald asked, releasing her and crossing his arms over his chest.

Jessamine was no longer being held in place, but she found she could not move. "Whatever are you talking about? I'm going to ring for my carriage, of course."

"Your carriage isn't here, my pet," Reginald replied, his smirk broadening. "I had an inkling you might decide to abandon the celebration earlier than propriety demanded, so I took the liberty of sending your carriage home. Your driver agreed you could hardly have a safer or more suitable ride home than a conveyance from the palace itself, and I must say that I heartily agree. What objection could you possibly have, my dear?"

Jessamine ground her teeth together in frustration. "I despise you," she whispered through her tears.

"The basis for many a successful marriage, or so I'm told." Reginald sighed. "Heavens, you aren't going to sulk for the rest of the night, are you? How tedious."

And he left her standing by the door, whistling cheerfully as he went.

19

A RCHIE WARD HAD BEEN MADE AWARE of the carriage now sitting parked outside his place of business. The moment it had entered the lane, the boy he paid every day to hang about down at the corner came racing up the rickety outside steps to announce the news to him through the shattered back window. Archie tossed the boy an extra *venia* and he scampered. Then Archie rolled a cigarette, lit it on the stub of a candle, and sucked on it as he moved to the front window, twitching the curtain aside so he could watch his guest without being spotted.

The carriage was plain, but by no means shabby, with a seal painted on the door that marked it as a public carriage for hire. This was enough to pique Archie's interest, as there were no licensed carriages for hire in the Barrens, which meant this particular conveyance had made its way from the Commons or perhaps even the Dignus districts. The occupant had not yet emerged from the curtained interior, but Archie's mind was already racing about who it could be, and what they would be asking of him.

Archie Ward had a reputation, you see; a reputation that no respectable person would ever admit knowledge of, but which many a respectable person had nevertheless managed to take advantage of to their own benefit. Archie Ward was a fixer. For the appropriate remuneration, he could make a man's problem vanish like a copper from the palm of a magician. Or a woman's problem. After all, Archie was not one to discriminate on the basis of gender where money was concerned.

At last, after several minutes of stillness, the curtain in the carriage window twitched and the door opened. A tall, thin man unfolded himself from the interior and straightened up, keeping his hat pulled low over his face, so that his features remained in shadow. Archie squinted through the grime-covered glass, but had no luck in his attempts to identify the man. He took a long drag of his cigarette until the embers came nearly to his fingertips, then he dropped it to the floor and ground it out beneath his boot. His hand drifted to his hip, where he kept his knife sharpened and holstered. He would have to be on his guard with this man, whoever he was. A man with a suit of such fine quality and such a shine on his boots could mean a large payday or a whole mess of trouble, and Archie needed to be prepared for either.

Archie settled himself behind his desk, attempting to look as unbothered as he could. He listened for the familiar sounds from below: the rap upon the door, the low, gravelly voice of his man, Enoch, as he questioned their guest. The exchange was very short—so short, in fact, that Archie found himself unable to pull his hand away from the knife at his hip. Footsteps were already pounding up the staircase, two sets of them, followed by Enoch's familiar knock and grumble.

"There's a gentleman what wants to see you, Mr. Ward," Enoch said.

Gentleman was code for "Dignus." Archie took a deep breath to steady himself. "A gentleman, you say? Well, by all means, Enoch, show the gentleman in."

The door scraped open and Enoch lumbered aside, revealing Archie's anticipated guest standing in the doorway. The guest did not wait to be told to enter the room, but did so without hesitation, his expression dripping with distaste. He gave the room a quick but thorough sweep with his eyes, displaying the same kind of shrewdness Archie himself would have shown if he'd been the one stepping into another man's office. The suit alone might have been enough to earn respect from most inhabitants of the Barrens, but a fool could look fine in a suit, as Archie knew well. He squared his shoulders and prepared to deal with a man whom, it was clear, ought not to be trifled with.

"A gentleman indeed," Archie said, inclining his head in the suggestion of a bow. "And what brings you to this fine establishment today, Mr...?"

"Smith. John Smith," the man replied. He made to sit down in the chair in front of Archie's desk, took a closer look at it, and seemed to decide against it. He remained standing, his hand closed tightly over the head of a carved walking stick.

"Well, *Mr. Smith,* would you like to lay your hat and walking stick aside? Make yourself comfortable?" Archie asked, his voice dripping with overdone politeness.

"I thank you Mr. Ward, but I have no intention of making myself 'comfortable' in such surroundings. Besides, your associate was very thorough in checking my walking stick for hidden weaponry."

Archie chuckled. "Yes, well, a man can't be too careful in my line of work."

"We have that in common, Mr. Ward," replied the man who was decidedly *not* named Mr. Smith.

Archie knew better than to inquire as to what that line of work might entail, so instead he said, "What can I do for you today, Mr. Smith?"

"I am looking for a man I can trust to clean up a mess discreetly. Have I come to the right man?" Mr. Smith asked.

Archie grinned in a self-satisfied sort of way. "I have been known to clean up a mess or two in my time. Perhaps you could tell me a bit more about this particular mess, and we'll see if I ain't the right bloke for the job."

In answer, Mr. Smith reached into his pocket and pulled out a velvet pouch, which he tossed onto Archie's desk. It made a very loud, satisfying clinking sound as it landed.

"I require your silence above all else, Mr. Ward. And I also require that you agree to the job before I share the details."

Archie raised a brow. This was highly irregular. He was not used to customers trying to set the terms of his arrangements. Then again, he was not sure so heavy a purse had ever been tossed across his desk. He gestured to the pouch as though asking permission to examine the contents. Mr. Smith nodded.

Archie took the pouch between his fingers and tipped it upside down. The coins that clattered forth were not mere *venia* or even silver marks. They were solid gold coins, the kind that could slip back and forth across the borders without difficulty. Archie let out a low whistle. "It must be quite the mess," he muttered.

"Does that mean you accept my terms?" Mr. Smith asked.

"Mr. Smith, for this kind of money, I'd accept the Devil's terms. You may put yourself at ease, we have an arrangement, sir."

Archie stood and thrust out a hand. Mr. Smith looked at the proffered hand but made no move to shake it. Archie let it dangle there for a moment longer and then dropped it, grinning broadly.

"The Riftmagic doesn't rub off, Mr. Smith. It ain't catching, you know."

Mr. Smith replied with such a scathing look that Archie quickly dropped his features into a more businesslike expression, shaking his sleeve down to cover the faded Riftmark that branded him as an Influencer. Mr. Smith, it seemed, would not be remembered fondly for his sense of humor, and while Archie loved himself a good joke, he wasn't ready to risk that pile of gold for a laugh.

"Now, Mr. Smith, to what task, specifically, am I applying my skills?" Archie asked, sitting back down. Mr. Smith hesitated a moment before finally relenting and perching himself lightly on the edge of the chair.

"In all honesty, Mr. Ward, there are two tasks for which I require your assistance. I have paid you handsomely to embark upon them both. When they have both been dispatched, and neatly, I shall pay you as much again."

Archie's mouth went dry. As much again? If he managed to carry out whatever this man was asking of him, he could retire to a life of leisure like a proper gentleman. He took a liberal swallow of mead to wet his whistle and pasted on his most placating smile. "I'm still listening, sir. What of these two tasks, then?"

"I assume that news of the fire at Bethlem Hospital has reached you in your… hidey-hole," Mr. Smith said, wrinkling his nose as he gave his surroundings another distasteful glance.

"Oh, sure. There ain't a corner of the Barrens what hasn't heard all about that. A strange business to be sure, lunatics runnin' around on fire! I understand the Praesidio has had quite the job roundin' 'em up."

"That's just it, Mr. Ward. The Praesidio, formidable though their numbers and skill might be, have not succeeded in recapturing all of the escaped patients. That's where you come in."

For the first time, Archie felt his confidence falter. He did not like the idea of having to associate with lunatics. Archie was good at what he did because people, in his opinion, were remarkably predictable, which made them easy to manipulate for his purposes. There was nothing predictable about a lunatic.

Mr. Smith did not miss the hesitation—the man was shrewd, damn him. "Do I detect a hint of reluctance, Mr. Ward? I will be quite put out if I have wasted my time and risked my own unsullied reputation in coming to see a man who does not live up to the tales of his deeds."

Archie stiffened. He did not take kindly to attacks on his person, however elegantly delivered. "No reluctance here, Mr. Smith. You've come to the right place, I assure you, for discretion. I must admit though, even this purse will be stretched thin if you mean to have me spend all my time chasing down a horde of lunatics. I do have other business affairs to see to."

"Well, then, you will be glad to know that it is not a horde of lunatics that needs capturing. It is two particular patients I am trying to locate. Two women."

Archie could not help but expel a relieved sort of chuckle. "Two women, yeh say? And you think you need my help for a job of this nature?"

Mr. Smith's face hardened at the sound of Archie's laughter. "You're a man of the world, Mr.Ward. Do you mean to tell me you don't know just how dangerous a woman can be?"

Archie felt the smile fade momentarily from his features. "Aye, guv' that's true enough, to be sure. So, these two women— why are they dangerous, exactly?"

"They are examples of the most dangerous kind of lunatic: the lunatic who appears sane, but beneath that veneer lurks a diabolical streak fearsome to behold. Either one of these women could charm you into her bed and then slice your throat while you were still smiling. Do you take my meaning?"

Archie gave only a nod in reply. Even Archie, who had ventured many a bold question to men above his station, did not dare ask the question that niggled at him now: whether this man knew of these women's wiles because he had fallen victim to them himself. It was hard to imagine such a man as this allowing himself to sink to the level of bedding a Riftborn woman, but then again, Archie was well acquainted with the murky depths to which men could sink when provoked. In fact, he rather relied on it.

Mr. Smith went on, "I have here all of the information that I have deemed helpful in tracking them down." He produced a thick envelope from his inside breast pocket and tossed it across the desktop to Archie.

E.E. Holmes

"And when I do manage to track them down? What then?" Archie asked, picking up the envelope and placing it carefully in his own pocket. He dared not say, "*if* I manage to track them down."

"I need them disposed of. Neatly, and without a trace," Mr. Smith replied shortly.

Archie merely nodded. He'd expected as much and found himself not at all troubled. "Very well, Mr. Smith. And the second task?"

"The second task is going to require a bit more... fortitude," Mr. Smith said.

Archie raised an eyebrow. More fortitude than murdering two dangerous madwomen? "Consider me intrigued, Mr. Smith. Do go on."

"Before I explain to you what this second task will entail, I need you to understand something. I am in a position to protect you. The risk, if your task is carried out successfully, will rest solely on me."

"I see," Archie replied. His palms felt suddenly clammy. Something terribly close to regret was trickling through his veins and yet, he knew he was in too deep to back out now. "Well, as much as I welcome the reassurance, Mr. Smith, I'd very much appreciate you getting to the point."

"I require you to kill Elder Carpenter."

The words hung in the air between them, irretrievable. Mr. Smith stood casually leaning upon his walking stick, watching Archie carefully as he waited to see how he would respond. Archie could feel the color draining from his face, could feel the tremor in his hands, but he succeeded in keeping his features smooth and composed.

"Mr. Smith, I am beginning to wonder if you might misunderstand the circles I run in. A pair of Riftborn lunatics hiding in the gutters is one thing, but an Elder of the Illustratum? I'm not sure if there's a place where a bloke like me can get within an 'undred paces of a man like that, but it sure as hell ain't this great city of ours. Men like Elder Carpenter himself have seen to that."

"I assure you, I am quite serious, Mr. Ward."

"Oh, I can see that," Archie replied, patting his hand against the money pouch so that it jangled dully against his chest. "And while I appreciate your confidence, sir, there are limits to what a man in my position can do."

"Well, never fear, Mr. Ward, for there are almost no limits at all to what a man in my position can do," Mr. Smith returned. "I have

180

formulated a plan, and if you will take a moment to hear it, I think you will not be so quick to write my request off as an impossibility. And just imagine the life of luxury and leisure you could live on that first purse alone, never mind the second you will have earned when the job is done."

Archie worried at his lip with his teeth. He'd never been a man who backed down from a challenge, especially when money was involved. Then again, he'd always prided himself on being the kind of man who knew when to scarper. Saving his own hide had always been his strongest instinct. Still, he could not help but blurt out his next question.

"Why me?"

Mr. Smith furrowed his brow. "Pardon?"

"A man like you—you despise men like me. You treat our Riftmagic like it's the bloody plague. Why would you want to hire someone like me?"

Mr. Smith looked thoughtful, as though he hadn't considered the matter. Then he leaned forward, clenching and unclenching his hand upon his walking stick. "Your magic is not a plague. It is a tool, to be wielded in the name of the Creator and no other. I seek you out to do His will. In service to me, you are in service to Him. Do I make myself clear?"

For perhaps the first time in his life, Archie found himself without a smart reply. The walls of his office seemed to be closing in on him, as the realization hit him like a slap to the mug. He would have no choice but to do whatever this man asked of him. Mr. Smith, whatever his real name, was not only a wealthy man, but a powerful one as well, and now Archie was trapped. He had been trapped from the moment the man had knocked upon his door.

Mr. Smith smiled, and though he had heard each and every one of Archie's thoughts, as though Archie's realization had pleased him beyond measure, a cat with a mouse dangling in his claws. Archie swallowed, trying to compose himself as he inclined his head toward the man sitting across from him—the man who now held his life in his hands.

"Very well, Mr. Smith. Let's hear this plan."

20

P ENNY WAS DISTRACTED. This was less than ideal because, in her line of work, distraction was dangerous. It was almost enough to make her regret throwing herself into Resistance plans—almost, but not quite.

The past week had been a flurry of meetings, messages passed back and forth, and a multitude of tiny tasks, such as tidbits of information that needed to be skillfully extracted or officials who needed to be diverted. No lunatics had, as yet, been relegated to the attics, but otherwise, Lavender's warnings that illicit activity would be seeing an uptick had quickly come true.

While some of the girls found the change unnerving, Penny had never felt so alive. The truth was that she had always pushed the boundaries of her profession, using her various talents to charm, manipulate and otherwise scheme her way into much more than a few coppers for her time and attention, often out of pure boredom. But now, with a cause to work for and a goal in sight that could change the very shape of her world, Penny started each night's shift with a thrill of excitement rather than the dull aching dread that had once been her constant companion.

Tonight, her task was simple: keep an eye out for Zeke and relay his message to Lavender. An exciting breakthrough in Cora's work meant that the Resistance could begin to lay the groundwork for their plans. Just two nights ago, she hit on the antidote for Riftmead, an herbal concoction that rendered the stuff practically harmless. Hoping to strengthen the magic of the general population in the lead up to their bid for power, the Resistance would attempt to introduce the antidote at the source, in the very facilities where the Illustratum produced and bottled the Riftmead. If they were successful, Zeke was to come here and pass the information along. The worst part would be the waiting—it could be hours before he arrived, and Penny would be forced to go through the motions of a regular shift while she waited on pins and needles, and with only a single whiskey to sustain her, bugger it all. Even the hand of cards she was playing could not occupy her mind, though there was the added benefit of the coins she'd won now occupying her pocket.

There was a secondary distraction, and that was the fact that she had neither seen nor heard from Daniel in the last week, and she had begun to wonder if she had misplayed her hand where he was concerned. She still believed, in her gut, that she could trust him, but not all trustworthy men will throw their lives away on a gamble such as she had offered him. Perhaps it was too dangerous, too uncertain. The Resistance plans would go on without him, but Penny could not help but feel a little pang of emptiness that she might have scared him so far off that she would not see him again. She scoffed at herself, at this tiny chink in her armor, but there it was, raw and soft and exposed, and she had no idea how to heal it.

There was a sudden nudge against her leg and Cate hissed in her ear as she passed. "Oi! Pen!"

Penny looked up from her hand of cards to see Zeke dropping into a threadbare chair by the fire. He wasn't looking at her—he was occupied with loosening one of his boots. Cate had already swept over to him, gesturing to the bar. Zeke grumbled something in reply and she floated away. Penny looked over at her partner, so deep into a bottle of whiskey that she'd have been surprised if he'd been seeing any less than two of each card in his hand. After pretending to consider her own hand for a moment, she put down a jack of clubs and laid her cards down.

"How the devil did you still have a club? What is this, witchcraft, or are you keeping trumps up your sleeve?" the man grumbled, his nose an inch from the card she'd just placed on the tabletop.

"Just a lucky trick," Penny replied. "Besides, everyone knows I keep my spare trumps in my cleavage. Would you excuse me? Lilah, why don't you take my spot for a bit. You'll like Lilah, Mr. Kerry, she's terrible at cards."

Penny got up from the table, allowing the crimson-cheeked Lilah to slide into her vacated seat. Lilah would probably try to get Mr. Kerry upstairs before Penny could get back—that was just like Lilah, opportunistic to the core and interested in nothing but survival. But Penny had already considered this and had decided it was worth it to let Mr. Kerry and his textiles factory money go—she had more important things to worry about, like why Zeke was back so damn early. She hadn't even planned to keep an eye out for him for another hour or two yet. She intercepted Cate halfway across the room and plucked Zeke's tankard from the tray. A few seconds later she had sunk languidly into Zeke's lap and thrust the tankard into his hand.

"There you are, love," she cooed, wrapping her arm around Zeke's neck and pulling herself in close to him so that they could speak without being overheard. "What's gone wrong? Why are you back so soon?"

"Always the optimist," Zeke murmured into her hair, his face now obscured. "Who's to say we didn't succeed more quickly than expected under my impressive leadership?"

"I've seen your leadership in action when you've been dealing with your patrons. Now, come on, out with it. What's happened? Has someone been caught? Did you have to scrap the whole thing?"

"Naw, this time, for maybe the first time ever, I can report that one of our operations went off without a hitch," Zeke said, and Penny's fingers tightened on his shoulders. "The foreman was a layabout drunkard. I barely had to distract the man while the other boys joined to queue for the shift. They had slipped out again before I'd even managed to feed him my cover story—that I was looking to change my delivery schedule for the pub. I'd be surprised if he even remembered the conversation tomorrow—either that or I'm going to be getting surprise midnight deliveries of twice as much mead as I ordered."

"So you mean to tell me they did it? They got Cora's antidote into the barrels?" Penny breathed.

"Every single one. Storage room was unlocked, and no one gave us a second look—they were all still half asleep at the start of the evening shift. We could have stolen a barrel or two, just carried it out on our shoulders, and I don't think anyone would have so much as questioned us."

Penny snorted. "No offense, Zeke, but that sounds more like

general incompetence on their part than it does brilliant strategy on yours."

Zeke chuckled, grabbed the tankard, and downed the contents in one. Penny unfurled herself from his lap, satisfied she had enough information to pass along to Lavender, who would be very keen to know how the plan had gone. She was, after all, going to be a crucial touchstone in the further distribution of the now harmless Riftmead. Her connections to business owners all over the Barrens and the Commons meant that she had more sway behind the scenes than the whole of the Illustratum. She had volunteered to use her clout to make sure the harmless Riftmead filled as many businesses as possible, a feat that would require every ounce of her considerable influence. So much had rested upon the success of today's mission at the factory. Now it seemed like that part of the plan, at least, could proceed as they had hoped.

If only the other elements were coming together as easily, she lamented silently to herself. There were still too many gaping holes, too many obstacles that they had not yet foreseen and so could not plan for. And as she looked up, the most handsome of those obstacles strode right through the front door.

Zeke must have felt Penny's body stiffen, for he suddenly froze, becoming alert. "What is it, lass? Trouble?" He set his empty tankard down and reached for his belt, where he kept a well-sharpened knife sheathed.

"No, no, it's not trouble. Just… someone I've been expecting," Penny murmured. Her heart was starting to behave like a frightened bird trapped in her chest, fluttering and flapping madly. She snatched a glass from a passing tray and threw it back for courage. Then she stood up, smoothed her skirts, and sauntered toward the door just as Daniel Byrne spotted her. His face broke into a relieved sort of smile.

"I'm glad you're here," he said as she closed the last of the distance between them.

"I'd hardly be anywhere else, at this time of night," she replied, taking his hand and leading him out of the brightly lit center of the room and off into one of the shadowy booths tucked in the front corner. Daniel looked around him warily, his smile slipping.

"Are we hiding from someone?" he asked.

"No, but I hardly think you want people to suppose you're a regular around here, do you?" Penny sounded almost incredulous.

"Praesidio uniforms draw enough attention without putting them on parade in the middle of the room."

Penny caught Tabitha's eye as she passed and gave her a quick nod. Tabby was the only other girl who knew about Daniel, and she knew to keep an eye out for Lavender if he showed up at the brothel again. She'd keep the watch while she could, but if a customer took a fancy to her, she'd have no choice but to entertain him. Penny would have to make this quick.

"So, what brings you 'round Lavender's again? Did you fancy one of the other girls? I could introduce you, you know..." she said lightly. She dared a glance at his face. His expression was utterly bemused for a moment before breaking into a smile again.

"Ah, I see. That's very funny," he said.

Penny shrugged. "Ah, yes, well, the customers come for the tits, but they stay for the jokes." Daniel's face reddened, and Penny cursed herself. She'd scare him off as like as not if she didn't remember he wasn't just another customer, and that she couldn't talk to him like one. She cleared her throat and tried again, remembering she didn't need to perform for him.

"Sorry. It's just the habit when I'm... when I'm here," she said. He opened his mouth, but she forestalled him, suddenly terrified of what would come out of it. "Well, what is it, then? What have you come for?"

Daniel, his mind returned to his purpose, looked suddenly glad that they were settled into such a quiet corner. Even so, he leaned across the table toward Penny and dropped his voice to a whisper in an effort not to be overheard.

"You told me to come see you if I was sure. Well, I'm sure. I want to join up."

Although Penny had been waiting anxiously for Daniel's answer for a week, she did not comprehend his words right away. For several seconds, she merely stared at him, her brain working furiously to keep up.

Daniel's brow crinkled in confusion. "Penny? Did you hear what I said?"

Penny blinked, dragging her sluggish brain forward into understanding. "You're... you're not serious?"

"Shouldn't I be?"

"No! No, of course you should, dead serious, it's only..."

Daniel looked almost affronted. "I wonder why you asked me if you thought I was a lost cause?"

Penny's face broke into a grin. "You? A lost cause? I'd never be fool enough to drag my arse all the way down to the north wall before the sun was half up for a lost cause."

"Then what's got you looking all shocked, then?" Daniel asked.

Penny sighed. "It's only… well, Lavender told me not to recruit you, but I've gone and done it anyway, as is my custom, and now I'm realizing I was half hoping you'd say no, only so I wouldn't have to face her."

Daniel looked suddenly concerned. "Look, Penny, I don't want to cause you any trouble—"

Penny flicked her hand impatiently. "Don't be so presumptuous, soldier. I cause my own trouble just fine, thanks." Her eyes narrowed. "I've just got to have myself a proper think and figure out just how I'm going to tell Lavender and the others."

"So Madam Lavender is part of this as well, then?" Daniel asked, realization sinking in.

"Madam Lavender's a part of everything," Penny snorted. "It's Lavender's London, Daniel. The rest of us are just living in it."

"Well then, what do I need to do?" Daniel asked, leaning eagerly forward again. "Surely there must be something I can do to prove to Lavender or anyone else that I'd be useful to the cause."

Penny's eyes lit up. "Yes! Of course, we've got to think of something you can do to help now, a sort of good faith gesture. If you deliver something to them that they could never hope to get on their own, they'll have no choice but to take you on."

"Something they couldn't get on their own? Like what?"

"I'm not sure yet… like I said, I've got to have a think on it, and—"

"Penny, Mr. Weston's here, and he's looking for you. In a bit of a mood." Edith popped her head into the booth, her face twisted with aggravation.

Penny cursed under her breath. She was never in for a particularly pleasant night when Mr. Weston was in a mood, but she was handsomely paid for it, and there was usually a bauble or two thrown in if he drank enough. "Tell him I'll be right with him, Edith. Get him a whiskey, can you?"

Edith made a face but swept off to get the whiskey. Penny turned her eyes reluctantly back on Daniel. "Duty calls," she said with a rueful smile.

Daniel looked like he wanted to protest, but swallowed back whatever objections were rolling around in his mouth. "Of course." He started to stand when Penny's hand, seemingly of its own accord, as she did not recall deciding to move it, shot out and caught Daniel's before he could remove it from the table.

"Wait... there may be something you could do... well, it's *completely* mad, but..."

Daniel's eyes lit up with interest. "I have been known to do a mad thing or two in my life," he said with a smirk. "What did you have in mind?"

Eliza—

I'm sure you're surprised to be receiving a letter from me. I'm dead surprised that I'm sending you one, so there's a scrap of something in common, anyhow. I need to speak with you, and it can't be at one of the meetings. I can't risk the others overhearing. Can you meet me in the High Street on Tuesday morning at eight o'clock, before you and the other manor girls start your rounds with those charity baskets? I wouldn't ask, but it's an important matter, one that could help the cause, and I don't know who else to ask for help.

Don't reply to this letter, it's too risky. If you decide you want to help me, I'll be waiting for you in the market square. If you decide not to help me... well, I guess I'll have gotten up early for nothing.

—Penny

21

ELIZA CLUTCHED THE LETTER IN HER HAND, as though she needed the reminder that it was real, and that what she was going to do was not just some mad whim, because that was exactly what it felt like — madness.

In the first place, she didn't have the time. Between the preparations for the wedding that would never happen and her clandestine work with the Resistance, she was running on little more than broken sleep and a healthy dose of fear. She had a list of errands a mile long that she had to get through before another dress fitting that afternoon, and then she would be up late that night, practicing her Influencer magic and taking her turn manning Sully's printing press. The days left until the wedding were slipping away, and though she constantly found herself wishing for more time to prepare, there was a part of her that was glad the day was looming up so quickly. If she had to go on like this for months, she thought she might just drop dead.

But apart from all of that, there was the fact that Penny just didn't like her. It had been obvious from the first moment of their meeting that she resented Eliza's presence in the Resistance. Penny shared a disdain for manor servants endemic to the Riftborn of the Barrens, but there was something deeper. It was the poker-stiff pride of a woman who knew that other women looked down on her and try as Eliza may to be friendly to her, the walls Penny had built to protect herself were high and strong and covered in barbs. Never mind that Penny's assumptions about Eliza were at least as disdainful as anything Eliza might have assumed about Penny. And so, as Eliza looked down at the letter again, she wondered for the hundredth time whether it wasn't all just some trick. Why would Penny be writing to her, of all people? It didn't make sense. And yet, Eliza had never, for even a moment, considered not answering the summons. This was a chance—however slim—to prove to Penny that she was worth trusting, and she wasn't about to squander it.

When Eliza rounded the corner into the High Street, charity baskets dangling awkwardly from both arms, Penny was already there. Eliza spotted her perched upon a water barrel, jiggling her foot and devouring a steaming bag of roasted chestnuts in small, anxious nibbles. Their eyes met from across the little market square, and Eliza, desirous of blending in, began a slow inspection of the wares in the various carts until she had reached the cart of apples beside which Penny had placed herself. Under the guise of examining the apples, Eliza spoke first.

"You asked to see me?"

Penny kept her eyes on her chestnuts as she answered. "I wasn't sure if you'd come."

"Well, here I am. So, what is it? I haven't got much time before the other girls will be here, and then I'll be missed."

"Right, okay, here's the problem. I've got a chance to get some very valuable information for Sully and the others, but it's from an... unusual source."

Eliza fought the urge to look up at Penny, selecting another apple instead. "Unusual how?"

Penny's voice sounded tight. "He's a Praesidio guard."

This time, Eliza could not help it. Her head snapped up and she stared at Penny for a moment before she came to her senses and dropped her gaze again. The vendor who owned the cart poked his head around the side of the display.

"Anything I can help you with, miss? Sweetest fruit you'll find this side of the Thames!"

"I'm just looking, thank you," Eliza said, layering on an air of superiority that manor servants were often known to use when speaking to Riftborn from the Barrens. "I shall ask for help if I require it."

The man bowed and mumbled himself around the corner of the cart and out of sight. Eliza returned her attention to Penny. "A Praesidio guard? Have you taken leave of your senses?"

Penny snorted. "I recall asking Eli the very same question when he dragged you into Lavender's."

Eliza wanted to protest, but she could not in good faith. Instead, she pivoted. "Very well, then, making the enormous assumption that this guard is to be trusted, what is it you want me to do?"

There was no denying the relief in Penny's voice that Eliza had not already walked away. She explained in a whisper, "He believes he may be able to get his hands on Praesidio security plans for the day of the wedding. Someone needs to meet him outside the Praeteritum so that he can hand them off. That someone needs to copy out as much information from the documents as they can overnight, and then meet him again so that he can return them, hopefully before anyone notices they're missing in the first place."

"That sounds... quite dangerous."

"Oh, I reckon it is, yeah," Penny said mildly, popping another chestnut into her mouth.

"And you thought particularly of me for this little adventure?" Eliza asked, just as mildly.

"That's right. Just the woman for the job," Penny replied.

Eliza sighed and set down her baskets, pretending to be examining the contents as further cover for their conversation. "Look, Penny, I'm not saying no, but... I suppose I don't really understand why you can't just meet this guard yourself? He already knows and trusts you from the sound of it. Why bring me into it?"

"I've met him at the wall once already. I can't go making a habit of it, or the guards will take notice," Penny said.

"A manor girl at the Praeteritum wall is going to draw a lot more notice than someone who already belongs in the Barrens," Eliza argued, "so unless you've got a better reason than that, I don't—"

"All right!" Penny bit her lip and hesitated. Finally, she huffed loudly and replied, "It took me the better part of an hour just to write that letter I sent you, and that was barely three lines, for Creator's sake. But you... I've seen you reading and writing at the meetings. You've been taught, proper-like. And you won't have trouble getting your hands on some paper and ink. I had to nick my writing supplies from Lavender's office; otherwise, I'd get a thousand bloody questions about what I needed 'em for."

Eliza nodded. It was an answer to the question, and yet, it completely avoided the heart of the matter. Most of the Resistance could read and write, and some of them, Sully included, were likely remarkably better and faster writers than she was.

Penny was watching Eliza's face anxiously, analyzing every blink, every twist of her mouth. Whatever she saw did not please her, for she sighed, and her shoulders slumped. "All right. The truth is that you... well, you're an outsider to the group. I ain't sayin' that to hurt your feelings. It's just how it is."

Eliza nodded. She was painfully aware of it herself every time she walked into a Resistance gathering. She wasn't from the Barrens. She didn't understand what life was like for those Riftborn, not really. Her proximity to the Dignus meant she would always be met with wariness and mistrust at first.

Penny went on, "Daniel is an outsider, too. He's Praesidio. It's mad to trust him. It's like inviting a fox into a hen house. And yet..." she trailed off and looked up at Eliza, willing her to understand where the words were failing her.

"And yet, you trust him," Eliza finished for her.

Penny nodded. "I do. I can't explain it. But I do. And I know that we need him. I just need the others to realize it, too, and the only way to make that happen is to show them just how useful he can be."

How could Eliza argue? Hadn't Eli made the same plea on behalf of herself? And hadn't she been valuable to the cause? Hadn't she been able to feed them information no other Resistance member could possibly have access to? Hadn't she proved her mettle in a hundred ways since? She could hardly argue with the fact that having a Praesidio guard on their side would be an invaluable asset.

"You didn't trust me at first," Eliza said, "but you trust me enough now to ask my help. I can only assume that's because I've proved myself to you in some way."

Penny shrugged. "That's right. You've put your neck on the line, like the rest of us."

"Then I trust that this Praesidio guard has proven himself to you as well?"

Penny's expression lost its edge. In its place, there was nothing but bare earnestness. "Yes," she whispered. "It was when he first came to me, at Lavender's. He wasn't there for company—didn't so much as glance at any of the girls in that sort of way. He was looking for someone, see: his younger sister. She'd vanished more than fifteen years ago, just like Eli and Jasper and likely a hundred other Riftborn children born to Dignus families. He's been searching for her ever since their parents died, digging through the gutters of the Barrens every night, shoving her picture under indifferent noses, desperate for a flash of recognition. He'd do anything to find her, even if it meant razing the Illustratum to the bloody ground."

Eliza listened in a state of shock. So many families torn asunder. She had known it, and yet to be confronted with yet another person whose life had been forever changed by this deep fear, this loathing born of ignorance... it tore at her afresh every time.

"This man's sister—she couldn't have been much older than a baby when... and still he looks? He must know how unlikely he is to find her," Eliza replied, her voice coming out in a whisper.

Penny shrugged. "I told him as much when I first met him, but he won't be dissuaded. As long as there's still a chance, he'll keep looking, I reckon." Then she added, upon sudden inspiration, "Look, I know it's a risk. I ain't made it this far in the Barrens without that much sense. But you know it's not impossible to trust a Dignus. From what I've heard, you've put a lot of trust in that mistress of yours, and none of that has been misplaced."

The mention of Jessamine struck Eliza like a blow. Another sister and brother whose family was dismantled and destroyed. If the daughter of an Elder, with the promise of every power, privilege, and comfort, could be sympathetic to the cause, surely a Praesidio guard with far less to lose could do the same. It was possible.

Eliza nodded once briskly. "That's good enough for me."

Penny gasped, and it was clear to Eliza at that moment that Penny had never expected her to agree. "Really?"

"Are you suggesting I *shouldn't* rely on your instincts in regards to which men to trust?" Eliza asked.

Penny's face broke into a cautious smile. "Ain't no better instincts to be found inside Lavender's or out."

Eliza smiled as well. "That's what I thought. And as I am merely a clueless, spoiled manor girl, I will trust you not to lead me astray. Now when and where am I to meet him?"

§

The very next morning, as Eliza stood in the shadow of the Praeteritum wall, she found herself clinging to that trust rather

197

tentatively. It wasn't that she thought Penny had double-crossed her somehow—her worry all lay in this mysterious Praesidio guard sympathetic to their cause. The Praesidio had always been, at least in her limited experience, some of the most aggressive and virulent in their hatred of the Riftborn, and so it was difficult to imagine one so different from his fellows. Of course, she was surrounded at Larkspur Manor by other Riftborn servants who cherished a deep loathing for the Riftborn that resided in the Barrens, and so she knew what it meant to be the exception to the well-established rule. But at least Eliza *was* a Riftborn, albeit a privileged one. She had a horse in the race, so to speak. Why a Dignus born and bred would fight for the Riftborn, she wasn't sure, but Penny promised he had his reasons, and Eliza must put her faith in that.

She glanced again at the clock which hung outside the cobbler's shop at the end of the alley, though she'd looked at it so frequently, she was sure that no real time could have gone by. Daniel Byrne's shift ended seven minutes ago. That meant, at any moment now, he should appear. Eliza shuddered. Never had she so heartily wished for a gift like Colin's, so that she could vanish into the darkness of the alleyway, cloaking herself in shadow and protecting herself from discovery.

To calm herself, she reached down into her cloak pocket and wrapped her fingers around the prayer book she had brought with her. It was common practice for devout Riftborn to come to the wall and read from the book—a sort of solitary missionary outreach to the heathens on the other side of bars. Eliza found no comfort in the book itself anymore—the words were empty to her now, fueling rage and disgust where once they fueled hope. No, the comfort came from knowing that she had an excuse for being where she was; if a guard questioned her, she could spout some verses and say she came to pray for the lost souls behind the wall. Her book was as good as Colin's magic in this respect—a ready-made disguise.

The sound of boots sent Eliza's heart galloping up into her throat. A soldier approached, his head down as he walked. She had no way of knowing whether it was Daniel Byrne or not: Penny had not described him. But he was meant to know her by her uniform and the Hallewell family crest stitched onto her cloak. She held her breath, shaking hands still clutching the book, ready to present her excuse if this were not the soldier for whom she waited.

The soldier looked up and spotted her, stopping in his tracks. He looked behind him, back toward the wall, to ensure they were alone, then he strode forward, closing the distance between them. Not until he whispered, "Eliza?" did she remember to breathe again.

"Yes," she whispered back. "Daniel?"

"That's right," he said, inclining his head respectfully, a gesture so out of character for any Praesidio guard Eliza had ever encountered that she felt the iron grip of her fear loosen at once. Her face must have retained its expression of wariness, however, for Daniel went on, "Don't worry. I made sure the patrol passed just as I left the barracks. We have five minutes easily before another guard turns up."

"That's a comfort to know," Eliza replied. "Penny said you would have—"

"Yes! Yes, I've got them here," Daniel said eagerly. He slipped his hand into his breast pocket and pulled out a thick envelope. Eliza wasted not a moment reaching out for it and tucking it safely into a hidden pocket she had sewn into the lining of her cloak.

"Penny said you're going to copy them over?" Daniel asked.

"Yes, tonight. I shall return them to you tomorrow at the same time so that you can replace them quickly."

Daniel nodded. "I hope the leaders, whoever they are, will be pleased. I was quite lucky to get my hands on those. They're classified, Elders and Praesidio leadership only."

Eliza shuddered to think about what she was carrying, and hastened her departure. "Well, thank you, Daniel," she said. "I... I suppose I shall see you tomorrow."

She turned to go.

"Wait!" Daniel called out to her. She whirled around in alarm, but it was only him standing there, looking a bit sheepish.

"What is it?" Eliza hissed.

"I guess I was just... I wondered how a manor servant becomes a member of the Resistance," Daniel said.

"Much in the same way a Praesidio guard does, I imagine. Against all odds and completely by chance."

Daniel smiled. "That's true enough, I reckon."

Eliza gazed into Daniel's eyes for a moment. The vulnerability etched there gave her the courage to ask the question she'd been wondering about since she'd agreed to this mad scheme.

"Penny told me you have a Riftborn sister?"

Daniel looked surprised for a moment and Eliza wondered if she had overstepped.

"I'm sorry. I'm sure Penny didn't mean to break your confidence, if there was a confidence in this matter. It was simply that she needed to convince me that you were trustworthy, and—"

Daniel held up a hand to silence her. "Please, say no more. There was no confidence. I am glad Penny told you, if it helped you decide to come here today."

"I don't know what will come from all of this, but I will hope, for your sake, that finding your sister is among the outcomes," Eliza said.

Eliza couldn't be sure, but she thought Daniel's eyes grew brighter. He certainly seemed lost for the proper reply, for he said nothing, instead pressing his lips together and inclining his head, yet again, respectfully in her direction before marching purposefully down the alleyway and out of sight.

22

L IGHT POOLED LIKE A PUDDLE OF WATER upon the desktop, but Josiah hadn't worked in hours. He hadn't written a word, nor shifted a memo. The papers beneath his gaze had long faded to a blur, his eyes focused instead on the thoughts that chased each other through his mind like predator and prey.

He ought to stop it.
He could not stop it.
There was still time.
He was out of time.
There were things that could not be undone.
He did not wish for them to be undone.

Days were slipping past him like grains of sand through his fingers, days and hours and minutes during which he could do nothing but wait and pray and hope and dread, and it was this inaction, this helplessness that ate away at him until he thought he would go mad. Waiting for the wedding day to arrive. Waiting for Archie Ward to carry out his orders. Waiting for the dreaded word that the High Elder had expired. Waiting to see if the escaped patients were captured. Waiting, waiting, waiting. If one more person told him to just be patient, that person would find himself flat on his back.

His whole life had been patience, strategy, and careful tending of slow-blooming seeds in the faith that his work would be rewarded. Now he saw that the most careful of gardeners could be thwarted with one unseasonable frost, one rodent sneaking through his defenses. Years of work, all for naught. He could not let it happen. He would not.

He sat back in his chair and squinted at the clock. It was nearly seven o'clock. He was expecting Brother Goodwin back from his nosing about, gathering information about the small meetings that continued to happen in the conference rooms without him, about the whisperings that floated from one servant to the next, about the rumors bandied about by barbed tongues.

It had been a week since the High Elder had been seen within the walls of the Illustratum. A full week in which his absence had drawn more eyes and more tongues than his presence had drawn in years. As Francis said, there was no use in trying to hide it anymore. The only hope was to stop the whisperers from approaching too closely to the truth. And after that afternoon's meeting of the Elders, that hope was fleeting.

"They know," Josiah had said to him only that morning.

"They don't," Francis had replied, entirely too comfortably. "They only think they know," he added at the foreboding look on Josiah's face. "It's not the same thing, Josiah. As long as there is doubt, there is room to move forward without interference."

"I see very little doubt in the expressions of our esteemed colleagues," Josiah said, glancing around the room as it filled with Elders. The atmosphere was somber, bordering on funereal. The empty seat at the top of the hall drew the eye like a coffin flung wide, its grisly contents on display. No one seemed to want to speak above a murmur, and even the most boisterous of their members were shuffling about in chastened silence. The call to order, when it came, was hardly required.

"We open the floor to new business from our committee heads," the Moderator announced, his voice ringing sharply through the room, "and we shall then proceed to our pre-scheduled votes. No more debate will be heard at this time on the items to be voted upon."

Josiah did not so much as blink when Elder Carpenter rose to his feet and cleared his throat, signaling his desire to be heard. The Moderator recognized him, the Scribe poised his pen above his roll of paper. Francis made to place a warning hand on Josiah's arm, but Josiah waved him away. He felt a cold calmness inside him.

"I would like to raise a concern of many among us that has not yet been voiced within this chamber, as regards the well-being of our illustrious leader, High Elder Morgan," Elder Carpenter said, his voice taking on the slightly nasal quality it always did when he was straining to be heard.

"And what is this concern, Elder Carpenter?" the Moderator asked, a warning in his voice that Josiah was sure that Elder Carpenter would not heed. Sure enough—

"The seat of the High Elder within this chamber has been empty these past seven days," Elder Carpenter said, "and it has not escaped the notice of the assembled company that the High Elder has been in poor health of late. We wish to be reassured that he is well enough to carry out his responsibilities."

There was a murmur of agreement, but it was soft and uncertain, as though the speakers wished to maintain deniability. They all knew this was uncharted territory in the Illustratum—a High Elder had never yet died while still holding his post. Even the very first High Elder, the very prophet and creator of their current system, had passed the mantle of power down to his son well before his own demise.

"I have not been made aware through the proper channels that there is any reason for undue worry," the Moderator replied.

This was the answer Josiah knew he must give, for Josiah himself had seen to those official channels with Francis' help, and they were all parroting the same line: the High Elder was ill, but not seriously so, and would be back on his feet in no time at all.

"Yes, I have heard the... ah, *official* report as to the High Elder's health," Elder Carpenter said, a definite sneer in his voice. "However, the unofficial reports have left many of us doubting what we have been told."

"You mean to call into question the official reports that are being relayed to us directly from the palace?" the Moderator asked, looking down over the top of his spectacles.

"I mean to remind every man in this room that our first duty is to the Creator and the carrying out of his will, and that we must do everything in our power to ensure that that work continues on as effectively as it can," Elder Carpenter said, dodging neatly around the question. "If we have doubts about the High Elder's ability to do his job, I think we must voice them, in the interest of the greater good."

"The High Elder communes directly with the Creator," the Moderator replied, his voice rising. "He takes his direction from on high. Do you mean to doubt the divinity of his instruction?"

Every head turned to see how Carpenter would extract himself from a very barbed exchange, and even Josiah could not continue feigning indifference, but stared with the rest.

"I have implied no such thing. The Word comes through the Rift into the ear of the High Elder, that is the highest truth. But I have it on good authority that the High Elder has not communed with the Rift for a full ten days. My concern is not that the Word is untrue, but that the Word is unable to reach him."

The Moderator's mouth twisted like he had tasted something sour. Then he said, "And how do you propose we ease this... concern of yours, Elder Carpenter?"

Elder Carpenter clasped his hands in front of him and adopted an expression that might have been appropriate for a funeral. "I'm not sure that we have any choice but to consider a vote of no confidence."

A rumbling broke out, but it was impossible to interpret the prevailing tone. Many looked angry, but still others were nodding in agreement. Josiah took in as many faces as he could in rapid succession, and all he could conclude was that the room was both passionate and passionately divided on what Elder Carpenter had just said. He glanced at Francis, who looked somewhat bewildered as he too tried to understand just what was happening. For all his smug confidence that he had everything under control, it was clear that all his well-placed informants and collectors of tidbits had failed him this time; the bid for a vote of no confidence had shocked him utterly, and that in itself was unnerving.

"The audacity," Francis mumbled.

"Indeed," Josiah muttered back.

"I do not wish to alarm my colleagues," Elder Carpenter's voice cut through the uproar. "But I do think it foolish not to give the matter serious thought."

"We will hear discussion on the matter," the Moderator said after a moment of deliberation. The drop of his gavel silenced every voice. Elder Carpenter settled back down into his chair, looking like a cat with canary feathers caught in his whiskers.

Elder Smythe stood, wobbling on his cane. "I think it's blasphemy to even consider a vote of no confidence in the Creator's hand-chosen representative on earth!" he shouted. "I will never vote for such a measure, but I will pray for those who do!" He sat down again as smartly as his creaking joints would allow, and his words were met with a smattering of applause and "hear, hears!" from the old guard.

Elder Primrose leaped to his feet. "I am also uncomfortable with a vote of no confidence, especially when the High Elder is not here to speak on his own behalf. We cannot decide upon such a measure without seeing the truth of the matter with our own eyes."

"So a man gets sick for a week, and rather than letting him recover so that he can return, we sweep his legs out from under him? That hardly seems sporting," Elder Garrison bellowed, not bothering to rise from his seat.

"He's been sick for longer than that, and you know it," Elder Ross said. He was a smarmy little weasel, clearly in Carpenter's pocket, for he made his argument like he had memorized it out of a book, with Carpenter nodding along beside him. "And getting worse by the day, if his absence is any indication."

"But the updates from the palace indicate—"

"The updates from the palace are well-meaning, I am sure, but I believe they are meant to placate us as much as to inform us," Elder Carpenter said.

"So the palace doctors are lying?" Elder Garrison asked, clearly gobsmacked at the audacity of the accusation.

"I don't mean to cast aspersions on anyone's honesty. But hope can skew our judgment, and what would the doctors be if not hopeful that their ministrations are working?" Elder Carpenter asked.

"Elder Carpenter, that is nothing more than speculation!" Elder Garrison blustered.

"Very well, then, let us hear from Elder Hallewell," Elder Carpenter said, turning a thin smile on Josiah. "He has been to the palace recently, if I am not much mistaken. What was your assessment of the High Elder's condition?"

Josiah felt Francis stiffen beside him. His own hands clenched briefly into fists before he managed to loosen them. Having no choice, Josiah stood up and cleared his throat.

"It is true that I went to see the High Elder at the palace. This was over a week ago now, and so I cannot speak to his current condition."

He knew he would not get off that easily, and he was right.

"Well, speak to us about his condition last week, then!" Elder Carpenter pressed, crossing his arms truculently over his chest.

Josiah had only a moment to make a decision. He could not consult Francis. He could not plot or plan or carefully draft his words. He had just this one moment to decide what he would do, and he had

205

to decide it alone. Well, he had taken the reins already behind Francis' back, and he wasn't going to hand them back over now.

"I will not insult the intelligence of any man here by trying to make light of the situation. The High Elder is very unwell, that is true. However, he was sitting up and speaking when I spoke to him, lucid and focused. Whether that is all still true, I do not know. None of us does, though Elder Carpenter would seem to want us to make a decision based solely on his own speculation."

Elder Carpenter's face turned a blotchy red. "This is not—"

But Josiah held up a hand, silencing him. "I am not desirous of arguing with you. In fact, I think your suggestion is a good one." Josiah took a moment to relish the shocked expression on Elder Carpenter's face before continuing, "It is incumbent upon us to make sure that the High Elder can continue in his post, for the good of all his flock."

"You... you are agreeing to the proposal?" Elder Carpenter spluttered.

"I am, but not in the hasty and flagrantly insubordinate manner you are suggesting we pursue it," Josiah said, relishing the words even as he flung them at Carpenter. "Your well-intentioned concern has blinded you, Brother, and I would not have you stumble about in a manner that could land you in the path of an official charge of insubordination or worse."

Elder Carpenter's face froze, a mask of indignation. Josiah did not give him a chance to thaw, but plowed on, his voice becoming stronger.

"I propose that we inform the High Elder of our collective concern. Perhaps we even draft an official letter, formalizing it all for the record. Then we ask that he allay those concerns so that we can decide what steps to take next."

"And if he cannot allay those concerns?" Elder Carpenter countered, his voice bordering on shrill.

"Then we come together and decide if the vote of no confidence is our next step," Josiah said, being sure to keep his own voice mellow and calm, a counterpoint to Elder Carpenter that made the latter sound almost hysterical by comparison. "Unless, of course, you think the High Elder of the Illustratum, the leader hand-picked by the Creator Himself, does not have the right to defend himself against charges of incompetence levied at him by an Elder who is not even a member of his cabinet?"

The chamber went silent. Josiah managed to stop himself from smirking, but it was a near thing. He knew it was well done, every word of it. Out of the corner of his eye, he caught the shadow of a nod that meant Francis approved of the maneuver. Josiah stood with his face deliberately blank, staring at Elder Carpenter, waiting for him to make the only answer he could possibly make to such a question. And at length, after what appeared to be a mighty internal struggle, he made it.

"An excellent point, Elder Hallewell. If you care to make the motion to draft this letter, I will be only too happy to second it," Elder Carpenter said, the words slightly strained as they forced their way out between his clenched teeth.

Josiah smiled indulgently. "I wouldn't dream of it. This was your proposal, really, and a good one at that. All I've done is temper it a bit. By all means, you should go on the record to make the motion." And then he stood by and waited while Elder Carpenter was forced to stand and swallow this bitter little pill in front of the entire assembly.

§

"That was masterful," Francis said an hour later as they filed out of the room.

"Someone had to put the brakes on that jumped-up little blighter," Josiah murmured. "But all I've really done is buy Morgan more time, and very little time at that."

"Yes, that's true enough," Francis said, his eyebrows drawing violently together. "What do you propose?"

"We've got to get Morgan here. He has to commune with the Rift and tell the others that the Creator continues to have faith in him," Josiah said.

Francis' face went slack. "And what if we do manage to get him here, before the Rift, and the Creator does not communicate such a thing? What then?"

Josiah did not speak, knowing that his silence would do the talking for him. Francis looked grim but did not press the matter.

"Do you think he will come?" Francis asked instead.

"I do. He has no choice, really. He can't allow a decades-long reign to end in the disgrace of a no-confidence vote. No, he'll just have to find a way to arrange it. If the blasted doctors have to carry him in, he'll make damn sure he gets there, of that I am certain."

"We'll have to find a way to keep others away," Francis said. "If he is truly as ill as you say—"

"He is, I assure you."

"Then we will need to find a way to avoid prying eyes. Carpenter and his faction will not squander the opportunity to witness the High Elder's condition for themselves," Francis said.

Josiah simply nodded. He had his own plans for Carpenter, but he could not speak of them. Francis would never approve of taking matters so far. And that, he thought, was why Francis would always remain comfortably near the top, but never right at the pinnacle. He didn't have the stomach for it.

But Josiah did. He had stayed up late into the night for weeks, praying. The Creator was testing him, he had concluded, testing his mettle and his faith. Soldiers did as they were told, but generals took the reins, forged their paths, and made decisions that won wars. Josiah was in his own personal battle for the soul of his country, and he would make what decisions were necessary. It was the only conclusion he could draw; the Creator had given him the tools and he must wield them.

However, there was the possibility that Archie Ward would fail— he had yet to find the Braxton woman or the scullery maid. Josiah could not count Carpenter as out of his path, not yet. And so they had to buy what time they could.

"So, we must go to Morgan," Francis said. He didn't sound happy about it.

"Yes, we must. As his Councilors, no one will think it strange that we are the ones to deliver the letter, once it has been finished. His doctors will protest, no doubt, but we must convince him to come, to play the part, or it's all over."

"Do you think this will change his mind, about putting your nomination in writing?" Francis asked.

"Perhaps," Josiah said, though his gut told him no. Morgan knew what he was holding out for, and that would not change just because the other Elders were getting restless. "But whether it does or not, we must make the necessary arrangements. Morgan does not have a choice. If he doesn't convince the others of his relative well-being, he is in danger of losing his seat in the most humiliating of ways. It cannot be borne, that I know for certain."

And arranging to meet an hour later in Josiah's office, the two men parted. Josiah had only made it a few steps down the corridor when he heard a snide voice call his name. He knew whom he would see standing there before he had turned his head.

"I suppose you are pleased with yourself, Hallewell?" Carpenter said, his face stretched into a smile that did not reach his eyes.

"Moderately pleased, yes," said Josiah dryly.

"How long do you think you can keep up this charade?" Carpenter asked, taking another step toward him. "You're not fooling anyone. The halls of the Illustratum are all but echoing with the rumors of the High Elder on his deathbed. What good does it do, covering for Morgan like this?"

"I am not covering for anyone," Josiah replied. "I am, however, ensuring that we proceed as civilized men, and not guttersnipes scrambling over each other for the scraps that fall onto the kitchen floor."

"The High Elder's seat is no mere scrap," Carpenter said.

"That is very true. But it is also occupied, a fact that seems to continuously slip your mind."

Carpenter's smile widened with genuine amusement now. "Propping a corpse up in a throne will not stop the fight to come, you know. I'm not sure what you think you gain by continuing to play the lapdog to a man whose time has passed."

"I suppose we will have to wait and see," Josiah said.

"I don't wait," Carpenter hissed, his smile slipping from his face. "And I don't play by whatever rules you've convinced yourself we've all agreed to. There is no gentlemen's agreement here."

"I've surmised as much," Josiah said, maintaining his composure.

"I'm glad to hear it. So, you're smarter than you appear," Carpenter said, relishing the opportunity to insult Josiah to his face. "The others may be content not to look beneath the surface, but I know you're no saint, Josiah Hallewell. I won't hesitate to pull back that veneer and reveal you're rotten to your core. I'll keep digging until I find whatever it is that you're hiding."

Josiah felt his smug expression waver. He stepped forward as well, closing the last of the distance between them. Anger burned through his veins, but his voice was calm as he replied. "I'll lend you the shovel," he said. "It will make it so much easier to bury you if you've dug the hole already."

And he walked away, leaving Carpenter white-faced and speechless in his wake. The long walk to his office did not calm his ire. The anger built and boiled over until he reached his office door, managing to shut the door behind him before letting out a roar of frustration. Behind him, a shriek sounded in response and he spun around to find that Brother Goodwin was standing there at his desk, a piece of paper clutched in his hand and a look of pure terror on his face.

"Goodwin! What the blazes are you doing in here?" Josiah shouted, all the angrier for having been taken by surprise in his own office.

"I-I-I'm terribly sorry, sir," Brother Goodwin stammered, his face as white as the envelope he now held out to Josiah. "Y-you asked that I inform you immediately if any news came from a certain quarter, and I—"

Josiah's rage imploded, condensing into a hot pulsing ball of anticipation lodged in his ribs. He charged across the room, snatching the envelope from Brother Goodwin's shaking hand and tearing it open immediately. He stared down at the message, a single word, scrawled in an unpracticed hand.

"Tonight."

23

T HE SUN HAD GONE DOWN and twilight hovered gently over
the city like the ever-present smog. Eliza stood stock still upon
the pavement, watching the figure approach her from the other
end of the street with a mild fluttering of panic under her ribs. Not
until she recognized the swagger of the step and the flash of a lacy
bodice did she feel her body begin to relax.

"Oi there, manor girl," Penny said as she sidled up to her.

"Oi there, yourself, brothel girl," she replied archly. Penny snorted
her amusement and Eliza's nerves unclenched by another degree.

"I've got to make this quick. My shift at Lavender's starts soon.
Was this really the earliest you could get here?"

"Our shifts run at slightly different hours, Penny," Eliza said. "I
got here as quickly as I could."

"Well, come on, then. Let's get this over with," Penny replied, and
Eliza could hear the nerves jangling beneath the girl's defenses. She
was just as nervous as Eliza, although for slightly different reasons.

Eliza had copies of confidential Illustratum documents sewn into
the lining of her cloak, and she was quite keen to get rid of them.
Once she had done so, her concern in the matter of Daniel Byrne was
over. Penny was much more invested and stood to find herself in very
hot water when Madam Lavender discovered Penny had gone behind
her back, for there was no hiding it any longer. Eliza only hoped the
consequences wouldn't be too severe. Despite Penny's best efforts,
Eliza was rather starting to like her.

Side by side, they slipped down the alleyway that led to the kitchen door and knocked. Louise's sharp gaze met them, and then the door opened.

"Sully expecting you?" she grunted.

"No," Eliza said.

"Right, then. She's in the printing room. Have a pasty." Louise replied, pointing a flour-dusted finger at a plate of still-steaming pasties. Her expression was so severe that they dared not refuse, each snatching a pasty off the plate and biting into it. Penny groaned with delight and crammed two more into her pockets at once.

"Can't get food this good at Lavender's," she said through a mouthful of meat and potatoes.

They hastened to finish their food, Penny licking her fingers exuberantly, and then made their way down the stairs into the basement. Voices drifted up to meet them, and they knew that Sully wasn't alone. Eliza knocked gently on the door at the bottom of the stairs and Sully's sharp bark of a voice answered.

"Louise?"

"It's Eliza. And Penny."

"Come on in."

Eliza pushed the door open to see Sully, Eli, Jasper, Cora, and Zeke sitting around the long, low worktable. A small stack of pamphlets sat between them. Eli half-stood, catching Jasper's eye, but then settled again when Eliza acknowledged him with a nod and a smile, trying to reassure him nothing was wrong.

"Well, you two make quite a pair," Jasper said with a chuckle. "Having a poke around the shops, were we? Out for tea?"

Penny cheerfully replied with a hand gesture Eliza had never made in her life, while Eliza wasted no time tearing out the seam in her cloak to retrieve the papers she carried. Without a word, she tossed the papers onto the table. Sully eyed her beadily as she reached for them.

"What's all this, then?" she asked.

"Have a look," Eliza said.

She watched with satisfaction as Sully's eyes widened and her mouth dropped open. "Are these... this can't be—"

"The Praesidio security plans for the day of the wedding," Eliza replied.

Even Jasper forgot to look smug. Everyone at the table stood up at once, crowding around Sully to get a better view of the gift that had just fallen into their laps.

"Bloody hell," Sully whispered.

"Are these originals?" Zeke asked.

"No. I copied them over. The originals have already been replaced, we hope."

Sully's face shot up. "You hope? Don't you know?"

"Well—"

"Eliza, how did you get your hands on these?" Eli cut in.

"I didn't," Eliza said. "This is all down to Penny. I'm going to let her explain it to you."

Every face turned in unison to Penny. Jasper grinned.

"If you tell me you swiped these from some poor blighter's pants while they hung over your bedpost..."

Penny took an aggressive swing at Jasper, who laughed and fell back onto his stool to avoid her fist. The stool toppled over as he overbalanced and fell, still chuckling, to the floor. Cora leaned over and kicked him in the shin for good measure.

Sully was barely paying attention to the mild hijinks that had broken out, too busy poring over the papers like someone had just handed her a lost document from Alexandria. "You don't mean to tell me that Lavender—"

"No!" Penny cried. "No, Lavender didn't... she doesn't know about them yet."

Sully and Zeke exchanged a look. "You sure about that, lass?" Zeke asked.

Penny raised her chin defiantly. "She's a madam, Zeke, not the bloody bollocking Creator." And then, losing a touch of her nerve, "Look, I daresay she'll know soon enough, but I wanted to bring it here first. I wanted to prove how useful he can be."

Sully raised an eyebrow. "He?"

Penny looked at Eliza who nodded encouragingly. "Go on," she whispered.

"His name is Daniel Byrne. He's a Praesidio guard and these documents are a gesture of goodwill. He wants to join the cause."

"So why does Eliza have the documents, then?" Eli asked.

Penny took a deep breath. Within a few minutes, all was told. Not even Jasper dared to crack a joke once the story of Daniel's Riftborn sister hung like a cloud over the room. Eli had gone pale. Sully's voice was sharp with suppressed emotion as she finally broke the silence.

213

"You trust these documents are real?" she asked, directing the question at Eliza.

She nodded at once. "They had official seals on them. And signatures as well."

"He could have forged them," Sully pointed out.

"To what end?" Eli asked.

Sully shrugged. "I don't know. It's just a possibility."

"Yes, well it's also possible they fell out of the sky onto his head, but we don't have to waste time pretending that's very likely," Zeke grunted. "The Praesidio seal their documents with ring seals, and they are unique to the commanders who wear them. Unless this guard stole rings off the hands of his own commanding officers, used them, and put them back without their noticing, I think we can all agree these are real."

"What does Lavender know about all of this?" Sully asked, her eyes narrowing.

Penny lifted her chin defiantly. "I told Lavender about Daniel, right after I met him. I told her I thought he would be able to help us, and I was right!"

"But I don't suppose you told her about any of this madness, did you? Exchanging documents under the nose of the Praesidio? Dragging Eliza into it? I find it hard to believe that Lavender would have allowed any such risks to be taken."

Penny opened her mouth to argue but it was Eliza who piped up first. "She didn't drag me into it! I made my own decision. And for what it's worth, I've met Daniel Byrne twice now, once to take the papers from him and once to return them, and I agree with Penny. I think he's truly on our side."

She expected them to scoff, to continue arguing about the many risks, perhaps even to chastise her for being too foolish or too trusting or too naive. What she didn't expect was for Sully to nod her head and say, "Very well, then. It sounds like he's a risk we are going to take."

Eli and Jasper exchanged looks that said they were just as surprised as Eliza felt. Jasper pulled one of the papers toward him and started examining it eagerly in more detail. Eli, however, stood up and came around the table to Eliza.

"I wasn't expecting to interrupt a meeting," she said, lowering her voice. "Has something happened?"

"We're deciding who to give this first batch of pamphlets to," Eli said, gesturing to the pile of freshly printed paper on the table, now swept aside with the introduction of the security plans. "Lavender's connection Mr. Harlowe is printing most of them, of course, but we decided to treat this first batch from Sully's press as sort of... invitations."

"Invitations?"

"That's right. We'll send them out to hand-selected people, people we think would really not just join the cause, but help us to organize it on the day. It gives us a little more time, you see, to get them all on the same page. Then, in the wee small hours before the wedding, the bulk of the pamphlets will go out to the rest of the Barrens and the Commons."

"The night before the wedding?" Eliza asked.

"Can't do any earlier," Eli said. "There's too good a chance we'll be rumbled and then everything will fall apart before it even has a chance to begin."

"What if someone does warn them? The Praesidio, I mean?"

"We just have to hope that too many gears are already in motion, that it will be too late to halt it all. After all, they won't have the manpower to spare to investigate a threat like that on the day of the wedding. They'll be stretching their resources to the breaking point as it is."

"Aren't you afraid they'll simply cancel the wedding?" Eliza asked.

Eli raised a quizzical eyebrow. "You know Elder Hallewell better than the rest of us. Can you imagine him canceling or even postponing a political alliance of this magnitude?"

Eliza considered for a moment, but there was nothing to consider. There was not a chance that Elder Hallewell would postpone the wedding, not with the High Elder at death's door and the chance of his taking the highest seat. Eli watched the conclusion form on her face and nodded his satisfaction.

"There you have it. The wedding proceeds regardless of whatever nebulous threat makes its way to Praesidio ears on the day. Once the pamphlets go out, there will be no turning back. The crowd that turns up—and whatever they might do in their rage—will be almost completely out of our control."

"That's a scary thought," Eliza muttered.

"Nothing more terrifying than the power of the people," Eli

agreed. "And no one knows that better than the Illustratum itself. They live in terror of the day that they finally reap what they have sown."

Eliza arched an eyebrow. "And you'd like nothing better than to personally serve them that day," she said.

Eli's face split into a grin. "On a silver platter, just like they're accustomed to."

Eliza felt a tap on her shoulder and turned to see that Cora had gotten up from the table and was standing behind her.

"Cora! Hello! How is my mother? I was planning to pop upstairs and see her before I left," Eliza said, giving the woman a hug.

"I was going to send along a message for you tomorrow," Cora said, a contented smile nested between her round apple cheeks.

"A message?"

"The antidote. I've been administering it to your mother and it's made quite the difference in her health," Cora said.

Eliza felt her heart lift, like it had sprouted wings in her chest. "Really?"

Cora chuckled. "Really. I am hopeful we've found something that can help the victims of Riftsickness after all, now that we understand that Riftsickness is simply Riftmead poisoning."

"Can I… is it okay if I go see her?" Eliza asked.

"Of course," Cora said. "Bridie has been keeping her company."

Eliza looked at Eli, who smiled and nodded. "Go on. I'll make your excuses to Sully."

Eliza fairly flew up the stairs and yet hesitated before tapping, ever so lightly, upon the door. She listened, heart fluttering, as a chair creaked, as footsteps crossed the grumbling floorboards. Bridie's face appeared in the crack of the door and her eyes lit up at once.

"Eliza!" she cried in an excited whisper. "I didn't know you were coming tonight! Usually Cora or Sully let me know!" She pushed the door wide enough to fling her arms around Eliza's neck.

"I didn't know myself until the last minute," Eliza said, matching Bridie's whisper. "Cora told me my mother is doing better?"

"Yes, she's made progress!" Bridie said, and then held up a book. "I've been reading to her. Sully's lent me all sorts of books, and this Jane Austen is truly—"

"How is she?" Eliza interrupted. She had not a spare corner in her mind for novels at the moment.

"Well, see for yourself," Bridie said, pushing the door wide.

Emmeline lay with her head upon a stack of pillows, her face peaceful in slumber. Eliza could see an improvement in her immediately. There was color in her cheeks, which seemed a bit less hollow than the last time she had seen her. Her skin no longer looked waxy and sallow, and her expression was a peaceful one, her forehead no longer creased with lines that spoke of pain and exhaustion. Someone had washed and brushed out her hair—it lay around her face like spun gossamer. Her eyes were closed, and her chest rose and fell easily, evenly.

"I don't want to bother her when she's sleeping," Eliza said, feeling suddenly guilty.

"Don't be silly, she'll want to see you!" Bridie said, prodding her in the back so that she stumbled through the door. The little lamp on the bedside table cast a golden pool of light onto the chair in which Bridie had been sitting only moments before. Bridie pulled Eliza by the hand and guided her to the chair. Then, before Eliza could do more than open her mouth to protest, she reached out a hand and brushed a tendril of hair from Emmeline's forehead, speaking as she did so.

"Emmeline, wake up. Eliza's here to see you."

Eliza held her breath as her mother's eyelids fluttered open and her wide grey eyes, familiar and yet clouded, struggled to focus on her. "Eliza?" she whispered.

"Yes, I'm here," Eliza replied, her voice cracking under the assault of more feelings than she could possibly wrangle. "It's me."

"I thought you were a dream. I told myself you were a dream," Emmeline said. It seemed to take every bit of strength she had to keep her eyes open. Eliza caught a glimpse of movement out of the corner of her eye—her mother trying to reach for her hand. She caught up her mother's hand at once, cradling it between her own. Emmeline gave a contented sigh.

"She's still on the sedative tea, but Cora thinks we'll be able to wean her from it soon. There's been an enormous improvement since she started with the antidote," Bridie whispered.

"I can see that," Eliza whispered back.

"I... have so much to... to tell you..." Emmeline said, fighting to pluck each word from the mantle of sleep she was wrapped in.

"And there will be plenty of time for you to tell it to me," Eliza replied soothingly. "Ages and ages together, I promise you."

She said the words not because she knew they were true, but

because they both needed them to be true. But her mother was not content to wait. Emmeline fought the wave of slumber that kept batting at her eyelids, knocking them lower each time.

"The letter... they made me write it... so you would think I left," she mumbled, the words beginning to slur together. "I never... never would have..."

"I know, mother. Please, I understand. Don't exert yourself, you need your rest," Eliza said, reaching out to stroke her mother's forehead. The motion caused her mother's eyelashes to droop right down onto her cheeks.

"Your father... he knew... he..." But sleep overtook her, and she could say no more, her slurred speech slipping seamlessly into quiet snores.

"What was she saying? Something about your father?" Bridie asked, stepping forward to tuck Emmeline's blanket around her.

"I don't know. It doesn't matter right now," Eliza said. She had already decided she could not trust her father with the knowledge that her mother had escaped. It was just one of the many secrets teetering in an ever-growing pile inside her. She only hoped she could keep them hidden until the wedding day.

For then, there would be no secrets anymore. Only consequences.

There was a sharp knock on the door and Eli opened it without waiting for an answer.

"You've got to get home. Something's happened."

Eliza jumped up from her chair, her heart hammering against her ribs. "What is it? What's happened?"

"Colin's just come to tell us all. An Elder was just killed outside Madam Lavender's place."

Eliza's hand flew to her mouth, trying to hold in her horror. "Who was it?" she asked, her fingers snatching at the words, muffling them, but Eli understood.

"We don't know. Penny and Sully have just set off for the Barrens, and Colin's gone with them, to give them cover, just in case. The Praesidio will be swarming the place. But that means you should get home while you still can."

"Yes, of course," Eliza said. She looked anxiously over her shoulder at Bridie, who stepped forward to pull her into a swift hug.

"Be careful," Bridie squeaked, her eyes swimming in fearful tears.

"Always," Eliza replied, trying to give her friend a reassuring smile, but her face felt numb with the same fear that was flooding through the rest of her body. She turned back to Eli and followed him down to the kitchen door.

"When will I see you again?" she whispered as he opened the door to let her out.

He reached out and took her hand, lifting it to his lips and depositing a kiss on the soft underside of her wrist. The touch of his lips made her shiver.

"Unless you hear from me, we will meet again on Saturday night at ten o'clock in the back room of the Bell and Flagon. That gives us three days to get the pamphlets to all our hand-chosen recipients, and to convince them to show up. We may need to discuss another meeting place, further from Lavender's, if things take a turn in the Barrens over tonight's events."

"Won't you find some way of letting me know what's happening?" Eliza begged. She had never more fervently wished that she was free to come and go to Sully's as she was at this moment. Her place at Larkspur Manor felt more like a gilded cage than ever it had.

But Eli smiled. "You're likely to hear more at Larkspur than we are here, but I will try to get a message to you if I can manage it safely. Just try to stay out of trouble until Saturday."

"You as well," Eliza said.

An embrace and one swift, heart-stopping kiss later, Eliza was hurrying down the sidewalk, away from Sully's, when she heard a voice call after her.

"Eliza! Wait!"

Her heart thundered in her ears as she turned, but it was only Jasper jogging toward her. Glancing nervously around, she ran a few steps to meet him.

"Jasper! What is it? What's happened?" she whispered.

Jasper waved her questions away. "Nothing, nothing. Well, nothing new. I need to talk to you."

Eliza took a deep breath to calm herself. "You couldn't have spoken to me while I was inside? You scared me half to death!"

Jasper grinned sheepishly. "Sorry about that. But I needed to get you on your own."

"That seems to be a pattern recently," she muttered, thinking of Penny. "Very well, what is it? And I don't have much time."

"It's this idea I've had, for the day of the wedding," Jasper said, looking much more serious than he usually did. "Everyone keeps going back and forth about the best way to ensure we get a Riftborn on the floor of the Elder Council chamber, and I've had a thought. It's slightly mad, of course, but then again, this whole plan is slightly mad."

"And you need to tell me about this plan alone?" Eliza asked.

"Yes, because it involves you. Or at least, I think that may be the only way it will work," Jasper said. A distant sound of a horse made him glance around. "Let's move into the alleyway here," he added, looking wary.

Safely shrouded in the shadows of the alleyway, Jasper looked earnestly down at her. "Did you mean it when you said that Jessamine Hallewell wants to help our cause?"

"Yes, I did," Eliza replied.

"Just how far do you think she would be willing to go?" Jasper asked.

Eliza bit her lip. "After everything her father has put her through, I think she would do almost anything to help us."

"I'm glad to hear that because this plan won't work unless both of you agree to it," Jasper said.

"Has anyone else heard this plan?" Eliza asked.

"Not yet. There was no point in suggesting it without your approval."

"Why?"

Jasper rolled his eyes. "Because everyone will just say I'm being reckless and ridiculous, as is tradition."

Eliza raised a quizzical eyebrow. "And are you?"

Jasper's smirk faded away. "I don't think so, not this time. But people like Eli won't see it that way."

"Eli? It was my understanding that you've had a fair bit of luck getting him to go along with your more questionable plans."

"Not where you're concerned," Jasper said, a knowing smile tugging at one corner of his lip. "Not anymore."

Eliza felt the heat rising to her cheeks, but hoped the darkness would prevent Jasper from seeing how his words had made her blush. "And what makes you think that I'll go along with this plan, whatever it is?"

"I'm glad you asked, and the answer is twofold," Jasper said.

"First, it ensures that your mistress and Eli's sister are kept out of harm's way. And secondly, it's absolutely bloody brilliant."

Eliza couldn't help but smile. "Very well, Jasper. I'm listening."

24

A BRIGHT GIBBOUS MOON HELD COURT over the
shadowy streets of London as Alexander Carpenter stepped out
to meet the carriage. He took a deep breath of the night air and
held it, savoring it in his lungs before blowing it out again. He didn't
hold with what doddering old men said about the detrimental effects
of the night air. And while it was true that any deep breath within a
stone's throw of the Thames must by reason carry a rather pungent
stench, he did not care. London's night air revived him. It smelled like
the city. It smelled like progress.

It smelled, this evening, like power.

It had been an exceptionally long day, but Alexander was not
tired—in fact, he was downright giddy with exhilaration. His
schemes, dismissed at first as juvenile overreach and political
strutting—all noise and no substance—had, quite suddenly, it seemed,
solidified itself into something much more promising. Josiah
Hallewell's pedestal, upon which he had been so firmly perched for so
long, seemed in imminent danger of toppling, and though Alexander
could by no means be sure that he would be the one to take his place
upon it, still he was gratified.

His father hadn't been able to stomach the man, and Alexander
had inherited that same disdain for him, though not for the same
reasons. His father had detested Josiah's rise to power because he had
wanted to be in his shoes. But if he had been the one at Morgan's right
hand, he would have done very little differently. Alexander's father
and Josiah were part of the old guard, a generation of men content to
do things the way they had always been done, smug and satisfied in

their seats of power with no dreams beyond turning to dust in those same seats.

But Alexander had a vision. He knew the Illustratum's power was still in its infancy. Riftborn magic was cropping up all over the world, and yet the Illustratum had not dared even to discuss the idea of extending their power beyond their borders. A pitiful handful of missionaries whining about the Book of the Rift on European street corners was a poor substitute for true empire building. Their country had once been a global power, extending its reach all across the world, bending other nations to its will. Now, it was closed off, shriveling and decaying, held captive by fear. But Alexander was not afraid. He was ready for the Illustratum to become an international seat of power once again. And he was determined to be at the helm when that vision set sail.

Not that Hallewell was making it easy, but Alexander had never supposed he would. The man was cunning, and he knew how to play the long game better than anyone. His Achilles heel, as Alexander saw it, was in the short term—how to restrategize when there was an unexpected move on the board. Alexander smothered a smile. Despite Hallewell's gambits to maintain control, Alexander had done what he'd hoped: he'd gotten the majority of the Elders nervous enough about the High Elder's health to agree to the drafting of the letter. He had also managed to shorten the time frame within which the High Elder must appear within the walls of the Illustratum. Two days. Forty-eight hours. That was all the time Hallewell was able to buy him. It would not be enough.

Hallewell wasn't the only one with sources on his payroll. Alexander had managed, after some exhaustive digging and a negligible bit of blackmail, to find a nurse within the palace's medical staff who would feed him information. The High Elder was at death's door, and Alexander planned to be right there to hold it open for him. Like the rest of the old guard, Morgan was too stubborn, too tied to pomp and pageantry to skip the official nomination process. If he couldn't show up to nominate Hallewell in person, Hallewell was finished, Alexander was sure of it.

Alexander paused impatiently at the gates while the guard stationed there fumbled with his keys to allow him passage, and then crossed the cobbles to the waiting carriage. He nodded once to the driver, a weathered looking old man who had been driving Illustratum coaches for ages and stepped inside, closing the door behind him.

He closed his eyes, laid his head back against the seat, and wrinkled his nose; the leather upholstery had been recently brushed and oiled, and the sharp tang of it still hung in the air. His body was exhausted, but his mind was racing ahead into the night, outstripping the coach, catapulting him into a fever dream of what could come to pass within the hallowed halls shrinking into the distance behind him. His imagination sparked with vivid images; his own hand tightened on the arm of the High Elder's seat; the view of the palace from an approaching carriage; his daughter Sadie, the belle of every ball; his attendants, blessing his sashes before laying them carefully over his shoulders.

He shook the images away. Daydreaming was all well and good, but he was getting ahead of himself again. Still, he had made great headway this week. Perhaps he deserved a moment or two for a flight of fancy. His meeting with the other Elders behind closed doors had gone much better than he could have hoped. The resentment aimed at Josiah Hallewell ran deep through the benches. He had stepped over many a colleague to reach the place where he now stood, content, it seemed, to simply rest on his laurels and let the highest seat in the country fall into his lap. The man had built the last few steps of his ascent of little more than vain assumptions and a healthy dose of self-congratulatory smugness. But Alexander had been watching and waiting, knowing those last few steps were the most precarious of all. He might not succeed in tipping Hallewell from his pedestal, but the man would be clinging to it for dear life by the time Alexander was done with him, and that was enough for now. Alexander was younger than Josiah by fifteen years. He had time to lie in wait and plot his next move, even if Hallewell did manage to scrape together the support he needed to be named Morgan's successor.

Alexander wondered vaguely if his cook had set aside a plate for him from the dinner that had come and gone hours ago. He was positively ravenous.

An unexpected jolt to the carriage nearly sent Alexander toppling to the floor. "Watch the road, man," he grumbled, more to himself than to the driver. He thought for a moment the old man might have heard him. He could hear his somewhat muffled voice calling out from the driver's bench above.

"What's that?" Alexander called, drawing back the curtain and releasing the catch on the window. A gust of damp foggy air whirled into the carriage, along with a strangled sort of scream. "Hastings?" Alexander called again, his voice a bit sharper now as annoyance gave way to fear. For Creator's sake, the man was ancient. What if he was having an episode up there at the reins?

"Hastings! I say, man, are you quite well?" Alexander called again, this time sticking his head out of the carriage window to try to get a glimpse of the driver. With a shout he pulled himself quickly inside again just as Hastings' face appeared beside the window, bobbing about like a ragdoll, eyes unseeing, a terrible scarlet stain blossoming on his white collar. Hastings mouthed wordlessly, dragging one finger across the glass, leaving a ghastly red streak, and then there was another jolting bump and Hastings dropped to the ground with a sickening thumping crunch from the carriage wheels. Alexander gagged with horror, clapping a hand to his mouth to stop the bile or the scream from rising—he could not be certain of which. The carriage was now barreling down the road at breakneck speed. Surely the horses had been spooked, but what the devil had happened to Hastings?

Alexander slapped himself about the face to force himself to focus. If he didn't get a grip on himself, he would be as good as dead. He had to get control of the horses somehow before they took a corner too sharply and he was dashed to pieces on the ground as surely as Hastings had been. The thought made him dizzy with fear but he struggled to his feet, bracing himself securely against the seat with his feet before pushing the door open.

He caught the merest glimpse of the ground rushing past beneath him before he squeezed his eyes shut, his stomach roiling. His eyelids snapped open again almost immediately, though, at the sound of another voice shouting into the wind. Alexander leaned out as far as he dared, clutching madly at the door frame, and turned his head to peer up at the driver's seat.

It was not empty. A man's hunched figure sat there, snapping the reins and struggling to regain control of the horses. He wore a ragged suit jacket and his hair was unkempt and filthy, but this was not what sent an icy shard of fear through Alexander's already thumping heart.

The moonlight glinted off the edge of a knife the man held clenched between his teeth—a knife already smeared with blood.

226

Alexander flung himself back inside the carriage, pulling the door closed with a snap. He stared around wildly, as though the interior of the carriage might propose some kind of plan to him. What was he to do? His carriage had been hijacked. That man—whoever he was—had just murdered Hastings and taken over the reins, and Alexander had never been in such a precarious position in all of his life.

"Think, Alex, think," he hissed at himself through clenched teeth, slapping his hands against the sides of his head. He slumped back onto the seat. There had to be a way out of this, there simply had to be.

The first thing to discover was where in the bloody blazes they were going. Alexander pulled back the curtain and peered out into the night. The lantern swinging wildly from the coach made his head spin, but he thought he recognized the road. The driver—no, *murderer*, he thought frantically—had taken the left fork at the crossing after the bridge, which meant his carriage was careening not toward his house, but toward the Riftborn districts. Alexander forced himself to take several long, slow breaths. The Praesidio patrolled the streets in the Riftborn districts in much higher numbers than they did in the Dignus neighborhoods. Surely a patrol would see the Illustratum seal on the side of the carriage and realize something was dreadfully wrong. Surely they would help... But even as he said it, he knew it was no good. By the time they caught up to the carriage...

"Pull yourself together, man," he growled to himself. He looked out the window again. The streets were growing less and less familiar. If he didn't jump for it soon, he'd surely become the next victim of the blade clutched in that blackguard's teeth, and yet if he didn't time the jump carefully, he'd probably be dead anyway.

He got to his feet and braced himself firmly in the doorway, wedging his feet up against the bottom of the seats and grasping the handle with one hand while pushing the door open with the other. This time, the sound of the door opening caused the attacker to turn, and Alexander looked him dead in the eyes. The man's face was scarred and poorly shaven, and as he opened his lips to swear, he revealed a mouthful of rotted teeth.

"What the devil are you doing, man? Don't you know who I am? I am an Elder of the Illustratum! Stop this coach and flee, or you will swing from the gallows, I promise you!" Alexander shouted, though the whipping wind stole most of the power from his voice.

The man did not reply except to sneer, a sneer that told Alexander that this man already knew exactly who he was. But before this realization could sink in, the attacker reached a filthy hand down and shoved against the door, slamming it back into Alexander and knocking him backward onto the floor of the carriage. Alexander heard the crack of his skull against the opposite door and his vision bloomed white for a moment as the pain blinded him. Awkwardly, he shifted first to all fours, then to his feet. He felt disoriented and slow even as the adrenaline pumped through him, like a dreamer who finds himself running through sand. There was nothing for it. He would have to jump and pray the man did not give chase. If he could sneer at the fact that he had abducted an Elder, there was nothing he would not do. It did not matter where the coach was now headed; nothing but danger waited for him there. He had to stay in public, had to get someone's attention.

Still frightfully unsteady, he pushed against the other door, but only opened it just enough to peer out of it. He had to take stock of his surroundings and decide where to make his exit. The street had narrowed considerably, the further it twisted and turned through the Riftborn district, and Alexander doubted very much he'd be able to open the door wide enough to escape the carriage while it was moving. Unless he could time the jump while they passed an alley or an intersection with another road...

He peered up ahead, relying on the passing flutter of gaslights to illuminate enough of the dank and darkened street to allow him to see what was coming. Sure enough, just a hundred or so meters ahead, he saw the street corner open wide onto another intersecting road. He bent his knees and braced his hand against the door handle, waiting.

Any moment now. Steady on, old boy, wait for it...

Just as the gaslight on the corner flashed past, he made his move. Holding his breath, his heart thudding like the horse's hooves, he flung the door wide and leaped into the darkness. For a moment there was only rushing wind, and then he hit the ground so hard he might have jumped from a rooftop. He could not even cry out—every bit of breath was knocked from his body as he slammed into the cobbles. He felt his left leg fold under him, heard the snap of his bone like a gunshot just as his left side smashed into the ground. He felt no pain at first, though whether from shock or adrenaline, he could not have said. He stared at his leg for a frozen moment, squinting down at it, sure his eyes were playing tricks on him, sure it could not possibly have been bent at such a dreadful angle.

A clattering of hooves and an angry, echoing shout brought Alexander out of his daze. The pain arrived, blinding him with its intensity even as he craned his neck to see what had become of the carriage. The man had discovered his escape and was frantically attempting to get the horses to stop. Alexander stared wildly around. The doors on either side of the street looked like shops, their doors and windows shuttered. Cursing, he twisted around, craning his neck to see further down the street they had just entered; one building, in particular, was lit up at every window, and as he spotted it, a woman took a man's arm and welcomed him in: a brothel.

Throwing all caution to the wind, Alexander started shouting at the top of his lungs. "Help! Help, please! Someone help me! Murderer! Lunatic! Someone, anyone, please!"

He continued to shout, as the carriage turned around in the road, as his attacker cracked the reins like a whip and the horses exploded out of the darkness toward Alexander, snorting and neighing frantically. Alexander began trying to drag himself out of the middle of the road, but the pain in his leg doubled the moment he shifted his weight and he screamed and wretched with the blinding agony of it. His desperate eyes sought out help or hope of any kind.

From the homes above the shops, faces peeked warily between drawn curtains. Doors remained closed and locked. A few people seemed to have stopped to stare down the road at the brothel, but no one came running to rescue him, not here of all places. *And why should they?* he suddenly asked himself in a moment of perfect, terrible clarity. *What right did he have to their magic or their pity?*

The carriage bore down upon him, the driver's face in the passing gas lamps glowed with a manic light.

Alexander closed his eyes, and his unanswered prayer was silenced upon his lips.

25

Q UIET CHAOS REIGNED IN THE HIGH STREET when Sully and Penny arrived. From their position, carefully cloaked in Colin's shadows, they felt the seismic shift of what had occurred, a vibration of fear and anxiety that chattered every set of teeth and made every heart pound.

Nothing could be seen of the body. It had been covered completely by a length of white fabric, though blood had seeped through it, forming a dreadful map of the man's injuries. Praesidio guards had set up a sort of perimeter in order to keep gawking Riftborn at a safe distance. The music and laughter that usually flooded out of the windows and doors of Lavender's place were absent, replaced by fearful murmurings and ghastly whispers. Snatches of it caught at Sully's hearing.

"…said it was an Elder…"

"…saw the livery on the coach…"

"…rode off like the dickens, sure they'll not catch him now, whoever he is…"

"…will have abandoned that coach, unless he's mad…"

"Of course he's mad!"

"…suppose they'll question people?"

"I'll not stay around to find out. I'm not getting dragged into this."

Guards were indeed questioning people, but they were met with little more answer than shaking heads and shrugging shoulders. Those who had seen it didn't want to speak of it, and those who hadn't had nothing to offer but their own morbid curiosity.

Uneasy about being spotted, Sully and Penny crept around the back of the brothel, thanking Colin for the cover as they did so.

"You get yourself home," Sully ordered, looking the boy square in the eye. "I know there's excitement in these streets tonight, but it's the kind you run from, not the kind you run to, you hear me?"

Colin nodded his head, eyes wide, and scampered off. Sully and Penny slipped through the back door and closed it swiftly behind them.

"Are you coming up to see Lavender?" Sully asked.

Penny grimaced. "I'd rather not face her wrath tonight. No doubt she'll tear me to pieces in the morning."

"What do you want me to tell her?" Sully asked.

"Tell her the truth," Penny said. "She'll listen to you before she'll listen to me. If Daniel has been useful, say as much."

"Right, then," Sully said. Then, with a nagging feeling that she ought to acknowledge the girl's efforts, "You risked a lot, getting those documents. They'll make a real difference."

Penny looked confused but pleased, like she hardly knew how to accept a compliment, which Sully supposed made sense, seeing as how she hardly knew how to give one. They gave each other awkward nods of acknowledgment and then parted ways, Penny headed for the tavern room to find herself a customer, and Sully for the stairs leading to Lavender's office. Lavender's door flew open before Sully could even finish knocking.

"Get in here quickly," Lavender said in a low rumble of a whisper. Sully complied, closing the door behind her.

"Well?"

Sully blinked. "Well, what?"

Lavender pointed a finger at the window behind her. It overlooked the commotion in the High Street. "Did you have anything to do with that?"

Sully's mouth dropped open. "Murdering an Elder? Not bloody likely!"

"And the others? None of them would do something so foolish, would they?"

"Of course not!" Sully cried. "Jasper's a bit rebellious, it's true, but they would never have been involved in something like this."

"They broke into Bedlam without telling you," Lavender pointed out.

"To rescue someone, not to murder Illustratum leaders!" Sully shot back. "For Creator's sake, Lavender, we had nothing to do with this!"

Lavender deflated. Her head drooped into her hands and she sighed. "No. No, of course, you didn't. I don't know why I even—"

"It's because you're scared. On edge. And so are the rest of us," Sully said. "What have you found out?"

Lavender flopped onto her chaise. "Drink?"

"Are you offering or asking me to pour you one?" Sully asked.

"Both?"

Sully crossed to the table where Lavender kept her stash and selected a bottle. She was so shaken she would have drunk Riftmead if that was all that was on hand. Luckily for both of them, Lavender had recently acquired some rather compromising information about a local merchant, and since then, crates of high-quality bootlegged liquor had made regular mysterious appearances on her doorstep. No note, no explanation, just a mutual understanding. One sip, and it was clear why she had kept that information to herself. You couldn't find wine like this outside of a manor house dinner party these days. Sully savored it for a moment in the silence that had fallen between them and allowed Lavender to do the same. Lavender drained half the glass before she spoke again.

"It's Elder Carpenter," she said. "You'll have heard of him."

Sully nearly choked on her wine. "I have. He's the one that's been pushing through all the imperialist nonsense. He wrote that essay in *The Word* last month, didn't he? The one about expanding our military to fight Riftmagic abroad?"

"That's the one. A real nasty piece of work," Lavender confirmed, her nostrils flaring in disgust. "Let me tell you, there are many a man who would love to silence Carpenter, and not all of them are Riftborn."

"Are you telling me you think a Dignus did that?" Sully asked, hitching a thumb toward the window that looked over the continued chaos outside.

"I think there's a good chance the Illustratum itself is responsible," Lavender said, dropping her voice to little more than a murmur so that Sully had to crouch forward on the edge of her seat to catch it. "Word in the High Street is that the carriage that ran him down had the Illustratum seal painted on the door."

233

"And the person driving it?" Sully asked.

"I can't confirm it, but the rumbling suggests Archie Ward," Lavender said.

Sully swore under her breath. Everyone in the Barrens knew about Archie Ward. His name was only ever spoken in a whisper, or else shouted, as a threat. Tangling with him was always a mistake, as many a desperate Riftborn with nowhere else to turn had learned the hardest of ways.

"Surely Archie has more sense than to get involved in the murder of an Elder," Sully said, shaking her head. "He's a devious blighter to be sure, but I wouldn't call him a fool."

"Every man turns into a fool if you dangle enough money in front of his nose," Lavender declared, and it was hard to argue with her.

"If that's the case—"

"Ward will be dead before the week is out if he hasn't already made a break for the border," Lavender said. "Whoever hired him will want to cover their tracks."

Sully knocked back the rest of her drink and stood to pour a second. "This is going to up the security in the Barrens again," she said through clenched teeth. "If the Illustratum is involved, they'll want to cast the blame as far from themselves as possible."

"Which, I expect, is why they hired Ward in the first place," Lavender said. "But you're right. Expect more patrols, more searches, and more arrests. They'll have to make a proper spectacle. That's going to make things harder for you lot."

"Aye, I daresay it will," Sully said. "But we've come too far to abandon the plan now. We'll just have to tread carefully."

"Speaking of treading carefully, Tabby told me Penny arrived with you," Lavender said.

Sully turned. "Did she? Got your girls spying on each other now? Hard to keep the peace that way."

"Don't be daft, she was out in the street when you arrived," Lavender said. "I asked her to keep an eye out for you."

Sully pursed her lips but didn't press the point. It was up to Lavender if she wanted to preside over a building full of bickering alley cats.

"So I take it Penny's told you, then? About the Praesidio guard?" Lavender asked with a sigh.

Sully blinked, but recovered quickly. "How did you know?"

"I saw the look on her face when I told her he wasn't worth the risk, and I knew she was going to take it anyway," Lavender said. "Penny's a good girl, but she's stubborn as all hell."

"She came to me, yes. And she knows I've got to tell you everything."

Lavender cackled. "No wonder she's been avoiding me. I thought she might be drinking. Let me guess: you were afraid she hadn't told me about him." It wasn't a question.

"I wasn't sure. But I knew if she had, you would have done your research," Sully replied.

Lavender raised her glass and gave a knowing wink. "You're bloody right, I have." She reached onto the mantel behind her and lifted down a small leather satchel. She tossed it to Sully, who caught it automatically and unzipped it at once. It was full of documents.

"Dug up everything I could on the lad the moment I had his name," Lavender went on, swirling the wine in her glass. "It's all in there. Full name Daniel Matthew Byrne. Born the eldest child of Matthew and Millicent Byrne. Father was a fairly wealthy Dignus merchant, owned a lovely home in Baker Street. Mother died a few years ago of influenza and the father just recently of heart troubles. Daniel enlisted with the Praesidio at eighteen after he graduated from Eton. His father had political hopes for him and thought a short stint in the military might strengthen his chances of a seat in the Illustratum. Apparently, he was meant to take over his father's shipping business as well, but thus far he has left his father's business partner in charge of things and has shown no sign that he means to run for office, as his father intended. Instead, he seems quite content to remain in the lower ranks of the Praesidio, where he has been using his position to search for this lost sister of his."

Sully paged through the documents as she listened: a military registration form, a doctor's release for service, several business agreements, and a copy of Matthew Byrne's will. "And what of this mysterious Riftborn sister of his? Have you been able to find anything about her?"

Lavender let loose a derisive snort of laughter. "They've covered their tracks well, as far as that goes, but I'd expect nothing less from Dignus with that kind of money and clout. There is a birth announcement in there for the girl, as well as a death certificate. There is also a grave in the family plot. Empty, we must assume, unless they went so far as to procure another body."

"You're sure they didn't just have the girl killed? Plenty of them do, you know," Sully said.

Lavender shook her head. "It appears not. My sources tracked down a servant who used to work for the family. The woman says the child was packed off in the middle of the night, though she could not tell them where. The next day the staff was told the child was ill upstairs, and to stay clear of the contagion. Two days later they were told the child had died. All they saw of her was the tiny coffin being carried down the stairs. When the servant was allowed upstairs again, every trace of the child had been removed. Not an article of clothing, not a toy remained."

Sully swore under her breath and drained her wine glass, holding it out to Lavender, who refilled it at once, her expression unusually somber. She remained silent while Sully finished thumbing through the documents, her eyes flying over the text. Finally, Sully closed the satchel with a sigh.

"What of the soldier himself? Daniel. What can you tell me about him?" Sully asked.

"Well, top of his class at Eton, but seems to have been a bit of a disappointment since. Turned down an apprenticeship in Elder Smythe's office, which ruffled a few feathers. Also foreswore a promotion in the officers' ranks to continue on guard duty. However, it seems he's been using that position as a wall sentry to search for his sister. Multiple requests to visit the Praeteritum archives, which are full of records dating back decades. He's also become well known in the Barrens for flashing the child's picture around in even the most squalid of neighborhoods. He'll be lucky to escape the notice of his superiors if he keeps it up."

"I didn't see a picture of the child in here," Sully remarked, opening the satchel again.

"It seems that the photograph in his possession is the only surviving one. Like I said, the Dignus do a thorough job of covering their tracks," Lavender said.

"All right, then, to the real questions, then," Sully said, fixing Lavender with her most penetrating gaze. "Can we trust him?"

Lavender swirled the dregs of wine left in her glass, considering. "You know me, Sully. I don't suffer fools gladly, and I don't tolerate

236

foolishness from my girls. If you're going to work here, you're going to show me you've got some damn sense. A girl with no sense has no business in my establishment, or in this line of work, for that matter."

Sully nodded her agreement. A girl had to look out for herself, true enough, but some more than others, and perhaps none more so than a girl working at a place like Lavender's.

"Penny has always been one of my most streetwise girls. She's smart, and a damn good actress too, which is probably a girl's most important asset in this business. She's always read people well; she knows when a client needs his ego stroked, and she knows how to extricate herself from messy situations. She doesn't often miscalculate. So as much as I can trust anyone in this world, I trust her."

"But?"

Lavender pressed her lips together. "This Daniel Byrne isn't like the men she's used to dealing with. In the first place, he's not trying to bed her, or hasn't admitted as much yet. He's been respectful and polite. And the fact that he's earnestly looking for a Riftborn girl means he doesn't think Riftborn girls are worthless but for the occasional tumble in the sheets."

"You think he's toying with her?"

"I think he's disarmed her," Lavender clarified. "And I'm not even convinced he's done it on purpose, or that that purpose is nefarious. I just think her defenses are down, and they bloody well shouldn't be."

"That doesn't mean we can't trust him," Sully pointed out.

"That's true enough," Lavender conceded. "But it does mean Penny shouldn't trust herself around him."

"So what are you saying, Lavender? That we shouldn't try to recruit him?" Sully asked.

"I didn't say that," Lavender sighed. "I think the child's gone and fallen for him. I don't think she even knows it yet, but she will, and I'd rather she didn't figure it out while risking her life. Do you catch my meaning?"

Sully nodded. "You want me to keep them apart?"

"I think they'll be better assets to you if they aren't fawning over each other," Lavender clarified. "Use them however you think best, but use them separately."

"Fair enough. And I should tell you that Byrne has taken quite the risk to prove himself trustworthy."

"Is that so?"

"I should say it is. He only went and procured us a copy of the entire Praesidio security plan for the wedding day."

It was a rare phenomenon, catching Lavender by surprise. Sully took more than a little enjoyment from watching Lavender's mouth fall open in shock.

"Well, I'll be damned," she muttered. Then she let out a laugh. "Murdered Elders. Rogue guards. Spying manor girls. My, my, my, the cracks in the façade are certainly beginning to show themselves, aren't they?"

"I just hope they run deep," Sully said.

"Just so," Lavender replied, nodding sagely. "And to that end, I've made some decisions. I've played this game for many years, and the stakes are getting dangerously high. You can taste it in the air tonight, like a storm coming."

Sully narrowed her eyes. "I can't say I'm surprised. Are you getting out, then? After all, you've done all we could ask of you, arranging for the leaflets."

Lavender smiled, a slow blooming smile that spread over her features like molasses, sweet and thick and sticky. "Oh, no, that's certainly not all that you could ask of me. And, no, I'm not getting out. I'm saying, I'm in. All in."

Sully blinked. "Pardon?"

"Come now, old friend. We both know I've got no one to run to anymore—no arms waiting for me. I've no desire to start over again in a new country. The thought of abandoning all I've built here and starting from nothing again is enough to make a woman want to start digging her own grave."

"So... are you saying you want to fight?" Sully asked, watching Lavender closely.

"I'm saying every resource I have is at your disposal. My girls are ready. My network is on high alert. We answer to you now. I'm tired of walking the tightrope, Sully. It's time for a new act," Lavender said.

Sully raised her glass, and Lavender did the same. It was as good as a blood oath.

"To your new act," Sully toasted.

"Light the hoops on fire and find me a lion," Lavender said with a broad grin. "If I'm learning a new act after all this time, I intend it to be a showstopper."

26

THE MESSENGER ARRIVED shortly after midnight. Josiah had expected him, but could hardly imply as much, and so he had changed into his night clothes, gotten into bed, and stared at the canopy of dark fabric above him, waiting for the inevitable knock on the door, the shuffling of servant footsteps upon the stairs, and the tentative calls to rouse him that drifted through his keyhole. He played his part, shouting for his carriage, dressing in haste, and setting off for the Illustratum again in record time. No man watching his performance would have dared to suggest it wasn't genuine, but Josiah knew it was only a dress rehearsal for the performance he would have to give among the Elders. That was the only audience that mattered tonight.

The Praesidio were in an uproar as the carriage pulled up. He had to step out, and every inch of the carriage was searched and his own driver questioned before Josiah could even be allowed beyond the gates. He submitted to it all silently, hiding his impatience behind a solemn and resigned exterior. He thanked the Commander for his diligence and requested a report from leadership upon his desk as expediently as possible.

He bypassed the Elder Council chamber, the doors of which were flung wide, a proscenium framing the performative chaos within. Josiah could have sat down right there and watched it all unfold with no small amount of satisfaction, but he kept walking. He knew Brother Goodwin would be waiting for him and sure enough, as he rounded the corner into the corridor where his office was located, he saw

Goodwin pacing in front of the door, his round face pale and dewy with mounting anxiety.

"At last!" he heard Goodwin murmur as he scurried toward him. Josiah stilled him with a look and pointed to his office. Blushing to the roots of his hair, Goodwin took the hint and opened the door, stepping back and folding himself into a ridiculous bow as Josiah swept past him. Josiah glared at him until the door was closed carefully behind them.

"Well?"

"Elder Carpenter is dead, run over by the Illustratum carriage he traveled in. The driver was overpowered, it seems, and the carriage was stolen with Elder Carpenter still inside. The carriage was driven off course into the Barrens. Elder Carpenter attempted an escape by leaping from the carriage in the High Street, but his assailant turned the carriage around and…" Brother Goodwin's voice trailed off, his bottom lip wobbling like a child's.

"And the assailant?" Josiah pressed.

"Has thus far eluded the Praesidio's attempts to find him," Brother Goodwin chirped at once. "The leadership has a description from bystanders, but it was dark and the carriage was moving quickly. Witnesses have been very… hesitant to cooperate with the soldiers who are investigating the incident."

Josiah smothered a smile. "Thank you. Has a time yet been set for the Elders to formally—"

"All Elders are requested in the chamber in twenty minutes," Goodwin replied, consulting a fussy little pocket watch for accuracy.

"Thank you, Goodwin," he replied, crossing to his desk and removing a sealed envelope. "I require that you see this is delivered directly."

Brother Goodwin hesitated, dabbing at his face with an already damp handkerchief.

"Goodwin," Josiah repeated, holding out the envelope.

Brother Goodwin opened his mouth and closed it again, his eyes alight with unspoken doubts. He looked down at the envelope as though he thought it might explode.

Anger flared inside Josiah, and he had to clench his teeth around his next words to hold it back. "Am I to understand it is your intention to make me ask you again?"

What little color was left in Goodwin's face drained away and he hurried forward to snatch the envelope from Josiah's hand. Josiah held onto it a moment longer than necessary, holding Goodwin's eye, warning him, before letting it go. Goodwin practically ran from the room. Josiah watched him go, and the brief flare of satisfaction he felt at being obeyed twisted into something ugly and heavy. For the first time, it seemed Goodwin had obeyed him not out of loyalty, but fear.

It was something of a nasty shock that the realization had given him tangible pleasure.

Josiah leaned against his desk, staring into the cold dregs of the evening's fire. From the moment the messenger had arrived at his door, he had been waiting to feel something—anything at all—about the death of Elder Carpenter. At first, there were too many other thoughts crowding his brain; he needed to hurry, he needed to appear shocked, he needed to look grim, he needed to decide what to say and to whom, he needed to deflect suspicions if there were any cast in his direction. Now that he had arrived at the Illustratum, now that he stood in the quiet and the dark, he felt... nothing.

No remorse. No regret. No sadness. No shame. Simply... nothing.

His mind probed tentatively at the edges of this empty space, and then pushed it away. He could not wallow in self-reflection now. There was too much to be done, too many schemes in motion. If he lost his focus now, his grand plans—the Creator's plans for him—could all come to nothing. He could not let that happen.

The minutes ticked by. Josiah shrugged into his procedural vestments. Goodwin had laid them out for him, along with a band of shiny black material that was to be worn around his arm. A mourning band, in honor of Carpenter. Josiah slid it on over the sleeve of his robe, straightened it, and started for the Elder chamber.

At the end of the hallway, he passed Francis' office. The door was open, and Josiah heard him clear his throat from inside. He backtracked and peered inside to see Francis standing with his back to the door, staring out the window into the dark city below.

"Francis?"

Francis didn't turn. He didn't reply. Josiah tried again, more loudly this time.

"Francis, are you going down to the chamber?"

Francis still did not turn. But he spoke.

"Is this what it's come to, Josiah?"

"I'm sorry?"

241

Francis turned and looked his friend in the eye, and the look burned away any pretense between them. "How did we get here?" he asked.

Josiah swallowed back his denial. What would be the point? Finally, he answered quietly, "I hardly know."

"You should have come to me."

Josiah hesitated. "Perhaps so."

"I want no part in it, do you hear me? Tell me nothing, so that I don't have to lie when they come asking me questions."

"They won't."

"They bloody well better not. And I will have no part in cleaning it up, either, do you hear me? This is your mess."

"There will be no mess, I assure you," Josiah said, thinking of the letter he had just dispatched with Brother Goodwin.

"I don't want your assurances," Francis said. "They have lost their luster."

Josiah pressed his lips together and let the comment pass. "Will you come down?"

"I will," Francis said. "But not with you. You will walk into that room and you will face this the same way you created it: alone."

"You think there will be accusations?" Josiah asked, somewhat incredulous.

"Not out loud."

"They would not dare," Josiah muttered.

"After what you have dared, Josiah, who is to say anymore what they might dare? You cannot expect them to follow rules of decorum when you've lit the rule book on fire."

He did not sound angry, or even resentful. He sounded tired. Josiah reached down into himself, looking for the frustration, the anger to defend himself and his actions, but the well seemed dry, and he came up empty. What could he say? He had made his own choice. Francis was entitled to make his. Still, he could not help but ask, "This Sunday, Jessamine and Reginald's Purification Ceremony. You will still preside?"

Francis looked at him for a long moment. "If I refuse, does that make me your enemy, Josiah?"

"Of course not! Surely you know me better than that," Josiah scoffed.

"Yesterday I would have said the same, Josiah. But today I'm half-convinced that I don't know you at all."

Francis turned back to the window and Josiah, recognizing the dismissal, walked to the Elder Council chamber alone.

§

All of the lights were on in the servants' quarters when Eliza arrived back at Larkspur Manor. The arrival of the messenger had roused half the house and now a handful of servants sat huddled around the scrubbed wooden table, hands clutched around cups of tea gone cold, heads bowed together, whispering in the candlelight. Eliza spotted them through the window as she passed, but she did not stop. As far as the rest of the staff knew, Eliza was up in Jessamine's quarters at her mistress' request, and she could not very well stroll in the back door without a proper explanation, desperate as she might be for news about the killing in the Barrens. Instead, she crept quietly in through the service entrance near the pantries, skirted the kitchen by a back corridor, and slipped up the warren of servant staircases to the third floor, where a door hidden in the paneling opened onto Jessamine's corridor. It was silent and dark, the only light crept its pale-yellow fingers underneath the door to Jessamine's quarters. Eliza pushed the door open and found Jessamine perched on her settee by the windows. At first glance in the wavering firelight, she appeared to be sitting upon a cloud, but Eliza blinked and the fanciful image folded in on itself, revealing the cloud to be nothing more than a pile of white fabric gathered in Jessamine's lap.

"Miss Jessamine?" Eliza's voice was tentative in the silence.

Jessamine looked over at her, and her face, for a moment, looked like that of a lost and bewildered child. "Eliza! Thank goodness you're all right! I wondered..." Her voice trailed away.

"Of course I'm all right," Eliza said, trying to smile. "Why wouldn't I be all right?"

Jessamine frowned. "Eliza, I may be the sheltered daughter of an Elder, but I'm not a fool. I know it's dangerous when you leave here at night."

Eliza sighed. "Of course. I'm sorry, miss. I don't mean to... you're right. It is dangerous. But I am very careful."

"Is it true, what the servants are saying?" Jessamine asked. "They are saying an Elder was killed in the Barrens. My father left in a rush."

"Yes, it is true," Eliza said. "I wasn't in the Barrens when it happened, but word reached us and I hurried home."

Jessamine looked Eliza directly in the eye. "Did your friends have anything to do with it?"

Eliza had expected the question and was relieved that she could answer it truthfully. "No, I can promise you they did not."

Jessamine closed her eyes for a moment, breathing out slowly, and then turning back to the window. "Do you know who it was?"

"I do not."

"I'm not sure what I'm meant to feel," Jessamine said, still talking to her own pale reflection in the window. "I suppose I'm scared. Something is coming, and it needs to come, it needs to happen, but it will not come peacefully or quietly. People will get hurt and die. I haven't wanted to think of that part of it, but now it's arrived, and I've no choice."

Eliza ventured a few steps across the room. "I understand what you mean. I've been struggling with that myself." She stared down at the pile of white fabric around Jessamine's body and started. "Miss Jessamine, what… is that…?"

Jessamine looked down at where Eliza's finger was pointing and looked, for a moment, almost surprised to see the cloud of white fabric around her. "Oh. Yes. It's a wedding dress."

Eliza frowned. "I don't— your dress is still at the dressmaker's, is it not?" She knew she had been exhausted and overwhelmed with her double life, but she was quite sure she would have remembered the wedding dress being delivered.

"It's not my dress. It's my mother's," Jessamine said quietly. Eliza watched her hands run over the fabric and noticed for the first time that it was quite tattered and torn apart, edges fraying, lace trailing.

"What's… happened to it?" Eliza asked.

Jessamine let out a shaky sigh. "It was the dressmaker's idea. She thought we could take some of the embellishments from my mother's dress—some beading perhaps, or some lace, and work it into my own dress. You were off running errands, so I asked Liesel to bring it down and unpack it for me."

"And this is what it looked like?" Eliza asked, venturing to perch herself on the very corner of the chaise. Her fingers longed to touch the tattered dress, the sight of it making her heart ache, like seeing a wounded animal.

"Oh, no," Jessamine said, her voice strangely hollow. "No, it was pristine. But I put it on, you see. I decided to practice what it would be like, to stand there in the dress, to walk down the aisle of the Illustratum, to promise myself to—" She swallowed hard. "I thought if I practiced, perhaps it wouldn't be so bad. Perhaps I could convince myself that I could go through with it if I had to."

"Miss Jessamine, you won't have to. I've told you, we'll find a way out of this," Eliza said, trying to sound soothing.

But Jessamine closed her eyes, and two fat tears rolled out from beneath the curtain of her lashes and dropped heavily onto the fabric clutched in her hands. "I know you've told me that before, and I'm trying to trust you, to trust that you have a plan and that it will work, but—"

"It *will* work," Eliza said.

"You can't know that. No one can, for certain," Jessamine said, shaking her head as though Eliza's placations were attacking her. "And so I wanted to try... to see myself as the bride I might be. And I... I..." she gestured helplessly down at the dress, and Eliza understood. Jessamine had torn the dress to tatters with her own two hands.

"It's all right," Eliza said. "It... it doesn't matter. No one needs to know."

"I destroyed my own mother's wedding dress," Jessamine whispered. "What is wrong with me?"

"Nothing is wrong with you!" Eliza said firmly. "If your mother could have gotten her hands on it, I daresay she would have done the same."

Jessamine looked startled. "What do you—"

"Miss Jessamine, I am asking you to trust me, for just a few more days, and then I promise I will tell you everything. I am only trying to keep you safe, but to do it, I've had to keep you in the dark, and darkness does not feel safe to the person who has to maneuver through it. I know it is hard to trust in anything anymore, but I am begging you to trust in me."

"I'll try, Eliza," Jessamine whispered, taking another deep, shaking breath.

"I'm glad to hear it," Eliza replied, a businesslike snap returning to her voice as she reached forward and gathered up the remains of the dress. Jessamine allowed it to slip through her hands. "Don't worry about this dress. I shall salvage what I can from it and send it along to the dressmakers tomorrow. In the meantime, I want you to get some sleep if you can."

"Will… will you stay with me?" Jessamine asked, her voice small, childlike, as though she was half ashamed to make the request aloud.

"Of course I will," Eliza said, and she reached out a hand. Jessamine took it, and Eliza led her over to her bed, holding back the coverlet so that she could climb in and then tucking it gently around her. Then she piled the remains of the dress into a chair, unlaced her boots, and climbed up onto the bed as well. Jessamine rolled her head onto Eliza's shoulder with a contented sigh. Eliza stroked her hair, humming an old Riftborn lullaby under her breath, trying to remember the words.

Her mother had sung it to her…

Such a long time ago…

Both girls were asleep before a single word of the melody could find its way to her tongue.

27

T HE FOLLOWING TWO DAYS PASSED with agonizing
slowness. Eliza had never been so anxious and distracted. She
slept fitfully and could not concentrate. She would stop in the
middle of hallways, having forgotten what she was doing and where
she was going. She left tasks abandoned on tables and forgot to come
back to them. Liesel and Mrs. Keats both had to scold her for absent-
mindedness. If Jessamine had not been party to the great heaping pile
of secrets she was keeping, Eliza was quite sure she'd have been out
of a job. As it was, both young women were doing their best to hold
each other together while trying not to fall apart themselves.

The news of Elder Carpenter reached them the morning after his
murder. Eliza, who knew nothing of the man, felt the knowledge but
little. Jessamine, however, seemed greatly rattled by it. She was well-
acquainted with Sadie Carpenter, after all; and though she detested the
girl, still she dwelt with great distress over the news that Sadie had
lost her father, a feeling no doubt amplified by the guilty knowledge
that she had never been very friendly with Sadie. In an effort to avoid
thinking about her upcoming wedding, now only a week away, and
also to assuage some of her own guilt, Jessamine arranged with the
rest of her charity circle to meet and assemble flowers and gifts to
be delivered to the Carpenter home. She set out on Saturday evening
in the carriage, having notified her father of the plan and receiving
his permission to go. He had been home barely an hour since the
messenger had brought news of the murder, but had left strict
instructions that Jessamine was not to leave Larkspur Manor without
his express approval. Eliza saw her off with a sense of relief, knowing

247

that Jessamine would be occupied with something constructive to do while she herself had somewhere else very important to be.

Eliza knew that this was the night that would make or break all of their plans. The pamphlets had gone out to the select group of Riftborn that the Resistance had wanted to recruit. Zeke, Eli, Jasper, and the others had done all the coaxing, prodding, and convincing they could manage, but none of them were very confident about who, exactly, would show up in the end. Eliza had heard very little from them, agreeing that correspondence should be limited due to the number of extra patrols out in the streets and around Larkspur Manor. And so, as she arrived at the back door of the pub and knocked quietly, she held her breath and waited, hoping. Eli's face appeared at the crack of the door before he swung it wide to admit her.

"Thank goodness you made it," he said. His face looked strained, his eyes tired. It had been a couple of days since he had shaved, and a shadow of stubble darkened his jawline.

"Of course I made it," she answered briskly. "Of all the things you should be worrying about right now, I am not one of them. I can look after myself."

Eli smiled. "Of course you can. I apologize if I sounded like I was underestimating you. It was not my intention, I assure you."

"You're forgiven," Eliza said with a smile that folded almost immediately back into a scrunched-up frown of concern. "Has anyone shown up? Please, please tell me that at least someone has shown up after all you've done to recruit them."

Eli's face was inscrutable. "See for yourself," he said, gesturing down the narrow hallway to the room beyond. Eliza inched past him, placed a hand on the door, and pushed.

The room was packed to the rafters. People had crammed themselves into every available seat and stood three deep all around the walls. Still more people had perched themselves on top of crates, whiskey barrels, and upturned buckets. As she scanned the room, Eliza saw that every face was tense and anxious, and aside from the occasional hiss of a whisper, the room was almost completely silent. Eliza turned and looked at Eli, who smiled tightly. It seemed as though every person they had recruited had turned up and, by the look of it, not a single one of them had come alone. Taking her hand, Eli guided Eliza through the crowd to the table at the center, where Sully, Zeke, Cora, Seamus, Jasper, and Bridie waited, huddled together in a knot. Eliza pressed in beside Bridie who reached down and slid a cold, work-roughened hand into hers and gave it a welcoming squeeze.

"I'm still not sure about this," Sully was saying as they joined the group. Her eyes behind her spectacles were surveying the room anxiously. "This is a lot of folks."

"We need a lot of folks, Sully," Jasper said, gritting his teeth in an effort to hide his exasperation.

"I know, but even so..."

"This was your idea!" Jasper cried, giving up on restraint. "You were the one who said we needed to recruit! You were the one who said we've reached a tipping point and we need to grow to meet the moment or miss our chance!"

"This is more people than we agreed upon. There are more people here than just the ones you handed those pamphlets to," Sully hedged.

"We told them to bring anyone they trusted to be sympathetic to the cause," Eli said patiently, his tone a calm counterpoint to Jasper's frustration. "We discussed that as well. Don't you see that this is a good thing? We needed bodies, and we've got them!"

Sully's hands were twisting in her lap. "I suppose you've realized that any one of these people could leave this place tonight and go straight to the Praesidio to turn us in. Unless, of course, you're counting on it for a little excitement," she said, her tone acidic.

"Of course I have!" Jasper said. "We all have, and not because we're hurting for excitement. I think we can all agree Bedlam was excitement enough. But listen to yourself, even if you won't listen to me. For once, we were all in agreement. The time has come to take the risk! We won't have a better chance than this."

"He's right, Sully," Eli replied, his voice quiet but firm. "And if John Davies was here, he'd tell you the same thing."

"If he weren't six feet under," Sully murmured.

"Don't you dare, Lila Sullivan" Zeke said, his usually boisterous voice unexpectedly gentle. "Davies didn't regret what he gave for the cause and you know it."

The sound of her full name seemed to startle Sully, and her face snapped up so that she met Zeke's eye. He simply nodded at her, and it was as though the spell that her fear had cast on her was broken in that instant. She pulled herself up, and something hardened in her face—something very like resolve. She turned to Eli, in full command of herself once again.

"You spoke to Penny, didn't you?" she asked Eli.

"Yes," Eli replied. "She agreed not to bring the soldier to the meeting. She understands that people would panic. And she's agreed to act as the messenger, communicating all plans to him, as well as to Lavender. She should be here soon."

"Right. Well, then. I suppose we'd better get started," Sully said, almost to herself.

Zeke clapped her heartily on the back. "The longer we wait the more restless this crowd is going to get. It's time."

Something shivered through the group at his words, a shared understanding. This was the moment at which there was no turning back. The fuse could not be unlit.

When Sully spoke again, it was to the gathering crowd, and her tone was commanding. Beside her, Eliza could feel the tension rolling off of Eli's body in waves. His fingers twitched, as though he longed to reach out and shatter a glass with his Riftmagic, just to relieve a modicum of the tension. Catching her eye, he shoved his hands into his pockets.

"Right, well, let's get started. Everyone sit down and shut it. Things are really heating up in the Barrens and we haven't got time for chitchat."

The room fell silent, the tension settling over everyone like a blanket, muffling the whispering and rustling. Every eye in the place that wasn't fixed expectantly on Sully was darting around suspiciously, taking in the faces of the other people who had risked their safety to be there. Sully seemed to decide she wasn't visible enough, and hoisted herself up to stand on a chair with a quiet groan.

"There are a lot of new faces in this room tonight," Sully said, addressing the obvious. "And there are some old faces as well, faces I wasn't sure I'd see here again. I don't know if you'll want to stay after hearing what I've got to say, and that's grand. I only ask that, if you choose to walk away, you do so with your mouth bloody well shut. You don't have to join us, but neither can you speak freely of what you hear tonight without the expectation of repercussion. Believe me when I tell you that we will be looking out for ourselves, and for each other. That's the only warning I'll be giving you on that score, so I suggest you remember it."

No one spoke. A few people shifted uncomfortably. Eliza could feel the weight of the silent decisions being made pressing down upon them in the flickering lantern light. Sully seemed to feel it, too. She allowed the silence to stretch, for her words to sink beneath everyone's skin before she continued.

"Many of you have questions. I'd like to try to address some of them now, before we dig into the real substance of this meeting," she said, pausing a moment to set the tip of a lighted match to the leaves packed into the bowl of her pipe. She sucked it with relish for a moment, blew a smoke ring, and continued. "To those of you who are wondering about the pamphlets: yes, it's all true. That text came directly from the official records of the Illustratum itself. They were obtained by stealth from the desks of the very doctors using the stuff in Riftwards, workhouses, and asylums all over the country."

Her words created a ripple of muttering. She let it die out before continuing.

"I'm not going to ask you to take my word for it. I simply want you to look back over the last month, during which the Illustratum has been supplying the Riftborn of this city with additional Riftmead. I'm sure it was a welcome gift, at first. I'm sure many of you thought of it as a stroke of good fortune, a blessing even. After all, life is hard in these streets, and a drink at the end of the day is a welcome respite, especially when that drink is given from on high, as it were. But now I want you to think for just a moment and answer me this: how have you been feeling since?"

And she blew another smoke ring while she waited out the murmuring and uncomfortable shifting of feet and clearing of throats.

"Noticed a bit of trouble, have we, with our Riftmagic? Responses a bit slow? Minds a bit cloudy? Have to work a bit harder to get through your day?"

In the corner of the room, a young woman's eyes were shining with unshed tears as she dandled a baby on her hip. Surreptitiously, she worked two of her fingers together, eyes narrowed. At last, she coaxed the tiniest of sparks from one fingertip, a single flash that was gone before it could flare. Then she looked up at Sully again, eyes bright not with tears anymore, but with understanding.

"That's right," Sully said, reading the room. "That's what they've done to control you. They're not trying to save your souls. They fear your magic. All they're trying to save is themselves and the power they cling to. Riftmead is a lie. We've proven it. And you've all felt it for yourselves."

251

Sully turned and jerked her chin at Bridie, and Bridie, recognizing her cue, stood up, shaking from head to toe like a leaf in the wind. Sully acknowledged her with a flick of her wrist, and Bridie spoke.

"My name is Bridie Sloane. What Sully's telling you, it's true. I was sent to Bedlam and they used Riftmead on all the patients, including me. Several times a day they were forcing us to drink it, and in greater quantities. Within a week I was sicker than I'd ever been in my life, and couldn't produce even a spark."

"Isn't she one of those holier-than-thou manor girls who's always handing out baskets?" a shrill voice called from the far corner.

"Aye, that she is. I recognize her!" another voice chimed in.

"Strange company you keep these days, Sully. What is she doing here, wallowing in the gutters with the rest of us? What can she possibly know about our life here that hasn't been fed to her on a silver spoon by the Elders themselves?" the first voice called again.

There was a rumble of agreement. Bridie sat back down smartly, dropping her eyes to her lap, but Sully's voice broke over the crowd, a clarion call.

"Yeah, and I want you to think on that. A manor girl, one of the chosen few who hasn't had to drag herself up in a place like this. A lifetime of obedience and licking Dignus boots from dawn to dusk, and where does that land her? If they can do that to a manor girl without batting an eye, imagine what they could do to the rest of us, if they took the notion?"

"And they have taken that notion. I'm living proof."

The voice was quiet but strong. There was mettle in it that turned every head in search of the speaker. Even Bridie ventured to raise her beet red complexion to seek out who had taken up the thread.

"And if you don't want to take a manor girl's word for it, you can take mine." Every eye was upon the lanky, rail-thin man as he struggled and grunted his way to his feet. A tiny woman stood beside him, her arm wrapped around his waist, endeavoring to help take some of his weight. She looked at him with the kind of fierce pride that stole Eliza's breath from her lungs. Beside her, she thought she heard Jasper swear under his breath, but when she ventured a glance at him, his expression was smooth.

"Many of you know me, though I doubt you thought you'd ever see my ugly mug again," the man went on with a rusty attempt at a smile; the effort looked painful. "For those of you who don't, my name is Peter Neill, and I've lived in the Barrens all my life. Grew up right over in Butler Street as a lad, and if you had a cart in the High Street, it's likely you had to chase me off with a broom and tell me off for nicking something. I got meself on the straight and narrow, though, when I'd grown. Worked as a bricklayer, finally making something of meself. And then last year, I tried to break up a fight down the pub in Harrow Street and wound up getting arrested instead. Thought I'd have to spend a night or two in a Praesidio holding cell until I could get things sorted out. Imagine my surprise when they locked me up in Bedlam instead. I kept screaming for someone to let me out, that it was a mistake. But no one listens to you in a place like that. No one cares."

The rapt quiet that followed was broken only by the cracking of a log in the fireplace. Peter adjusted his hand on the cane he was using to help keep himself upright.

"Everything they told you in those pamphlets is true. Force fed Riftmead three times a day, I was, sometimes more. I was healthy as an ox when they arrested me last year. Now look at me—a cripple what can't hardly hold a trowel anymore, never mind lay bricks. And if it wasn't for that fire, I'd have died in that place. Tillie never would have known what happened to me." He looked down at the tiny woman who smiled back at him, her eyes fierce with love and pride. "There's a lot what can be said about Peter Neill, but there's not a man what knows me that can call me a liar. The manor girl speaks the truth. The pamphlets, too. If you ain't sure where you stand, if you ain't sure you want to fight, ain't no one goin' to blame you. But you all deserve to know what side the truth lies on, at least. If you stand with Sully, you stand with the truth, and that's not nothing."

The effect on the room was immediate. Where moments before there had been a constant undertone of skepticism, now there had fallen a quiet heavy with understanding and fear. Eliza realized that many of the people in the room had come to this meeting hoping to be told that the rumors they'd been hearing were false or exaggerated. They had hoped to walk away having disproven the unsettling evidence that their eyes and ears had been presenting to them over the past weeks and months; that not all was as it seemed with the Illustratum. But now Peter's admission had sucked all of that hope from the room, and in the vacuum that remained, everyone was looking around as if to say, "Well, now what do we do?"

And Sully, hearing the unspoken question, was ready with an answer. "Do you see it now? Each time we get close to exposing the truth, the Illustratum works twice as hard to bury that truth. It was only a few months ago that we flooded the Barrens with books— books explaining the truth about what the Dignus do to Riftborn children born into their own families. I thought that information alone would have been enough to start a rebellion from every corner of the Barrens, but no. The Illustratum was a step ahead of us, distributing enough Riftmead to dull any minds we'd managed to sharpen. But no more."

She reached onto the fireplace mantel behind her and grasped a dusty brown bottle by its neck, raising it high into the air. The candlelight glinted off the golden seal of the Illustratum pressed onto the label. "Every home in the Barrens has had bottles like this delivered for weeks now. Have you been drinking it? Perhaps even giving it to your children? How does it feel to know that you were poisoning yourselves and your families, dulling your own magic and damaging your bodies, all so that the Elders could sleep more soundly in their great estates? Would anyone like a swig now?"

She offered the bottle around the room. No one wanted to go near it.

"Are you calling us stupid, then?" a cantankerous voice bellowed from somewhere near the door. "What the bloody hell else is a man supposed to drink around here? What else is there?"

"I'm not calling anyone stupid, so don't you be putting words in my mouth, Samuel Barber!" Sully barked back, narrowing her eyes at the round-bellied man who was scowling back at her, arms crossed over his barrel-like chest. "This isn't a matter of intelligence. This is a matter of being lied to. Manipulated. Poisoned and repressed by tiny men who fear gifts they cannot understand because they do not possess them."

"If people are getting sick, it's merely Riftsickness. Their souls are blackened with sin," another man proclaimed boldly.

"It is Riftsickness all right," Sully shot back. "Sickness, caused by Riftmead. Just ask yourself, if Riftmead is supposed to cleanse you, bring you closer to the Creator, if that were truly its purpose... then why would drinking more of it make you sicker?"

"That Riftmead is blessed by the High Elder, and the Creator himself!" came a quavering voice, a woman's this time.

Sully opened her mouth to reply, but it was another, deeper voice that rang out instead. "That Riftmead," Jasper said, standing up so everyone could see him, "came off a wagon from a bottling factory in Yorkshire. I know, because I followed the wagon, and I watched the men offload the crates. They were delivered to the Praesidio barracks, where they were heaped onto carts and delivered to your homes. At no point did the High Elder come anywhere near those bottles. They've never seen an altaria or even the inside of a church. No Elder, High or otherwise, has ever laid a finger on them. And as for the Creator, well..." he snorted derisively, '...unless He's on holiday in a Yorkshire bottling factory, I think it unlikely He's had a hand in it either."

Zeke suppressed a snort of laughter under the ensuing wave of muttering. Eliza felt like she could see the tide in the room turning; their fear of the truth was being overtaken by the strength of that truth.

"So what if it did?" another voice called, belonging to a young man with a bulbous nose and a scraggly mustache. "What are you proposing we can do about it?"

"You can stop bloody drinking it, for a start," Sully said. "Don't take my word for it. See for yourselves what happens if you take every drop of Riftmead in your house and pour it straight out."

"That's sacrilege!" a woman cried.

Sully raised an eyebrow. "And poisoning people is the Lord's work, is it?"

The woman did not respond.

Sully sighed, clunking the bottle of Riftmead down on the table. "Friends, I can't convince you of something you don't want to believe. I can only tell you what I know to be the truth and hope you'll have the sense to see it. If you want to walk out of this pub tonight and forget everything I've told you, I'll not try to stop you. Creator knows I wish it wasn't true. But denying the facts won't make them disappear. The Illustratum are poisoning you... poisoning your children... because they fear your magic. Fear. That's all it is. Now, I say we bloody well give them something to fear. I say we stand up. Stand up and say no more. If you don't want to stand with us, we'll understand. Go home, and bury your heads. But if you've had enough of the shame and the guilt and the lies and the poison, stay. Join us."

Eliza had hoped for a ringing cheer, but silence followed. These people were torn—torn by the very real fear that they would lose more than they could possibly gain—that the cost would be too high. And

255

Eliza could not blame them. She had lost so much already, and would surely lose a great deal more before this was all over. But what choice did she have? She couldn't continue on, not now that she knew the truth.

A woman stood up. Her face was flushed, but set. A small child clung to her skirts, yawning sleepily. She placed her hand on the child's head, anchoring herself. "What if we do decide to join you?" she asked, and there was no trembling in her voice. "What is it we'll be expected to do?"

It took Sully a moment to answer; her eyes had fallen on the little boy and a lump seemed to come into her throat. She cleared it harshly. "First, I ask you to stop drinking the Riftmead. If you do nothing else, please, for your own sakes, stop drinking it."

The woman looked down at her child and nodded. "We can do that. But surely that's not all?"

"Spread the word," Sully said. "To everyone you know. Tell them all the Riftmead is tainted. That it's making them sick. Keep telling them until they believe you."

"And if they don't?" a man asked.

Sully shrugged. "Then they don't. We can't save everyone, and I'm not trying to sell you a fantasy that we can. Some Riftborn will choose the Illustratum over their own lives, and never look back."

It was a grounding, sobering thought, but it was true. Not everyone would believe them. Many would go on poisoning themselves. It could not be helped. Fear worked in both directions, and the Illustratum inspired as much fear as it fed upon.

"Look, if the Illustratum is telling you the truth, then it means that the Creator put you on this earth to be poisoned, shamed, and exploited. Only you can answer for yourself if you really believe that's true. But I can tell you that I've made it my life's work to understand what's going on in the world outside of our borders. I've read countless books from as many countries as possible, and there are places all over this earth where Riftborn are not treated like the dirt beneath the Dignus boot. They are holding office and teaching at universities and working as doctors, lawyers, and inventors. They are thriving, contributing to their communities with their gifts, and living in freedom. And yet, with all the books and newspapers I've consumed, I've yet to read a word about the Creator parting the clouds and sending a thunderbolt to strike them down for the sin of existing."

"Other countries allow the Riftborn to just... walk free? Do as they like?" a young man asked, voice full of wonder. He was barely a man—not more that sixteen.

"Other countries don't even call them 'Riftborn,'" Sully said quietly. "It's only here that the concept of the Rift even exists. Address a Riftborn on the street as such in Paris or Rome or New York City and they'll look at you like you're mad. We are not the only country that has fallen back on our worst and most dangerous weaknesses, but I assure you, life does not need to be this way. We do not need to accept it."

"But surely it's not enough," the woman with the small boy piped up again. "Simply stopping drinking the Riftmead won't change our lot."

Sully seemed to steel herself. "You're right. It's not enough. We will have to rise up. Stopping the Riftmead will strengthen us and lessen their hold on us and our gifts. But we will still need to stand up to them."

"How?"

"Sheer numbers," Sully replied. "The number of Riftborn in this city alone would be enough to put up a rollicking good fight."

"Fight? With what?" another voice cried. "They have all the weapons, all the soldiers."

"We fight with what we've always had, what they've always feared. We fight with magic," Sully said. "Without Riftmead coursing through your veins, you will be astonished at what your magic can do. A bit of training and careful planning, and the Illustratum will be in for the surprise of their bloody lives."

People had begun to look at each other, to whisper together. Eliza felt an excitement building in the room, catching like dry kindling set to a match. Eli seemed to feel it too. He jumped to his feet and spoke to the crowd.

"The wheels are already turning," Eli said, his voice eager. "Our recent discovery of the research on Riftmead means we finally know what's in it, and that means we can render it harmless. Cora?" He gestured to Cora, who looked startled at being asked to address the group but stood up smartly just the same.

"That's right. Most of you know me. I've been midwife to many of your children, and cured many an ache and pain. I've spent years trying to better understand what Riftmead is and how to counteract its effects, and I'm pleased to say I've finally succeeded, thanks to what we learned from Bedlam. I've brewed what I believe will be an effective antidote. I've already started testing it on some patients, with good results." Here she threw a smile to Bridie, who returned it gratefully. "I hope to find more Riftborn diagnosed with Riftsickness who want to test the effectiveness of the antidote by trying it for themselves."

"You can put my name at the top of that list," Peter Neill called out. "I'll try anything if it might get me back to me old self."

Cora nodded. "Thank you, Peter. I urge all of you, if you know anyone ill with Riftsickness, send them to my shop. I'll be brewing this antidote day and night."

"And that's not all we're doing with it," Eli added. "Zeke and Jasper have already infiltrated the bottling factory in Yorkshire, the one the Illustratum has taken over to produce the Riftmead."

"That's right," Zeke said, chiming in. "I've got connections, see," he added, gesturing unnecessarily to the fact that they were all sitting in the back room of his pub. "The plan was to contaminate the supply right at the source—slip Cora's magic elixir there right into the barrels before they were shipped out across the country. We've succeeded with one shipment already, and we plan to do it again."

"So, for those of you asking how you can help, Zeke cannot do it alone," Eli said.

"But surely he won't need more than a few of us?" a man replied.

"That's true," Eli said. "A dozen or so men could get it done. As to the rest of you, we have another plan."

The door to the bar opened quietly and Eliza saw Penny slip through it, taking care to close it silently behind her. She bent her head toward Fergus, who listened for a moment, nodded his head, and waved her in. She settled herself against the wall, arms folded over her chest, listening as Sully took the lead once more.

"One week from today they are going to open the gates of the Illustratum to the city. Elder Hallewell's daughter is marrying the High Elder's son and they have decided to stage a citywide blessing to celebrate the momentous event. You've likely seen the announcements being pasted in the shop windows by now. Every Riftborn in the city is invited to pray for the new couple and receive a blessing while they watch the wedding carriage procession. We want as many people there as possible who know the truth."

"Let me guess," Samuel Barber boomed, "You don't want us there just to pray, do you?"

Sully's head bobbed. "We want to stage a demonstration. We want the whole city there to witness it. We want the Riftborn of London to rise up and demand our freedom from the Illustratum, from their lies, and from their poison."

The room erupted in discussion now. And though Eliza could see some heads shaking, there was a shift in the energy in the room; a kind of anticipation was building.

"But how could such demands work?" the woman Tillie spoke up now, her expression shrewd. "The Illustratum will be absolutely crawling with Praesidio guards at an event like that."

"That's true, Tillie, but they won't be expecting confrontation," Eli said. "Don't forget, they'll think we've spent the last month poisoning ourselves, weakening our bodies and our magic, rendering us harmless to them. They won't realize we've destroyed their most powerful hold over us, and that we have come not for blessings, but for justice."

"And when they stamp us out like the insects they think we are, what then?" a man called out. He was leaning against the wall, an amused smirk on his face. "I came here tonight expecting to hear a real plan, and all I've heard so far is that I'm supposed to sacrifice myself as pre-wedding entertainment."

Eliza bristled at the man's tone, but not as much as Jasper, who jumped up from his seat again. "As entertaining as it would be for fully two-thirds of the people in this room to watch you get strung up, Keegan, there's a bit more to the plan than that." Raucous laughter met these words, and Keegan, reddening, opened his mouth to speak again, but Jasper forestalled him. "While the large crowd creates the distraction out front, we will be staging several attacks on the Illustratum itself from various points of entry. We are counting on the Praesidio to be so engaged with the crowd in the front that we will find ourselves at an advantage at other points around the building."

"We can't just assume they're going to be easy targets," Keegan continued to argue. "You have no way of predicting how the Praesidio will be planning to protect the Illustratum that day."

"I'd agree with you, Keegan, if we weren't in possession of the full Praesidio security plans for the wedding day," Jasper said, crossing his arms over his chest.

Keegan's face went slack with shock as murmurs rippled through the room.

"There is also another element to the plan," Sully barked, "one that will drastically increase our numbers, but we haven't yet figured out the details."

"Well, come on, out with it," a woman called. "You said you need our help. What is it?"

Sully bit her lip, clearly hesitant to reveal this element of the plan when it was still on such unsteady footing. Jasper, however, took it out of her hands.

"We're staging a mass break out from the Praeteritum," he announced. The gasps that greeted him filled the room like a gust of wind.

"Criminals? You think we should throw in our lot with a bunch of criminals?" a man shouted.

"Oi! My brother's locked up in there, and he ain't no criminal!" A woman stood up, face florid with resentment. "He's a hard-working man who fell on some hard times. He did what he had to do to feed his children, and now he's being punished for it. Five years of hard labor for poaching a few rabbits."

"My son's in there for missing a tax payment on his farm. No warning, no chance to make it up. Just a pair of handcuffs and a three-year sentence," another man chimed in. "The Illustratum took his farm. Now he won't even have a place to come home to when he gets out."

"Don't you all see?" Eli called over the bickering. "Other Riftborn aren't the enemy here. Are there some real criminals in the Praeteritum, people who deserve to be locked up? Sure, I suppose there are. But much more than that, the Praeteritum is full of good people who need help, not punishment. You've seen what happened to Peter, and to Bridie as well. They weren't mad, and yet they would have spent the rest of their lives wasting away in Bedlam if not for the happy accident of the place burning to the bloody ground."

"And was that just a happy accident, or has Jasper been playing with matches again?" a voice shouted, followed by some boisterous laughter. Jasper grinned and opened his mouth, but caught Sully's eye and closed his mouth again at once.

"The point we're trying to make is that the folks in the Praeteritum could be a valuable resource. If anyone has any leads or ideas about gaining access to the place, talk to Sully," Eli said. "In the meantime, we do not ask any of you to give us a firm commitment tonight. We only ask that you think about what you've heard, and ask yourself if you want to be a part of it. We'll meet again the night before the wedding, but not here. We'll get word around to all of you when we find another meeting place."

"Until then, please, stop drinking the Riftmead. Even if you want nothing to do with what we've discussed tonight, please do that much, for your sake and for the sake of your families," Sully added.

"What if we don't need to think about it? What if we already know we want to help?" Peter Neill said. A rousing chorus of shouts answered him. Eli's chest swelled, though he was carefully controlling his face, trying not to look too pleased with the response.

"Then we invite you to stay," he replied. "The rest of you, mull it over. You know where to find us."

"Before the rest of you all rush out of here, remember, we're trying not to attract attention to the pub," Zeke called, his voice booming over the chorus of scraping chairs and booted feet. "So we'll be leaving in shifts out the back door. Some of the men can make their way out the front, but only a few at a time. Queue up at the doors and Jasper and I will tell you when the coast is clear."

Eliza stood up and picked her way through the room to Eli amidst the exodus. "I think that went well," she told him.

"Do you think so?" Eli looked anxious. "I was afraid we were going to lose them when we started talking about the Praeteritum. I still think it might have been a mistake."

But Eliza shook her head. "No, I think it was important. It's like you said, the Illustratum purposefully divides us. They don't want us to trust each other. It strengthens us. I seem to remember no one other than you trusting me at first."

Eli smiled. "Further proof that no one should ever listen to me."

Eliza punched him lightly in the arm. "That's enough cheek out of you," she said, but Eli's smile was already fading.

"This is it, Eliza. It's finally happening. Succeed or fail, we're finally going to stand up to them."

Eliza simply nodded, her throat tight. She didn't know how to express the emotions swirling around inside her, making her dizzy and breathless. Pride, that they had worked so hard. Fear, that it would all end in tragedy. And something else, something she at once desperately needed to say and also prayed would never cross her lips. Something aching and lovely and terrifying.

"Ouch!"

An elbow had caught Eliza sharply in the side as Penny shoved past her. Eliza caught one glimpse of her face and reached out to catch her arm.

"Penny? Are you all right?"

Penny hardly seemed to hear her. She was staring at the back door of the pub where people were queued up to leave.

"Penny!"

This time Eliza's sharp tone got Penny's attention. She tore her eyes from the doorway and looked at Eliza as though she hadn't even realized she was there.

"Are you all right? You look as if you'd seen a ghost!" Eliza said, genuine concern creeping into her voice.

"I... yeah, no, I'm all right. I thought... it's nothing," Penny said, shaking her head as though to clear it.

"Are you sure? You seem—"

"Penny! Come here, lass!" Zeke was calling, waving her over. With a tight smile, Penny nodded to Eliza and then slipped away to answer Zeke's summons just as Eliza and Eli heard a summons of their own.

"Eliza! Eli! Come here!"

Sully was motioning to them. Jasper stood beside her, looking a bit jumpy.

"Jasper's just told me about an idea he's had. He says Eliza's agreed to it as well," Sully said.

"What idea?" Eli asked.

"It's good, isn't it?" Jasper asked Sully, ignoring Eli's question.

"It's clever, I'll give you that. And I think there's a damn good chance it could work, but it will take very careful planning. And of course, the Hallewell girl has to agree to it as well."

"She'll agree to it," Eliza said at once.

"Agree to what?" Eli asked.

"You're sure of that, are you? I still think it's mad to trust a member of an Elder family in all of this," Sully hedged.

"Now, that's not fair, we trust Eli, after all," Jasper said with a wicked grin.

262

"I am absolutely sure," Eliza insisted, with such a tone of finality that Sully swallowed what remained of her doubts.

"Is anyone going to tell me what the bloody hell we're talking about?" Eli cried, throwing his hands up in the air in his frustration.

"We will, but you're not going to like it," Sully said baldly.

Eli looked suspiciously from Sully to Eliza who nodded solemnly. "She's right," Eliza said. "You're going to hate it."

Eli turned his gaze on Jasper, his nostrils flaring. "What have you done now?"

Jasper sighed. "I'll get him a drink."

28

E LIZA HAD NEVER FELT SO ALIVE as she did on the journey home from the night's Resistance meeting. So many times, traveling back and forth in the darkness, her only companion had been fear, and perhaps a feeling that she was in over her head. But now a fire was kindled in her belly, fed by the determined faces and powerful words of the army they were slowly beginning to build. For the first time, she was not afraid that all they had worked for would be snuffed out. For the first time, it felt powerful; a nameless something that could survive whatever the Illustratum tried to throw at it. She did not feel safe—indeed, she had rarely been so frightened of what was to come—but there was a quiet knowledge that even if she was caught, even if she hanged, she was part of something that would continue to grow and fight even without her. She couldn't say why she found it so comforting, so bolstering, and yet, she did.

If only Eli felt the same way. Eliza had known he wouldn't like Jasper's plan, but she hadn't expected him to storm out of the pub. She had nearly gone after him, but Sully stopped her.

"Just let him walk with it for a while," she'd said. "He'll come around."

Eliza hoped he would, and also that his worry wouldn't turn to anger at her. Committed though she was to the idea, she knew it would be much harder to go through with it if Eli couldn't forgive her for it.

Peter had left the door to the back pantries unlocked as they'd agreed, and she slipped into the house without anyone seeing her. She stopped in the silent kitchen to hunt down something to eat; nerves about the meeting had meant that she had done little more at dinnertime than push her food around her plate. After a cursory search, she located a plate of scones Mrs. Keats had left upon the counter, wolfing two of them down ravenously to silence the growling of her stomach. Now sure her hunger wouldn't prevent some much-needed sleep, she tiptoed down the hall past the other bedrooms until she reached her own. She pushed open the door and froze.

Someone was sitting on the edge of her bed in the dark. Whoever it was did not move or speak when she appeared. She nearly turned around and fled, but curiosity, stronger than her fear, caused her to reach out her hand to switch on the sconce. The gas lamp flared to life, illuminating the face of her visitor.

"Father!" The word escaped her in a whooshing gasp of relief. But then her eyes adjusted and she saw the look on her father's face, and the fear tightened like a fist around her heart again. "What are you—"

Braxton looked up and met his daughter's eyes. For the first time in her life, he looked old to her—impossibly old. When had that happened? He did not speak right away, letting the silence spiral horribly before he sighed. The sound seemed to empty him completely.

"Eliza, where have you been?" he asked quietly.

Eliza could have cursed herself. Why hadn't she formulated an excuse? To give herself time to think, she asked, "Where is Sarah?"

"She came to me when she woke and found you missing. I sent her to bunk with Millie," he replied. "You haven't answered my question."

She shrugged, trying to sound unconcerned. "Oh, I… I was just… I couldn't sleep, so I…"

"Please do not insult my intelligence with a poorly constructed falsehood," Braxton said. "You are not in your nightclothes, and you still have your boots on. You've been somewhere. Where did you go?"

Eliza didn't reply. Her hands were clenched into white-knuckled fists at her sides. She did not want to do this, not now. Not with her father.

"I must have been a fool not to see this coming," Braxton said, rubbing at his eyes, as if he, too, would rather be anywhere in the world than in his daughter's room having this conversation. "You are nineteen, after all, and for all your obedience and piety, you were bound to meet this temptation at some time or another."

"Temptation?"

Braxton sighed, looking at her again. "What's his name, Eliza?"

Eliza blinked. "I'm sorry?"

"What is his name?" Braxton repeated slowly. "This… boy who's tempted you beyond the bounds of your good sense? Who is he?"

The realization of what her father was talking about hit Eliza so suddenly that she actually laughed with shock, a laugh she instantly regretted. She composed herself quickly and replied. "I apologize. I didn't mean to laugh, truly. You're accusation simply caught me off guard, Father."

"Well? Are you going to answer my question, or not? Though I suppose it does not really matter. You won't be seeing him again, whoever he is," Braxton said.

"There is no 'he,' Father," Eliza said, trying to keep her voice calm and even. "I cannot give you a name. I have not been out gallivanting with young men, I promise you." Even as she said it, the promise felt strained. Then, she reminded herself that she was at least innocent of her father's interpretation of events, even if the truth was a hundred times worse.

"I'm very tired, Eliza," Braxton said, in a tone that made it clear he did not believe a word of it. "The preparations for the wedding have stretched our time and resources to the limit. You yourself have surely never worked so hard as you have these past few weeks preparing Miss Jessamine, which is why I'm frankly shocked that you would choose now of all moments to behave so very selfishly."

It was all Eliza could do to keep from screaming. "Selfish?"

"I'm at a loss as to what else I'm meant to call such behavior—sneaking out at all hours, tiring yourself when you are meant to be giving every ounce of your skill and attention to the event of the Dignus season. How can you possibly concentrate on Miss Jessamine when you've got your head in the clouds with some ridiculous romantic frivolity? It won't do, Eliza. You are going to be in danger of losing your position if you cannot focus on the task at hand!"

"Father, for the last time, I am not involved in some romantic entanglement!" Eliza cried. "Romance—or anything like it—is the very last thing on my mind right now."

Braxton's eyebrows drew together in confusion. "I don't understand."

"Of course you don't! You were so busy trying and convicting me of a crime I didn't commit, that you've paid not the slightest attention to what I've been saying!" Eliza replied. "I regret to inform you that the fatherly speech you've undoubtedly prepared about the perils of romance is wholly unnecessary."

It took a moment for Braxton to gather himself after this blow to his perception of things. He cleared his throat three times before he finally managed to say, "Well, then, what in the world are you doing sneaking into the house at this time of night?"

Thankfully, the intervening nonsense about moonlit trysts with anonymous gentlemen had given Eliza enough time to settle on her lie. "I was looking for Bridie," she announced.

"You... you've been doing what?" Braxton asked, his eyes going wide.

"I've been looking for Bridie," Eliza said, shrugging out of her cloak and hanging it on the back of a chair. "After what you told me, about her not returning to Larkspur Manor, I knew it would be my only chance to see her again."

Eliza was not sure what kind of reaction she had expected—a stern admonishment, perhaps, or even a lecture on the contagion of Riftwards. What she certainly did not expect was for her father to jump up from the bed with the energy of a man who had just sat on a pin. He leapt to his feet, his face suddenly pale and trembling.

"What do you mean by doing such a thing? I told you not to get involved! I told you I would see to it!" he cried, his voice rising in a way Eliza had never heard before. She took an involuntary step back.

"I'm sorry, but I'm worried about her," Eliza said.

"You have no need to be worried about her! She is being well taken care of, I am sure," Braxton blustered.

"Well, I'm glad you feel so certain of that, but I haven't any proof that it's true," Eliza replied, anger coming to her defense now.

"What have you done? Where have you been poking around?" Braxton demanded, shouting now.

"I... checked at some hospitals in the city that have Riftwards to see if I could—"

"You are never to do such a thing again! What can you have been thinking? A respectable young woman from a manor house does not traipse around the slums of London in the dead of night!"

"I wasn't traipsing!" Eliza cried, and even though her story was a lie, she found herself desperate to defend it. After all, she would have torn down every corner of London to find Bridie, if she hadn't already known where she was. "I cannot just forget about her, Father! I can't just pretend my friend doesn't exist anymore."

"You can and you must!" Braxton replied, his voice thunderous now. "Eliza, there are situations that are best left alone, situations where poking and prying will only lead to disaster. You must take heed and understand that you cannot go looking for Bridie. You must stop at once."

Something was wrong. Eliza stared into her father's red, quivering face expecting to see anger glaring back at her, but no. His eyes were feverishly bright with something else altogether, something she had rarely seen in his face before, something that drove a shard of ice cold understanding right through her heart.

Fear. Her father was afraid.

She took a step back from him, narrowing her eyes. "What are you afraid of?"

The question only served to unsettle her father even further. "I... I beg your pardon?"

"What are you afraid of?" Eliza repeated, almost under her breath, for the realization had indeed snatched her breath right from her lungs. "That is fear I see in your eyes. You're afraid of something."

Braxton seemed too stunned even to deny the accusation. He spluttered and stammered incoherently as he struggled to gather himself, which only fed Eliza's conviction that she was indeed correct.

"You weren't afraid when I walked in the room. It wasn't until I told you I went looking for Bridie that your demeanor changed. You were disappointed, perhaps angry when I came in, but now... now you're afraid. Why?"

"Eliza, this has gone far—"

"You're afraid I'll find Bridie—or you're afraid I'll find out what happened to her," Eliza whispered. It wasn't a question. She could see it in his face, as clearly as words scrawled upon a page. She knew her father had lied about where Bridie was, had tried to keep them apart, but this was something different, something more.

"What happened to Bridie was her own fault, for poking her nose in where it didn't belong!" Braxton cried out. Eliza watched as his pupils dilated, as the realization of what he had just uttered sank in, as his hand reached out into the space between them as if to pluck the words back out of the air. Eliza watched because she, too, wanted to snatch the words away, crumple them up, and burn them. It couldn't be true. It just couldn't be.

"You knew." The words escaped before Eliza could close her mouth to cage them in. And once those first two words escaped, she was powerless against the rest. "You knew where Bridie was, didn't you? All this time, you've known."

"Not—not at first," Braxton said, with the air of a sinking man snatching for life preservers, "No, it was only when Elder Hallewell informed me. He... he knew I would need to know, so I could set about hiring her replacement."

"But Elder Hallewell knew," Eliza said slowly. "And he knew why she was there. He knew what happened, at Clerkenwell."

But Braxton had suddenly gone the color of cold porridge, and the sharp pain in Eliza's heart twisted still deeper.

"And you knew as well. You've known all along."

Braxton's face sagged. What would have been the point in denying it? She already knew it was true.

"You knew that mother hadn't left me. You knew they'd caught her, and that she was locked away in that workhouse."

"I was trying to protect you," Braxton groaned.

"Protect me?" Eliza cried out. "From what? The truth?"

"Yes! Your mother was a criminal! She betrayed our Creator himself when she interfered with that child, and I couldn't risk you ever being tempted in that direction yourself. We'd worked so hard to raise you in the light of the Creator's grace. I had to help you stay the Path."

"So, you told me my mother abandoned me instead?" Eliza gasped, sobs building in her chest, heaving up upon each other like waves crashing over rocks. "How could you not have known the havoc that would wreak upon a child like that? I thought I'd done something wrong! I thought there must have been something wrong with me, that she didn't love me enough to stay."

"That's nonsense, Eliza—"

"No, that was my *life!*" Eliza shouted, a sob breaking in her chest, choking her. "For fifteen years, that has been my life! That has defined me, in every decision, in every belief! I formed my life around it, and now I simply orbit it, a lost and lonely moon in the darkness. I weighed and measured each fiber of myself, trying to grow into something that someone would think worthy of keeping! That is what your protection wrought!"

Whatever words Braxton had been saving to hurl at her next, he quite forgot them. He simply stood, staring in abject horror at his only child, upon whose face were etched the unmistakably sharp lines of hatred. Eliza could feel them on her features, unwelcome strangers.

"Did you know what they were doing to her in there?" Eliza asked, the question clawing its way up her throat.

Braxton blanched again. "No, I... I don't know what... what do you mean, what they were doing to her?"

"Well, you knew she was a prisoner. You must have realized it wasn't going to be a pleasant experience for her. Didn't you ever wonder what they were doing to her in that place?"

"It... it wasn't my place to question the judgement of the Elders. Whatever they decided, in the light of the Creator, would be the just and rightful consequence," Braxton bleated, sounding like little more than a child reciting a lesson.

"How many times did you have to say that to yourself before you believed it?" Eliza hissed.

Braxton shook his head, mouth working uselessly.

"Well, you should know I've seen her," Eliza said, her voice calm and cold. "I've seen her. She's alive. Not that you've asked. Not that you seem to have had the slightest interest in what became of your wife when the hellhole she'd been chained up in caught fire."

"I didn't know she was in there!" Braxton blurted out—that one last desperate reach for a life preserver. "I swear to you I didn't know they'd transferred her there!"

"It doesn't even matter. You'd have cared as little either way. You'd already scrubbed her from my life, what did it matter if she was scrubbed from the rest of the world as well? Very tidy for you."

"Eliza! That's unfair! I never... I always wanted to... to—"

"I'm not interested in what you always wanted. Not anymore," Eliza said. She suddenly felt very sure—very calm. "She's alive. But very weak, and very ill. She needs rest and quiet if she is going to recover. If you tell anyone at all that she's alive—or that I've been to see her—I swear that I will throw myself down upon the *altaria* and swoon and cry and swear upon the Book of the Rift that my father was the mastermind of the plot to free my mother, and that I was only following his orders."

Braxton swayed on his feet, throwing out a hand to the bedpost to steady himself. "He would never believe you," he whispered.

"It won't matter whether he believes me or not. The die will be cast," Eliza said, her tone now bordering on didactic. "Once your trustworthiness is questioned, your reputation will be tarnished beyond repair. Elder Hallewell will be forced to sack you just to save face. You will be out in the street regardless, and no one will dare employ you after a scandal like that."

Braxton pressed his lips together, his knuckles going white where he gripped the bedpost. "You would ruin me? Your own father?"

"To save her from you again just once, I would ruin you a thousand times over," Eliza spat. "But you are stalling, Father. Your silence, or your ruination. That is the bargain I am offering you. Take it, for I shall not offer it again."

Braxton stared into his daughter's eyes, and Eliza watched the recognition fade from them. "Who are you?" he whispered. "The daughter I knew would never—"

"The daughter you knew was never allowed to know herself. She has since rectified that oversight. So if you find me much changed, father, then just know that who you see now is the girl I managed to become in spite of you. Now, please leave my room. I am tired and wish to go to bed."

The dismissal seemed to snap the man's very last thread, and he left the room, unraveled. Eliza sank down upon the edge of her bed, in the very place her father had sat just now, before he turned into a man she could hate.

And she sat there, hunched and aching with the weight of that hatred, until the rose-gold of dawn stole the grey from the room.

(excerpt from an article in *The London Clarion Call*, issued 30 June 1888)

"...Late last night, Praesidio officers were called to the banks of the Thames River near the Battersea Bridge with a report of a body floating in the waters below. With the help of local fishermen who lent the use of their skiff, soldiers were able to recover the body and bring it to shore, where it was quickly identified as that of Archie Ward, 43, of the Barrens, a notorious Riftborn criminal who had a long and sordid record of misdeeds, arrests, and sentences in the Praeteritum. It can be argued that the list of people who might want to see such a man dead is very long indeed, but it appears that the Praesidio will not be questioning suspects. Officers at the scene indicated to our reporter that Ward died from a gunshot wound to the right temple and a flintlock revolver, consistent with the injury, was found with the body. It is the conclusion of the Praesidio that Ward's gunshot wound was self-inflicted, and his death has been ruled a cowardly act of suicide, an insult to the Creator Himself, granter of life, who..."

29

T HE DOOR TO BRAXTON'S OFFICE remained closed all of the following day. Mrs. Keats announced to the staff at large that Braxton had a headache and had left them an extensive list of tasks to prepare for the next day's Purification ceremony, as well as the wedding reception. The blank looks of shock from the staff, along with the low, concerned muttering revealed the whole of downstairs was flabbergasted that Braxton, who had never missed a day of work in his life, was leaving them to fend for themselves when so much was at stake; but Eliza was not surprised. She knew what her father was grappling with, knew the existential crisis he must be staring down, and yet she found she could not care. The gravity of everything that lay before her over the next few days left no room in her heart or mind for such a man as her father had revealed himself to be. Perhaps the empty space he left behind would ache eventually, but for now she felt freer for the absence of him.

She wondered if this meant she was a terrible daughter, and then decided that, whatever kind of daughter she was, she was the daughter he had made her.

Eliza went through her day in a kind of haze, exhausted and yet filled with a manic kind of energy. Her mind wandered constantly off to the Barrens, buzzing with frustration that she was here, pressing garments and arranging flowers for a farce of a ceremony while Eli and the others were recruiting, planning, training, and organizing. She wanted to scream, and had to constantly remind herself that she was doing her part, for the façade was just as crucial to their plan as all the clandestine pieces coming together behind it. The Purification ceremony must happen, or the wedding could not take place, and so she worked through her tasks with manic fingers and a tongue that was growing sore from having to bite it so often.

Although the only topic of conversation downstairs ought rightly to have been the wedding preparations, there was a constant hum of gossip circulating about the murder of Elder Carpenter. All the newspapers were calling it "a heinous act of evil" and "the work of a Riftborn madman," which had the entire staff on edge. Many of them had never even set foot in the Barrens, and so they were able to indulge their morbid fascination without fearing for themselves. Others though—Mrs. Keats and Liesel, for example, who knew more about the darker side of the Illustratum—took a much grimmer view of things. They would not engage in idle speculation about escaped lunatics and murderers running loose through the streets, and instead spent most of their time barking at the others to stop whispering and get back to work as the hours ticked steadily by.

§

The evening of the Purification finally arrived, and the entrance hall was like something out of a fairy tale. White flowers clustered and bloomed and dripped from the banisters and the tabletops. Candles seemed to float in their own golden bubbles of light. The leather-bound, gilded copy of the *Book of the Rift* had been placed upon an intricately carved wooden pedestal, ready for Elder Potter, who would be performing the Purification at Elder Hallewell's request.

Jessamine stood by the doorway to the library, clad in a simple white sheath. She wore her dark hair pinned back from her face but allowed her curls to cascade down her back. She wore a single white rose tucked behind her left ear. Eliza thought Jessamine had more natural beauty in such simplicity than any woman could have had, even if adorned head to toe in the finest of jewels and fabrics. For a long moment, she simply stared at her, drinking her in, like someone admiring a painting. Jessamine caught her gaze and her hands began fluttering around her hair and dress, looking for something out of place.

"What? Why are you looking at me? Does something need fixing?" she whispered.

"Not at all, miss. You look perfect."

"I feel ill."

Eliza pretended to tuck a curl back into place as she replied, "Remember, none of this matters. No matter what happens, you are not walking down the aisle to that man."

Jessamine bit her lip. "Do you promise?"

"I do."

"Could you... help me calm down?"

Eliza felt startled for a moment. "Are you sure?"

"Yes, of course! I asked, didn't I?" Jessamine pointed out.

"Well, yes, you did, but—"

Jessamine reached for Eliza's hand. "One day you're going to stop thinking of your magic as a curse and start thinking of it as the wonderful gift it is," she said softly. "I know my father has turned it against us both, but when we're gone from here, out from under his control, you'll realize that it's truly a wonderful thing you can do. You're going to help so many people. You've already helped me many times."

Eliza's voice caught in her throat, and it took her a few seconds to reply. "Do you really mean that?"

"I certainly do," Jessamine insisted. "Now for heaven's sake, will you please help calm me down before I flee for the garden wall?"

Eliza chuckled and pulled a glove from her hand. Then, resting it gently against Jessamine's cheek, she closed her eyes and felt a deep, abiding calm flow through her. It came so easily, with hardly any effort at all, and Jessamine gasped as she felt it. Eliza's eyes flew open at the sound of the gasp, but there was nothing to fear. Jessamine's face was full of wonder.

"That's remarkable," she whispered. "You've been practicing, haven't you?"

Eliza nodded. She certainly had, every chance she got, and with no more Riftmead clouding her abilities, her magic was more powerful, more focused than ever. With everything else going on, she'd barely had time to appreciate the strides she had been making. Now, as she pulled her hand away from her mistress' face, she felt true pride in herself.

Jessamine closed her eyes and took a deep breath. When she opened them again, her features were aglow with true composure. "Very well, then. Let's get this charade over with."

There were still several long minutes to pass before the ceremony.

A string quartet was quietly warming up in the corner. Braxton had emerged from his office that morning and had thrown himself into the preparations so completely that only Eliza noticed the way he was avoiding her. She watched him now as he bustled around, straightening and adjusting things that were already perfectly straight and in no further need of adjusting, his eyes carefully focused on anything but the daughter who stood only a few feet away from him. A quiet rumble of voices drifted in from the adjoining sitting room where the Morgans, Elder Hallewell, and Elder Potter had all gathered to wait. It was traditional for the young woman to reveal herself to the assembled company only when the ceremony began, which suited Jessamine just fine. The less time she had to spend in Reginald's company, feigning delight at the idea of being married to him, the better.

Eliza had never attended a Dignus Purification ceremony before, but she had attended several Riftborn ones for older servant girls over the years who had chosen to marry. She had looked on in dreamy-eyed wonder at the time, convinced as she was in the power of the words being spoken. The idea that someone could speak words over you, like an incantation, and what was rotten or wrong in you would just vanish… poof! It was beautiful.

It was also a lie.

Suddenly, the door opened and Elder Hallewell entered, closing the door carefully behind him so that Jessamine was not yet revealed to the assembled guests. His usually composed face was pale and drawn, and there was a tightness to the corners of his mouth.

"The High Elder is not in attendance," he said, his voice strained and snappish. "He is too unwell to venture out today. We will carry on without him, in the hopes that a few more days rest will see him fit to attend the wedding."

Jessamine simply nodded her head. "We will pray to the Creator that his condition improves," she said meekly.

Elder Hallewell nodded once, sharply, and then turned to Braxton. "All is ready. We can begin."

"Very good, sir. I shall alert the musicians," Braxton said, bending into a very low bow and then following his master out the door, closing it behind him.

Jessamine and Eliza waited for a few moments in tense silence, and then the musicians took up their instruments and began a slow, lyrical rendition of the chosen hymn. The start of the music was Jessamine's cue to enter. She threw one last, conflicted look at Eliza, who gazed back solemnly.

"It means nothing," she mouthed. "Whatever else happens, you will never belong to that man."

Jessamine repeated it under her breath, lifted her chin, and turned to face the doors as they slid open.

Elder Potter led the party, dressed in all his most sacred habiliments. A golden sash stretched across his ample belly as he shuffled out across the entrance hall, his face serious and contemplative for once, though he did have the mercy to twitch his mouth into a small sympathetic smile when he saw Jessamine. She did not return it.

Behind Elder Potter came Elder Hallewell, looking so pleased with himself and with the proceedings that Eliza momentarily saw red. She took her own advice and repeated the mantra under her breath.

It means nothing. It all means nothing. Let them have their pageantry. Let them have their charade. It will all come toppling down soon, the entire house of cards.

Mrs. Morgan came next, looking like a sugared pink confection, her face obscured by the delicate mist of the veil she wore draped from her hat, followed by Reginald's two younger sisters and their husbands, all with carefully controlled expressions. They filed in, the most somber of processions, looking more like the attendants at a funeral than what ought to have been a joyful pre-wedding ceremony. The absence of the High Elder hung like a storm cloud over the proceedings. One of the Morgan sisters even had a handkerchief pressed to her mouth, as though to stop herself from making any sound. Her eyes, as they fell on Jessamine, were wide and misty.

When the entirety of the company was gathered on either side of the pedestal, Reginald strode into the room. He was also dressed simply, in white, but unlike his future wife, the ensemble did little to recommend his appearance. His hair usually had a somewhat messy elegance, but now looked merely unkempt. Without his usual foppish accessories, he looked rather unremarkable, the regularity and pleasantness of his features insufficient to distract from his bloodshot eyes and the dark circles beneath them. Even his usual rakish smirk did little to lessen his resemblance to a small boy who had been dragged out of bed before he was ready to get up.

279

Whether Jessamine had noticed any of this, Eliza could not tell. Her mistress had retreated into herself and snipped the strings to the reality of the moment. She would go through the motions and then it would be over.

The music swelled and Jessamine and Reginald moved toward each other like sleepwalkers, coming to a stop in front of the podium where Elder Potter stood, the *Book of the Rift* open in his hands, and an uncharacteristically solemn expression upon his face. He cleared his throat dramatically and the music quieted beneath him, though it did not cease.

"May this day's Purification ceremony please the Creator, uplift His works, and glorify His name," he began, and as one, every head bowed in prayer.

"Please join your hands," Elder Potter instructed. Reginald extended his hands toward Jessamine, cocking a waggish eyebrow at her. She hesitated only a moment, and then placed her own hands in his.

"Bravo," he mouthed.

Jessamine did not take the bait, bowing her head again and closing her eyes, determined to get through the ceremony. But Elder Potter had barely begun his prayer when a gasping scream caused everyone to start and look around at Mrs. Morgan.

The rosy tone of her veil could not conceal the deathly pallor of her cheek, nor her mouth still open in silent continuation of her shriek. She did not seem able to make another sound, but she did not need to. Instead, she raised a shaking finger and pointed to the top of the staircase. Everyone turned to look.

A figure stood upon the landing, the ghost that had long been rumored to haunt the house made corporeal at last. Everything in the room below had frozen in time—the very flames on the candles gone unnaturally still. Not a soul dared draw breath—the figure had stolen all the air from the room. Until…

"Mother," Jessamine whispered.

"Mother?!" Reginald repeated, horror-struck.

Lillian Hallewell began to slowly descend the steps, her bare feet utterly silent upon the treads. The long white nightgown she always wore hung haphazardly off her wasted shoulder, one lace cuff torn and fluttering along like a tail of smoke from a cigarette. Her eyes were dark, burning pits in the sharp white planes of her face. Her dark hair dripped down around her, twisted and knotted and wild with struggle. All was colorless, in black and white, like a photograph come terrifyingly to life…

Except for the blood. The bright and terrible scarlet streaked upon her cheek, smeared upon her hands and wrists, spattered upon the starched creaminess of her gown.

Eliza clutched at the table behind her as her knees turned to water. The blood. Where had it come from?

There were three footmen and a dozen Praesidio soldiers in the room, but not one of them moved as Lillian floated down toward them, each one of them immobilized in a shared spell of horror. With a sound like a sigh, Mrs. Morgan fainted. One of her sons-in-law reached out reflexively and caught her before she could hit the floor.

It was Francis Potter, the *Book of the Rift* still open to the ceremony and shaking in his hands, who broke the silence.

"What in the blazing *hell* is going on, Josiah?"

Elder Hallewell jumped as though scalded, and then stared around the room. Elder Potter's voice had broken the spell his wife's appearance had cast upon him, and now he stared around him with dawning horror that the shameful secret he kept locked away in the attic had revealed itself to everyone present.

"Braxton, please see our guests into the library," Elder Hallewell said, only a slight edge to his voice.

Eliza's father leaped into action at once, gathering Reginald, the other guests, and the musicians around him and ushering them quickly out of the room. The two sons-in-law had taken up Mrs. Morgan between them, carrying her easily. Francis held up a hand, refusing to be moved from his place at the podium. Reginald grabbed Jessamine by the elbow and tried to drag her with him, but she tugged her arm out of his grip, looking positively murderous.

"No, Reginald!"

"Jessamine, what are you playing at? The woman has a weapon!" Reginald said, his eyes fixed on the pair of scissors dangling from Mrs. Hallewell's hand.

"She's not just some woman, she's my mother!" Jessamine shot back at him, her voice venomous. "Go cower in the corner if you want to, I'm not coming!"

Braxton attempted to intervene. "Miss Jessamine, I must really insist…"

"Just leave her, man!" Reginald growled, his panic rising as Mrs. Hallewell drifted further and further down the staircase toward them, closing what was quickly becoming a very short distance. The last thing Eliza saw before her father closed the library doors were the faces of their guests, wide-eyed and pale with terror, craning their necks to get one last glimpse before they were closed off.

Elder Hallewell leaned in toward the nearest footman and whispered in his ear. Eliza was just close enough to hear him.

"Go upstairs and fetch Mrs. Spratt at once." The footman nodded then took a cautious step backward, and then another. When Lillian did not so much as acknowledge the movement, he turned tail and fled to the far side of the room, fumbling with a hidden latch in the paneling before slipping into the rabbit warren of servant passages hidden behind the wall. Peter Bennett watched him with a half-desperate expression, and it was clear he was fighting the impulse to run after him.

Lillian had reached the bottom of the staircase now, one hand lingering lazily on the banister as she stared straight at Josiah, who was fighting like mad to keep his composure. He wrestled his face into a semblance of a smile, and spoke, his tone light, friendly, and shaking like mad.

"Lillian, my darling, what are you doing out of bed?"

Lillian cocked her head to one side, still staring at her husband. "I heard the music."

She gestured to the corner where the musicians had abandoned their instruments in their haste to escape the sight of her, and their absence struck her. Her bottom lip trembled as she added, "Oh, dear. Is it over? I've missed it haven't I?"

"Yes, yes, all over," Elder Hallewell said, with an attempt at cheerful airiness that fell far short of the mark. "I'm sorry we disturbed your rest, dearest, but you really should be—"

But Lillian was humming, a hoarse snatch of the tune the musicians had just been playing. It was a traditional Illustratum hymn, common to many ceremonies and celebrations. Eliza had known the gentle lilt of it as long as she had known her own name.

"That hymn. We played it at our wedding. And at William's naming. Do you remember?"

It could not have been clearer that the sound of his son's name shook Elder Hallewell to his core. Just behind him, Elder Potter lost what little color he had left.

"I... I do remember, of course. But my darling, we really must get you back upstairs to—"

"I used to hum it to him. He used to smile at the tune, almost like a lullaby," she interrupted. "I thought perhaps if I followed the sound..." Her face spasmed, and she looked around at the people who remained behind, unable to find the face she sought.

"Where is he, Josiah? Where's my sweet boy?" she asked.

"Really, Lillian, you'll only upset yourself. Someone's gone to fetch Mrs. Spratt, and then we'll get you all settled d—"

"Mrs. Spratt isn't coming," Lillian whispered.

Elder Hallewell's face went ashen. "What do you..."

Lillian shook her head violently. "She wouldn't let me follow the music. She stood in front of the door. It was calling me, and she wouldn't let me answer."

"Lillian, what did you—"

"I had to answer, Josiah. Don't you see that I had to answer?"

A muffled shout cut through the air, followed by pounding footsteps above them. A moment later, the footman appeared at the top of the staircase.

"She's... she's dead, sir. I think she's dead. There's... there's blood everywhere—" He dropped to his knees and retched violently.

Elder Hallewell and Elder Potter exchanged looks, and then Elder Hallewell turned to Peter. "Peter be so good as to have Doctor Filbert fetched here at once. Bring him in through the servants' entrance please, and then alert Mrs. Keats, but no one else. Tell Mrs. Keats to keep everyone downstairs. Under no circumstances is anyone to come above stairs, not for anything, do you understand?"

Peter looked for a moment as though he had not understood in the slightest. But then he gave his head a shake, bowed, and hurried out of the room. Lillian watched him go with a curious, childlike expression, as though he was a furry little mouse scurrying across the room.

"We'll have to tell the doctor something, Josiah—give him some excuse," Elder Potter muttered.

"I'll think of something," Josiah murmured back, before turning to his wife again, but she was no longer watching him. Her eyes had fallen on Jessamine instead.

"I was so young. So very young," she whispered. "Could I really ever have been so young? Or beautiful?"

Elder Hallewell's eyes darted back and forth between his wife and his daughter. He seemed to decide it was best to play along, for he replied, "Of course you were. The most beautiful girl I'd ever seen."

Jessamine whimpered, her eyes swimming with tears. Lillian took two more steps toward her, tentatively, like she was approaching something dangerous.

"I was so happy. So lovely," she whispered. She continued to close the distance between herself and Jessamine. Jessamine looked at once longing for her mother's touch and terrified of it. Elder Hallewell danced on the spot, fighting the urge to throw himself between his wife and his daughter, his eyes darting repeatedly to the bloodied scissors still clutched in Lillian's hand. It was clear he scented danger, but he did not want to make any sudden movements that would startle his wife into doing something rash, so he stayed where he was, practically vibrating with tension.

"So lovely," Lillian whispered brokenly. She stood right in front of her daughter now, fighting an urge to touch her with a trembling hand. Jessamine could only draw a shuddering breath in reply, watching her mother's fingers float toward her. A sob bubbled up from deep in Lillian's chest as she tenderly stroked Jessamine's cheek. Jessamine closed her eyes, and for a moment there was nothing and no one in the room but the two of them.

"So lovely," Lillian repeated.

Elder Hallewell broke the spell, inching closer to them, his voice shaking. "Yes, my darling, and you can be that happy again if you'll just listen to—"

Lillian's face snapped to his so suddenly that he stepped back in fear. "Listen? To you?" she hissed, and venom dripped from every syllable. "When has that ever brought me happiness?"

Elder Hallewell stepped back again, flustered. "I... that is to say... we had many happy..."

"You promised to care for us. To protect us. And now? All is ashes. Ashes and sorrow and..." with a glance down at her own hands, "...and blood."

Elder Hallewell's mouth worked silently, but no words came to his defense.

"He was so beautiful, too. So sweet and brave. Where is he now, Josiah? Where is William?"

The name was like an incantation, the room immediately captive to its sound. Eliza pressed the back of her hand to her mouth to stifle a sob. The knowledge of William's whereabouts suddenly felt like a lump of hot metal in her chest. She ached to shout the truth, to end Lillian's agony, but she knew she could not.

"Our only son. Our *only son*, Josiah!" she whispered, tears spilling over her cheeks and down her face. Elder Hallewell's eyes lit up with panic. He rounded on Eliza.

"Can't you do something to calm her down?" he ground out between his teeth.

Eliza's heart dropped like a stone into her shoes. She shook her head. "Please, sir, I—"

"Is that all the answer you can give? Is that all you can say?" Lillian cried out, her voice cracked and broken from disuse. "Just say it out loud, can't you? Just tell them. Tell them all you killed our little boy!"

"Lillian, that's enough!" Elder Hallewell cried out, losing his tenuous hold on his self-control for the first time. "You are talking nonsense, you are ill, please, stop these ludicrous accusations!"

"Nonsense? Nonsense," Lillian repeated the word, rolling it around in her mouth, tasting it before spitting it out. "We could have loved him, couldn't we, in spite of the magic? Couldn't we have loved him anyway?"

All of her life, Eliza had thought of Elder Hallewell as a giant of a man, carved of stone in his manner and his mind. But as she stood and watched his wife's words strike him like physical blows, she realized he was small. So very, very small, in every sense of the word.

"We must trust to the Creator," he whispered back. It was as cowardly an answer as he could have given, and perhaps he knew it, for all the surety had drained from his voice.

"I trusted you, Josiah. And you took him from me. You took him..." Lillian's fingers tightened around the scissors in her hand, and she took a step toward her husband, something dark and decided solidifying in the depths of her eyes. Eliza watched it happen, horror dawning in her mind, and yet her body was too slow to catch up. Lillian let out a tortured cry and swung her arm back, lifting the

285

scissors into the air, staggering toward Elder Hallewell, who was too stunned even to move.

Everything seemed to slow down. Sound distorted, like they had all been dropped underwater. Eliza's brain was screaming at her body to move, to somehow stop what was about to happen. Out of the corner of her eye she watched as the remaining Praesidio guards started forward with the same intention. Elder Potter might have been carved from stone, seemingly unable to do anything but stare. Not a single one of them was going to be able to prevent it, they were all too late...

It was Jessamine whose muscles responded quickly enough. It was Jessamine who leaped forward, catching her mother around the waist with one hand and grabbing her scissor-wielding wrist with the other. Both women toppled to the ground before anyone could reach them, and the pair of scissors skidded across the floor, leaving a gruesome trail of blood upon the stones.

"No! I won't let you! I won't let you do this!"

Jessamine was gasping, and Lillian was howling like a wounded animal, her vengeance unquenched, her grief overflowing. She struggled against Jessamine's body, but Jessamine held her tightly and began stroking her hair and kissing her cheeks.

"It's all right. It's all right now. It won't bring William back. It will only break your heart again. Shh. Shh, it's all right now."

Lillian's struggling slowed and then stopped. She curled herself into the curve of Jessamine's body and cried stormily.

"Couldn't we have just loved him anyway?" Lillian whispered over and over again.

"Of course we can. He may not be here but we will always love him, you and I," Jessamine murmured, tears spilling out of her eyes and over the apples of her cheeks, now flushed pink with emotion and exertion.

Lillian raised her tear-stained face from the floor to look at Jessamine. "Don't make the same mistake again. Don't listen to Josiah. Save him. Save them all."

Jessamine could barely form the words around the onslaught of sobs. "I will. I promise. I'll save him this time."

Lillian's lips curved into a tremulous, watery smile, and then she buried her face in her daughter's neck, sobbing to wring the pain from her broken heart.

For what felt like a very long time, there was nothing but the sound of her crying and Jessamine's cooing. Then the room slowly seemed to wake from its collective nightmare; Elder Hallewell dropped into a chair, pressing his hands over his face. Elder Potter stepped back from the podium, closing the *Book of the Rift* and swearing under his breath. The door to the library slid open just a crack, anxious faces craning to catch a glimpse of what they had heard unfolding in the entry hall.

"Sir?" came Braxton's tentative voice. "How would you like us to proceed, sir?"

Elder Hallewell pulled his face up out of his hands with what looked like great effort. He looked around as though unsure where he was or what had happened. It was Jessamine who took charge.

"Eliza, please help me to get my mother back upstairs. We will bring her to my room. She should not be brought back to her own quarters until..." her voice cracked, "until someone has seen to Mrs. Spratt."

Elder Hallewell was trying to pull himself together. "Jessamine, I really—"

"Eliza, you can stay with her and ensure that she stays calm until the doctor arrives," Jessamine pressed on as though her father had not spoken. "She may need the kind of assistance that only your magic can provide. Will you please do that for me? For her?"

Eliza nodded, brushing errant tears from her cheeks and hurrying forward at once. Mrs. Hallewell's sobs continued unbroken as the two girls worked together to get her onto her feet. Having satisfied himself that Mrs. Hallewell was no longer a threat, Braxton eased the library door open further, and emerged with the rest of the guests, faces blank with shock.

"I'll, uh... ring for the carriages, shall I?" Elder Potter said, his voice loud and jarring in the stunned quiet of the hall.

Elder Hallewell stood up suddenly. "No. Eliza can settle my wife in Jessamine's room, and we will proceed with the Purification ceremony."

Elder Potter's mouth fell open. He threw an anxious look, first at Mrs. Hallewell, and then at Mrs. Morgan, who was still being held upright by her sons-in-law. "Josiah, I'm not sure if now is the proper—"

"Nonsense. We are all here. Everything is prepared. We need not worry about another interruption." He was rapidly regaining his authoritative manner, along with an energy that was almost manic. "Eliza, you heard your mistress. Get Mrs. Hallewell upstairs."

Braxton started forward, and it was clear that he was deeply troubled with the idea of his only daughter being sent upstairs alone with a woman who had just, in all likelihood, murdered someone. "Elder Hallewell, sir, perhaps I should—"

"Braxton, I would like you to have some tea brought up for our guests. Then I would like you to wait for Dr. Filbert and see that he is taken directly to my wife when he arrives," Elder Hallewell said sharply.

His feeble attempt at resistance crumbling at once, Braxton threw one last anxious glance in Eliza's direction before mumbling his assent and hurrying away.

"Everyone, please come back out here and join us," Elder Hallewell went on, in a tone that would brook no opposition. "I extend to you all my sincerest apologies on behalf of my wife, who has not been well for many years, since the kidnap and murder of our son by the Riftborn Resistance. She has never recovered from the shock, and over the years has grown more anxious and confused. Recently, she has fabricated in her mind this fallacy of our son having been Riftborn, and she blames me for his death. In truth, I often blame myself that I could not protect him from my enemies, but I will not allow the past to tear apart our future. I am sorry that she frightened you all. I have struggled over the years wondering if I ought not to have her committed, but I could never bring myself to do it. I trusted her to the hands of a servant—clearly a mistake. But I can promise you she will not interrupt us again. Let us all have a drink and a few moments to recover, and we can proceed as planned."

"Elder Hallewell, a woman has been killed!" Reginald piped up, pointing a shaking finger at the bloodied scissors that still lay on the floor. "Surely this all can wait!"

But Elder Hallewell shook his head. "She was naught but a Riftborn drudge, derelict in her duties. If she had done her job properly, this never would have happened."

"Even so—"

"The Purification must continue!" Elder Hallewell nearly shrieked, looking for a moment nearly as mad as his wife. "The *Book of the Rift* is clear, the marriage cannot take place without the Purification prior. The wedding date cannot be pushed back any further, too many preparations are already underway. We will not dishonor the Creator's blessings by flouting His word!"

No one dared argue with him further. The musicians shuffled back to their chairs, a couple of them still sniffling loudly. The Morgan daughters led their mother to a settee where they sat with her, patting her hands and whispering together behind their gloves. Recognizing defeat, Elder Potter dropped all ceremony and began pouring generous measures of whiskey and knocking one back in a single go before handing the other glasses around to the men, all of whom accepted them gratefully.

Eliza looked down at Mrs. Hallewell, who had retreated once again inside herself, completely oblivious to everything except her own tears. Then she looked at Jessamine, whose face was quite impassive.

"What would you have me do?" Eliza whispered.

Jessamine stroked her mother's face tenderly for a moment before answering.

"Please do as my father says. I will join you in my chambers as soon as the ceremony is over."

Eliza placed a hand on Mrs. Hallewell's cheek and closed her eyes. She felt the calm and the peace flooding through her own fingertips, felt it leave her, felt Mrs. Hallewell's body sag and relax with a deep and sudden sigh. Mrs. Hallewell looked up and found Eliza's face, with a flicker of fear in her eyes.

"You're using your magic on me, like she did. You're trying to make me forget him," she whispered.

"I will never let you forget him," Eliza whispered back. "No matter what, I promise you that. No one will ever try to make you forget him again."

Mrs. Hallewell let out a keening cry, and buried her face in Eliza's neck; however, she allowed herself to be set on her feet and guided back toward the staircase. But as Eliza began to ascend them, someone caught her by the arm. It was Elder Hallewell, and there was panic burning in his eyes.

"You are more powerful than Mrs. Spratt, aren't you?" he hissed.

Eliza swallowed back anger like bile. "I cannot say, sir. I knew little of the woman."

"But you can subdue her, can't you? This cannot happen again. I cannot risk any further outbursts."

"I will do my very best to keep her calm and quiet, sir. But you should know that there are feelings too deep to compel away. There are places my magic cannot touch."

Elder Hallewell looked startled at this. "What do you mean?"

"It means I cannot control your wife to her soul. And that is how it should be," Eliza said calmly. "Wouldn't you agree, sir?"

She met his eye calmly, impassively. His expression twitched with something dark and repressed, but whatever it may have been, he mastered it. He nodded his head once, slowly. "Yes, of course. A Riftborn should never have that kind of power."

A dozen images flashed through Eliza's mind at once. Jessamine, broken-hearted, walking like a puppet onto the dance floor. Her own mother, huddled in a broken heap on the floor of her cell at Bedlam. Mrs. Spratt, bloodied and forgotten upstairs. Riftborn shoving filthy hands through the bars of the Praeteritum, begging for scraps. Mrs. Hallewell sobbing for her son, and that same son, aching to belong.

"No, sir," she said softly. "There is nothing more dangerous than power in the wrong hands."

30

J OSIAH STARED AROUND THE ROOM. The remnants of the
Purification ceremony had long since been tidied away by a
veritable army of solemn-faced servants, including the streaks of
dried blood from the banisters and floors. Dr. Filbert had arrived and
his silence had been handsomely purchased. While the ceremony had
proceeded in the front entranceway, Mrs. Spratt's lifeless body had
been discreetly removed through one of the servants' entrances and
hurried away to the ignominy of a Riftborn burial plot, just another
sinner dumped unceremoniously into a mass grave. If her daughter
was lucky, news of her death would eventually reach her. Josiah
certainly did not trouble himself with such matters.

The High Elder's daughters, their husbands, and the musicians had
been escorted to their carriages and sent off into the night. Josiah had
paid the musicians such a sum that he felt fairly confident of their
silence, but he would have to trust the discretion of the Morgan family
to ensure that the news of his wife's outburst would not become the
talk of Dignus society. Here, he also had little to fear; the Morgans
were now to be associated with the Hallewells through marriage, and
it seemed very unlikely that they would sully their own reputation by
damaging Josiah's. No, all in all, he felt as sure as he reasonably could
that the matter would slip quietly behind them, lost in the splendor
of the coming wedding pageantry, and even if it did eventually make
its way into the mouths of gossiping busybodies, it would be too late.
The wedding and his rise to High Elder would already have taken
place—let them shout it from the rooftops, then, if they liked.

Taking a deep breath, he opened the door to the library where

Francis, Reginald, and Mrs. Morgan waited for him. They all looked rather the worse for wear; Mrs. Morgan's hand shook as she raised a teacup to her lips. Francis and Reginald looked slightly more in control of themselves, though it had taken several generous measures of whiskey to achieve it. Josiah cleared his throat.

"Mrs. Morgan, I trust you are feeling better?" he asked solicitously.

"Yes, thank you," she replied, her voice still weak and fluttery.

"I would like to apologize again for my wife's outburst. I am very sorry it cast a damper on what was otherwise a blessed evening," he said.

"Bloody hell, I don't think I'll sleep for a week," Reginald muttered into his glass. Francis said nothing, his expression stony.

"I believe it is important for us to discuss the mandate that was handed down by the Elder Council," Josiah went on as though he hadn't heard Reginald's words, "that the High Elder commune with the Rift and seek guidance on the fate of his position in the highest seat."

"*That's* why you kept us here?" Reginald asked, incredulous. "How can you think about that after the night we've just endured?"

Josiah glanced at Francis, looking for support, but Francis was determinedly not looking at him. His silence spoke louder than any words could have: *you're on your own.*

"I appreciate that we are all shaken, but the fact remains that we have a duty, to your father and to your commitment to my daughter. We must see this through; after all, it is your father's most profound wish that you be settled and the Illustratum be kept in safe hands."

"And by safe hands, you mean your hands," Reginald shot back.

"That is your father's wish, yes," Josiah said.

"Do you deny it is your wish as well?" Reginald asked.

"I do not," Josiah said in a voice of determined calm. "But I have always been guided by your father in my ambitions. If he were to commune with the Rift and learn that the Creator has different plans for me, I will of course follow whatever guidance I am given."

"What, you mean you'll just walk away from the highest seat in the land?" Reginald challenged him, with something very close to a jeer in his voice.

"Certainly, I will. I have no desire to interfere with the Creator's plan for me," Josiah said. "And I shall bend my mind, body, and duty to His will, as always."

Reginald looked mildly chastened and slouched over to the cart in search of another drink. Francis continued his silence.

"I thought I made it clear when last we spoke of this matter," Mrs. Morgan said, setting down her teacup, "that my husband is in no fit state to leave the palace, let alone traverse across the city to commune with the Rift."

"And I understand your concern, Mrs. Morgan," Josiah said, smiling patiently at her even as impatience burned in his chest. "But you must understand that, as High Elder, your husband has a duty to his title that supersedes all else."

"You would have him sacrifice himself to carry out this mandate?" Mrs. Morgan asked, tears in her voice now.

"I would have him do the Creator's will and nothing more or less," Josiah said. "And I am sure your husband would say the same, if you asked him."

"My husband," Mrs. Morgan replied, the words struggling out around clenched teeth, "has no regard for his own physical well-being. He will certainly squander what little health and strength remain to him if he embarks on this foolish pilgrimage."

"A foolish pilgrimage, is it, to seek direct communion with the Creator?" Josiah asked, his eyebrows raised.

"Th-that's not what I mean!" Mrs. Morgan cried out, half-rising from her seat, but finding herself still quite unsteady. "The point of this trip to the Illustratum would be to prove that he is well enough to continue carrying out his duties, but it is all in vain! He is not well enough, and the effort to prove otherwise will surely kill him!"

"I wish you had the same faith in the Creator as you seem to have in your own declarations," Josiah said. "He shall surely sustain your husband through whatever spiritual exertions are required of him."

Mrs. Morgan opened her mouth to argue, but what could she say? If she continued to oppose Josiah, she would be flirting dangerously with blasphemy, and even her concern for her husband would not allow her to venture that far. Josiah watched with satisfaction as she gave up, dropping her eyes to her own lap and sniffing to hold back tears. Frankly, he was surprised at her fiercely protective manner. It was an odd match from the beginning, with John Morgan being so many years her senior, and yet, it seemed she had developed a sort of affection for him. At the very least, she cared whether he lived or died, which was more than he could say for half the Elder Council marriages, and certainly more than he could say for his own, having survived his wife's violent attack only hours before.

"Well, I for one think he should get on with it," Reginald said, a bit loudly. "He's not fooling anyone by hiding in the palace. He's got to face it. Show the Elder Council the true state of things and let them get on with replacing him, if that's what they need to do."

"Reginald!" Mrs. Morgan cried out. "How can you say such a thing!"

"Quite easily," Reginald said with a careless shrug. "Rolls right off the tongue, really."

"I've never been so ashamed of you!" Mrs. Morgan replied, fishing in her reticule for a handkerchief.

"Well, you can't have been paying much attention, then," Reginald muttered, turning his back on her and strolling toward the windows.

"Come now, let's not have any arguments, here," Josiah said, raising his hands. "I know John would not want it so. I agree with Reginald that the journey over to the Illustratum must take place, but I promise, Mrs. Morgan, to ensure that it is as safe and gentle an excursion as possible. We shall enlist the help of your husband's physicians to accompany us. We shall arrange the trip for nighttime, to avoid traffic and delay on the roads, as well as to avoid prying eyes. It shall be over and done within a matter of a couple of hours at most."

Mrs. Morgan bit her lip and did not respond. Josiah suspected she still disapproved of the plan, but it seemed she would not vocalize her doubts any longer. That battle won, Josiah turned to Francis, who was still doing his damnedest not to acknowledge him.

"Very well, if we are all in agreement, Francis and I shall arrange everything for tomorrow night."

Mrs. Morgan's voice was choked with tears. "I would like to go home now," she mumbled.

"Yes, of course. It has been a most trying evening for all of us." He reached out and took her hand, helping her to her feet. "I hope we can count on your discretion about this evening's events, Mrs. Morgan. My wife is unwell, and I would hate for her to become some kind of public spectacle due to idle gossip."

Josiah heard a noise come from Francis, a sort of snorting, choking

294

noise, but still he said nothing. Mrs. Morgan, however, dropped into a curtsy, her cheeks reddening.

"Of course, Elder Hallewell. I certainly have no intention of gossiping, and I shall pray that the Creator heal your wife's regrettable condition and grant her peace."

"I thank you," Josiah said, and looked to Reginald, who shrugged, drained his glass once more, and followed them toward the door. Josiah saw them into the custody of the footmen and returned to the library, where Francis still stood silently.

"Have you nothing to say?" Josiah asked at last, barely able to keep a testy edge from his voice.

Francis snorted again. "My God, Josiah, why did you never tell me?"

Josiah pressed his lips together. "You knew she wasn't well. You knew I had to keep her with the nursemaid."

"Josiah, she almost committed a double murder tonight with a pair of sewing scissors, for Creator's sake! There's a damn good bit of difference between being unwell and being a raving, murderous lunatic! You're going to have to commit her, there's no way around it. If word ever got out about what she is—about what she *said*..."

"No one will believe what she says," Josiah snapped.

"Plenty of your enemies will want to believe it, Josiah, so you'd best pray that the people gathered here tonight keep their word so it doesn't get out," Francis replied. He slammed his glass down on the table. "Damn it all, I just want this to be over," he roared.

"There we are in perfect agreement," Josiah said, endeavoring to keep his voice calm.

Francis turned and looked Josiah in the eye. "I will do this. I will help get Morgan to the Illustratum to buy us all a little more time. But that is all. You have brought this quest for power to the brink of lunacy, Josiah, and I refuse to walk over the edge with you. No more surprises. No more, or you're on your own, do you hear me?"

"I assure you, I do," Josiah said. "You must see that this is a test, Francis! The Creator is testing me, challenging me, to prove myself worthy of His favor. I cannot let him down now. I cannot give up. We cannot give up."

Francis crossed the room so that he stood right in front of Josiah. "Do not confuse the success of the Creator's plans with the failure of your own," he said.

And then he left, leaving Josiah alone in the gathering dark to grapple with all that had befallen him, and all that he had brought upon himself.

§

"She looks so small," Jessamine whispered. She was sitting cross-legged on the edge of her bed, looking down on her mother, who was sleeping soundly. Once in a while her breath would hitch, as over a sob that still lingered in her chest, but otherwise, she was peaceful.

"Grief can diminish you," Eliza said quietly. She was bustling around the room, tidying the evidence of the night they had all endured. Lillian's nightgown was nothing more but a pile of ashes smoldering softly in the fireplace grate. Lillian herself had been bathed and changed into a clean nightgown of her daughter's, her hair brushed and braided, and settled down to sleep before Jessamine had so much as plucked the wilting rose from her own curls. Then Eliza had helped her out of her own gown and into her nightclothes. Throughout it all, Lillian never spoke another word. Eliza's magic worked to calm and soothe her, keeping the dark shadows in her mind at bay.

"Poor Mrs. Spratt," Jessamine whispered.

Eliza bit back tears as she answered, "Yes. She did not deserve what happened to her, but your mother couldn't have known that."

"But Mrs. Spratt was her caretaker," Jessamine said, and there were tears in her voice as well.

"Mrs. Spratt used her magic to keep your mother in this state," Eliza said. "She's been a prisoner all this time, and she has only ever understood Mrs. Spratt to be her jailer. Who can blame her for making a bid for freedom when she had the chance? As terrible as all of this is, your mother is not responsible."

Jessamine's hands clenched into fists. "But my father is."

"Yes, I daresay he is," Eliza agreed.

"I've never heard her speak of William like that before," Jessamine choked out.

Eliza felt her whole body stiffen. She did not reply, but her mind was racing. This was the moment she had been anticipating since the word "magic" had escaped Lillian's lips.

"I wonder how she convinced herself that William was Riftborn,"

Jessamine murmured, staring at her mother's face as she said the words, as though wishing she could answer. "Madness is such a strange, twisted thing."

Eliza's throat had gone dry. Eli had agreed that, when the moment presented itself, Eliza would be the right person to tell Jessamine the truth. Try as she might to deny it, the moment had arrived. She swallowed hard, wet her lips, and launched into an explanation before she could talk herself out of it.

"Miss Jessamine, I have something to tell you. Let's come sit over here so that your mother can sleep undisturbed."

Jessamine hesitated a moment, loathe to leave her mother's bedside, but she did as Eliza bid her and sat down beside Eliza in front of the fire. When they had settled there, Jessamine looked Eliza in the face, her expression so innocently clueless, and Eliza could hardly force the words out. When at last she did, they tumbled over each other in a rush.

"Your mother was telling the truth. Your brother was Riftborn," she blurted out.

The words expanded like a bomb, filling the room, the air crackling with a truth set free at last. Eliza could feel the enormity of what she had spoken aloud pressing against her eardrums, buzzing against her skin like a current. "He was born with Riftmagic, and when that magic was discovered, your father knew it would destroy his career and his reputation, everything he had worked so hard to build and preserve over his lifetime."

Jessamine sat statue-still, a study in evolving grief. Eliza went on before the look of devastation on her mistress' face could drive her into silence.

"Your father planned to stage William's death. Your mother discovered his plan and tried to thwart it. She asked for my mother's help in smuggling him to safety."

"It can't be true," Jessamine mouthed.

"It is true."

"But how could you possibly know such a thing?"

"Your mother told me."

Jessamine's whole body shuddered in revulsion. "My mother hasn't spoken a word of sense in more than fifteen years. She's raving."

"No, she's grieving. And she's been silenced on your father's orders. She wasn't being kept calm, she was being kept quiet. Mrs. Spratt has seen to that," Eliza said, trying to keep the bitterness out of her voice. After all, Mrs. Spratt was as much a pawn in Elder Hallewell's game as the rest of them.

Jessamine shook her head violently, her dark curls falling all over her face. "No. I don't believe this. I can't believe that—" But her voice trailed off and a spark of realization came into her eyes. "Oh, no. Your mother. She disappeared right after... they caught her, didn't they? That's why they locked her away?"

Eliza nodded solemnly. "She's not crazy, Jessamine, no more than your mother or Bridie. She was locked away so that no one would ever find out about William."

"But then... what happened to my brother?" Jessamine whispered, the words escaping around the fingers pressed to her mouth, fingers that looked desperate to keep the question from coming out because the answer must be too terrible to face.

"It's all right, Jessamine," Eliza said, reaching out for her mistress' hands and pulling them down into her own to squeeze them tightly. "My mother succeeded. William was safely delivered into the hands of those who would protect him. He's safe. He's alive."

"William... William is *alive?* But how could you... where is—" Jessamine's questions tumbled out over one another.

"He was rescued and raised by members of the Resistance—a group of Riftborn citizens committed to defying the Illustratum. At the time, your father used the capture and exposure of the Lamplighters Confederacy to mask what had happened. He claimed your brother was kidnapped and killed as revenge for the capture of John Davies, but none of it was true. The Lamplighters Confederacy was trying to rescue and smuggle out Riftborn children from Dignus families before they could abandon or harm them. Your brother was the last one they managed to rescue, just as it all fell apart."

Jessamine was shaking her head, as though trying to force all the new information to sink in. "My brother is alive," she said, almost experimentally, like trying to speak a new language for the first time.

"You've met him, Jessamine. At Bedlam," Eliza said quietly.

Her eyes widened in alarm. "Do you mean to say he was a patient in that horrible—"

"No, no," Eliza said, snatching at Jessamine's hands again. "He helped us rescue Bridie and my mother, do you remember? He goes by Eli now."

"Eli... you mean the man who... he had looked familiar to me... Eli... William *Elias*...

Eliza held her breath as all the color drained from Jessamine's face, sure her mistress was about to faint dead away. But instead, a remarkable thing happened. A bubble of sound escaped her lips—a sound halfway between a sob and a laugh. Then another escaped, and another, until she was laughing and crying hysterically in equal measure. She flung herself forward and launched herself at Eliza in a hug that knocked her flat to the floor. Before Eliza could even get her breath back, she found she was laughing and crying too, and before long the two girls lay together with their arms around each other. At that Eliza got a grip on herself.

"Shh, or we'll wake your mother!" she murmured.

"My brother is alive," Jessamine whispered again. "I can't believe it."

"I know," Eliza said. "It was just how I felt when we discovered my mother."

Jessamine rolled onto her side so that her tear-tracked face was nearly nose to nose with Eliza's. "But I still don't understand how you know any of this?"

Eliza sighed. "I can hardly understand it myself. It was pure chance that I met your brother in the first place. A chance encounter on the street. I used my Riftmagic on him and he realized how powerful I was and who I worked for. And he rescued me, that day in the Barrens when you insisted on dressing in Bridie's uniform to accompany me—you saw him talking to me when you and Martin found me.

"That was William?!"

"Yes, it was. I would have been killed in that riot if it wasn't for him." *Oh, and I fear I may be madly in love with him*, she added silently to herself. She wasn't quite ready to let *that* part of the truth slip out.

"Did he... did he know who I was when we met at Bedlam?"

Eliza shook her head. "No. Well, yes, of course, he knew who *you* were. But he didn't yet know who *he* was. It was only after we found my mother that he discovered the truth. He knew he was a Riftborn child of a Dignus family, but he only just learned he's a Hallewell."

Jessamine's face fell. "But why didn't you tell me right away?"

Eliza's heart sank. "I know, and I'm so terribly sorry about that. But I needed to be sure."

"Of what?"

"Of you."

Jessamine frowned. "What do you mean?"

Eliza sighed and chose her words carefully. "You and I have always been friends. But it was only recently that we became much more friends than mistress and servant." Eliza took Jessamine's hands and folded them, one on top of the other, in hers. "I must ask you something, and it is very important that you tell me the absolute truth."

"Of course I will, Eliza."

Eliza took a deep, steadying breath. She didn't realize how afraid she was of the answer until that very moment. "Do you believe what the Elders preach? About Riftmagic being a sign of moral weakness? Do you believe I am less of a person than you are, less worthy of freedom? Less worthy of love from the Creator?"

Jessamine's lips trembled. "Of course I don't. I love you, Eliza, you know that, don't you?"

"I do know that," Eliza said calmly. "But I also know that you can love a dog or a cat. It does not mean that you do not believe them to be less than you are."

Jessamine looked as though she had been slapped in the face, but she recovered quickly. Some part of her must have known it was fair. "I think..." she said slowly, "that there was a time when I might have believed that. No, that's not the truth. I *did* believe that. And it wasn't very long ago, either. When I was younger, when I had never taken a moment to think for myself. And even now it would be... *easier* not to question the things my father has taught me."

Eliza waited patiently as Jessamine searched for the words. She had to be sure.

"But I've realized my father only cares about one thing. Power is the love of his life, and our family has been obliterated because of it. Nothing could ever be more important to him than his ascension to the seat of High Elder, not my happiness, or my mother's sanity... or even my brother's life." Jessamine sniffed loudly. "The only time your Riftmagic has ever harmed me was when my father forced your hand. Riftmagic isn't the danger, I know that now. It is those who would use and abuse that magic for their own ends who are the real danger, and no one has been more guilty of that than my own father."

Eliza nodded. "And would you like that to end? Not just here in this house, but everywhere?"

"Yes," Jessamine whispered. "I want him to pay for what he did. I want my brother back."

Eliza's mouth stretched into a smile. "Then I can finally tell you everything."

Jessamine looked weary. "You mean there's *more?!*"

"I'm afraid so," Eliza said. "You remember I told you that you wouldn't have to marry Reginald on Saturday?"

"Yes, but you've still refused to tell me exactly how," Jessamine grumbled.

"That's because it was part of a much bigger plan," Eliza said. "And if we succeed, you won't be the only one gaining your freedom."

Jessamine's eyes shone with fevered excitement. "Well, what are you waiting for? Tell me!"

31

T HE NIGHT WAS SLIPPING QUIETLY AWAY, receding
from the sky and withdrawing its inky fingers from corners
where the shadows gathered and pooled. The last of the
customers who were fit to walk had stumbled their way out of Madam
Lavender's, some whistling unconcernedly, others wracking their
whiskey-addled brains for an excuse as to where they had been and
why their pockets were empty. Not one of them noticed the young
men entering the place, caps pulled low over their faces, expressions
carefully blank. The newcomers did not go to the bar, but slid into a
booth in the farthest corner of the place, arranging their chairs so that
they had a clear view of the doorway. Then they waited.

Eli and Jasper glanced at each other, each realizing they should
probably be laughing or making some idle conversation for the sake
of appearances, but neither of them quite had it in them. They'd been
run ragged over the last few days, coordinating plans, recruiting and
training members, assigning tasks, and helping with the continued
distribution of the now harmless Riftmead being carted into the city
from the bottling plants the Resistance had infiltrated. On top of all
of this, Eli was battling constant anxiety over the many risks being
taken by people he cared about, Eliza and Jessamine at the very top of
the list. He knew his sister didn't know him from any other Barrens
guttersnipe, but that didn't mean he wasn't half-mad with fear that
she'd been caught up in their schemes.

"Aren't you going to buy me a round?" Jasper asked idly.

"No."

"And why ever not, pray tell?"

"Because I'm still mad at you," Eli replied, though there was no heat in his voice.

"Ah, no you're not, not really," Jasper said easily, sounding so much like the lanky kid he once was that Eli almost grinned. "You know it's the right thing to do."

"Yeah, maybe," Eli allowed.

"And also, you're sore that you didn't think of it yourself," Jasper added.

"Now, there you're wrong. I never would have suggested something like that."

"Well then, you should feel lucky that you have someone like me to do it for you," Jasper said. When Eli didn't rib him back, Jasper took a closer look at Eli's face. "Oi, mate, I'm only muckin' about. I know you... no one wants to put Eliza in harm's way."

Eli's face seemed to fold in on itself. He hadn't told Jasper what had happened between him and Eliza, but Jasper seemed to have figured it out anyway, and he didn't bother asking how. Instead he said, "I know. I know, but isn't that exactly what we're doing?"

"Look, I was wrong about that girl, okay? I admit it. I was a fool for thinking she'd be useless just because she's a manor girl. She's damn brave, actually. And we wouldn't be planning this attack without her. But even if we didn't use my plan, what did you think she'd be doing, sitting at home with her needlepoint?"

Eli blinked. "I... well, no, of course not, but—"

"Then what's left but to be in the thick of it? She wasn't going to cower in a corner while we charged ahead. She was always going to fight. And if I know that, mate, then you most certainly do."

Eli sighed, and even in his own ears, it was a defeated sound. "I just... I don't know what I'd do if... if something happened to her."

The last dregs of merriment drained from Jasper's face. He quirked his lips like he was trying to find the right thing to say. Then, he seemed to decide that he just didn't have the words, and so he put his hand on Eli's shoulder and gave it a sympathetic squeeze.

And Eli felt bolstered. It was exactly what he needed at that moment—the chance to just sit with his fear, to face it, without having to fend off well-meaning placations and empty promises that made his ears ring with their hollowness. Tomorrow was not promised to any of them, and the sooner he looked that truth dead in the eye, the better he'd be able to face what was to come.

"I hope you two aren't looking for companionship, because the pickings are slim at this time of the morning."

Eli and Jasper looked up to see Penny smirking down at them.

"All right, Penny?" Jasper asked by way of greeting, pulling out a chair for her.

She flopped into it. "I've been worse," she replied, rubbing at her eyes and stifling a yawn. "What's the word, then?"

"I'd say we're cautiously optimistic at this point," Eli said. "Organizing has gone off without too much trouble. We've got more volunteers than I ever thought we'd get, and more keep showing up at the Bell and Flagon every day. No Praesidio have come snooping around, none of us have been stopped, so I think we've managed to keep a lid on our plans. Now we've just got to make it until Saturday."

"So close yet so far," Jasper said. "Still a lot of time left for things to go to hell."

"That sounds uncharacteristically dark for you," Penny remarked. "The Jasper I know turns positively gleeful at the thought of things going to hell."

Jasper acknowledged the truth with a grin, but it faded quickly. "As a rule, sure, but not this time, Pen."

"I'm surprised Lavender agreed to let us meet here," Eli said. "She's usually too careful for that kind of thing."

"Yeah, well, times change. Jasper's avoiding risks while Lavender's taking them. Bloody world's turned upside down, hasn't it?" Penny snorted.

"I'll say," Jasper mumbled.

Penny threw an expectant look at the door, and then lowered her voice. "You say you know everyone who turned up at that first meeting?"

"Of course," Eli said, frowning. "It was by invitation only, you know. Couldn't risk the plan by opening it up to strangers."

Penny bit her lip.

"What is it, Pen?"

"I saw someone there, a girl, and I thought she looked a bit like—"

"Sorry I'm late."

All three of them looked up, startled to see that Daniel Byrne was standing right in front of them.

"Blimey, Daniel! I almost didn't recognize you without your

uniform!" Penny gasped, her hand clutching at her chest as though she could reach right through it and calm her racing heart.

Daniel chuckled. "I'm not sure whether I should be insulted or pleased that I blend in so easily."

"Daniel, this is Eli Turner and Jasper Quinn," Penny said, gesturing between them. "Eli, Jasper, this is Daniel Byrne, defected Praesidio guard and our ticket into the Praeteritum."

Daniel made a stunted motion like he was going to hold out a hand for them to shake, but he seemed to think better of it. He gave a nod instead, which Eli and Jasper returned, somewhat warily. Jasper went a step further and pulled out a chair. Daniel looked relieved as he dropped into it, as though he had just passed some test he thought he might fail.

"I thought it best to change out of my uniform before heading over here," Daniel explained. "Thought I'd draw less attention that way."

Eli just nodded again. He knew Sully, Lavender, and even Eliza had decided to trust Daniel Byrne, but the sheer weight of what he had to lose if the soldier betrayed them was making it hard for him to show that same trust.

"So, what can you tell us? Anything?" Penny pressed since the men on either side of her were still tight-lipped.

Daniel leaned forward, clearly eager to prove himself. "The Praeteritum will be operating on the wedding day with only a third of its regular staffing," he said. "They reassigned dozens of soldiers to the procession route, to keep spectators at bay."

Jasper nearly smiled. "Excellent."

"Your best chance of infiltrating the Praeteritum is to create a diversion somewhere along the north wall," Daniel went on. "The patrols will have no choice but to respond to it, and when they do, you should be able to infiltrate along the southeast corner, where the fences are."

"How much time do you think we'd need?" Eli asked.

"Ten, maybe fifteen minutes?" Daniel said, his expression thoughtful. "It would be more effective if the prisoners were ready and waiting for you, prepared to make a run for it."

"What about getting a message to them?" Penny asked. "Warn them to be ready and waiting?"

"It's risky," Eli said, rubbing meditatively at the stubble on his chin as he spoke. "But if the prisoners know why they're being

306

released, there's a better chance more of them will join us in the fight rather than just running as far from the Praeteritum as they can."

"Many of them will still do that," Penny pointed out.

"Sure, the real cowards and criminals will," Jasper replied. "But who wants them anyway? I want the angry ones. I want the wrongfully imprisoned ones, the ones who sit all day with vengeance smoldering their blood. Those are the prisoners we need."

"Oh, I think you'll have plenty of them," Daniel said. "I'm very sorry to say that's the majority of the people trapped behind those walls."

"Walls that you've been guarding," Jasper said evenly.

Daniel did not shy away from the accusation. He looked Jasper dead in the eye as he said, "I'm not proud of it. I've known it was wrong for a long time now, and regardless of what happens on Saturday, I will not be doing the Illustratum's dirty work ever again."

"I hope we all get the chance to hold you to that promise," Eli said.

"So do I," Daniel said.

Penny's eyes darted back and forth between the men, reading the moment, it seemed, before she attempted to steer the conversation back to the details. "So, the message then? What do you think is the best way to get it to the prisoners?"

Daniel thought about it. "There's this one man. Waits by the bars of the fence every single day for hours on end, in the hopes of catching a glimpse of his son. The boy is an apprentice in the cobbler's shop and has to walk within view of the fence every day. We've formed a bit of a... rapport him and me."

"What do you mean a rapport?" Jasper asked, looking intrigued in spite of himself.

Daniel shrugged. "I've talked with him a bit. He told me about his son. So, I stop by the cobblers once a week to get my boots shined up. Talk with the boy a bit, and take the news back to his pa. The boy doesn't know, of course."

"So, this man trusts you," Eli said.

"That's right," Daniel said. "Well, as much as a prisoner can trust his jailer, anyway."

"What's he in for?" Jasper asked.

Daniel met his eye again. "Broke into an apothecary and stole medicine he couldn't afford. Saved the boy's life."

Jasper swore under his breath. Eli rubbed his hand over his face again, feeling suddenly as exhausted as he'd ever felt in his life.

"If you write it and I give it to him, I think he'll see to it you've got as many prisoners ready and waiting to join you as you could hope for," Daniel said.

Eli looked at Jasper and a silent understanding passed between them: this was as good an opportunity as they were going to get.

"All right, then. Penny will get the message to you, once Sully's crafted it. Do you think you could pass it along on Friday night?"

Penny frowned. "That won't give the prisoners much time."

"We don't want to give them much time," Jasper said. "The less time they have to talk themselves out of it, the better."

"I think I know a bit about that," she muttered. All three men knew exactly what she meant, but had the decency to ignore it.

"Are we agreed then?" Daniel asked, looking levelly at Eli and Jasper, and all three of them knew there was a deeper question lying beneath the surface.

Again, Jasper and Eli looked at each other. Again, a silent understanding passed between them. It was Eli who stuck out his hand first.

"We are agreed."

§

Josiah stood in front of the great golden doors, staring up at them with undisguised longing as he had done every day for months. Each time he found himself troubled, unsure, undecided, he came and he stood right here, to remind himself what it all was for.

To walk through those doors. To feel the connection. To hear the Words and feel them in his soul and never to doubt himself again.

To the outside world his faith appeared unshakable, but Josiah had found himself shaken many times in recent months; the whispers of doubts in his ears, in voices he did not recognize. Sometimes, he thought he must be going mad, that the thoughts intruding on his surety must be malevolent in nature, outside forces of evil, trying to steer him from the Path he had worked so hard to climb very nearly to the top.

"The journey will get harder, the farther you travel along the way," his father had once told him. "Each hardship is a test you must pass, and pass it you will, for this is your Calling." No doubts ever crept into his father's words or hid in the depths of his eyes. Josiah could not allow them to infest him either.

Behind those doors was the *Sacrum Odium*, a place where only the High Elder could enter, the only place where a mortal man could hope to speak directly with the Creator. It was said that when the High Elder was in commune with the Rift, the connection was so powerful that the very air would spark and hum, and the High Elder would taste the pure power on his tongue and feel it in his skin. What utter bliss it must be to be chosen, to be enveloped in a truth so profound you could never doubt again.

John Morgan would do it tonight, one last time. And then it would be Josiah's turn.

Josiah was shaken from his waking reverie by the sound of the door opening at the end of the hall. Brother Goodwin appeared, followed by a man Josiah recognized as one of the palace physicians. He turned on his heel and walked to meet them.

"Dr. Thomas, welcome," Josiah said with an ingratiating smile. "I trust your journey from the palace went smoothly."

"You should trust no such thing," Dr. Thomas said stiffly. "I have repeatedly advised against this excursion on medical grounds."

"And I am sorry that I had to insist upon it, on spiritual grounds," Josiah said. "But we shall not interfere with the High Elder's recovery again, I assure you."

Dr. Thomas snorted. "Recovery? Have you read a single word of the letters I've been sending to you? There will be no recovery; the man is dying, and all the more quickly for having been made to leave the confines of his chambers."

"Ah, yes, I sometimes forget that men of science are rarely men of faith," Josiah said, and there was a denunciation clear in his voice.

Dr. Thomas' eyes darted to the great golden doors over Josiah's shoulder before answering, carefully, "I have always considered myself to be a man of both."

"Then today is an ideal opportunity to demonstrate that," Josiah said. "All is prepared. You may bring the High Elder along."

"We are working to stabilize him in the outer chambers," Dr. Thomas said, the words making their way out through his clenched teeth. "When his heart rate and breathing are under control again, we will bring him down."

Josiah bit back an impatient reply and nodded curtly instead. Almost unconsciously, he touched the breast pocket of his jacket, as though checking to see that the envelope he'd tucked away there hadn't somehow vanished. It was the nomination letter, the one Morgan had refused to sign before the wedding. Josiah was not planning to waste this chance to importune him to reconsider signing it without delay. Given the incredible ordeal it had been to get him to the Illustratum, Josiah hoped that Morgan might be just a bit more pliable, a bit more cognizant of how ill he really was, and why he could not afford to delay in making his wishes known for the future of the leadership. He would wait, however, until Morgan's communion with the Rift was over.

"Let us go to him, then, and see how he fares," Josiah said, gesturing back along the corridor the way they had just come, turning his back reluctantly on the seductive call of what lay promised behind the golden doors.

32

ELIZA WOKE SUDDENLY AND COMPLETELY as though someone had spoken her own name into her ear. She stared around, startled, but she was alone. Mrs. Hallewell lay in Jessamine's bed, sleeping soundly. Jessamine, too, was breathing deeply and evenly, curled up under a blanket on the settee. Eliza stood up out of her chair stiffly and stretched. Her head had drooped onto her chest and she had a kink in her neck. She massaged it with her fingers, wondering what could have woken her, and had just begun to think it might have been a dream when she heard a quiet tapping on the door.

She hurried across the room, glancing over her shoulder to make sure that Mrs. Hallewell and Jessamine hadn't been disturbed, then pulled the door open.

Her father stood in the doorway and, beside him, Brother Goodwin, sweaty-faced and visibly shaking from head to toe.

"Whatever is the matter?" Eliza managed to ask, her heart leaping into a gallop.

"Miss Braxton, I n-need you to follow me," Brother Goodwin whispered.

Eliza did not move. "Where are we going?"

Her father's mouth twisted unpleasantly. "Elder Hallewell has sent for you. You are to go with Brother Goodwin to the Illustratum."

If Eliza hadn't already been holding onto the doorframe, she might not have been able to stay on her feet—her legs had suddenly turned to custard. "But why? What could he possibly want with me?" she squeaked.

Brother Goodwin opened his mouth as though he had every intention of giving her a thorough explanation when her father cut him off with a sharp, "It is not for you to question an order from Elder Hallewell! He has sent for you and you must go."

"It is a matter of some urgency," Brother Goodwin added, his lips trembling. "Time is of the essence."

"What are you just standing there, gaping for? Get a move on, child!" her father hissed, his eyes quite wild, and still Eliza's feet refused to move.

"But... Mrs. Hallewell. I've been ordered not to leave her," she said.

Brother Goodwin looked completely at a loss as to how to deal with this complication, but Braxton huffed loudly. "I will get someone to tend to Mrs. Hallewell! You must go!"

"I'm the only Influencer in the house! What if she—"

But Braxton's shallow pool of patience had run dry. He reached out and grabbed Eliza by the arm, pulling her roughly through the door and into the hallway. She reacted instinctively, the magic surging through her, unchecked by the dulling influence of Riftmead. Her father's hand flew from her arm as though some invisible being had tugged it violently away. He was thrown off balance, stumbling backward into a table. He lifted his head slowly, staring at her as though he had no idea who or what she was.

"I will not be mistreated in such a manner," she said, and though her voice was quiet and even, the rest of her was blazing with anger. She straightened the sleeve on her dress and smoothed her hair. "Very well, Brother Goodwin, I shall come with you."

"I... that is... thank you for... this way please," Brother Goodwin replied, eyes wide.

"Father, I suggest Liesel come sit with Mrs. Hallewell. Mrs. Keats will be too busy in the kitchen, and Liesel is the only other staff member she might recognize, should she wake before I return." She turned back to Goodwin and asked the question that roiled in her stomach. "When shall I be returning?"

"Oh, I do think very soon, miss. The matter... well... it's soon to be over." His voice trailed away in a whisper.

Eliza nodded her head, and her panic lessened by a fraction of a degree. She found that her feet would, at last, obey her and she let them carry her down the corridor, down the stairs, and out of the main entrance hall. A carriage was waiting in the gravel drive, the horses pawing and snorting nervously.

When the carriage had exited the gates of Larkspur Manor, Eliza asked, "Will you truly give me no reason for this late-night venture?"

"I am terribly sorry, Miss Braxton, but I am not at liberty to say. I was instructed not to tell you anything," Brother Goodwin mumbled.

Eliza considered for a moment merely reaching across the narrow space between them and compelling him to tell her everything, but decided against it. She would know soon enough, and it hardly seemed worth a sentence in the Praeteritum for using Riftmagic upon an unsuspecting Dignus. Instead, she vibrated with tension against the seat, wondering what in the world could cause Elder Hallewell to summon her to the Illustratum in the dead of night, her mind presenting one terrifying possibility after another. She knew it must have something to do with the Resistance. Something must have happened, someone must have betrayed them. Had it been one of the people they'd recruited? Had someone perhaps been caught, someone like Zeke or Jasper or… her brain would not allow her to even think his name.

She thought the ride would feel agonizingly long, but instead the minutes slipped past her with frightening quickness and, much sooner than she ever would have thought possible, she found herself staring up at the imposing façade of the Illustratum, a sight which once upon a time had filled her with awe and reverence, but now left only an icy chill in her heart and a sheen of cold sweat on her brow. Her legs kept trying to fold beneath her as she walked through the echoing halls, up a flight of stairs behind a door, and along the upper halls of the Illustratum, where she had never been before. With every step, her heart threatened to beat straight out of her chest.

At last, they turned a corner and Eliza froze in her tracks, a gasp escaping her lips before she could slap her hand over it. The hallway ended in a pair of towering golden doors, two stories tall, intricately carved, and engraved with words and symbols. She had never seen those doors before—she was not sure any Riftborn ever had—but she had heard them spoken of in awed whispers: the doors to the *Sacrum Odium*: to the very Rift itself.

"Miss Braxton, come along!" Brother Goodwin's harried cry broke through her shock. She hastened to follow him, each step bringing them closer and closer to those doors.

"We... we aren't g-going through there, are we?" she asked in a strangled whisper that nevertheless echoed around the cavernous hallway.

"Of course not!" Brother Goodwin snapped. "We aren't allowed through there!" And then he turned, stopping in front of a perfectly ordinary wooden door, and knocked sharply.

"Who is it?" came a muffled voice. Deep. A man's. Eliza could not be sure if she recognized it; the pounding of blood in her ears was deafening.

"It's Brother Goodwin, sir. I brought the Influencer, as you requested."

"Bring her in, bring her in!"

The door was flung open and Eliza was thrust unceremoniously through it. She barely managed to stay on her feet. She gazed around, her fear peaking and then, suddenly, draining away as confusion took its place.

There were no gallows, no instruments of torture, no grim-faced row of Elders waiting to pass judgment. Instead, Eliza found herself gazing upon a makeshift hospital room. Nurses bustled around the metal bed frame, adjusting blankets and administering remedies. Even as she watched, a young woman injected a syringe of something into the wasted arm of a man Eliza did not recognize—at least, not at first. But then the man groaned and turned his face upon his pillow so that the light threw his features into sharp relief.

Eliza stared in horror at the High Elder, and the High Elder's hollow, pain-riddled eyes stared back.

Eliza stumbled backward against the wall. Her brain felt electrified as it tried to understand everything she was taking in, but her body was already trying to flee. Somehow, before her brain had even caught up, her body seemed to know that something was very, very wrong.

"Eliza! There you are! For Creator's sake, what took so long?"

It was the only voice that could have ratcheted her fear any higher. Elder Hallewell emerged from the darkened corner of the room, invisible at first because of his dark suit and cloak. His pale face seemed to float forward, disembodied, twisted and contorted with a kind of maniacal panic. His eye twitched, his hair was in disarray, and when he spoke again, that terribly familiar voice was tight and shaking.

"We are in need of your Riftmagic, child. Remove those gloves at once!"

Every single pair of eyes in the room was upon her. Behind Elder Hallewell was a knot of other men, all with the same harried, exhausted look to them. One of them she recognized as Elder Potter. Another was wearing the white coat of a doctor and an extremely grim expression. The others were mere specters in the wavering light, all staring at her, eyes gleaming with expectation. As she stared at them, Brother Goodwin scuttled past her and joined them, blending into the shadows and turning his eyes on her like the rest of them.

"Eliza, come here at once." Elder Hallewell did not even wait for her to comply, but shuffled forward with those fevered, gleaming eyes and pulled Eliza toward the bed by the crook of her elbow. She flinched away from him, terrified to look at him.

"This is the High Elder of the Illustratum," he said, as though she didn't know exactly who he was, as though she had not attended his services every week of her life and journeyed to the palace with them. Eliza did not know what to say, and so she said the first thing that came into her head.

"H-he looks very ill."

"He is dying." The words fell to the floor like stones with a blunt finality. No one reacted to them. Everyone in the room had already absorbed this terrible truth, everyone except for Eliza, and so her quiet gasp was the only sound in the silence that followed. Everyone simply continued to stare at her while she stared at the High Elder, watching in growing alarm at the sound of his labored breathing, and the way his eyes seemed to be moving rapidly back and forth beneath his partially closed eyelids. Jessamine had told her, of course, that he was ill, that they had even moved up the wedding date because of his ill health, but that information had not prepared her for the sight of a man clearly teetering on the precipice of death itself.

When no one spoke again, she tore her eyes away from the dying man and found Elder Hallewell's face again. "Why am I here, sir?"

"I need you... we need you... to help him," Elder Hallewell said.

Eliza darted a look back at the High Elder. His face was coated in a sheen of sweat. He looked delirious, his mouth moving in a constant, silent muttering of sorts.

"I... I don't understand, sir. I'm not a healer. I know nothing of medicine. How am I to help him, sir? Surely his doctors and nurses can do that, if anyone can," Eliza replied.

"Of course, I know you aren't a healer, you ridiculous child. It is not medical assistance I require of you. It is your Riftmagic," Elder Hallewell snapped. Eliza flinched, but she did not back down.

"My Riftmagic cannot stop a man from dying," she whispered. "I do not possess the power you require, sir. No Riftborn does."

"I am not asking you to save his life!" Elder Hallewell cried, slamming his hand down upon the bedside table, sending a mortar, pestle, and several small bottles clinking and clattering to the floor. The nurse at the High Elder's bedside leaped backward until she was pressed against the wall. Her face was pale and exhausted, her eyes bright not with fever but with fear. Eliza wondered what she had been asked to do, and if she would be punished for failing.

"Then what, sir?" Eliza asked, her voice barely more than a whisper.

"The High Elder was meant to sign some official documents before he fell into this fever. We need you to compel him to write his signature upon them before he is incapable of doing so."

Eliza's stomach twisted. "Documents?"

"Yes."

"What documents?"

"That does not concern you," Elder Hallewell hissed through his teeth. "I did not bring you here to submit to your inane questioning. I brought you here to do as you are bloody well told, and you will do so or face my wrath, do you understand me?"

But though Elder Hallewell's words struck her like projectiles, she could not help but notice that the other men in the room looked deeply uncomfortable. They were not looking at her, but staring at the floor or else whispering together in hushed but intense tones. Every face was awash with misery and something else—something that looked very much like shame.

"Josiah—" began Elder Potter, his tone very grave.

"Francis, I do not want to hear it! I have made up my mind!" Elder Hallewell shouted, his face twisted so that he looked more beast than man.

Elder Potter did not respond, but he looked at Eliza and shook his head in what could only be described as a silent apology.

Eliza opened her mouth to speak, though she had no idea what she was going to say—but she was saved the trouble of figuring it out because at that moment, the last of Elder Hallewell's scant patience ran dry. With an angry grunt, he stepped forward, grabbed Eliza forcefully by the arm, and dragged her the rest of the way across the floorboards until she stood at the High Elder's bedside, her leg pressed up against the bedpost. She leaned away from him instinctively.

"Don't be a fool, child. He's not catching, or none of us would be here with him," Elder Hallewell said. He reached out a hand across the bed and snapped his fingers impatiently. Brother Goodwin hurried forward into the circle of light in which the bed stood, a sheaf of papers clutched in his hand. He passed the papers to Elder Hallewell, and Eliza spotted the official wax seal and emblem of the High Elder's office. She knew it well—she'd seen it all her life, stamped upon the notices put up around the Barrens and cast in bronze upon statues and in solid gold upon the front of the *altaria*. The sight of it had always awed her, as though the very hand of the Creator himself had reached down and left its mark upon the mortal world. Tonight, like everything else about the scene, it filled her only with dread. She spotted the ring with the seal on it, lying upon the tabletop beside the candle and a stick of purple wax. They had taken the ring from him and used it to make the seal right there over his failing body.

Elder Hallewell took the papers in one hand, using the other to push Eliza down into the chair that had been placed at the High Elder's head. Then he thrust the papers onto Eliza's lap and pointed to the fountain pen that lay upon the bedside table among the pile of spent medical debris.

"You will compel him to sign, there at the bottom of the first page," Elder Hallewell said shortly.

Eliza looked down at the paper, bewildered. It seemed to be a kind of declaration. She spotted Elder Hallewell's name.

"But what is—?"

The blow knocked her sideways in her chair, and she only just managed to stay in it by grasping the metal pole of the bedframe beside her. Her vision went momentarily black, and then little white lights popped behind her eyes.

A man's voice called out, "Josiah, control yourself, man! I see no need to—"

"No need? We are nearly out of time, and this insolent little chit thinks she can question me?!" Elder Hallewell shrieked.

317

Eliza opened her watering eyes to see Elder Hallewell towering over her, rubbing at the back of his right hand and glaring down at her as though she had just struck him rather than the other way round. Her right cheekbone throbbed and burned. How could she ever have believed this man to be the embodiment of goodness? She could see nothing now but the monster who had always been lurking in the depths of his eyes.

And she could not defy the monster and live to tell it this time. His eyes were telling her so.

Pressing her lips together so that she would not risk another question slipping out, Eliza removed her gloves, adjusted the papers in her hand and picked up the fountain pen. Then she reached out and placed a violently trembling hand upon the High Elder's shoulder. His eyes flew open at her touch, his face twisting on the pillow to stare at her with glassy, feverish eyes.

His expression was such that she nearly pulled her hand away. She cleared her throat, but it took two attempts for her voice to claw its way out of her mouth.

"High Elder Morgan, sir."

The High Elder searched her face as though the answers to a thousand pressing questions were written upon it.

"Who are you?" he whispered.

"I am here to help you, sir. It's all right. Everything's all right," Eliza said, and as she said the words, she sent them down her arm and out of her fingertips and into the man who lay gasping before her. She felt the energy enter him, felt his body shudder and relax just a little as the compulsion took hold. She also felt something else, something she had never felt before—energy pushing back, a sort of desperate pressure, fighting against what the magic was telling him to do.

Drawing a deep and ragged breath, Eliza picked up the fountain pen and placed it in the High Elder's hand. His fingers twitched but did not close around the pen, and he gave no sign that he even noticed he was now holding it. Eliza willed him to grasp it, and his fingers tightened of their own accord for a moment before falling limp again. She snapped her head back over her shoulder to glare at Elder Hallewell.

"I realize you think I can force anyone to do anything, but the High Elder is in a very fragile state, and he is slipping beyond the reach of my magic. If you want me to help you, you must help me, too." Her

318

voice was icy, cold enough to melt through a bit of Elder Hallewell's anger. His face twisted, but he approached the bed again.

"What must I do?" he said flatly.

"Help him sit up. Help him remember how to grip the pen," Eliza said.

Elder Hallewell hesitated for the first time. He glanced up at the other men in the room, but not one of them would meet his eye. Even the doctor and attending nurses had turned their backs, pretending to busy themselves with the medical supplies as though by not watching, they could claim ignorance.

"Sir, we are nearly out of time. I assure you that I cannot compel a corpse," Eliza said, a quiet ferocity in her voice.

Her words jolted Elder Hallewell out of his indecision. He wedged his hands under the High Elder's shoulders and, with a grunt, lifted the man into a slumped sitting position. Then he slid himself behind the High Elder's back, using his own body as a sort of cushion to prop him up. The High Elder groaned, his pallid face rolling from side to side. Elder Hallewell could scarcely bring himself to look at the man as he reached down and wrapped his own fingers over the High Elder's so that they had no choice but to hold the pen.

"Get on with it," he murmured, his face twisted with revulsion.

Eliza did her best to focus only on the dying man in front of her. She sent the request down her arm, through her fingers: *Sign the paper. Just sign it.*

The High Elder seemed to stiffen again. A kind of clarity came into his face, and he looked down in surprise, first at the papers in his lap, and then at the pen in his hand. Then he looked back at Eliza, bewilderment draped on every feature like a shroud.

"Go on," she whispered. "Go on and sign it. Then you can rest."

The High Elder's lips trembled and spittle gathered in the corners of his mouth. Eliza pushed harder, feeling it drain her, a pitcher being poured out. Slowly, his body shaking, the High Elder dragged his hand toward the paper. Elder Hallewell pulled his own hand away as though burned, as though Eliza's magic would seep into him as well. With painstaking effort, the High Elder managed to scrawl his signature on the paper, beside the wax seal. The moment it was done, Josiah snatched the paper with a cry of triumph and held it out for Brother Goodwin, who scurried forward to receive it. Elder Hallewell extricated himself from behind the High Elder, allowing the latter to slump back once again into his pillows. Then all of the men present pulled together into a knot, whispering, gesturing, and conferring; their peerless leader all but forgotten as he struggled for breath.

Eliza looked down once again into the man's eyes. They were glazed and fevered again, looking without seeing. She wasn't sure what she was looking for. She had never been so close to him, never spoken a word to him before this moment. She wondered if she ought to hate him. After all, was he not an architect of the world in which she had been so degraded and shamed? She supposed she should be happy he was dying, but she could not dredge up anything resembling happiness. She felt only pity. Pity, and just a bit of curiosity.

This man was the mouthpiece of the Creator on earth. Why should he fear death? The fear in his eyes brought the question to her lips, but she pressed them down upon it, biting it off. She could not ask him this. Surely a human being was allowed to feel his own mortality as he faced it.

And then, as though he had heard her thoughts out loud, the High Elder suddenly turned his head so that he was staring directly at Eliza. She pulled back, frightened of the intensity in his expression, but her movement startled him, and he reached out, grasping her wrist with a pressure she would surely have thought him too weak to exert upon her. She threw a panicked look toward the other Elders, but they were still whispering excitedly over their newly signed papers and had not a glance to spare for the Riftborn now that they had gotten what they wanted from her.

"I... I must tell... must tell you..." The High Elder's voice was strangled, his lips faintly blue.

Eliza was too scared to move, too afraid even to remember that she could compel the man's hands off her with a single thought. Horrified fascination left her rooted to the spot, unable to talk, to think, to act...

The High Elder pulled her closer so that she sank to her knees beside him, her face so close to his she could count the broken blood vessels upon his whiskery cheek. He strained upon his pillow until his lips were nearly brushing her ear.

"They... must... know... tell them... tell them..."

A ragged, labored breath dragged itself up his throat. This man had moments to live, Eliza could feel it. She was both desperate not to see it and unable to turn away.

"Tell them... the Rift... is a lie."

The moment the words had escaped him, Eliza felt his hand clench, just once more upon her wrist, then fall limp. She looked into his face just in time to see the light leave his eyes, like windows being shuttered. One moment he was there, and the next, he was simply... gone. How surreal it was to see him there, the most powerful man in the world, reduced to a hollow, shrunken husk.

"What's happening there! What are you doing? Get away from him!"

Eliza looked up to see the Elders hurrying toward her. She struggled to her feet, stumbling and falling back into the chair the High Elder had pulled her from. The Elders crowded the bed. Eliza watched the realization settle over them.

"Doctor! Doctor, come here at once!" Elder Hallewell cried out. The Elders parted as the doctor and his nurses descended upon the bed, listening and searching and feeling in the absolute quiet that death had left behind.

The Doctor backed away, shaking his head. "He is gone. The Creator has taken him home."

Every head dropped immediately in silent prayer, all but Elder Hallewell, who was still staring at the High Elder's body, his face blank and white with shock. Then he turned his gaze upon Eliza.

"He spoke to you."

It was not a question and so Eliza didn't answer it. She was still in shock, still processing the fact that she had just watched a man die so close to her that the stench of his last breath lingered in her nostrils. She felt faint and feverish.

"He spoke to you, I saw it! He whispered in your ear! What did he say?"

"I... he..." Eliza stammered as she tried to disentangle herself from the horror of the moment, but Elder Hallewell, whether mad with grief or something more sinister, growled with impatience. He shoved a nurse out of his way as he strode around to the other side of the bed where Eliza sat cowering in the chair. He grabbed her by the arm and yanked her to her feet, shaking her violently.

"Those were the last words of the High Elder of the Illustratum, you insolent little wretch! Now tell me what he said to you!"

Eliza looked up into Elder Hallewell's face, twisted into something ugly, and her answer rose to her lips without conscious thought.

321

"Nothing, sir."

"Nothing?!"

"He tried to speak, sir, but all he managed was a sort of groan."

Elder Hallewell blinked confusedly at her, as though her words made no sense.

"I'm sorry, sir," she added softly. "Whatever it was he was trying to say, he did not manage to say it."

For one trembling moment, Eliza thought Elder Hallewell might strike her again. But then he sagged, folding in on himself like a puppet whose strings had been cut. He ran a shaking hand over his face, looking for just a moment like he had lived a hundred years since the last time Eliza had seen him. Then he jerked his head toward Brother Goodwin.

"Take her back to Larkspur Manor."

Eliza felt relief flood through her, and at that moment she realized that she hadn't expected them to let her leave. What she had witnessed, what she had done—surely they wanted to keep that a secret? The silence expanded in the room, a living, pulsing thing that seemed to have sprung to life the moment the High Elder had departed it. Then Elder Potter crossed the room to the bed and took up the livery that was hanging over the headboard. It was the High Elder's, the one he always wore draped over his shoulders when out in public. Elder Potter ran his fingers over it, tracing the delicate golden embroidery. Then he turned and, with a somber look, draped it over Elder Hallewell's shoulders.

Eliza skittered backward, knocking her chair over and causing every pair of eyes to turn on her. But she did not care. She was too busy trying to absorb the meaning of what she had just seen.

"Why… why are you wearing that, sir?" she whispered, though she could feel the answer as though it was tapping on her shoulder, coaxing her to look around and face it.

Elder Hallewell did not answer at first. He was staring down at the sash upon his own chest as though unsure whether it was really there. Just as Elder Potter had done, he ran his fingers delicately over the glimmering threads. Then he turned and looked down his nose at her, a gleam of triumph in his dark eyes.

"You are addressing your High Elder elect, child," he said, in a voice that rang with the same victorious note.

Eliza shook her head wordlessly. It could not be. She would not believe it.

"And, ironic as it sounds, I believe I must thank you, Eliza," Elder Hallewell said, his lips sliding into a twisted smirk. "If it weren't for your magic, the High Elder would never have been able to sign the papers in support of my interim appointment."

He held up the papers. Eliza could see the signature upon them, the ink still glimmering faintly in the dim light, not yet dry. Anger rose inside her like bile. Her hands clenched into fists at her sides. She hadn't been helping a dying man at all. She'd used his last moments on earth to force a political coup.

"Uneasy is the head that wears a crown," Eliza whispered, the words rising unbidden to her tongue.

"What did you say?" Elder Hallewell asked, his voice suddenly sharp.

But Eliza did not repeat the words. Instead, a dam broke inside her, and every thought she had that was too dangerous to speak came rushing out of her, and she was unable to stop them. "You fear the Riftborn will use our magic to take what we want because we're so weak, so selfish. And yet, here you are, using my magic to do the same. How are you any better, sir?"

A shadow passed over Elder Hallewell's face. "You understand nothing. This was already meant to be," Elder Hallewell replied. "It was the will of the Creator."

Eliza laughed—a bitter, caustic thing, the sound of which drove the smugness from Elder Hallewell's face. "The will of the Creator, to use a dying man's last moments to ensure your own power? Yes, I suppose you'd have to tell yourself that, wouldn't you, sir? However else would you live with yourself?"

Elder Hallewell opened his mouth to reply, but at that moment, Elder Potter thrust out his hand, pressing it to Elder Hallewell's chest. "Let the child go, Josiah."

Elder Hallewell looked incredulous. "Let her go? She dares to—"

"She is confused. And frightened by what has passed here tonight. She knows not what she says. And besides, you need her to keep your wife subdued. It was risky to take her away even for this long. Let her go."

Elder Hallewell turned to Eliza again. "You will speak of this to no one. Not Jessamine, not anyone. If you do, you will be thrown in the Praeteritum so fast that no magic can save you."

Brother Goodwin scuttled over to Eliza, but after what he had seen, he looked too scared to actually touch her again. "C-come along, M-Miss Braxton…"

Eliza turned her back on Elder Hallewell and walked slowly toward the door, rage pulsing through her, a fire she had never felt burn so fiercely before. A voice rang out behind her. Elder Hallewell's voice, cracked and hysterical.

"It was the will of the Creator!"

Eliza turned and stared the man squarely in the eye. There was no heat from that fire in her voice, but it rang with certainty. "And you needed Riftmagic to make it happen. Think on that, sir."

The last thing she saw as the door closed behind her was Elder Hallewell's face, pale and shaking, wiped blank with her last words.

Eli—

Creator help us all, I don't know what I've done. High Elder Morgan is dead, and Elder Hallewell is the new High Elder—or at least he is for now. I think the other Elders still need to elect him, but Elder Potter put the vestment of High Elder upon him. I watched it happen.

The High Elder was dying—I mean, truly dying, and Elder Hallewell forced me to use my Riftmagic on him, forced me to make him sign some papers that meant Elder Hallewell would be the next High Elder. At least that's what I think they said—no one was much troubled to explain to me what was going on until I'd already done as they demanded.

And then I watched him. I watched High Elder Morgan die. It was terrible. I don't know what this means for all that we've planned, but I had to alert you right away. There are no plans to delay the wedding as far as I know. I don't know what's going to happen when the rest of the Elder Council finds out, but it must surely add to the chaos of the wedding day.

I'm not sure what else to say, except that I have never been more determined than I am in this moment to carry out my part in Jasper's plan. This must work. It must. Your father must never be allowed to reign supreme over this country. If he does, it will be all my fault.

—Eliza

33

E LI STOOD WITH HIS HANDS THRUST DEEP into his
pockets, watching Sully read the letter. When she finally looked
up, her expression was blank with shock, a slate wiped clean.

"Saints alive," she whispered. "A political coup in the dead of
night."

"What does it mean?" Eli asked. His whole body was vibrating
with tension, and he clenched his teeth against it.

"I don't know," Sully said, sounding frankly bewildered. "This
has never happened in the history of the Illustratum. A High Elder
has never died while still in his position, except for the very first,
but he had already made a public declaration that he wished his son
to become his successor, and the rest of the Elder Council had voted
upon his impending ordination. But this..." She shook her head.

Eli began pacing. Jasper, on the other hand, stood motionless in
the corner, his mouth hanging open.

"But what does it mean for our plans?" Eli growled. "Does this
ruin everything?"

"Well, it's like Eliza said, isn't it? It's too damn late to stop
this, there are too many parts already in motion," Sully said. "The
pamphlets have been printed and are being delivered tonight. Our
recruits have their assignments, the harmless Riftmead has been
distributed throughout the city, and Daniel Byrne is likely delivering
your message to the prisoners of the Praeteritum as we speak. Even if
we wanted to call it all off, I don't think we could."

Eli could barely think, barely see the room in front of him through
his rage; a rage that caught him completely off guard, and was all

the more difficult to control because of it. He had never been able to reconcile the idea of his father with what he knew of Elder Hallewell. But now, suddenly, knowing that the man was now the High Elder of the Illustratum, he couldn't keep the truth at bay. Something about knowing that his father was the very face of the system they were trying to take down chilled his blood like no fear for his own mortality could. And to think he'd used Eliza to carry out his own dirty work, used the very Riftmagic he claimed to despise to get what he wanted… Eli could feel his gorge rising, his heart pounding, his blood raging and the magic tingling in his fingertips, itching for release.

"Eli?" Sully's voice was tentative.

"Yeah?" With great effort, Eli dragged himself up out of his own thoughts to look at her.

"You all right, lad?"

He took two sharp breaths, breaths that flared his nostrils and burned his lungs. "I don't know," he finally said. "I guess I shouldn't be surprised. After all, I was an obstacle to his rise and he had no hesitation about removing me."

"Compelling a dying man to sign papers putting him in charge," Sully muttered, shaking her head again. "I'll give the man credit, he doesn't back down, does he?"

"No, he doesn't. And I expect he'll put up a damn good fight tomorrow," Eli said.

"Then I guess it's good we're ready for him," Jasper said, speaking at last. His face looked as set and angry as Eli's. "Come on. Let's go."

"Go? Where?"

Jasper grabbed Eli by the arm and yanked him toward the door. "Out."

Sully frowned. "Jasper, I'm not sure that's a good—"

"Well, I am," Jasper said, still hauling Eli toward the exit. "I'm dead sure. We'll be back soon."

And without another word, he dragged Eli straight down the hallway. Eli tugged against him.

"Are you going to tell me where we're going?"

"No."

"Can you at least stop manhandling me? I can walk, you know."

"Do I have your word you'll come with me?"

"Sure, but—"

"Well, come on then."

Eli followed Jasper out the front door and down the sidewalk, practically jogging to keep up with him as he barreled down the pavement. They spoke not a word as they cut through the early morning gloom. A handful of dock workers slunk sleepily past them; eyelids heavy, faces badly shaven, and last night's whiskey still on their breaths, but otherwise, the street was completely deserted in the cold grey light of pre-dawn London.

Jasper didn't slow down until he reached the very banks of the Thames, across which, through the thick rolling threads of fog, they could see the Illustratum rising up like a ghoul to haunt them all. Then he stood, staring across the water at it in silence until Eli finally spoke up.

"Look, Jasper, no offense, but looking at the Illustratum isn't likely to make me feel any better. In fact, knowing that my father's now in charge of the place is only going to make me feel worse."

"We're not here to look at it," Jasper said, his voice unusually calm. "We're here to yell at it."

Eli blinked. "Uh... what's that?"

"I said we're here to yell at it," repeated Jasper, looking at Eli as though he was the one suggesting something ridiculous.

"Jasper, mate, I... have you gone mad?"

"No, but you might, if you don't bloody well listen to me," Jasper replied, looking back at Eli at last. He pointed a finger violently at the great hulking outline of the Illustratum. "You can't focus on what you've got to do tomorrow if you don't have out with it."

"Have out with *what?*" Eli cried, exasperated.

"With this. With that place. And with him!" Jasper shouted. And with his finger still jabbing mercilessly in the direction of the Illustratum, Eli didn't need to ask him again.

"Tell me what you think of him," Jasper said, crossing his arms over his chest.

"I don't think of him," Eli said shortly.

"Bollocks. You think about him much more than you want to admit to anyone, especially yourself. And if you hold onto all of that tomorrow, it's going to weigh you down like stones in your pockets."

It was Eli's turn to cross his arms. "Maybe it will motivate me."

"Oh yeah, sure, motivate you right into an oncoming horde of armed guards, for example," Jasper said, rolling his eyes. "Eli, you can't think straight like that. And if there's one thing you've got to be sure to do tomorrow, it's think straight."

"This is really rich, you know," Eli returned. "You, lecturing me about making good decisions."

"As it happens, I'm exactly the right person to lecture you about decisions," Jasper shot back, "seeing as I've built my entire public reputation on making bad ones. Who knows more about how to cock up a situation than I do? You should consider this a lesson with one of the great masters."

Eli snorted, with a mocking bow of deference. "Ah, yes, the DaVinci of cock-ups. How could I be so rude?"

"That's right," Jasper said, sounding satisfied that Eli had caught on so quickly rather than annoyed at being insulted. "And as such, I'm telling you that you've got to exorcise some of what's burning in you right now."

"You have no idea what you're talking about."

"Oh come off it. You think just because you know who your family is that you're angrier than I am?" Jasper asked. "At least you have a target. I've just been spouting off at any poor sod who crosses me at the wrong moment. I've been mad at the world, and so I've moved through it like an enemy. And not once has it done me a lick of good. I don't want that for you on any day, but especially not tomorrow. So we yell."

He said it with the air of someone who had just proved a hypothesis beyond a reasonable doubt, and Eli, recognizing defeat, decided it would be easier just to have done with his tomfoolery than to keep fighting against it. He sighed, slumping.

"All right, you win. We'll yell."

Jasper grinned. "Excellent. You first."

Eli felt like a fool, but he took a deep breath and shouted. Jasper snorted at him.

"You call that yelling?" Then Jasper threw his head back and unleashed a stream of expletives that would have made a sailor blush. Eli looked over his shoulder.

"Bloody hell, Jasper, do you want to send every patrol in the Commons running?"

"We'll be long gone before they get here," Jasper replied. "Now you give it a go."

Eli sighed. Then, filling his lungs, he stared straight at the

Illustratum and shouted the first words that came to his lips, "I hate you!"

Jasper laughed and slapped him on the back encouragingly. Eli didn't want to admit it, but it felt good. He dragged the words up from his very toes.

"I hate you! I despise you! I hope you rot in hell!"

It was as though a dam had broken inside him. His feelings flooded through him, rushing in his veins, all tangled up in his magic, and he seized an empty bottle from the muck at the river's edge and flung it into the air. Then he focused all the hatred and all of the magic on the bottle's rising shape against the brightening grey and thrust his hand forward with a howl of rage. The bottle exploded, shards of glass raining down into the water below.

Jasper whooped with approval and snatched up another bottle. He flung it into the air and Eli shattered it. Again and again, with shouts of pure fury, Eli made bottles explode like fireworks in the sky until, with one last scream of rage that tore up his throat like a clawed thing, he fell back onto the ground, exhausted and panting and drained. Jasper plopped down beside him, still hooting with laughter.

A voice suddenly shouted out from somewhere up in the road, "You tell her, lad! All women come straight from the Devil!"

Eli and Jasper looked at each other in surprise and then both burst into roars of laughter even as Eli was wiping tears of rage from his face, even as sobs threatened to burst from his chest.

"Thanks, Jasper," Eli said when they had, at last, gasped themselves into silence.

"Don't mention it," Jasper replied.

A pause. Then...

"I'm scared, Jasper."

"Me too, mate."

They didn't try to talk each other out of it. The danger was real, the fear was warranted, and they needed to feel it. For once there was no bravado, no cocky half-lies about how everything would be fine. For just a moment they were two scared boys with no answers and no idea what tomorrow would bring, just as they'd been on the day the world had thrust them haphazardly together into brotherhood.

§

Across the city, Larkspur Manor was waking up, shuffling through the dawn with sleepy faces and aching feet, but minds already humming away with to-do lists and last-minute preparations. The wedding was a day away, and the whole staff knew that there had never been a bigger test of their efficiency and skill than they would meet upon the morrow. But even as bread was baked and table settings were laid and silver was polished and flowers arranged, there were those within the house who knew that no one would ever admire the flowers, or dine from the place settings, or admire the sparkle of the cut crystal. It was all for nothing, an exercise in foolish futility, and yet they must let it play out, watch everyone work their fingers to the bone, all for naught.

Upstairs in Miss Jessamine's chambers, Eliza and Jessamine huddled together on the rug by the fire. Eliza wasted no time upon her return to wake up her mistress and tell her everything that had transpired, despite Elder Hallewell's orders that she keep the night's events to herself. Jessamine had listened with wide-eyed horror, and it was many minutes before she could find her voice to respond.

"What do we do?" she whispered. "He... he stole the seat. The other Elders... surely they won't allow him to..." She clamped her hand over her mouth, her dismay swallowing the rest of her words.

"Unless someone who was in that room tells them, I don't think they'll be able to stop him," Eliza said. "Your father threatened me with hanging if I spoke of what I saw... what I... I *did*." Her voice broke.

Jessamine reached out a hand and traced a finger along the bruise blossoming purple on Eliza's cheekbone. "Eliza it wasn't your fault. He would have killed you if you hadn't done as he asked."

"Maybe I should have let him," Eliza whispered.

"And what would have been the point of that?" Jessamine cried, sounding angry before throwing an anxious glance at her mother's sleeping form and lowering her voice again. "You can't carry out tomorrow's plans if you're dead, and those plans are the only way to make sure my father loses what he's stolen."

"What if it doesn't work?"

"What if it *does* work?"

Eliza stared into Jessamine's fiercely scowling face and sighed. "You're right, of course. I'm just..." She gestured helplessly, but Jessamine didn't need an explanation.

"I know. So am I." She pulled her knees up to her chest and wrapped her arms around them. "What do we do now?"

"We make all our preparations for tomorrow as though you will be a blushing bride dancing the night away among a crowd of admirers. We play our parts," Eliza replied.

"And my mother?"

"We prepare her as well. We can't leave her behind. She'll have to come with us."

"Surely she isn't well enough to travel?"

"She will be fine. She's stronger than she looks," Eliza said.

"Well, *that's* certainly true," Jessamine agreed. She gnawed worryingly on her lip for a few seconds before adding, "Should we tell her? About William?"

Eliza shook her head. "No. Only as a last resort. The less she knows, the safer she is until we get her out of here."

"Very well," Jessamine said, standing up and reaching out a hand to pull Eliza to her feet. "Let us get started then. There is much yet to be done for the wedding that will not be."

Eliza managed a smile. "Let's start with packing your trunk. A girl can't make a daring escape without a wardrobe."

§

Long black draperies hung on the walls in the Elder Council chamber like tall dark soldiers standing sentinel over the empty seat at the top of the hall. Black bands adorned the arm of every man who stood within its walls. The bustle of activity and chatter that usually preceded morning meetings was replaced by a silence so heavy that not a soul dared to break it, not with a whispered exclamation or even a prayer. Every eye was turned to the man who now wore the vestments of High Elder, standing at a lectern beside the empty seat. The Moderator took his position at the top of the benches, and called the room to order, though the words had never been less necessary, and the sound of his gavel echoed in the silence like a gunshot.

Josiah looked around the room, letting his lungs expand, breathing in the moment. He let his eyes stop on every face, willing himself to imprint every detail on his memory so that he might always be able to close his eyes and remember, with absolute clarity, the first moment he stood here, wearing these vestments, standing at this podium. Then he looked down at the papers in front of him and began the most important speech of his life.

"My fellow brothers in the Creator's love, I speak to you today with the heaviest of hearts. Our great leader, High Elder John Francis Morgan, has flown this mortal realm to take his place at the Creator's side after a valiant battle with a terrible illness. I ask, before another word is spoken, that we honor him with a moment of silent prayer."

Josiah bowed his head and closed his eyes. He heard the slight rustling sound from all around the room that signaled the others were doing the same. The silence stretched, tense as a bowstring, until Josiah raised his head once more.

"I ought to have been better prepared to speak to you now, but I am sorry to say that my love and respect for High Elder Morgan would not allow me to imagine this moment, much less prepare for it. He was my mentor, my compass, and my friend. I watched him carry out his solemn duties with such admiration. He was unwavering in his commitment to the people of this great land, and to the Creator he served. I found myself in constant awe of his selflessness and faith. I know there are many in this room who share these feelings, and to those who count themselves as one of that number, I know the depth of your pain.

"My grief is heightened by the knowledge that John Morgan was so determined to experience the joy of seeing his only living son married upon the morrow to my own dear daughter Jessamine. To know that he was so very close, only a day away, adds a tang of bitterness to my tears. It feels unfair that the Creator should take him before he could know the satisfaction of seeing his child happily settled, but of course, we cannot divine the Creator's plans. We must simply submit to them and have faith that He knows best what moment we are to join with Him. I must admit that the loss of John Morgan in such a moment has been perhaps the greatest test of that faith for me."

He took a moment, lifted the end of his sash in his hand, and then let it flutter back down with a sigh.

"I will not embarrass myself with some lie about how I never dreamed I would be wearing these vestments. I have often dreamed of it. I had ambitions of one day inhabiting the seat of High Elder. I was actively seeking support from people in this room in the hopes of earning enough votes when the time came. But this..." He shook his head sadly, gesturing to the black draperies, and the empty seat beside him. "This is not how I wanted this to be. I wished to wear these vestments, yes, but not like this, never like this."

He paused, letting these words burrow in and find purchase where they might before he went on.

"As glad as I am that High Elder Morgan had faith in me, that he chose to select me as his successor should he succumb to his illness, still I am uneasy," he said. He felt Francis' eyes on him, burning through him, but he did not meet his gaze. He could not afford to be derailed. "I don't want to wear these vestments, this title, without the full support of the men in this room, my brothers in faith, my comrades in a battle waged for the soul of our country. Without you, this is empty. Without you, it is meaningless.

"Tomorrow my daughter will marry Reginald, and I wish for it to be a joyous celebration of all that we as a nation have built. Some of you may ask why we do not postpone the wedding in light of what has happened. I admit that was my first instinct, but then my better judgment prevailed. I asked myself, what was it that the High Elder wanted more than anything? What, indeed, was the one wish he had, the one event he so desperately longed to see before he passed on? The answer, of course, is the union of his son to my daughter, and it would be an insult to his great struggle against his mortality to delay it even a day longer. And so I ask this of you, esteemed Elders of the Illustratum; I ask that you will all join me, so that we may lift up in prayer both the young couple and our fallen leader. And then, the next day, when the dust has settled, I ask that you meet me here for our morning session. I shall offer my whole day to your questions, your concerns, your ideas, and your words. Let me earn your support. And then, at the end of the day, let us vote. And then, if and only if I have the support of the majority of people in this room, will I dare to sit in this chair or commune with the Rift. Only then will I consider myself anything more than a temporary guardian of these vestments and this title. Only with your full-throated support will I don the title and do my utmost to carry it in faith, dignity, and unwavering devotion to our Creator. And now, I would like to lead us all in a prayer for the soul of John Morgan for whom all of our souls weep today."

All around him heads bowed. Only Francis' head remained raised, and Josiah caught his eye. Francis' face was carefully blank. He had not spoken a word to Josiah since Morgan had passed. He had shut himself in his office, and Josiah was not foolish enough to disturb him. For the first time, he was as unsure of Francis' support as he was of any other man in the room. Josiah searched those familiar features for a sign, however tiny, of the friend and confidante that Francis had become to him. Then Francis dropped his head in prayer, shuttering any chance of finding it.

Josiah swallowed his doubts and raised his eyes to the vaulted ceiling, and began the prayer.

And though the prayers rose through the Illustratum, they could not match the fervor, the passion, the wild hope of the Riftborn planning and scheming all over the city. They could not spread faster than the word of rebellion through the stinking hovels of the Praeteritum. They could not rise higher than the hopes of young men practicing their magic and reviewing the parts they would play in the square the next day. They could not match the eloquence that flowed from Lila Sullivan's pen as she crafted the words they would speak if, by some miracle, they made it onto the Elder Council chamber floor. And they could not hope to match the passion of each and every Riftborn who turned their face to the sky that day and into the night, daring to dream that the next day might see a new world for them and for their children.

And while the skies over London swarmed with all these hopes and prayers and fears and dreams, a lady's maid worked quietly over a frothy white wedding dress, knowing the next day would change everything, for better or for worse.

34

A SHARP, SHRILL WHISTLE SOUNDED in the street below, but Colin was already awake. He lay in his bed with his boots still on and his cap in his hands, waiting. The clock read 4 a.m. At the sound of the signal, he was off the bed and across the room to the window before the whistler could draw another breath. He threw up the sash and stuck his head out.

"What's the news, then?" he called in a whisper that nonetheless carried in the still night air.

"Delivery time."

Colin nodded, and a thrill ran through him. They were about it, then. He'd get to do his bit after all, even if his father was still insisting he'd be stuck at home during the wedding later that day. But he supposed he'd have time yet to change his mind about that.

Quick and quiet as an alley cat, Colin slid through the window and clambered down the drainpipe. When he straightened up, he was grinning into the freckled face of Toby McGuinn.

"All right, Colin?"

"Never better," Colin replied. "Where are the others?"

"Me brother's roundin' 'em up. We'd better get a shift on."

The two boys took off down the narrow lane, burning off their nervous energy by jumping puddles and steaming piles of horse droppings. The streets were dark and empty, save the occasional rat and a Riftsick beggar or two who hadn't made it all the way to their doorsteps. Soon, the sun would hold its flame to the edges of the darkness, burning it away as it gradually turned the rooftops to burnished gold and bronze; but by then, Colin thought, their work would be done. As they ran, other boys joined them, leaping from shadowed doorways and tumbling out of windows, and swinging off of lampposts. Colin grinned as the group swelled behind him. He felt like the pied piper of grimy Barrens lads, and he quite liked it.

Mr. Harlowe's newspaper operated out of a large brick building right where the outer border of the Barrens met the Commons. For decades, young lads who could clean themselves up to a respectable degree could earn a few *venia* by lining up at his back doors in the wee small hours of the morning and taking a stack of papers to deliver. The term 'newspaper' was the very loosest of definitions, as nothing within the pages of what Mr. Harlowe printed could ever be considered "news." It was propaganda, printed and distributed for the glorification of the Illustratum, and to increase good will toward the Elders themselves by highlighting their good and charitable works. There were also a number of sappy stories about wayward Riftborn who found their way back onto the Path and were therefore deliriously happy every moment afterward. Colin's father was fond of saying the London Herald was good for little else than wiping his arse.

Today, however, it would come in very useful indeed.

By the time they had arrived at Mr. Harlowe's back door, a ragtag gang of twenty boys had gathered together, ready to do their bit. Toby jumped up onto the top step and knocked sharply once, twice, then twice in quick succession. Instantly, an anxious face popped into view behind the grimy little glass pane set into the door. Then the door opened with a squealing, scraping sound.

"You here for Lavender?" the man asked. His forehead was dotted with beads of sweat, which he swatted at anxiously with a damp handkerchief. Colin had never seen him before, but based on the silk of his tie and the gleam of his cufflinks, he thought he just might be staring at Mr. Harlowe himself.

"That's right," Toby replied.

"All of you?"

"Every one of us, sir."

The man shook his head in disbelief, and then turned and gave a sharp whistle over his shoulder. Almost at once, two barrel-chested men appeared lugging crates of papers. They heaved them onto the top step and disappeared again into the building.

"No one breathes a word about where these papers came from," Mr. Harlowe barked. "Is that clear? If it comes back to me that one of

338

you little buggers ratted me out, I will send one of my lads to rough you up, and you won't look too pretty when they're done with you, is that clear?"

The group of boys merely stared at him. A few smothered smirks behind their sleeves. Each and every one of them had weathered worse threats than that, most of them in the last week and from their own fathers, so a few harsh words from a Commons swell didn't exactly strike fear into their hardened little hearts. Harlowe seemed to realize it, but as there was nothing to be done about it, he mopped his brow again and gestured impatiently to the crates.

"Well, go on then. I haven't got all day to be waiting on you. Take your stack and be off with you!"

The boys descended on the crates, shoving handfuls of pamphlets into potato sacks or whatever else they'd scrounged up at home to carry them in. As soon as the crates were empty, Mr. Harlowe kicked them back through the door, gave one last nervous glance around the alleyway, and disappeared into his factory again. In another hour or two, his regular delivery boys would be lined up here with their matching caps and their branded bags, ready to deliver the official news of the day. Whether Harlowe would still be there, or whether he would have given in to his fear and gone into hiding somewhere, was anyone's guess. As for Colin, he was betting all his meager fortune on a Harlowe-shaped hole in the wall before the sun had properly risen.

If the Creator was really looking down on them, what would He see now, Colin wondered. A scattering of rats, it must look like from above, or perhaps insects, splintering off down every alleyway and street in the Barrens, tucking pamphlets into baskets and under doorways and through the drafty cracks around windows, ducking into dark corners and thresholds when the patrols passed by before taking off again, silent as shadows. Though only Colin had the gift to cloak himself in darkness, it was the first rule of survival in the Barrens to conceal yourself properly, and those boys had learned it well. Before long, every one of them was chucking aside their empty bag and heading for the relative safety of home.

And as the sun rose, as Colin returned at last to his own doorstep, as Mr. Harlowe hastily crammed some belongings and a great deal of cash into a bag, as the night patrols reported to their commanders that all had been quiet—nothing of note to report—the Riftborn of the

Barrens were waking up to a publication that would split their world wide open.

Colin whistled cheerfully and snatched a slightly withered apple off the window sill. Then he scampered upstairs, out his window, and up onto the roof. There, munching on his apple, he watched the sun rise on a brand-new day and thought, for the first time in his young life, that it might just be better than the day before.

35

T HE MORNING OF THE WEDDING DAWNED clear and warm. Mrs. Keats and Liesel were enlisted to help dress the bride, and they consented, despite the expectation of their presence downstairs. Even Braxton, who was so determined that everything should go perfectly, understood that a bride on her wedding day needs a village around her, and did not dare to question the mysterious feminine rituals that transform a mere girl into a bride.

And the ritual began, a dance nearly as old as time itself. Hair was curled and pinned, corset strings tightened and hundreds of tiny buttons hooked carefully into place. A tiara, a Morgan family heirloom provided by Mrs. Morgan, crowned the lacy, beaded confection, and a long white veil obscured the entire vision like glittering frost on a winter windowpane. They stepped back to admire their handiwork, breath caught in their throats.

"Absolutely perfect," Mrs. Keats sniffed.

"That'll do, I reckon," Liesel added, as close to a compliment as she ever came, though her voice shook.

A picture-perfect bride, the envy of all who would gaze upon her that day, stared back out of the mirror, back straight and tall, the embodiment of composure to anyone who didn't look too closely at her hands, which shook like leaves when she unclenched them. To hide the trembling she reached out for her bouquet, a delicate ivory cascade of spray roses, peonies, lilies, and baby's breath.

The clock on the mantel chimed nine o'clock, and every eye in the room flew to it. Four hearts clenched. Four mouths went dry. It was time.

In the mirror, the bride and the lady's maid stood side by side, one drab enough that no one would notice her, one splendid enough that she would draw every eye. Their fingers intertwined.

"Good luck."

"And you."

They had already whispered their fears to each other. They had cried and hugged and worried out loud, reviewed the plans until they could recite them by heart. There was nothing else to say, nothing else to do but face the day and what would come of it. They parted full of the breathtaking knowledge that they might not see each other again.

§

Down in the entrance hall, Josiah fought the impulse to pace. His heart was full as well, though the feelings that threatened to burst it could not have been more different than the ones causing his daughter's heart to pound upstairs. He felt in that moment the culmination of decades of scheming and dreaming. He felt a pride so buoyant he thought he would float away as he stared around at the elegance of the arrangements materializing around him; banisters and chandeliers festooned with flowers, elegant displays of cut crystal goblets sparkling on tables, towers of delicacies drifting by on trays, all of it came together around him in real time, as though he had waved a magic wand. Oblivious to the irony of that thought, he looked again at his pocket watch. Any moment now...

A gasp rose from the servants around him, and the magic seemed to freeze in the air as the figure appeared at the top of the stairs, white and silent as a ghost, and began carefully to descend the steps. Josiah felt a momentary shudder, his memory skipping back to only a few nights ago when another figure in white appeared at the top of those stairs and almost ended everything. He shook the memory away. He would not allow that—nor anything else—to darken this triumphant day.

His daughter floated down to him, light and graceful, a petal on the wind, and when she arrived beside him, he was nearly overcome. He could make out very little of her face through the traditional wedding veil, but he thought he could sense her trembling.

"You look lovely, Jessamine," he managed to say.

"Thank you, father," came the tremulous reply from beneath the veil.

"It is natural to feel nervous, my dear," he said, feeling the obligation to address her fears. "But all is prepared for you, every detail in place. It will be a glorious celebration, I promise you."

She nodded, and he did not push for further response. Instead, he offered her his arm and, after a moment's hesitation, she took it. They turned to the front doors and two of the footmen opened them, revealing the waiting carriage in the driveway. All of the servants who could be spared from their duties for a few moments stood lined up outside to see them off, the gentlemen stoic, the women starry-eyed and smiling, dipping into bows and curtsies as the regal pair processed past them. Josiah stepped aside and watched with bemusement the difficulties of maneuvering such a gown into a carriage, but soon they were settled and the carriage trundled toward the gates, beyond which Josiah could already see people lining the road beyond, hoping to get a glimpse of the bride in all her splendor.

"Let them gaze," Josiah thought comfortably to himself. "Let them feast on the joy of this day, for there is plenty to be had of it."

§

Three figures watched the carriage from the third-floor window as it disappeared around the bend, headed for London proper. Three sets of lungs exhaled in relief to see it vanish before three chests filled up once again with anxiety. It was only the first step in a plan that could fail at any juncture, and there was no time to lose.

"Creator above, I think she's done it," Liesel murmured.

"I don't want to speak too soon, but I think you're right," Mrs. Keats replied, her apron hopelessly wrinkled from twisting it violently between her anxious hands. "Do you agree, miss?"

Jessamine turned to the other women, her expression shining with hope. "I do. The veil is thick and we darkened her hair. I don't think my father has a prayer of realizing it's Eliza in that dress as long as she keeps quiet."

"Then we'll just have to pray she keeps her mouth shut, won't we?" Liesel grumbled. "Now let's get a shift on. We haven't a moment to waste."

The three women scattered; Mrs. Keats to the hallway so that she could return to the kitchen and keep the other servants occupied; Liesel to the trunk, finishing the fastening of the straps; and Jessamine, wearing Eliza's uniform, to the small chamber off her bedroom where her mother slept. She reached out a hand and shook her mother's shoulder gently.

"Mother, wake up. It's time to go," she sang, her voice a lullaby. Her mother's eyes fluttered open and she looked around her in confusion until she spotted Jessamine's face. At last, the maddening effects of constant Influencer control had begun to wear off, and Lillian looked into her daughter's face as though seeing her for the first time.

"J-Jessamine?" she whispered, and there was wonder in her voice.

Jessamine swallowed a sob at hearing her own name on her mother's lips. "Yes, it's me," she managed to choke out, trying to keep a firm handle on her emotions. "Can you sit up? We've got to go."

"Go? Go where?" Lillian asked.

Jessamine's face broke into a smile. "We're going to see William."

Lillian blinked. "My William?"

"Yes," Jessamine said, endeavoring to keep her voice and expression stern even as she longed to burst into tears. "But if you want to see him, you must follow all of my instructions."

Terror cracked in Lillian's voice. "But your father—"

"My father is not here. He's gone out, so we must hurry. If you do as I say, we shall soon be safely away from here."

"But where will we go?" Lillian whispered.

Jessamine mustered up her most encouraging smile. "Somewhere far from here. Somewhere we can be together, and we don't have to be afraid anymore. Is that what you want?"

Lillian nodded.

"Good," Jessamine answered, pulling back her mother's bedclothes. "Now, let's get you up and dressed, quickly. We don't have much time."

Jessamine managed to get her mother out of bed and into an extra maid's uniform that Liesel had smuggled up the servants' staircase with her. Then she lowered her carefully into a chair so that Liesel could lace a pair of scuffed boots onto her feet. Lillian's face broke into a rusty smile at the sight of her.

"You're Liesel," she announced.

Liesel looked up at her, startled. "I... that's right, madam." And then she bent her head back over the laces to hide the tears that had sprung up unbidden into her eyes.

Her boots laced and a ruffled cap pulled low over her face, Mrs. Hallewell was as well-disguised as they could hope. Liesel stuck her head out into the hallway, peering back and forth before scooting across the carpet on quiet feet and knocking on the door hidden in the paneling. It swung open at once, revealing James and Peter waiting for her. With just a nod, they strode into Jessamine's chambers, tipping their caps awkwardly in her direction, and trying not to gawk openly at their elegant Dignus mistresses in servant's attire, as they hefted the trunk between them and disappeared with it back into the hidden staircase. Jessamine and Liesel wasted no time guiding Lillian across the hallway and down the narrow steps, imploring her in whispers to stay quiet and keep her head down.

James and Peter were to go ahead of them and whistle if someone was on the other side of the door. When no shrill sounds met their ears, Jessamine and Liesel led Lillian down a narrow hall full of broom cupboards and linen closets, which was blessedly empty; the floors had all been polished and swept already, as well as the linens pressed and laid upon the tables. They didn't see a single servant until they had to pass by the pantries around the corner, and thankfully the new maid, Sarah, didn't so much as look up from her work as they snuck by. In order to reach the back door, however, they would have to walk right past the kitchens, and there would be no avoiding staff then. They were counting on Mrs. Keats to keep everyone on task so that they would have as few pairs of eyes on them as possible, but it was too much to hope that no one would see them at all.

They paused before turning the corner, listening to James and Peter shuffle through with the trunk. They heard them say something to Mrs. Keats. Then they heard Mrs. Keats say, "Come here the lot of you, I want you to see how Minnie's glazed these biscuits. This is how I want them done."

Liesel tugged them forward and they walked, heads down, behind her, straight through the bustling kitchen to the door. If anyone noticed them, they didn't speak up, and Jessamine, who had been holding her breath in terror, exhaled with relief into the morning air out on the grounds. Peter was already strapping the trunk hastily to the back of the carriage while James was climbing up onto the driver's seat.

345

"Go on, then!" Liesel hissed.

"Thank you for all you—"

But Liesel waved the thanks away impatiently. "You can thank me by getting the devil out of here!"

Jessamine led her mother forward and was just helping her into the carriage when a voice called out behind them.

"What in the Creator's name is going on here?"

It was Braxton, charging out of the door, horror dawning on his face as he took in the carriage, the trunk, and the faces of the two women now climbing into it.

"Miss Jessamine!" Braxton was sputtering, his face turning red. "You... but I watched you leave... your wedding!"

"I'm sorry Braxton," Jessamine said. "But the best thing you can do is go back inside and pretend you never saw us."

"I can't do that!" Braxton huffed, sounding insulted at the very idea. "Your father will be... I don't understand how you're still here, but you must come away from there, we must tell him that—"

"*We* must do nothing," Jessamine said, mustering up the most authoritative tone she could even as her legs shook beneath her. "*I* must get in this carriage. *You* must go inside and speak of this to no one."

"This is Eliza's doing, isn't it?" Braxton whispered, his face going the moist, pasty white of raw bread dough. "She put you up to this, didn't she? Where is she? What has she gotten you mixed up in?"

"She hasn't done anything but help me when I needed her help," Jessamine replied. "She hasn't mixed me up in anything. I am a grown woman and I can make my own choices. I am also the mistress of this house, and I am ordering you to go back inside and speak of this to no one, for your own sake as much as mine."

"But...but..." Braxton looked in serious danger of collapse. He dithered on the spot, arms flailing, unsure whether he should be doing as she said or charging forward to pull them both from the carriage before it was too late.

"You cannot prevent this from happening. All you can do is try to protect yourself. I am telling you one last time, Braxton. Let us go."

And still Braxton did not move. Still he stood there, unable to move aside, the idea of letting his master down so abhorrent to him that he could not seem to overcome it. Jessamine began to wonder if he would do something foolish, like stand in the way of the carriage when another voice entered the fray.

"William, come back inside and let them go, now."

It was Mrs. Keats, and her voice was very calm, a counterpoint to Braxton's mounting hysteria. He turned to look at her, his expression almost pleading.

"I can't let them do this," he said.

"You can and you will," Mrs. Keats replied, just as steadily. "They are making their choice, and you must let them go. For Creator's sake, William, look at them, won't you? Just look at their faces. He's put them through enough pain for two lifetimes." She didn't mention Elder Hallewell by name, but Braxton still flinched at the mention of the master of the house, as though the criticism were painful to him.

"Lettie, I—"

"He's destroyed your family, too, don't forget that," Mrs. Keats said, and there was an edge in her voice now that cut him clean to the bone. "Your blind devotion to that man has cost you more than you will ever have the courage to admit to yourself. But this... this is not your fight. Hallewell made his choices. You can't protect him from the consequences."

"But Eliza! Where is—"

"She's made her choices, too. And that's your consequence to bear," Mrs. Keats said quellingly. "Now come inside."

Jessamine watched, gobsmacked, as Braxton hung his head like a chastened child and walked back inside the house. Then she turned to Mrs. Keats, who had tears shining in her eyes.

"Go on, now. Take your life back, child. Go," Mrs. Keats told her, and hurried back inside.

Jessamine didn't need telling twice. She and Liesel finished getting her mother settled on the seat, and then Jessamine climbed in. Liesel stood with her hand on the door, her face twisted.

"Liesel, what is it?"

The words burst from Liesel like an explosion.

"I don't want to stay here. I want to come with you. I want to help."

Jessamine did not even hesitate. She scooted across the seat and patted the cushion beside her.

"I daresay we are going to need all the help we can get. Come on, climb in."

36

"**W**E HONESTLY COULDN'T FIND A BETTER PLACE to hide than this?" Jasper grumbled, shifting his weight away from the nearest rubbish bin. He and Zeke were crouched in a narrow alleyway outside of a butcher shop at the corner of the south fence of the Praeteritum.

"There is no better place," Zeke replied. "The alley is dark and it smells so bloody foul that no one ever comes down it."

"Exactly," Jasper said, trying not to retch. "I'd rather risk a patrol than have to smell the rubbish outside a butcher's shop in the dead of summer."

"And that's why I'm with you, you great prat," Zeke said, slapping Jasper rather too hard on the back. "To make sure you don't take any unnecessary risks rather than deal with a bit of stench."

"A bit of stench? My nostrils have all but caught fire!" Jasper hissed.

Zeke just chuckled. The man ran a pub, after all. There was nothing a dirty alleyway could dish out that he hadn't scraped off the floor of his own establishment with his bare hands. Jasper knew the real reason why Zeke had been chosen to accompany him on this job, but he bit his tongue. Zeke never spoke of the year he spent as a very young man as a prisoner in the Praeteritum, and Jasper wasn't fool enough to ask him about it. But when the final plans for the day were being drawn up, Sully had looked at him, grim but expectant, and Zeke had made a motion somewhere between a nod and a shrug that had nonetheless been taken as assent. No one else had the knowledge of the inside like he did, and he knew it.

"Here he comes now," Jasper muttered. Daniel Byrne appeared around the corner of the fence and, as promised, he was alone. Indeed, they had seen hardly a soul for over an hour since they'd first arrived in the alleyway. Most every shop had closed, treating the wedding as a sort of holiday; and the Riftborn of the Barrens had long since made their way through the streets in the direction of the Illustratum, knowing they would have to arrive early and shove their way through the crowds if they hoped to catch even a glimpse of the processional carriages. How many were going simply to gawk, and how many were going to join the fight remained to be seen, but regardless, the echoing emptiness they left behind them was unnerving.

They watched from the shadows as Daniel looked first left, then right. Assured that the coast was clear, he bent down to where the wall met the fencing and unlocked the chained padlock around a small metal grate set into the stone. It was used to allow the passing of supplies into the Praeteritum, but today it would allow Jasper and Zeke to get inside. The rusted hinges squealed in protest, but after a minute's tugging and scraping, the door hung open. Daniel then stood up and began to whistle an old hymn, chosen as the signal that Zeke and Jasper could approach. Wasting no time, they clambered out of their hiding place and ran straight for the wall.

"All right?" Jasper asked as they reached Daniel.

"They've stuck to the plans I passed along to you: one guard on each corner," Daniel said. "We should be all right as long as everyone sticks to their post, and they will. All three of them are barely out of short pants, and wouldn't disobey a direct order even if they were told to shoot themselves in the leg."

"And the prisoners?"

Daniel shrugged. "Gil Martin was convinced, but as to how he's done rounding up the others, I can't say," he said, referring to the man he'd passed the message to.

"Whistle the same tune if you spot another of the guards. Otherwise, we'll meet you at the gates. You managed to get the key?" Jasper asked.

Daniel patted his breast pocket. "Right here. Just a knobble-kneed kid guarding the desk inside. Sent him off for a cup of tea and swiped it right from the drawer. Couldn't have been easier."

Jasper grinned. "Well, if this goes to hell, I'll be happy to swing alongside you, Byrne."

Daniel grinned back. "Likewise."

"Let's go," Zeke said, looking edgy. The grins vanished as quickly as they'd appeared, and Daniel stepped forward to shield the other two from view of the street as they wedged themselves one after the other through the grate.

Jasper straightened next to Zeke and dusted off his clothes. The inside of the Praeteritum was eerily still and silent, much like the streets outside. A shiver ran up Jasper's spine as he took in the stinking trenches of human filth, the ramshackle hovels, some without so much as a ragged curtain hanging in the doorways, the rusting piles of old manacles and chains piled like sleeping snakes. Here and there, a gaunt face peered out from the shadows of one of the shacks. He suddenly regretted every snarky remark he'd ever made about not caring a whit about getting arrested and sentenced to this place. He caught Zeke's eye and couldn't decide whether to apologize or just let Zeke take a swing at him. Instead, he nodded his readiness and followed Zeke down a narrow lane between hovels.

"How will we know where to find them?" Jasper whispered.

"The message told Gil to gather what volunteers he could into the mess hall," Zeke said, pointing to a long, low tent-like structure about a hundred yards ahead of them. "If he's managed to convince anyone, they'll be waiting for us in there. We use our magic to remove restraints on anyone who wants to fight, and then we lead them to the gates."

Jasper turned his eyes back to the tent. It was impossible to tell if anyone waited for them behind the flaps. Jasper sent up a prayer to no one in particular, a desperate wish whispered to the universe.

Please let there be just a few. Just a few people to stand with us. Just a few ready to fight.

Zeke ducked under the tent flaps and vanished. Jasper hesitated and then did the same. It was dark inside, and he bumped into Zeke's shoulder, staggering backward a little. At the sound of his muttered curse, a spark flared. Then another, and another. Jasper forced his eyes to adjust to the newly wavering light. A crowd of hundreds of figures materialized from the shadows, a sea of dirty, determined faces, clenched fists, and fierce hearts. Then a figure detached itself from the heart of the crowd and stepped forward, a tiny flame cupped in the palm of his hand.

"The Resistance, I presume?" Gil Martin asked, inclining his head. "I managed to rustle up a few volunteers for you."

§

A carriage trundled up to the back of Madam Lavender's establishment, causing a flutter within. Tabitha closed the curtains through which she'd been instructed to watch and flew to the stairs, calling down over the banister.

"They're here!" she bellowed, and an answering cry rose up from the flurry of activity below. The tavern room of Lavender's was almost unrecognizable. The chairs had been stacked in the corners and the bar and piano had been draped in white sheets. Tables had been pushed to the corners to make room for dozens and dozens of cots that had transformed the space into a makeshift field hospital. Cora and a dozen other volunteers, including ten of Lavender's own girls, were scurrying between them, rolling bandages and organizing small tinkling bottles and metal instruments and pouches of dried herbs and salves onto small tables. As they worked, several pamphlets were passed around between them, exclaimed over, and then passed along to the next reader. Colin had delivered the last of his batch before the sun rose, and Lavender had made sure that every last girl had one to read. An hour later, she gathered them together and gave them all a choice.

"Stay and help, go to the Illustratum and join the fight, or clear out," she announced. Not a girl among them had packed a bag. A handful had armed themselves and set out to join the crowd at the gates. The rest had rolled up their sleeves and let Cora put them to work.

It was Penny who answered Tabitha's cry, abandoning her task of tearing scrap fabric into bandages and running for the back door behind the bar, unlocking it just as a tentative knock sounded against it.

Three figures stood on the threshold, white faced and dressed in maid's uniforms with the Larkspur Manor crest embroidered on the chest.

"We were expecting two of you," Penny said, her eyes flying between them.

"I decided to come and help. I can be useful," Liesel said at once.

352

"And you are?"

"Liesel Price. Manipulator."

Penny took one look at the woman's grimly determined expression and decided not to question her further. She stepped aside to let them pass, then closed the door behind them. Liesel barged ahead without waiting for instructions, heading straight toward the bustle of activity in the tavern room, already rolling up her sleeves. The other two women huddled just inside the doorway, hesitating.

"You're the Hallewell girl," Penny said. It wasn't a question. She'd never seen a person look so out of place in a servant's uniform.

"That's right," Jessamine said, drawing herself up and attempting an air of someone perfectly at ease in the back hallways of brothels.

Penny smothered a chuckle and gestured her forward.

"And this is my mother, Mrs. Lillian Hallewell," Jessamine added.

"I'd say it's a pleasure to meet you, but I've never been one for pleasantries. Were you followed?" Penny shot the question back over her shoulder as she led them toward the staircase.

"No," Jessamine replied. She had her arm wrapped protectively around her mother's shoulders, as though she could shield her from the indignity of her surroundings.

"Glad to hear that," Penny muttered as they reached the landing.

"Where are we?" Mrs. Hallewell asked tremulously.

"Somewhere safe," Jessamine replied, and left it at that.

"You can stay here for now," Penny said, pushing open the first door at the top of the hall. She had to give the Hallewell girl points for gumption. She didn't so much as hesitate as she settled her mother into bed, and though she eyed the gaudy surroundings warily, she swallowed her questions.

"Are you hungry? There are sandwiches downstairs for the volunteers," Penny said.

"I don't suppose we could get a cup of tea?" Jessamine asked wearily, in the same sort of tone Penny might wish for something stiffer.

"I think we can arrange that," Penny replied, smothering her amusement. Classic toffs, thinking tea was the answer to everything, even when the city was about to explode into inevitable chaos. Penny turned to leave when Jessamine's voice rang out again behind her.

"I'm sorry, I didn't catch your name."

353

"That's because I didn't offer it," Penny said. Then, deciding to play nice, added, "I'm Penny."

"Thank you for your help, Penny," Jessamine said, clasping her hands solemnly in front of her. "And when we've had a few moments to take tea, I would also like to help."

One of Penny's eyebrows arched. "Is that so?"

Jessamine licked her lips nervously. "Yes. My mother is still rather fragile, but I am perfectly capable if someone gives me a task. I'm afraid I lack any number of practical skills, but I can sew and tie knots and fetch things."

"And when the casualties start coming in?" Penny asked. "How's your stomach?"

Jessamine paled, but only a little. "Stronger than most, I think."

Penny smiled. "Today will be the judge of that, I reckon. I'll be right back with your tea, and then we'll put you to work, Miss Hallewell."

"Jessamine. Please."

"Jessamine."

Penny couldn't bring herself to curtsy, but she managed a respectful jerk of the head before closing the door. "Trading first names with an Elder's daughter," she muttered. "The whole bloody universe is upside down."

Lavender was standing further along in the gallery, watching over the progress below. She looked up as Penny rounded the corner.

"The Hallewell girl?"

"Safe in the corner room, along with her mother. They brought another manor maid with them. She's already rolling bandages I reckon," Penny replied.

Lavender nodded and resumed her silent observation. Penny left her there and headed back down the stairs. She needed to keep her hands busy. Every time she paused in her tasks, her mind spiraled into fear for Daniel, wondering what was happening at the Praeteritum; if they'd managed to stage the breakout, or if they'd been discovered, their plot foiled before they could carry it out. She thought she would go mad, choking on her own unanswerable questions she had to keep swallowing every time they threatened to burst from her.

At first, she had deluded herself that it was simply anxiety for all of her friends in the Resistance that left her feeling so desperately at loose ends. But that delusion was short-lived; after all, it was never

Jasper's face or Zeke's face she saw in those moments of weakness when her fears overwhelmed her. And so she grew angry with herself, angry that she had slipped up and allowed herself to care about a man in such a fashion. She'd spent years fortifying her defenses against men of all sorts, arming herself against every tactic they could throw at her. But it turned out that the one thing she had not prepared herself for was a man with actual integrity—likely because she hadn't ever encountered one—and now she was behaving like some brainless chit, constantly chiding herself in a voice that sounded suspiciously like Lavender's. But today she could not even muster such a pathetic defense. The fear rushed in like the tide and she simply let it rise, washing away every attempt to soothe it. Her one consolation was that she knew she was far from alone.

She had just reached the top of the stairs when a sharp cry rang out from the room below. With her heart in her throat, Penny flew down the stairs, prepared to meet some scene of tragedy, and instead arrived at the bottom just in time to see Liesel throw herself at another woman in a hug that nearly knocked both of them to the floor.

"You stupid girl! You stupid foolish girl, how could you worry me like that? What were you thinking?" The words were admonishments but they were lost in tender sobs as the woman called Liesel came completely apart at the seams, pulling the girl away from her to scrutinize her face, only to yank her against her bosom again a second later, until the word "stupid" sounded like the word "darling." When she had finally gotten a grip on herself, she released the girl, who was laughing and crying in equal measure, and Penny gasped aloud.

It was the girl from the meeting, the one she had seen from across the room. It had been the vibrant red of her hair that had caught Penny's eye, but up close, it was every single feature. She pushed right past Edith, who swore at her and almost dropped the tray she was carrying. Penny stopped in front of the girl, still gawking.

Bridie was wiping her eyes. "I'm sorry Liesel, truly I am."

"Oh, stuff your apologies, I don't need them now. You're all right and that's all that matters," Liesel replied as she tried to gather herself once again.

"But I don't understand, what are you doing here?" Bridie asked.

"I came to do my bit for the cause, of course," Liesel said stiffly. "You didn't think I'd leave you in this mess without me, did you?"

Bridie opened her mouth to reply but shut it again when she

noticed the way Penny was staring at her. She blushed and stammered, "I-I'm sorry. I'm sure Madam Lavender wasn't expecting us, but Eliza's mother couldn't stand waiting back at Sully's house with no news, so I brought her—"

"Eliza's mother?!" Liesel gasped, clutching at a chair back to steady herself. "Emmeline is here?!"

"I... yes, she's over there," Bridie said, waving a hand over her shoulder at a table in the corner where Emmeline was sitting in a chair, her head and shoulders draped in a shawl. Liesel lost not another moment crossing the room to see her, leaving Penny still gawking at Bridie.

"I... if you want us to leave, I suppose we could—" Bridie began.

"It's you!" Penny whispered.

Bridie's expression crinkled in confusion. "I beg your pardon?"

But Penny's face had broken into a positively euphoric smile.

"Someone's looking for you," she said.

§

Eli stood pressed against the bars of the gates to the Illustratum. On the outside, he looked like a curious spectator, craning his neck for a look at the wedding procession. On the inside, he was ablaze with fear and anticipation so intense he expected to burst into flames at any second. He kept his hands shoved in his pockets, afraid he would lose what little possession he had over himself and just start making things explode. The minutes ticked by interminably slowly and he watched them on the great clock face at the top of the nearest tower of the Illustratum, sure that if the events of the day didn't kill him, the waiting certainly would.

In an attempt to distract himself, he scanned the crowd, looking for the faces he knew, the faces with the same anticipation haunting their expressions. He found them, one by one, positioned where he knew they would be along the fences, upon the knoll by the gate, down at the corner of the square where the statue of the very first High Elder lifted his empty eyes to the sky.

But now, as the hour approached, he began to notice other faces in the crowd as well—faces that he did not recognize, and yet gave him pause. This was not the jubilant crowd the Illustratum had prepared for. For every fluttering little flag, there was a frown of concern. For every smile or cheer, there was a whisper behind a hand, a nervous glance. And once, as he turned his head, he saw one of their pamphlets folded and shoved into a pocket. It was then he began to realize just how many people in the crowd had come not for the wedding, but because the Resistance had asked them to. For the first time, his nervousness was shot through with excitement, a lightning bolt streaking across the sky.

It's happening. It's really happening and we're not alone.

He craned his neck so that he could see the far end of the square, where the carriages would appear. According to the route plan that Eliza had provided them, the carriages would make a circuit of the square and then proceed down the street to the east corner of the Illustratum, where they would enter the gates and be greeted by the full complement of Elders, before processing inside. That meant he should be able to get at least a glimpse of Eliza before all hell broke loose. If he could just see that she reached the inside safely...

"Eli Turner!"

A loud boisterous voice caused him to turn around. Samuel Barber stood before him, his face florid and his eyes bloodshot with drink at not quite ten o'clock in the morning. Eli cursed under his breath. Samuel was one of Zeke's regulars, always blustering about the Illustratum, but though he made no secret of his disgust for the Dignus, Eli had long thought him the kind of man who was all bark and no bite, so to speak. And right now, at the worst possible moment, he seemed determined to bark as loudly as possible.

"I see you've started the celebration early, Samuel!" Eli said, his smile not quite reaching his eyes. He darted a glance at a nearby Praesidio guard at attention against the gate.

"That's right. Not sure what we're celebrating yet, though, are we?" Samuel roared.

"Why, the wedding day, of course!" Eli replied pointedly, grabbing Samuel by the arm and squeezing it hard for good measure.

Samuel attempted a wink, at which he failed rather miserably. "That's right, that's right. Don't want to count our chickens before they hatch, do we?"

Eli ground his teeth together. He'd doubted the sagacity of including Samuel in their plans, but Zeke and the others had insisted he was loyal to the cause, and so he had let it pass. Now, he was heartily wishing he'd put his foot down. The bloody fool could ruin

357

everything if he attracted the attention of the wrong person—the Praesidio guard not ten feet from him, for example.

"Maybe we should lower our voices, Samuel," Eli said, endeavoring to keep his tone cheerful. "After all, the carriages should be here any minute and we wouldn't want to miss our opportunity to pray for the happy couple, would we?"

"Happy for how long, though, eh?" Samuel chuckled, wheezing. "What would you say, Eli? Not more than a few minutes now, I reckon!"

Eli acted before he could second guess himself. Ensuring only that the nearest Praesidio guard had his head turned in the opposite direction, Eli pulled back and punched Samuel in the face as hard as he could. The great lump of a man toppled like a statue, disappearing into the crowd, which promptly swallowed him and began stepping over him to get closer to the gates. A few people stared at his prone figure curiously.

"Ah, the poor man couldn't take the heat and all the excitement," Eli said loudly, shaking his head. With the help of another bystander, he heaved Samuel up against the edge of a post, although he was so aggravated that he couldn't decide if he cared whether or not the man got trampled. By the time he had finished and shoved his way to the back of the crowd, the first of the carriages was just rolling into view. His heart twitching in his chest, his magic thrumming in his fingers, he swung his gaze back up to the clock. It was nearly time.

§

There was something off about the crowds of people lined up to watch the processional. Josiah hadn't noticed it at first—he'd been far too focused on the details of the day—the livery and floral decorations on the carriages, the fantastic feather plumes on the heads of the horses, his daughter a vision in satin and lace—to pay too much attention to the spectators. The first mile or so was sparsely attended, further from the city, but there were smiling faces, waving flags, and children jumping up and down, craning their necks for a glimpse at the bride. It was all so surreal—so many months of scheming and planning, and all that had happened in just the last two days lent an almost dreamlike air to the day—that Josiah barely trusted his senses that it was all really happening. He imagined Jessamine must be feeling the same. Her gloved hands shook in her lap, but she sat straight and tall, leaning forward to be sure that the people who had gathered to see her had an unobstructed view of her finery through the windows. She did not speak, and he was not sure what to say to her. Her mother would have been better at... well, there was no point in dwelling on that.

But as they drew nearer to the city, and the crowds got bigger, a seed of uneasiness took root in Josiah's belly. The faces here were harsher. Many people stood staring without clapping or cheering. The waving flags and flowers became fewer and fewer. The tones of the shouts seemed to darken. It was a realization that crept upon him slowly, dismissed at first, and then growing, hardening into something solid and cold and troubling. Something his father once said to him rose, unbidden but clear from somewhere deep in his memory as he had stood on the edge of the Thames as a young boy, watching a dark bank of clouds roll in.

Do you feel that shift in the wind? That means a storm is coming.

The faces in the crowd felt burned into his memory even as they moved into the wider streets and across the bridge where the crowds were much further back, harder to read. If Jessamine had noticed anything, she did not mention it, and he certainly didn't want to make her any more uneasy than her wedding day jitters had already. He began to watch instead the Praesidio guards at attention all along the route. Many looked unruffled, expressions stoic as they manned their posts. But some of them—younger, less experienced—had an edge of panic to their expressions, eyes shifting left and right, hands drifting toward weapons. Josiah tried to reason with himself; of course they were nervous. For most of them, this was their first event of the kind, their first time holding such a crowd at bay. It was natural for them to look ill at ease.

A storm. A storm is coming.

But of course, the crowds and the soldiers and even Jessamine herself could only conceive of a tiny fraction of what troubled Josiah. The wedding itself, the reception, the processions, and the crowds were but a spectacle, a distraction from the truly important events of the next few days: the negotiations, the objections, the bargaining, and the vote wrangling that must precede his final ascension. And throughout it all, Josiah had to be sure that the events of the previous night would never be revealed, or everything would crumble.

359

For whatever reason, it was this reminder of the true stakes that calmed him at last. He was projecting his fears of the election onto the wedding; that was all it was. He must push down those fears—they would have their time when the last of the celebration was over.

The carriage turned the corner into the square and the front gates of the Illustratum came into view. The carriages from the palace had arrived as well, and Josiah and Jessamine's carriage fell into line behind them, as the bride would of course be the grand finale of the procession into the building. The full complement of Elders, all wearing their formal robes, sashes, and ceremonial caps, stood in formation upon the stairs, waiting for them. As the clock struck ten, Josiah would take his place at the head of them, and the city would see him in the vestments of the High Elder for the very first time. He would lead the crowd in a blessing over the couple, and then the wedding party would process inside. Across from him, Jessamine shifted in her seat, and he could hear her breathing pick up, turning fast and shallow.

"Calm yourself, my dear," Josiah said. "We're very nearly there."

Jessamine nodded, though her breathing did not slow.

At last, the line of carriages pulled to a stop in the shadow of the tower. Wigged and liveried footmen sprang down and opened the doors. Josiah stepped out into the heavy summer air, thick with the shouts and smells of the crowd. His senses reeled as he struggled to take it all in at once. Remembering to take his own advice, he took a deep breath and then extended a hand toward the open door of the carriage.

There was a moment—the tiniest space of time—when his brain acknowledged that the small, pale hand in his was bare—hadn't she been wearing gloves?—and then he could not think anymore.

The great bell over their heads tolled the hour, and chaos took the reins.

37

"**C**OME ON, COME *ON*," Keegan growled. The others had given up on telling him to stay still, and so resigned themselves to watching him pace like a caged animal as the minutes crawled interminably by.

"If he doesn't shut his mouth, I'm going to bloody well shut it for him," Fergus grumbled, but he made no movement to make good on the threat, so Sully let it pass. Hell, she'd have taken a swing at the blighter herself if she hadn't needed every warm body she could get her hands on.

"Easy now," Michael intoned for the third time. Perhaps it was the fact that he'd managed to stay off the Riftmead for the last week, but he'd been one of the calmest of the bunch since the morning dawned, and Sully, though she would have preferred Zeke, was grateful to have him there.

They were crammed into a groundskeeper's shed on the back corner of the Illustratum grounds, a handy suggestion of Daniel Byrne's which had enabled them to get as close as possible to the building without anything to obstruct their view. The plan to get them inside was a simple bait and switch, but a hundred things could still go wrong. They were counting on the guards abandoning their posts at the sounds of the explosions, but there was always a chance they'd have to fight their way in, and it seemed some of the more foolish among them were actually hoping for the confrontation.

"I say we just take them out now," Keegan hissed through clenched teeth. "There's only two of them, for Creator's sake."

"And that's why you're not in charge, isn't it?" Sully said.

"Aw, come on, we'd be doing our bit! Two less in the fray for the lads 'round the front."

"And when they see you coming across the lawn and shoot you, that'll be one less for the lads back here," Sully pointed out dryly. "Although if you prefer to be shot, by all means, keep talking and I might just take care of it for you."

Keegan unleashed a stream of profanity, but thankfully he did so quietly enough that Sully could choose to ignore him. He'd begged to be in the front crowd where Eli was, but there was a chance they might need an Influencer in their attempt to enter the back way, and Keegan was the best they had. He couldn't hold a candle to Eliza's Riftmagic, of course, but she couldn't be in two places at once, more's the pity. Sully looked at her pocket watch, and then at the clock face above them. They'd spotted the carriages processing around the perimeter of the square a few minutes ago. They were bound to have arrived in the courtyard by now. She strained her ears; she couldn't be sure if she was just imagining it, but she thought she detected a swell in the noise from the crowd, a surge of energy.

Sully flexed her fingers, her Manipulator magic singing in her bones. She twitched a finger toward a spade in the corner. It shivered and hovered a moment in the air before falling back to the rotted floorboards with a clunk. It had been a challenge, training herself to Manipulate more than the delicate pages of her books, but she knew that turning pages by Riftmagic was hardly going to help her today. Manipulating the inner workings of locks, on the other hand, would go quite a bit farther for the cause.

She looked down at her watch again. Any moment now. She closed her eyes and thought of Eli and Jasper. She wasn't a praying woman, but she focused on their faces, on seeing them again.

And as if in answer, the great bell tolled.

§

Within the frosted cage of the bridal veil, the world seemed to slow down. Eliza closed her eyes as the clanging of the bell vibrated through the square, and she knew what would happen next. All along the gates and fences to the Illustratum, explosions went off in almost perfect synchronicity, each one set off by a Catalyst. The crowd seemed to explode as well, first in a cacophony of screams and shouts, and then like a great tidal wave surging forward toward the gates that surrounded the inner courtyard of the Illustratum. She had one moment in which something caught her eye—the glove she had just removed, fluttering to the ground—and then her adrenaline kicked in and she remembered what she had to do.

Her fingers tightened around Josiah Hallewell's hand.

Take me inside where it's safe. Tell the Elders to follow.

Elder Hallewell's voice boomed like another explosion as he shouted to the crowd of panicking Elders around him. "Get inside! Up the stairs, now!"

Eliza caught sight of Reginald and Mrs. Morgan, whey-faced and terrified, already fleeing upward to the great doors which had been thrown wide to receive them, and then she was caught up in the tide, holding on for dear life to Elder Hallewell's hand, and she was buffeted and dragged into the sea of robes and shouts and stomping feet. Elders were climbing over each other, shoving and clawing to reach the safety of the entrance hall. The rows of Praesidio guards charged forward into the onslaught, weapons drawn, and Eliza knew a moment of pure terror. She wanted to charge after them, to compel each one to put down his weapon, to protect everyone somehow. She wanted to shove through the crowd until she found Eli, and Jasper, and Sully, and the others, and she wanted to gather them around her and run and run and run. She knew she could not. They were all depending on her. She had one job to do, and she had to do it, or any blood spilled, any lives lost today, would be for nothing.

With a greater effort than it had ever cost her, Eliza centered her whirling, terror-plagued thoughts on her magic and sent her command shooting down through her fingertips.

You know exactly what to do. You will lead the Elders to the Elder Council chamber. You will gather there for safety.

Elder Hallewell's shout cut through the madness. "To the Elder Council chamber! It is closer!" He dragged her behind him, and most of the others followed, though a few had scattered and taken off down other hallways in their panic. The doors were closed when they reached it, and there was a moment of screaming and confusion as they pushed in on each other, desperate to put some sort of barrier between them and the riot forming outside. Elder Hallewell and three other men managed to heave them open—they were not locked—and they spilled into the echoing space beyond. Eliza released Elder

Hallewell's hand at last and collapsed onto a bench, watching as the doors were thrust closed again as the last of the Elders limped and shuffled inside. Three Praesidio guards had been swept into the room with them, and they set to work piling benches and chairs up against the doors to bar them.

At first, no one spoke. The room was full of coughing and retching and gasping as they all struggled to catch their breath and take stock of their injuries from the mad dash to safety. Mrs. Morgan lay curled on the floor in a storm of sobbing. Three Elders had surrounded a fourth who was clutching his chest and struggling to breathe. Reginald was bent over, his head between his knees. One of his sisters was whimpering that she'd been separated from her husband.

It was a soldier who spoke first. "We've barricaded it as best we can," he said.

"What the bloody hell is going on out there?" Reginald cried out, still gasping.

The Elders began squawking and flapping over each other like a flock of spooked birds.

"I don't understand! It's a riot! Why are they rioting?"

"Of course it's a riot!"

"But what's set them off?"

"The explosions! Was that Riftmagic?"

"They were throwing Riftmead! Bottles of Riftmead!"

"It was blessed! That was sacrilege!"

"What were those papers they were waving? Didn't you see them? They were waving them in the air!"

"The sight of the carriages set them off!"

"No, didn't you hear them? They were riled before the carriages even arrived!"

As this went on, from the corner of her eye, Eliza saw one of the guards approach Elder Potter, whispering in his ear and handing him something—a trampled, filthy bit of newsprint. Elder Potter stared down at it, his eyes whizzing back and forth over the text as he took it in. Then he closed his eyes, shaking his head, and crossed the room, handing the paper wordlessly to Elder Hallewell.

Eliza watched with satisfaction as the realization broke over his features, the ruddy flush in his cheeks fading to a pasty grey color. The two men looked at each other, grim understanding passing between them.

Elder Hallewell stood up, and silence fell at once, every eye turning to him, every expression expectant. Eliza watched his dream of being the man they all look to crystallize into a nightmare before her very eyes.

"This has been a coordinated attack," he said, and his words echoed around them. "The crowd was lured here with this propaganda." He held up the battered pamphlet. "They are intending to rise against us."

A stunned silence met these words. Then individual voices began to murmur their shock.

"Lunacy."

"They'd be mad to try it."

"They *have* tried it!"

"Then they shall be crushed! Every guard in the Praesidio is out there!"

"And they outnumber them ten to one!"

"We needn't fear their magic! They've been subdued! The Riftmead—"

"They know about the Riftmead. They understand now what it does," Elder Hallewell called over the others, silencing them once more with another terrible blow. "This... document, whatever it is, wherever it came from, has angered them. And if those who organized this riot knew what the Riftmead does, then they will have stopped drinking it."

"So their magic?" prompted Elder Smythe.

"It will be more powerful," Elder Hallewell admitted.

"Do you mean to say that those explosions..."

"Catalysts," Elder Potter answered. "I'd bet my life on it."

Fear rippled through the room. Mrs. Morgan's sobs were turning to hysteria. One of Reginald's sisters had knelt beside her, trying in vain to calm her even as tears poured down her own cheeks.

"Even so, what can they hope to achieve?" Elder Garrison shouted. "They are many, but they are disorganized and unarmed, without resources, and will soon be quelled. The Praesidio has barracks full of weaponry. Their biggest advantage was the element of surprise, and they've spent it. All we must do is hold this place for a day or two and their pathetic rebellion will peter out."

"But can we hold the place?" another voice cried. "The gates are breached!"

"The building may not be," a third called. "They pulled the front doors closed against the crowd, I saw them before we turned down the corridor."

"What of the other entrances?"

"There are guards posted at all of them!"

"But they will have come running to the square at the sounds of the explosions, surely! That will leave the building vulnerable!"

Yes, if all went to plan, that's exactly what has happened, Eliza thought to herself. She felt invisible beneath the veil. No one had paid her the slightest bit of attention since they'd secured the room. She stood in the corner, the wilting bouquet somehow still dangling from her other hand, forgotten. She let it drop to the floor, a prop she no longer required.

"It matters not! The crowd is in the front! That is where they will be needed!"

"A crowd will spread! They will seek other ways in!"

The Elders descended on the guards and began shouting over each other, demanding answers they did not have to questions they could not hear. Meanwhile, the sounds of the riot outside grew louder, punctuated by more explosions, the sounds of shattering glass, and the whinnying of the horses still tethered to the carriages outside. A rumbling boom from the vicinity of the front doors meant that the fight had reached the top of the steps.

"We need a report on the security of the premises," Elder Hallewell commanded at last. "Double check every entrance on the ground floor and report back here to me."

"You're sending them away?! They're the only protection we have!" Elder Garrison barked.

"And their protection will mean nothing if that mob gets inside!" Elder Hallewell snapped. "Go now, do as I command you!"

The three soldiers hurried at once for the door they'd all entered through, but Elder Hallewell called them back. "No, you fools! Use the entrance at the top of the benches! We must leave this one barricaded!"

The soldiers turned and began to climb the benches to the top gallery that ran around the room. A brick smashed through one of the stained-glass windows that ran along the top of the room, no doubt flung from the mob below. Brightly colored shards of glass rained down on the benches, and everyone flung their hands over their heads to protect themselves from the debris. Reginald and one of his brothers-in-law stood up, dragging Mrs. Morgan and his sisters to the other side of the room, as far from the windows as possible.

"Jessamine, you'll be killed, get away from the windows!" Reginald growled. But Eliza did not move, and he made no attempt to reach her. Her eyes were on the door at the top of the room. Any moment now, if the plan had worked, if they'd made it into the building…

The guards were a mere ten feet from the door when the sounds of footsteps could be heard outside in the corridor. Instinctively, Eliza started forward as the guards, hearing the commotion, began to run. She knew she couldn't reach them, couldn't stop them, she was too far away.

The door burst inward with an ear-splitting crunch. The first guard was blasted off his feet, crashed down into the benches, and lay there, unmoving. The second two guards rushed forward, but they were forced back by the crowd spilling into the room. One was tackled, his weapon wrestled from his hands, and turned on him. The other plunged recklessly forward only to fall back shrieking and clutching his face: the result of running headlong into a Catalyst who grabbed him by the throat and unleashed a flare of magic so powerful that Eliza could feel the blast of heat like a hot wind. Within moments, all three guards had been overcome, and a dozen figures stared down into the Elder Council chamber, light spilling in behind them, and throwing them into relief like shadows. One stepped forward, her halo of curls crackling with triumph.

"Good morning, esteemed Elders," said Sully, pushing her spectacles up her nose. "I do hope you haven't started without us."

38

E LIZA CRIED OUT WITH RELIEF, but the sound was lost in the outburst of the Elders and the shrieks of the wedding party.

Only Elder Hallewell watched the newcomers appear without scrambling to move away from them. He gazed up at them, his face a mask of pure outrage.

"What is the meaning of this?" he bellowed. "How dare you demean this holy chamber with your sacrilege!"

Sully raised her eyebrows. "Sacrilege? I think not, High Elder. There is nothing written in the *Book of the Rift* that forbids a Riftborn from setting foot within the walls of the Illustratum, and you know that as well as I do."

"Explain yourself at once. I demand to know who you are," Hallewell continued, his voice ringing with authority.

"I'd be delighted to, sir," Sully said, sounding flattered. "My name is Lila Sullivan, Riftborn Manipulator. I am here on behalf of the Riftborn of London to invoke the rule of parley."

A muttering rose from the Elders, but Elder Hallewell actually threw back his head and laughed. "You cannot break into the Elder Council chamber by force and expect to be heard by this assembly! You have not been invited to bring your petition before this company."

Sully furrowed her brows. "Hmmm. That's right. We haven't been invited, have we lads? A slight oversight on our part, I'm sure. Interestingly, no Riftborn has ever been invited to bring their petition before the Elder Council in the 88 years of its existence. A slightly larger oversight on your part, I imagine."

Hallewell smiled; it was an evil thing, a taut leer that stretched his face. "And you thought you'd earn an invitation by sabotaging my daughter's wedding, did you?"

"Oh, not at all. We had no expectation of an invitation. The law itself does not expressly require one, as I'm sure you know. The language simply states, 'let the Riftborn with a petition but stand upon the chamber floor, and they shall be heard,'" Sully said.

Elder Hallewell's smile faltered for a moment, but he hitched it back into place almost at once. "Oh, very clever of you. A woman of learning are you, Miss Sullivan? Interested in exploiting a loophole in the law, as it were? Well, I am sorry to say that the language is clear. The Riftborn must stand upon the chamber floor, and there you stand in the gallery. There are over a hundred of us here, and merely a dozen of your scrappy little band of rebels. I assure you, we can prevent you from reaching the floor, despite the blasphemous use of your Riftmagic."

Sully's face broke into a wide smile. "I will grant you, High Elder, that your numbers within these walls are greater, though I'd wager that may soon change." She cocked her head toward the continued sounds of the struggle outside and smiled as though the sounds of fighting were music to her ears, while Eliza's stomach twisted, thinking of Eli, Jasper, Zeke, and the others. "But as to a Riftborn standing on the chamber floor, that goal has already been achieved."

Elder Hallewell laughed a bitter, ugly sound, and then stared around himself theatrically. "Is that so? Am I to believe that one of the Elders of the Illustratum is secretly a Riftborn?"

Sully was still smiling. "I would suggest no such thing. But perhaps you should ask your daughter to weigh in on the matter?"

For the first time, Elder Hallewell's expression faltered. He spun on the spot, staring into the corner where the figure in white had stood silent all this time. Indeed, every eye in the room now turned to stare at the bride as though they had only just that moment remembered her existence. Elder Hallewell's voice thundered.

"Jessamine? What is the meaning of this?"

Eliza's hands trembled as they reached for the edge of the veil, but Sully's voice rang out again.

"Before she answers that question, let me pose another," she said, and the expectation in her tone was delicious. "However did you wind up in this room, of all places?"

Elder Hallewell opened his mouth to reply and then froze. Eliza could see the question playing across his face as he asked himself.

"It's a puzzle, isn't it?" Sully went on. "After all, the *sacrarium* was much closer, and with only one entrance that led to an outer corridor. Larger as well, and located in the middle of the building, much easier to fortify against intruders."

Elder Hallewell's face spasmed, furious to have his error thrown up in his face in this manner, but he still managed a thin smile. "An error, perhaps, but an understandable one, given the pressure under which it was made. I assure you, I shall be happy to answer for my decision once we've had the pleasure of seeing you all hang."

"But surely you must be wondering how you made that decision," Sully went on, as though he hadn't spoken at all. "How the impulse dropped into your head, almost as though someone else had put it there. Because someone had."

There was no trace of a smile on Elder Hallewell's face now. "I can see that you enjoy speaking in riddles, Miss Sullivan. Perhaps you think you can spin this out like Scheherazade, delaying your fate, but it will not save you."

Sully actually threw her head back and laughed. "A literary reference! My goodness, Elder Hallewell, if you weren't using it to threaten my life, I'd be tempted to applaud you. But I daresay that your metaphor is apt, for the bravery of a young woman in the face of a tyrant was all the magic we needed."

And Sully turned to Eliza, who knew the moment had come and found she welcomed it. Let him see his folly. Let him see her for what she was at last.

And the lady's maid lifted her veil.

§

A single thought echoed through every cell of Eli Turner's body: Get to Eliza. From the moment he set off the coordinated explosions and the summer's day gave way to utter anarchy, it was all that propelled him forward. He clung to it, knowing it may very well be the only thing he could control. Whether Sully and the others would make it through the back entrance, whether Jasper and Zeke would arrive with reinforcements from the Praeteritum, all of this was in the Creator's hands. Eli had no choice but to trust his friends and their careful planning, for it took every ounce of his concentration simply not to be killed.

The Praesidio wasted no time firing into the crowds, indiscriminate of who they aimed for. The air was thick with smoke and the metallic tang of gunpowder. There was no telling which Riftborn had come to watch a wedding and which had come to fight. Weapons had been fashioned of whatever was within reach; Eli dodged jabbing sticks, broken bottles, improvised torches, and wildly swinging fists. Screams and agonized cries battered his eardrums, but he kept pushing forward.

A section of the wrought iron gate was hanging crookedly from its hinges as several young men threw their shoulders against it, trying to knock it loose. Eli threw an elbow to the face of an oncoming soldier and darted around him as he fell, closing the distance between himself and the gate. Shoving in beside the others, he grasped the bars and pulled with all his might, calling up his Riftmagic as he did so. The metal beneath his fingers grew hot, but he did not let go. He heard the sound of the hinges giving way, and the gate came loose in his hands, nearly knocking him to the ground. The surrounding crowd saw what they were doing, and suddenly there was a crush of bodies, and dozens of rebels hurried forward to grasp the bars. They pushed the gate upright again and lifted it from the ground in front of them.

"Forward!" Eli bellowed, and the others obeyed, joining his cry and shoving forward with all their might. The gate crashed into the crowd, sending bodies flying in every direction. The Riftborn scattered, but the Praesidio pressed shoulder to shoulder, determined to hold the line and protect the Elders and the other Dignus already escaping into the Illustratum. Eli caught a glimpse of white through the sea of red robes flooding through the doors, the only hint that Eliza had managed to get safely inside. It would have to be enough. The sound of screeching metal behind him made him glance back over his shoulder just in time to see the other gate come loose in rebel hands.

The crowd was fracturing apart now—even some of those who had come to support the cause were scattering as their anger gave way to fear for their lives. Eli had expected it, but it still sent panic through him to watch people run instead of fight. He began to wonder if they would have the numbers to get through the doors and into the Elder Council chamber. Everything hinged on their being able to get the numbers they needed to force the parley vote. If they couldn't get through, if they couldn't flood the place with Riftborn, all of this would be for nothing.

He pushed the thought away as he shoved against the line of Praesidio guards. No room for error. No room for hesitation or doubt. Only determination and grit and moving forward.

And they *were* moving forward. Impossibly, they were gaining, inch by painful inch, as Praesidio guards lost their footing and stumbled and their brothers struggled to fill in the gaps in their defenses. The men and women on either side of him were wild with rage and fueling themselves on every bit of progress they made toward the front doors.

And yet, Eli found himself despairing. Yes, they were moving forward, but even if they continued at this pace, inch by hard-earned inch, they would never reach the Elder Council chamber in time for what Sully and the others had planned. The parley vote would only work if they had enough manpower within the walls to gain a majority. The Elders had long since vanished into the building, and if Sully and the others had managed to enter around the back, they would likely be inside now as well.

Both gates were being used as battering rams now, slamming into the solid wall of soldiers trying to hold the line. Dozens more had finally worked their way from their posts around the building to the skirmish at the front, reinforcing the defenses, forming row after row of uniforms that the rebels would have to fight through. Bayonets began thrusting through the bars, and one by one the front line of rebels began to fall. The Riftborn crowd was throwing everything they could get their hands on, lighting things on fire and using their magic to propel objects through the air, but the forward progress began to stall. Eli heard explosions behind them and felt broken glass rain down over his head. A man was tossed through the air beside him and Eli watched as his progress slowed just before he hit the ground—a Temporal, using his gift to save himself from injury. And still they pushed, they shoved, they shouted and they fell. Eli dodged a bayonet blade a second too late and felt hot pain graze his side. Two men beside him grabbed a hold of the bayonet and tugged, slamming the guard still holding it against the bars. He crumpled, but another guard stepped up and immediately took his place. The rebels began to lose ground, and Eli tasted panic, sharp and metallic, on the tip of his tongue. His palms were sweaty, the bars of the gate slipping and sliding through his fingers.

If they couldn't get in, if they couldn't force their way into the Elder Council chamber...

But something was happening in the square behind him. The guards were staring beyond the rebels at the gates, focused on something over their shoulders, and whatever it was made their eyes go wide. Eli dared not take his eyes off the struggle before him to look behind him, but he felt a tiny bubble of hope swell in his chest.

Please. Please let them come.

And as though in answer to his silent prayer, a roar rippled through the crowd at his back. A tidal wave of energy surged forward—he felt it like a sudden gust of wind stirred up by an oncoming storm. The force of it shifted everything at once. Suddenly the soldiers before him looked terrified, and the rebels around him lit like fuses. And as the Praesidio guard right in front of him broke ranks and turned tail to flee, Eli, at last, ventured a glance behind him.

Jasper and Zeke had arrived, at the head of what looked like every single prisoner from within the Praeteritum. It was a ragged but fierce crowd, storming forward with all the recklessness of men who had nothing left to lose. Commanders were shouting instructions to their ranks, but soldiers were scattering right and left at the sight of the oncoming horde. Just before he turned his head, Eli watched as Jasper took the lead of a group of men who broke off to the right flank to help hem the soldiers in. They locked eyes, and Jasper grinned.

And the tide began to turn.

All at once, the gates were surging forward, knocking fleeing soldiers off their feet, the crowd trampling those who could not scramble up fast enough. Bayonets and pistols and blades were being wrested from Praesidio guards. Catalyst hands were thrusting through the bars, grabbing and burning every bit of flesh they could reach. Manipulators were rocking the stones under Praesidio feet, causing them to stumble and fall. Temporals were using their small pockets of power to slow down attackers and weapons so that people could dodge them. A Manipulator had gotten control over a plume of gunpowder smoke and was casting it into soldiers' faces, causing them to sputter and choke and fall back. One Manipulator, a girl no older than fourteen, was crouching against the plinth of a statue and quietly causing Praesidio bootlaces to knot up. Eli could have hooted with glee if he wasn't so focused on getting to those front doors.

At last, with an almighty roar, the Riftborn mob broke through the lines of remaining soldiers and moved in a great seething mass toward the main doors. Eli could hear the voices of the other Resistance members shouting instructions.

"Up the steps!"

"Use the gates to break through!"

"To the Elder Council chamber!"

"Parley! Parley! Parley!"

The crowd took up the chant as they mounted the steps, hurling debris at the building and shattering windows. The gates became battering rams, with the crowd shouting "Parley!" with every thrust against the doors. At last, they burst open, and the scrum to get inside thrust Eli up against the wall, pinned back by the crowd, unable to move. He craned his neck over the tumult, trying to spot any of the other Resistance members. Movement in his periphery caused him to turn and see a small knot of people near a statue.

Everything around him went silent.

Jasper. Jasper in a pool of blood.

Eli shoved mercilessly through the crowd which shoved just as mercilessly back until he broke through the sea of bodies. He pelted across the cobblestones, littered with bodies, until he reached the place where Jasper lay. Tillie and Peter hovered over him.

"What is it? What's happened to him?" Eli gasped.

"Went down in the final push, caught a bayonet and his leg's been crushed," Tillie replied. She was already ripping her skirt to shreds and tying the strips tightly around his thigh in an attempt to staunch the bleeding.

"We dragged him out, but it's bad, Eli," Peter said. "I think the bone's come through."

Eli did not allow himself any more than a half a glance at the mangled mess of Jasper's leg.

"Can you get him out of here? Back to Lavender's?" Eli asked.

Tillie nodded. "Zeke ordered a group of men to commandeer the carriages and horses. They're around the back of the building."

"Good. Take one of them, and get him there as quickly as you can," Eli said. He looked down into Jasper's face. His eyes had rolled back into his head and he was convulsing with the pain of his injury.

"You're going to be okay, mate. They're going to take care of you, all right?"

He couldn't wait to see if Jasper had understood him. He couldn't help him now. The only thing he could do was pray and get inside and finish what they had started together, and pray to whomever was listening that his brother was still alive at the end of it.

Feeling as though someone had punched his heart out of his chest, he turned and sprinted for the open doors.

§

Eliza knew that every pair of eyes in the chamber was upon her, but there was only one gaze that she cared to meet, and that was Elder Hallewell's. She watched with unbridled satisfaction as the realization broke over his features and settled into his body. His limbs stiffened. His spine straightened. His eyes grew wide and his lips curled over his clenched teeth. Eliza could think of a hundred things she would like to say to him in front of these people, words that would wound him, demean him, belittle him, just as he had done to so many others. But what she said instead were the words that Sully had written down for her, that she had practiced over and over again until she could recite them in her sleep.

"I stand before the Elder Council, a Riftborn upon the Elder Council chamber floor, to invoke my right to have my petition heard and call for a parley vote."

The words were met with ringing silence at first. Not a single Elder seemed to know how to respond. They were all staring at each other, asking without words whether this was really happening, and what they were meant to do about it. It was Elder Hallewell who spoke at last, and he did so as though he had not heard her words.

"Where is Jessamine?" he asked in a deadly whisper.

"She is gone, sir."

"Gone?"

"Left. Escaped. Regardless of what happens today, you will not see her again."

The answer wounded him, and Eliza took pleasure from that fact. But she did not want to allow him to dictate what happened next, so she calmly pulled a folded paper from her dress. Elder Hallewell stared as though she had just performed a magic trick.

"It has pockets," she said in explanation, before unfolding the paper and starting to read.

"As codified in the founding documents of this great institution, a Riftborn may seek a vote on any petition brought to a quorum of the Elder Council in the Council chamber. Furthermore, any Riftborn there present is entitled to vote upon the petition in question, and those votes shall be counted as having equal weight to the votes of the Elders. Our petition is as follows—"

"That is enough of this ludicrous charade," Elder Hallewell shouted. There was a dangerous edge to his voice now.

"Oh, I assure you this is not a charade, sir," Sully called from the gallery. "The petition that Eliza now reads from has been drawn up in a most serious manner, and has been signed by dozens of Riftborn citizens."

"It is a charade!" Elder Hallewell cried. "A feeble attempt to dress up your violence today in the trappings of respectability and orderliness. But your insubordination will not be rewarded. There will be no vote today, and you will be swinging from the gallows by morning."

"Is that so? Do you mean to say that the procedural rules of the Illustratum mean nothing?" Sully asked.

"I mean to say that they do not apply to blasphemers and criminals," Hallewell spat back.

"Criminals?" Sully asked, raising her eyebrows innocently. "Have we been charged with something? It's been a busy morning, but I rather think I'd remember something like that."

"When the Praesidio manage to make their way in here, you will be charged with every manner of crime we can throw at you," Hallewell sneered. "Oh, I daresay, you thought your plan was clever, Miss Sullivan, but I assure you, this is a farce, a spectacle of the most despicable kind, and I will not stand for it while I am High Elder."

"Sweeping declarations already, and you've hardly held that title for a day," Sully said. "Seems a bit ambitious of you, driving the cart off the cliff the moment you've gotten a hold of the reins, but I'm sure you have your reasons."

"I assure you, I am taking control, not losing it," Elder Hallewell snapped. "London shall not fall to your sinful demands."

"Yes, you've taken control of quite a lot in the past few hours, haven't you? The death of the High Elder happened at quite an

377

inopportune moment for you, didn't it? Luckily, though, as you say, you took control."

Elder Hallewell's whole body shuddered. "I stepped into the role the High Elder chose for me."

"And did he choose it?" Sully asked. "Was it truly the dying wish of John Morgan that you wear those robes today? Or was that yet another moment of taking control?"

Hallewell froze, tension rolling off him in waves. His eyes darted around the room, and each pair of eyes found to be staring at him ratcheted his tension even higher.

"What are you all doing, listening to this woman? Will no one else speak out against her? Am I to stand alone in rebuffing such lies and slander?"

"It is not slander. It's the truth."

Eliza's voice was small but steady, and every face swung around to watch her speak.

"I was there when Elder Morgan died. You sent for me," Eliza went on.

"You will not speak of it! I command you in the name of the Creator!" Elder Hallewell shrieked, spittle flying from his lips.

"Oh, what you would give for a little Riftmagic of your own in a moment like this," Eliza said, relishing the words. "Is that why you chased after those vestments? Because you could not have what you truly wished for?"

"I do not want your filthy, cursed magic!" Hallewell said, loathing dripping from every syllable. "I want nothing to do with it."

"Oh, I think you do," Eliza said. "I've seen you watching me when I've been forced to use it at your behest. I've seen the hunger in your eyes. You want that power for yourself, and you've certainly wielded it as though it was your own, haven't you?"

Elder Hallewell's face was contorted with rage that he could not seem to form into words.

"You sent for me because the High Elder would not do as you wished. He would not put your nomination in writing, and then time ran out. You needed an Influencer to compel him to sign the papers. I had no choice but to do as you commanded me."

"And you think the Elder Council is going to take the word of a lying, scheming Riftborn over one of their own brethren? Simple child," Hallewell scoffed. But Eliza thought she saw some glances traded between a few of the other Elders, and she took heart from it.

"He couldn't even sit up or hold a pen on his own. He wasn't lucid, and he certainly would not have been capable of it on his own. I forced his hand, and made the decision for him because you demanded that I do so."

"Is that so? And you have proof to support these wildly fantastical accusations?" Elder Hallewell asked, a soft sneer in his voice.

"I do not," Eliza said solemnly. "But I wasn't the only one in the room. Elder Potter was there, and so was Brother Goodwin. Perhaps they would like to tell everyone what happened?"

Brother Goodwin trembled where he sat, eyes cast down to the floor, refusing to acknowledge that he had so much as heard his own name. Elder Potter, though, was looking straight at Eliza as though he couldn't decide whether to strangle her or applaud her. He kept silent, however.

"If they'd rather not talk about it," Eliza went on, "I would certainly understand. It was a terribly sad night. But I don't need them to confess in order to prove what you did."

"Is that so? Then how will you prove it?"

Eliza held out her hand to Elder Hallewell. "You can tell them."

From above them in the gallery, Eliza thought she heard Sully smother a satisfied chuckle. Elder Hallewell, on the other hand, was staring at her fingers as though they were weapons she had just unsheathed.

"All you need to do is touch my hand. I can ask you what happened the night of Elder Morgan's death and you can tell them."

Elder Hallewell took an involuntary step backward, and the movement was as good as a confession, even as he continued to stammer about lies and sinners and tricks. Eliza lowered her hand.

"I see. Well, if you don't want to talk about High Elder Morgan, maybe we can get back to the matter of our petition."

She took up the paper to begin reading again, but a commotion in the outer hallway forestalled her. The sounds of hundreds of feet were pounding through the entrance hall. A repeated battle cry was heard above the tumult, a single word over and over again in hundreds of voices that sounded like one.

"Parley! Parley! Parley!"

The Elders began to panic, scrambling away from the doors and climbing up the rows of benches, but there was nowhere for them to go. The doors they had tried to barricade burst open with a deafening crash and the Riftborn barreled through it like an avalanche. Eliza turned to look over her shoulder, to watch the arrival of the rebel mob, and that moment of distraction was all it took. Elder Hallewell grabbed her arm, yanking her toward him. Eliza felt the petition flutter from her hands and reached for it, but Elder Hallewell was too quick for her, pinning her hands behind her back using his sash as a barrier between his skin and hers. In the madness of the roaring crowd, he half-dragged her far into the darkened corner beneath the gallery. He pushed his hand against the paneling and a narrow door popped open from where it had been concealed. Then he stepped through it, tugging her after him. Eliza's screams were lost, swallowed up in the cacophony as the door swung shut behind them.

39

"**W**HERE ARE WE GOING?"
The question bounced off the walls, its own echoes the only reply.

"Where are you taking me?"

If Elder Hallewell heard her, he gave no sign of it. His eyes were burning in his face, his muscles so taut that he looked like a man carved from stone. He dragged her along while muttering to himself, a steady stream of words so unbroken that Eliza thought they must be a prayer. Loud pops and bangs followed them down the corridor, but not once did Elder Hallewell respond to them. He pulled Eliza up the stairs and down another very long hallway that, even in her panic and confusion, knew that she recognized. By the time they turned the corner at the end, she knew what she was going to see.

The great golden doors to the *Sacrum Odium* gleamed and twinkled before them.

"What are we doing here?" Eliza tried again, and this time Hallewell answered, though the words seemed to be for himself alone.

"I will seek His counsel. I will know His word. He will tell me what to do."

Elder Hallewell did not hesitate when they reached the doors. He took no moment to reflect on the fact that he was going to walk through them for the very first time. He charged at them like they belonged to him and, with a mighty grunt, pushed them open.

Eliza's mouth fell open. She had expected a great palatial space beyond, vaulted ceilings and frescos of cherubs, and some kind of massive *altaria* full of mystical artifacts and scrolls of documents.

381

Instead, she found herself staring into a room that seemed to have been gouged out from ancient, solid stone. The rough-hewn walls reached way up above them, slightly rounded, like the inside of a tower. A few windows high above them allowed sunlight from outside to filter in, falling in narrow shafts across the dusty stone floor. Directly across from the doors, a huge, faded tapestry hung high over their heads. It depicted simply a pair of hands reaching up, and another, larger pair of hands reaching down; and between them, a great golden globe. A faded purple rug lay spread in the center of the floor.

Even in the dead of summer, the room was suffused with a damp chill. Eliza had the feeling of stepping down into a dank cellar, though she knew they were well above the street. Whether Elder Hallewell knew what he was going to see when the doors were opened, Eliza couldn't tell, but he gazed up at the tapestry with an undisguised hunger on his face.

"It's here. The Rift. I can feel it," he whispered.

He took the sash and tied it around Eliza's wrists, binding them tightly. Then he tossed her aside and resumed his examination of the tapestry.

"Sir, why are we here?" Eliza's voice was cracked with fear.

"We are here so that I can commune with the Rift," Elder Hallewell said without looking at her. "The Creator will tell me that I was right, that this was His plan for me all along, and then no one will question my authority again!"

"But why am I here?" Eliza asked. "You don't need me here to commune with the Rift. Let me go."

"Oh, no, I can't do that," Elder Hallewell said, a strange smile toying with the corners of his mouth. "You're my insurance."

And Eliza understood. If the Resistance came for him, he would use her to escape, his shield and his weapon.

"But whatever use I put you to, the Creator will guide me," Hallewell went on. "I am here at last, and He will reveal His plans to me."

Eliza gazed again around the *Sacrum Odium* of legend, cold and faded within these dank and dripping walls, and she thought she had never seen a place so devoid of the divine. The very motes hanging in the air whispered of emptiness.

Elder Hallewell did not hear these whispers—the call of his own longing was too loud in his ears. He stumbled forward until he stood upon the threadbare carpet, and then sank to his knees. His chin dropped onto his chest and his hands rose up in a gesture of supplication.

"Almighty Creator. It is by Your grace that I am here, upon my knees before You, seeking Your guidance. Let me hear Your voice. Let me know Your will."

Eliza sucked in a breath and held it, waiting for something—anything—to happen. The sounds of struggle were but a faint fluttering below them, and it carried on unabated. There was no charge upon the air, no sudden light or answering voice. All was stillness.

Undeterred, Elder Hallewell tried again. The hands over his head shook with the great effort of his concentration. This time, the answering silence struck him as though it had spoken his name. He raised his chin, lifting his closed eyes to the sky. He took deep breaths, filling his lungs. He opened his chest, spreading his arms wide to receive what was surely coming now.

The silence lengthened and twisted, a serpentine thing. Elder Hallewell let out a roar of frustration. He jumped to his feet and searched every inch of the room for something—some tiny clue as to what he might be doing wrong. When the room yielded nothing, he sank to his knees once more, his pleas becoming frantic.

"My Lord, I don't understand Your silence. I am ready and waiting for Your word. Please, do not leave me here in wonder as to what You would have me do. Guide me, oh mighty one! I am Yours to command! Speak to me!"

The answering silence stretched beyond the bounds of Elder Hallewell's patience. He let out an odd, shrieking cry and staggered to his feet again, tearing at his hair. Then his eyes fell on Eliza and he swung his body toward her, closing the distance between them in only three harried strides. He thrust a hand out, grasped her wrist, and hauled her onto the rug, forcing her down so that she too was on her knees.

"Help me, Eliza! Use your magic! Compel the answer to reveal itself to me!"

Eliza's throat felt like it was closing around the answer she had to give. "I can't do that, sir. It's not how my magic works."

"Don't you dare defy me! Do as I command you! The answer, where is it?"

383

"Sir, I cannot command the Creator Himself. It was He who wrought my magic and He cannot be commanded by it."

Elder Hallewell looked to the point of tears. He stared around wildly and then his eyes fell on his own hands. "Compel me, then!"

Eliza felt sure she had not heard him. "What did you say?"

"You must compel me! The Creator is speaking, but I cannot understand Him. Compel my understanding, make me see where I am blind!"

The sadness that spread through Eliza as she stared into the man's desperate eyes was almost too much to take. Even after all he had put her through—put all of them through—still somehow she found her heart aching with pity for him and the weight of the truth pressing down upon him. A truth she already knew, because a dying man had whispered it in her ear.

She swallowed, hard, and tried to wet her bone-dry lips. "I cannot do that. I cannot make a man hear when there is no voice."

Elder Hallewell scoffed. "Of course there's a voice. This is the Rift. There is no place upon this earth where the veil is thinner. This is where I will hear Him. This is where He has promised to speak to me."

And Eliza's understanding finally caught up to the truth. This was what it had all been for—not the titles, or the palace, or even the power. It was this all along that he craved—direct, unambiguous knowledge of the Creator himself. He thought his faith would be rewarded and instead...

...instead, he was staring down into the pity smoldering in the eyes of a lowly servant, and that pity angered him as nothing had before.

"These were the final words of John Morgan," she whispered. "The Rift is a lie."

Hallewell went quite still. Then, with a scream of rage, he drew back his hand, preparing to strike.

§

When Eli skidded to a halt outside the Elder Council chamber, the fight had exploded within its walls. Everywhere he looked, Riftborn were wrestling Elders into their seats. The few guards who had been swept in with them were scrambling to defend themselves, let alone the Elders. From the corner of his eye, he thought he saw Reginald

Morgan stumble to his feet and break for the door. No one tried to stop him.

Eli pelted up the risers of benches, trying to get his eyes on Eliza. They found Sully first.

"Sully! Where is she?"

Sully didn't need to ask who he meant. And from her vantage point up in the gallery, she had seen just where they'd gone.

"That way, Eli!" she shouted over the chaos. "Hallewell took her that way when the crowd broke in!"

Eli didn't wait for another word of explanation. He leaped from bench to bench, hurled himself over the heads of the last few men who were dragging the Moderator to his podium, and landed just in front of the door. A second later he was tearing down the hallway and up the stairs, listening for voices, looking for an open door, and at last, as he skidded around the corner he heard it: shouting from the massive golden doors at the end of the corridor. He ran as he'd never run before, bursting through them just in time to see his father raise his hand, preparing to strike the woman he loved.

"Father, enough!"

The word escaped him without his conscious thought, shocking him. His voice came out hoarse with breathlessness, but the cavernous room carried his words with more power than he gave them. They halted Elder Hallewell's hand in the air, and he turned to see who had spoken them.

Father and son stared at each other. It was impossible to tell if Hallewell had absorbed what had been said. His eyes were still lit with madness. He let his hand drop to his side, and then he spoke, voice subdued.

"What... did you say?"

"I asked you to stop."

"You... you called me father."

"I did."

"Why... why would you... who are you?" The question came out strangled, as though the truth was already closing in on him. Even as he spoke, his eyes were roving over the young man standing in front of him, cataloging the familiar features: the dark curling hair, the vibrant green eyes, his own square jaw, and aquiline profile. Eli did not have to answer the question; the answer was clear simply by looking at him.

"William," he whispered.

Eli took a step forward, and his father countered with a stagger backward.

"It's over. Step away from her."

"How are you... where did you... were you a part of this?"

"Like father like son," Eli replied with a bitter laugh. "We both saw our opportunity for power and we both grabbed for it. The difference, of course, is that I want to return the power to the people you stole it from, whereas you want it only for yourself. That ends today."

Elder Hallewell's mouth flapped open and closed uselessly. Eli took advantage of the moment to reach down and pull Eliza to her feet and then plant himself between her and his father.

"Are you all right? Did he hurt you?"

"I'm all right," came her tremulous reply.

His knees went weak with relief, and he turned to his father again. "It's over. The Resistance has taken control of the Elder Council chamber and it's only a matter of time before the parley vote; and with hundreds of Riftborn there to have their voices heard, we are assured of the majority. The Illustratum's reign of terror over the Riftborn of this country is ended."

But Elder Hallewell was shaking his head violently, like a child denied a boon. "No. This was His plan. His plan for me. He will not take me to the pinnacle and then abandon me here. He has chosen me," he said, the resolution in his voice wavering.

"Every step of this path was your own choice. At least be man enough to own your decisions," Eli spat.

"You're dead," Elder Hallewell whispered. "I do not argue with ghosts, nor listen to the ravings of specters."

Eli absorbed the words and found, to his surprise, that they did not hurt him the way he expected. This man, this hysterical shell of a man, was nothing to him. He might have been his father once, but he had severed all those ties when he abandoned his child, and Eli found himself remarkably free. Free from pain, free from the slightest inclination to give a damn. And so when he answered, the words fell easily from his tongue, and he did not regret a single one of them.

"Specters are all you'll be left with," Eli replied. "Every ghost of every person you sacrificed on the altar of your own insatiable lust for power: those will be your constant companions now. I hope, for your sake, that it was worth it."

And Eli turned, starting to pull Eliza back toward the door.

"You're just going to leave him here?" Eliza asked.

"Alone in his godless sanctuary, watching his ambitions crumble to dust around him? Yes, I think that's just the place to leave him," Eli said with satisfaction. "What else should I do? Beg him to love me? To accept me? He cares for nothing but the gratification of his own self-importance. As soon as the parley vote is over, the rebels will scour the building, and I daresay they'll find him right where we left him, still screaming fruitlessly at insensible stone."

On the other side of the golden doors, Eliza pressed herself to Eli's chest, relishing her freedom from the fear that had weighed her down like a stone from the moment the fight had begun.

"Thank heaven you're all right," Eliza whispered.

Eli chuckled. "You've stolen the words right out of my mouth."

"What about the others?"

Eli swallowed hard. "Jasper was hurt. They've taken him back to Lavender's place."

Eliza's hand flew to her mouth. "Will he be okay?"

"I don't know," Eli replied with a tight shrug.

Eliza frowned fiercely. "He will be all right. He has to be."

Eli swallowed his doubts and took her by the hand, heading back toward the Elder Council chamber. But as they reached the bottom of the staircase, a roaring sound erupted from the room, causing them both to stagger back in alarm. It took a moment for them to realize it was cheering—uproarious, celebratory cheering.

"What's happened? What does it mean?" Eliza gasped.

Eli felt a smile break over his face. "I do believe that's the sound of a majority."

"You don't mean..."

"We did it. Damn it all, we really did it."

And the joy in their quiet embrace could be matched only by the despair of the man on the floor above, who had shouted and begged and thrown things and had at last come to the unassailable conclusion that no one would speak to him; no one was listening. He stumbled from the *Sacrum Odium*, fleeing down the hallways that led to his office. It was quiet inside, and if he had not known the chaos that had taken hold downstairs, he would never have imagined anything was wrong. He did not pause at his desk, but proceeded directly to the doors that led onto his balcony. He pushed them open and staggered forward until his hands clutched the railing. Suddenly he was gazing down at a city he no longer recognized. His heart swelled with the kind of despair that can only come from watching the very foundation of one's life wash away, a sand castle when the tide comes in. He turned his face to the sky and begged once more for a sign, anything that might assure him. But bleak grey cloud cover had rolled in, obscuring the sun and, with it, all the hope that remained to him.

He did not remember making the decision, only knowing that it was made. Above him was insensible silence and below him, only consequences. And so Josiah Hallewell did the only thing he could do. He leaped into the emptiness and let it swallow him. His very last, fervent hope, was that the Thames below would bless him with oblivion so complete, that no more thoughts could find him.

And the Thames, in its infinite mercy, answered his prayer.

§

"After all of that, I didn't even make it inside," Jasper grumbled. "I didn't even get to vote!"

"Come now, don't sulk. I didn't get to vote either, you know," Eli pointed out good-naturedly.

He, Sully, and Eliza were sitting grouped around Jasper's bedside. His leg was set in a splint and wrapped in a gauzy mountain of bandages, thanks to the very deft skills of a Manipulator. His words escaped him in labored gasps as he struggled to deal with his pain. Cora had ordered him to gulp down a tea that would help and he had drained his cup as ordered, but it had yet to take much effect.

"You still managed to save the day, though, Jasper," Eliza said. "If it weren't for the Praeteritum reinforcements arriving when they did, I'm not sure the Resistance would even have made it inside."

Jasper managed a grin that twisted almost at once into a grimace. "Thanks. At least I can take credit for getting the Riftborn onto the chamber floor, eh?" He flicked a hand toward the white gown Eliza was still wearing.

"It was a brilliant plan," Eliza agreed. She'd have said almost anything to keep that hint of good humor on his face.

"I only wish it had been brilliant enough to keep us all safe," Jasper replied.

The day had not been without its losses. Dozens of Riftborn

had lost their lives in the struggle outside the Illustratum, including Fergus, whose weak lungs and frail body had succumbed to the pressure of the crowd. Zeke was injured as well, a blow to the head that had left him unconscious and badly swollen. It would be days, perhaps, before they knew how badly the blow had affected him. Cora would hazard no guesses as to the damage until he was awake.

The Elders were being held in the Praeteritum under heavy guard until they could be properly investigated for their crimes, along with many of the Praesidio guards. The people of the Barrens were flooding the streets, shouting and celebrating. The Dignus were hiding out in their houses, unsure what the future would bring for them. No doubt many would try to flee but, as Sully said, it wasn't anyone's wish to banish the Dignus to the gutters of society. Equal representation was all they wanted. To take any more than that would make them no better than the tyrants they replaced; and if there was one thing a scholar like Sully knew, it was the dangers of falling into a pattern of history repeating itself.

A soft knock sounded upon the door. It was Jessamine, a tea tray balanced in her hands.

"Excuse me, but Cora asked me to bring this up to... Eliza!" She froze, shocked into silence by the sight of who was gathered in the room. Her hands began to shake, the tea things rattling on the tray.

Eliza jumped up from her seat and snatched the tray from her before she dropped it. She set it carefully on the table and gathered Jessamine into an embrace.

"Eliza, I—thank heavens you're all right!" Jessamine whimpered.

"Didn't I promise you everything would work out?" Eliza asked, smiling.

"Well, yes, of course you did, but what else could you say?" Jessamine replied with a nervous laugh. "I don't think I've taken a proper breath since I watched you drive away in the carriage and..."

Jessamine's voice trailed away as Eli stood up. Now it was everyone else's turn to forget how to breathe. At last, Eli cleared his throat.

"Hello, Jessamine," he said, almost sheepishly, so that he looked for a moment like the boy he had been, caught at something naughty.

Jessamine laughed, a fragile sound that hitched with a sob at the end. "William," she whispered, and then gasped. "Oh, I'm so sorry. You don't go by William anymore, do you?"

Eli shoved his hands into his pockets. "You can call me whatever you like."

They stared wordlessly at each other for a moment, and then Sully took pity on them. "Well, I've got to meet with Lavender and check on Zeke. I'll leave you to it."

She shuffled out past them. Jessamine gnawed worryingly on her lip for a moment and then said, "Mother's upstairs. I know she's very anxious to see you if... that is if you'd like to?"

Eli straightened up. "Mother? She's... she's here?"

Jessamine held out a hand, a tentative smile on her face. Eli took it.

"Don't keep her all to yourself, Eli!" Jasper called after them. "She's the prettiest nurse in this place!"

Eli opened his mouth, probably to tell Jasper to leave his sister the hell alone, but Jessamine forestalled him, tugging on his hand and leading him from the room, though she gave Jasper a coy smile before she disappeared.

Eliza hesitated, unsure if she should leave Jasper alone, but then Cora appeared in the doorway to see to him, and she took the opportunity to slip out. She bumped right into Penny in the hallway.

"Oi, watch it! Just because you're the hero of the day doesn't mean you own the place!" she shouted, spoiling the effect with a wink and a grin.

"Oh, I'm not too sure about that title. After all, it was thanks to you that we liberated the Praeteritum. We ought to be calling you a hero."

"Very well, then. Does it come with a crown? I think it ought to come with a crown," Penny asked seriously.

Eliza broke into giggles. "I'll see what we can find."

Penny's genial expression melted away as she caught a glimpse into Jasper's room. "How is the bloody fool? I should have known he'd get himself near enough killed."

"He's doing all right," Eliza replied. "It's his leg. But as long as he avoids infection, Cora says he should be okay."

Penny's expression brightened. "Oh, right. Well, I'm relieved to hear that! But then, what are you all walking out of there looking all choked up for?"

"It's Jessamine and Eli. They've been reintroduced at last," Eliza said.

Penny suddenly gasped, slapping a hand over her mouth to stifle a raucous peel of laughter. Eliza blinked, confused.

"Is... is there something funny about that?"

"No, no, it's just... in all the mayhem today, I've not had a chance to tell you!" Penny said.

"Tell me what?"

But instead of answering, Penny grabbed Eliza by the hand and pulled her down the hallway to the railing of the gallery that overlooked the many beds below. She stopped right in the corner and pointed down.

"The Hallewells aren't the only unlikely family reunion taking place today."

Bewildered, Eliza leaned over the railing to gaze down at the place Penny had pointed out. There, sitting together on a cot, hands clasped together, were Bridie and Daniel Byrne. As she watched, Daniel pulled a small picture frame from his pocket with a heavily bandaged hand and opened it, placing it in Bridie's upturned palm. Between the shock and the exhaustion, it took a moment for Eliza to understand the significance of what she was watching. When the realization hit at last, her head snapped up, tears springing into her eyes.

"No! It can't be!" she gasped.

"It can and it is!" Penny crowed, slapping her hand down on the railing.

"I can't believe it!"

"Neither can I," Penny sighed. "Sisters-in-law with a manor girl. How will I survive?"

Eliza clutched the railing even harder. "You mean... you and... has Daniel Byrne proposed to you?"

"Saints above, no!" Penny chuckled. "But that won't matter. I've made up my mind, and when Penelope Lynch sets her cap for a lad, you can be sure she'll succeed. It's a talent of mine, you know."

Eliza laughed and threw an arm around Penny. "Now *that* I believe."

§

The sun was setting over the rooftops of the Barrens when Eliza found Eli again, standing in the open doorway and gazing reflectively out over the city they called home. As she sidled up beside him, he looked down at her and smiled.

"There you are! I haven't seen you all afternoon," he said, planting a kiss on the top of her head.

"I wanted to give you some time with your family," Eliza said. "How... how was it?"

Eli ran a hand through his hair. "I hardly know. I don't know what I'm feeling. But I think... I think it was good. Once I've gotten over the shock of it all, of course."

"Of course," Eliza agreed. Time would work its own special magic to heal the Hallewell family, of that she was entirely certain. Still, there was another shadow in Eli's eyes, something troubling him.

"Are you all right?" she asked him.

"I suppose so," Eli replied with a sigh that seemed to come from his very toes.

"You look so far away."

"I'm just thinking about everything we have still to do."

Eliza nodded. "Yes, I suppose that's a rather daunting thought, isn't it?"

"We'll be starting over. We will have to figure out the best way to move forward, starting with the Illustratum. Sully has the books that detail the Parliamentary system we had before, so I think we'll start there rather than trying to reinvent the wheel. And of course, if the royal family comes out of exile, that's a whole—what?"

Eliza was smiling at him. She couldn't help it. He looked like a schoolboy in his eagerness. She reached up and smoothed his hair back from his forehead. "We don't need to think about any of that right now."

Eli raised an eyebrow. "Eliza, we're rebuilding a country from the ground up, and if we don't start right away, we could lose our chance to—"

"Shhhh, I know. Tomorrow we will start that work. But right now, in this moment, just for tonight, let's imagine the hardest part to be over. We carried out the plan. We won the vote. And most importantly of all, we came back to each other. Let's let that be enough for tonight."

Eli smiled at her. "All right, then. Just for tonight."

"And since we came through it alive, I suppose there's no real reason to hold on to those words anymore," she hinted, intertwining their fingers together.

Eli's eyes widened. "Really? Are you sure?"

Eliza huffed. "Eli Turner, are you really going to make me say it first?"

He took her face in his hands. "I love you, Eliza Braxton."

"I love you, too."

And whatever else might come, that would always be enough.

Epilogue

HE BOY MOVED LIKE A SHADOW, silent and pressed to the dark places where the sunlight could not touch him. He kept his eyes fixed unblinkingly on his prey, watching every tiny movement so that he would know exactly when to strike.

The target in question was sitting in the grass and singing to herself, blissfully ignorant of the attacker waiting to pounce. Around her upon the blanket, she had assembled a most dignified group of companions, each sitting demurely before her own teacup, each patiently waiting her turn for the plate of toothsome currant jam tarts to be passed to her. They showed no impatience as their hostess chattered and sang, taking her time offering around the sweets. The boy harbored no such patience inside him, however; he groaned with hunger, and his stomach rumbled in ravenous harmony.

Just wait until she puts it down, he told himself. *And then, when she turns to reach for the teapot...*

"Oliver Elias Hallewell! What in the world do you think you're doing?"

The owner of the name jumped and yelped in surprise. His target, now warned of his presence, snatched up the tarts and guarded them jealously. Oliver looked up at his mother, heart full of the sting of betrayal.

"Aw, mummy, I only wanted a tart. Why'd you have to go and spoil it?"

Eliza reached down and ran her fingers through her son's silvery blonde hair. "You had your opportunity to share the tarts when your cousin invited you to her tea party. However, you refused that invitation, and now you must suffer the consequences."

"Those dolls won't even *like* the tarts," he argued.

"Perhaps so, but they're sitting on the blanket, taking tea and waiting their turn. I'm sure you could still do the same, if you really wanted one."

"Tea parties are boring," he whined.

"Not *my* tea parties," little Kate replied, her face scrunching up in indignation. "After we eat all the tarts we're going to storm the castle in the garden and then build a boat to sink in the fountain."

Oliver's face perked up at once. "Really? A boat?"

"Yes, but not until the tea party is finished."

Eliza watched with a carefully straight face as her son underwent a fierce mental struggle. Finally he sighed, stomped over to the blanket, and sat down between a porcelain doll and a stuffed dog.

"Okay, fine, give me some tea," he grumbled.

Kate raised a pert little eyebrow.

"Please," Oliver added grudgingly.

The teacup was filled, and Eliza walked away across the grass, laughing to herself. The grounds of Larkspur Manor were a riot of color on this summer evening. Here and there, some of the lodgers living in the converted east wing strolled about and enjoyed the last of the day's sunshine. A few waved to Eliza, who waved back. Turning the east wing into a boarding place for gifted young Influencers had been Eli's idea, but Eliza was even more pleased with the decision. When their training was done, they would be given help finding proper placements in the workforce, or they could go on to University.

The rumble of wheels on gravel signaled that Eli and Jasper had arrived at last. Eliza walked up the drive to meet them, arriving beside the carriage just in time to throw her arms around Eli as he emerged. She kissed him.

"Now that's what I call a proper greeting!" he declared, smiling down at her.

"I'll say, where's mine then?" Jasper called as the footman helped him out of the carriage and handed him his cane.

"You can speak to your own wife about that," Eliza chuckled. "How was your day?"

"Bloody exhausting. What are the children up to?" Eli asked.

"I believe the plan is to storm the castle in the garden," Eliza replied.

"The castle?" Jasper asked as he made his way carefully around to the other side of the carriage.

"That's what they call that old stone garden shed back behind the hydrangea bushes," Eliza explained.

"Ah. Well, I'm sure mother will be thrilled about that," Eli said, rolling his eyes.

"Don't worry, I've moved all of her gardening things to the shed near the stables. It's closer to the greenhouse, and the children aren't allowed over there because of the horses," Eliza said, patting his arm. Lillian's recovery had been considerably speeded up when she discovered she had a green thumb. Now she spent more time in the flower beds than the gardener. Eliza sometimes wondered if it had less to do with the flowers themselves and more to do with the freedom and the fresh air. After all, she'd been without either for a very long time.

"Where is my wife?" Jasper asked.

"Where else? Inside with the baby," Eliza laughed. "I haven't held my own child all day."

Jasper groaned. "I'll never get her to come home with me now. You'd better check her purse when we leave. Odds on she'll try to stuff little Emily in there and smuggle her out to the carriage."

Eliza laughed. Jessamine was delighted with her new niece. Eliza wouldn't be surprised if little Kate was expecting another sibling before long. It still made Eliza laugh to think how she and Jessamine had gone from mistress and servant to sisters and best friends. The weeks Jessamine had spent nursing Jasper after the rebellion had left them both so enamored of each other that they'd run off to elope as soon as Jasper was able to hobble around on crutches. When they'd returned, man and wife, the Resistance had thrown them a raucous reception at the Bell and Flagon, and Zeke had stood upon a table, proclaiming that their union was the breaking of the last barrier between the Riftborn and the Dignus. They now lived in the Commons together, Jessamine keen to start anew away from the house that had been much like a prison. But that didn't stop her from visiting several times a week, especially now that there was a new baby to nuzzle.

"Won't you stay for dinner?" Eliza asked. "We may be able to get her to leave if Emily's already in bed. And besides, Mrs. Keats has dressed pheasants."

Jasper and Eli groaned identically. Seven years later and the joy of devouring Mrs. Keats' cooking had still not lost a bit of its luster.

Life at Larkspur manor was a strange mix of new and old. Some of the staff, like Mrs. Keats and Millie, had chosen to stay on, though they had a great deal more freedom in Eli's household than they had ever had in his father's, and much better pay, too. Liesel was now the housekeeper in Bridie and Daniel's family home, where she scolded Penny and Daniel's children all day while secretly sneaking extra cookies into their pockets and extra fairytales into their sleepy little heads at bedtime. Others, like Peter and Sarah, had gone on to pursue new things—educational opportunities and professions that had been closed to them under the old Illustratum regime. Eliza did not know where her father had gone or if he had found a new place for himself in this new world they were building. When they had returned to Larkspur Manor a few days after the fall of the Illustratum, he was gone, along with his suitcase, his savings, and his copy of *The Book of the Rift*. Eliza's only wish for him was that one day he would open his eyes to his own complicity, and know some remorse for it. Beyond that, she did not think of him.

"Tell me more about the meetings today," Eliza urged as they walked together up the drive to the house.

"Boring as all hell," Jasper said with a yawn.

"We made progress on the treaty with France," Eli said. "Trade has been booming, so they are eager to renegotiate. And the education reform bill has come out of committees and it looks like we'll have the votes to pass it."

Eliza clapped her hands together. "With the provision for Riftmagic training?"

"Yes," Eli confirmed. "It should be a regular part of the curriculum from now on."

Eliza tucked her hand through Eli's arm. "I am so pleased to hear that."

"What about you? How was your meeting this morning?" Eli asked.

"We've voted in the new board of directors, but it will be some time before we are able to get the funds approved for the new wing at King's College Hospital," Eliza said. "In the meantime, we are going to have to work with the buildings we have, but the training programs are emptying the workhouses in record time, so I am confident we'll manage."

Eliza's work with the hospital and asylum reform had been so all-consuming that she had had to step away for several months before the baby was born, but she had since jumped right back in with both feet. Heavy investments in the Barrens meant that the workhouses were soon to be a thing of the past, and after what had happened to her mother and so many others, Eliza had made it her mission to overhaul the barbaric uses to which their asylums and hospitals had been put. She now had a reputation as a force to be reckoned with, a reputation that had nothing at all to do with her magic, and everything to do with her tenacity and passion. After all, as she had declared exasperatedly to Sully, "I can just as easily tear down a cruel system with a baby dandling on my knee as not!"

"Father, you're home! Did you bring it? Did you bring it?"

Oliver had spotted them and was flying across the grass to meet them. Eli crossed his arms and pretended to look offended.

"Is that all I get? Gone all day, and you just want to know if I've brought you something?"

Oliver rolled his eyes, hugged his father's leg, and then stepped back. "There, I've hugged you. *Now* will you tell me if you've brought it?"

Eli threw his head back and laughed, "Yes, I've brought it, you little monster, but first I need to know: have you been nice to your cousin while she was here today?"

Oliver bit his lip. "Well, I didn't steal her jam tarts, and I let her pour me tea."

"Model behavior, by any standards," Jasper said, nodding seriously.

"Very well then, here you are. With love from Sully, who says you're to come visit her before she'll lend you another," Eli said, yielding at last and presenting the boy with a small rectangular package. Oliver squealed with delight and ripped it open to reveal a copy of "Alice's Adventures in Wonderland." Without another word, he plopped down right there in the gravel and began to read.

"Oliver, why don't you bring it up to Grandma Emmeline's room. She'd love to have you read to her," Eliza suggested, and the child scampered off at once, castle storming and jam tarts forgotten.

"Shall we go in, then?" Eliza asked, starting forward.

Jasper went on ahead, but Eli stopped, staring up at the manor house with a dazed expression.

"What is it?" Eliza asked, frowning with concern.

"It's just… all these years later and I still can't quite believe this is my life," Eli murmured.

Eliza smiled. "Do you miss the way things used to be, then?"

Eli grinned back. "If I was still that lad, would you still have said yes? Worn my pawn shop ring and moved into a flat over a shop in the Barrens with me?"

Eliza kissed him. "In a heartbeat."

And they stood there together for a moment, lost in contemplation of how far they had come, how far they had still to go, and the joy of knowing that, through all the challenges and setbacks of forging a new and unfamiliar path, traveling it together was all the reward they could ever wish for.

E.E. Holmes is a writer, teacher, and actor living in central Massachusetts with her husband, two children, and a small, but surprisingly loud dog. When not writing, she enjoys performing, watching unhealthy amounts of British television, and reading with her children. Please visit www.eeholmes.com to learn more about E.E. Holmes, *The World of the Gateway*, and *The Riftmagic Saga*.

Printed in Great Britain
by Amazon